the Prisoner™
OMNIBUS

The Prisoner - Thomas M. Disch
Who is Number Two? - David McDaniel
A Day in the Life - Hank Stine

CARLTON BOOKS

This is a Carlton book

This edition published by Carlton Books Limited 2002
20 Mortimer Street
London W1T 3JW

First published in three separate editions as *The Prisoner; The Prisoner: Number Two; A Day in the Life*

The Prisoner
First published in Great Britain by Dobson Books 1979

Copyright © 1969 by Incorporated Television Co., Ltd

The Prisoner: Number Two
First published in the USA by Ace Books 1969
First published in Great Britain by Dobson Books Ltd 1981

Copyright © 1969 by Incorporated Television Co., Ltd

A Day in the Life
First published in the USA by Ace Books 1970
First published in Great Britain by Dobson Books Ltd 1979

Copyright © 1970 by Incorporated Television Co., Ltd

TM and © 1967 Carlton International Media Limited
Licensed by Carlton International Media

Design Copyright © Carlton Books Limited 2002

A CIP catalogue for this book is available from the British Library.

ISBN: 1 84222 531 6

CONTENTS

The Prisoner

PART I ARRIVAL

I have been studying how I may compare
This prison where I live unto the world.

Shakespeare, *Richard II*

Chapter One

The Connaught

"Have you been here before?" he asked.

"Wasn't it here that we came, the last time?"

"Not possibly. We were last together in . . . Trier, if my memory serves."

"Mine, apparently, does not. Coming across you again, everything gets very deja vu. The chandeliers, the flowers, even that waiter with the Hapsburg lip. They're all exactly the way I remember them."

"If this is what your deja vu's are made of, you've had an agreeable past."

"Small thanks to you, darling."

He touched her empty glass. "Once more?"

"Didn't you say you were in a terrible rush? Besides, it wouldn't show respect for the bisque. Which is already gliding to our table."

The waiter with the Hapsburg lip performed deft rituals with the bisque, while they, with the preliminary skirmish over, made minor modifications in their strategies. The wine steward brought the Solera, its brittle label flaking from the glass.

"Yes," he said. "Then, with the salmon, Coindreu Chateau Grillet."

"And I've seen *him* before too," she said. "Did you notice the funny ring he was wearing? No, men never notice how other men dress. It's delicious. If the venison is half so nice, I'll marry you. Would you like that?"

"I might. I've never had a wife."

"I'd make a very attractive wife for you, I think. You'd never have to feel embarrassed. I speak French, German, Polish, and probably something else. As I have my own income, I wouldn't even be expensive – except at Christmas – though I'd *look* expensive all the time. Whenever your self-confidence faltered—"

"It doesn't."

"—my skilful flattery would bolster you up. And I'm not *too* much younger. Am I?"

"Not at all."

"Do you fear I'd be too frivolous? Do you take exception to the coloratura passages? You, if anyone, should realise that my serious side is *just* as serious as yours. Make a serious face. Oh, like that! All those wrinkles – the strength of character they suggest."

"It's the supraorbital ridge that does that."

"It's so many things."

"You have good points too."

"Each complements one of yours. Imagine the two of us walking into the same room. We're surrounded with whispers, the cynosure of all men's eyes. The waltz swells above us, and you take me in your arms."

"What are they whispering?"

"That you're forty years old, and still single."

"Thirty-eight."

"*C'est la même,* darling. We'll both have little secrets tucked away in dresser drawers, behind our stockings. I would have thought forty more likely."

"You listen too much to the things people whisper."

"Let's leave them, then. They mean nothing to *us*. We'll go off by ourselves. To the Seychelle Islands? Meshed? The Philippines? They're said to be quite in now."

"We won't listen to what people say. We value our independence too highly."

"Where shall we go, then? You tell me."

"To Wales."

"Oh, not Wales! One must draw a line between independence and ennui."

"I've already signed the papers, love. I am committed."

"This isn't pretending, then?"

"I hope not, after all the money I've sunk in it."

"Where in Wales?"

"The Pembroke coast. It has one of the quaintest names on the map."

"Oh, I know just what it will look like – all the cottages built out of marzipan, and an abbey church from the 14th century, the rustics brawling in the pub, fishing boats, sunsets. You'll live in somebody's converted toolshed."

"A gatehouse, actually. I leased it through Chandler & Carr."

"Who showed you photographs."

"And a floor plan."

"Though smallish, it possesses every convenience."

"A majority, at least."

"I don't believe it. It isn't you. What about your *work*?"

He paused at this, the first point scored in the game.

"I've retired."

"I *don't* believe it. You? Though, of course, if that's what you're supposed to *say* . . ."

"It's been my impression that it's not at all what I was supposed to say. But I do say it, I have done it, I am retired."

"Why, in God's name?"

"That's a secret I've tucked away in a dresser drawer, behind my stockings."

Which tied it, one all.

"And the dresser? Off in the rural, implausible solitudes of Pembroke?"

"Still in London, most likely. I only bought it today. That's why we met here. I've been up and down Bond Street all day, furnishing the place."

"And *not* because we're so convenient to Grosvenor Square?"

"I thought that might make it handier for you."

"They won't buy it, you know. You can't just go and tell them you've lost interest in the whole thing, for heaven's sake!"

"On the contrary, Liora – you *can*."

"You called me Liora. That was nice of you."

"It's your name."

"It's not the name on my passport. You are a darling, and you really do believe in integrity and honour and all of that. Yes, thank you, just a wee bit more. 1872! And without an expense account?" When the steward had left them, she continued: "Is that what you'd call a Masonic ring?"

"I forgot to look."

"He also uses wax on his moustache. I've never kissed a waxed moustache. Remember where you kissed me, in Bergamo?"

"That was where I didn't kiss you."

A palpable hit. He moved into the lead.

"But you wanted to. Why are you looking seriously now? Is it about me?"

"Yes."

"No, it isn't. You're having second thoughts about all that furniture. What did you get? Where? How much did they make you pay?"

He itemised on his fingers. "Four Chinese Chippendale chairs, at Mallett's. A mahogany table from J. Cornelius, that copies one at the South Kensington. A Sirhaz carpet in the pear design. A Riesener secretaire that's very much restored. Oh, and odds and ends. I forget how much—"

"Fantasy, all of it."

"I did see them, and I might have wanted them. Actually I just picked out some bare essentials at Liberty's. Here's the salmon."

Bare and essential, the salmon was presented. The Coindreu was open, tasted, and approved. Richebourg '29 was suggested for the impending venison Diane. Their conversation, set against the backdrop of this restaurant, this meal, seemed to lack the element of chance. The ordered sequence of dishes dictated not only the wines they drank but also the words they spoke and the glances that passed between them. Even their errors were such as only the most expert players could have made.

Her serve.

"What do you intend to *do* in Wales? Fish? Think? Write your memoirs? Discover some new inner resource, or a hobby?"

"What's customary for a country gentleman these days?"

"Alcoholism."

Which might have tied the score again, if the glance that accompanied it had not, so noticeably, grazed the net. She tried again.

"When do you leave?"

"From Paddington, at half past eleven."

"Tonight?"

He nodded.

"How ridiculous! You asked me here . . . just to have dinner . . . and to tell me that you're leaving town?"

"I thought you'd enjoy eating out, and that you'd want to say goodbye."

"You don't give me time to say much else. I'd hoped . . . Well, you knew what I hoped."

"You didn't hope. You took for granted."

He had moved lengths ahead of her: she was reduced to being

forthright.

"Why *did* you want to see me? You won't say you love me, and you won't say you don't. You sit there and decorate yourself with wrinkles and irony. You know, if you can't trust *me*, you'll never be able to trust anyone. You sit there with your enigma dangling in front of you like some fat gold watch chain. You're just inviting someone to grab it my dear."

She leaned back in her chair, touching the emerald pendant on her throat, while these points were added to her score.

The waiter with the Hapsburg lip replaced the china on the table according to a strict and clandestine geometry. The dinner approached its climax.

"Do you think I look Jewish?" she asked.

"You look dark and mysterious. Your face expresses great strength of character."

"And you won't postpone your trip just one night?"

"There isn't a pullman every night. I'm sorry, Liora – I've made up my mind."

"Someone has – that's certain."

But the game was clearly his, for all that. She smiled, conceding it, and began to talk about nothing at all.

When they left the restaurant, at ten forty-five, the waiter with the Hapsburg lip, ignoring more pressing demands, cleared the cups and Tokaj glasses from the table. He pursed his mouth at the flower vase, from which the dark-haired woman had purloined the single rose.

He replaced the linen cloth with one slightly crisper, and on this, beside the new flowers, he put the small wooden plaque that indicated, in incised, gilt letters, the number of this table–6.

Chapter Two

A Round Trip to Cheltenham

The two identical Hartmann Knocabouts stood, already packed, beneath the false mirror in the foyer, like a demonstration of one of the less obvious axioms devised by the Alexandrian geometers. In the reception room the butler, a dumb and slightly Oriental dwarf, pressed the button that released the ornamental screen: he entered. The butler handed him his gloves.

"The telephone?" he asked.

In reply the butler removed the receiver from its cradle and offered it, as mute as himself, across the intervening space. Dead.

"Very good. The Locust is at the garage, I take it?" The butler nodded. "There's no particular hurry. When they've finished you can drive it on to Carmarthen. Wire me from there."

He turned for a last survey of the room. Depersonalised by dust covers, the furniture could not evoke so much as a flicker of sentimental regret. Like the monolithic pavilions of a defunct World's Fair, the room seemed already to be impatient for its own era of privacy, decay, and picturesque abandonment.

His fingers wriggled into kid gloves. Now there must be some gesture of departure, the closing of curtains, keys in locks. The butler stood at the opposite end of the room; he removed, from a pocket of his waistcoat, a key, turned, fitted it into the glass door of the bookshelves, turned the key.

"Not," he said, "the Dickens."

Obediently the butler reached, on tiptoe, to the fourth shelf and removed a slim sextodecimo volume of frayed morocco. Relocked the shelves. Crossed the room, padding on bare parquet, offered the book to its owner.

"Yes, that will do nicely." He slipped it in the pocket of his raincoat. "Goodbye, then."

The butler lifted a pudgy white-gloved hand and waved goodbye.

In the foyer he dipped his knees, caught a handle in each hand, and rose with the weight of the suitcases. The steel screen purred shut, sealing his past. He kicked open the front door. The taxi was waiting, aglow in the drizzle.

"Paddington," he said.

"It's fifteen after eleven, sir. No trains are running now."

"My train leaves at eleven-thirty."

The driver shrugged, and lifted the flag of the meter, which ticked off sixpences and fractions of miles along the Brompton Road, through Knightsbridge and past the floodlit Corinthian columns of Apsley House, turning left and turning left again along the perimeter of Hyde Park, then right into Gloucester Terrace.

The station clock said eleven-thirty.

"Thank you, sir. Thank you very much."

He walked with his two bags towards Gate 6. A blue-uniformed ticket puncher waved at him, across the intervening space, to hurry. But for the two of them, the station looked as deserted as a cathedral in one of those counties tourists never find. Liora had carried on about her cathedrals, Salisbury, Winchester, Wells, all through the bombes.

While the man worried the ticket with his punch, he glanced backward, thinking he had seen her. It was only a young American, in army surplus, seated on a knapsack, her back propped against the Sherwood green tin of W. H. Smith's, sleeping or seeming to sleep.

The conductor was waiting outside the blue sleeping car to help him with his bags. Before he had been shown to his compartment, the train had begun to move.

"I will arrive . . . ?"

The conductor glanced at the destination hand-written on the ticket. "At half past six. The engine is changed once in Bristol and again in Swansea."

He found the bed in his compartment already made, the sheet spread back to receive his body, the pillow plumped. He drew the blinds. He removed his raincoat, his gloves.

He began to read:

Escalus.

My Lord.

Of government the properties to unfold . . .

On the small screen in his own compartment, the conductor watched the swaying man turn the pages of his little book. Often, to his distress, he would turn them backward instead of forward, but not so often, after all, that he did not reach the end. He then rose, swaying, and began to undress, unknotting, first, the black bow tie, prying off the cufflinks from his cuffs. He shrugged out of the jacket, loosed the cummerbund, slipped the suspenders from his shoulders, unbuttoned his fly, stepped out of the trousers.

He hung trousers, jacket, shirt inside the closet of simulated wood, placed tie, cummerbund and cufflinks on the shelf above. He lifted the handle of the door to LOCK.

Then he moved for a moment out of range of the closed-circuit camera. The microphone picked up the sound of running water. He returned, naked now, to the bed and pulled the upper sheet loose. The conductor, who, though probably no older than this man, could no longer think of himself as fit, had time briefly to admire the sturdiness of these limbs, the trimness of the torso. Then the light blanked.

"The second camera," a voice commanded.

The conductor adjusted a knob at the side of the screen. It now showed a man's head, cradled in his hands, swaying. He stared directly at the lens concealed in the ceiling for several minutes. Even when his eyes had closed, his face did not seem to relax. It was a quarter past two.

The conductor picked up his copy of *News of the World* and read the captions beneath each picture. At a quarter to three, a buzzer, at E-flat frequency, brought him to his feet.

The man was now asleep.

The conductor flipped up the switch marked VENT beneath the screen and watched as the mask descended over the man's face. When the mask was retracted, the facial muscles at last showed some degree of relaxation.

He went into the corridor and pulled the EMERGENCY cord. He unlocked the upper half of the door, reached in, turned the handle down to OPEN.

He pulled the slack, naked, fit body out of the bed. Twelve cars ahead the engine whistled. He stood low for a better grip beneath the armpits. The floor lurched.

Four men had gathered in the corridor. They watched the conductor pulling the man across the beige Acrilan without offering to help. Lights flickered by outside the windows. The train was approaching Cheltenham well ahead of schedule. It came to a full stop by the siding of a cable warehouse. While the four men unloaded the limp body on to the boards of the siding, the conductor returned to the compartment for the two suitcases, and again for the clothes and the copy of *Measure for Measure*. There was barely time to place these on the platform before the train was moving again. Spools of heavy cable flicked past *accelerando*. The four men returned, each to his own compartment.

The conductor tidied the mussed bed, plumped the pillow, scoured the sink.

At Cheltenham the engine was switched. By four o'clock the string of cars was rolling back home to Paddington. Lights cut long arcs through the incessant drizzle.

Chapter Three

The Village

Woke.

Soft Muzak, sore limbs. He flicked flecks of sleep from the corners of his eyes. He was awake now. His shoes confronted him, propped on the two identical suitcases. Laces dangled from the eyelets.

He patted his breast pocket. He stood up. The cummerbund, unbuckled, slid down his wrinkled legs. The Muzak glided into *Oklahoma*.

The entire room – varnished benches, sooty windows, overheated air, the worn, well-swept floorboards, the twin slates for Arrivals and Departures, the ticking clock, the thick, inverted L of the stovepipe leading to the stove – was transparently probable.

It was, by this clock, III minutes after IX, a statement that the light slanting through the grimy lattice confirmed. CLOSED hung lopsides before the ticket window grille. Oh, what a beautiful morning!

There was one Arrival, at 6:30 am. There were no Departures.

He went out onto the platform, into the incontrovertible likelihood of sunlight, cirrus clouds, the scent of creosote. A white wooden planter, Property of the Village, welcomed him to ... ? For the entire length of the platform there was no sign to say. Well, to the Village then, in its most absolute sense.

He knotted his shoelaces, and in front of the mirror that sold chewing gum he tied a bow knot in his bow tie. His hair was not mussed by sleep. The cummerbund went into his raincoat pocket.

He returned to the platform with his suitcases and followed the arrows to TAXIS. A gravel path hedged with rhododendrons curved to the back of the station and debouched on a street of devastating neatness and typicality, at once folksy and abstract, like a Quaker chessboard. A Grocer, a Druggist and Meat confronted a Stationer, a Cafe and Dry-Cleaning; beyond these emblems of a community, trees and a steeple, admonishing, Italianate, of limestone capped with lead; then cirrus, and then blue sky.

The taxi stand was empty.

He carried his suitcases past the Stationer (whose windows celebrated the novels of B. S. Johnson and Georgette Heyer, various cookbooks and garden manuals, and Bertrand Russell's autobiography) and to the Cafe, which received him with a lush gust of gaseous grease.

The waitress said, "Ew!"

"Pardon me," he said, "but could you tell me—"

"We had *such* a fire!" She giggled, wiping her full red face with a dirty towel.

"—the name of this town?"

"You wouldn't of believed it. *Nobody* would!"

"Please."

"A cup of tea?" She drew tea from the steaming urn, set the cup before him. "There's milk." In a stainless steel pitcher. "And there's sugar." In a glass bowl.

She wiped the towel across the plastic joke that hung above the low entrance to the kitchen: YOU DON'T HAVE TO BE CRAZY TO WORK HERE – BUT IT HELPS! She glanced back to see whether he had noticed, whether he would laugh.

"Could you *tell me* the name of this town? Please."

"Village you mean." Pouting, she gave the plastic another swipe.

"Very well, the name of this village."

"Because towns are bigger. I don't care for towns, myself. They're impersonal. People forget that you're a human being. And we're *all* human beings, you know. Do you want toast?"

"No, thank you. If you—"

"Negg?"

"No. I—"

"You don't look like you've had breakfast."

"I'm afraid I got off the train by mistake. That's why I asked the name of this village. It does have a name, doesn't it?"

"You must take me for some kind of simpleton, Mister. I suppose next you'll want to know what year it is? And then maybe how many shillings in a pound?" New billows of grease blossomed from the doorway behind her. "Oh, the hell with it!" she shouted. She ran into the kitchen to swat at the burning griddle with her towel.

He left sixpence on the corner, for his tea, and went back outside. A tiny taxi was waiting at the taxi stand. The driver waved his plaid cap. "Hi there!"

A short man, blond and ruddy, a Scandinavian in miniature. He took the suitcases and swung them on to his luggage rack.

"Looks like you've had quite a night," he observed. His face suggested, but did not assert, bland strength and muscle contentment.

"Could be."

The driver opened the back door. His smile metered a precise quantity of bonhomie. "Hop in."

A cardboard sign was taped to the glass partition between the halves of the taxi. DRIVE CAREFULLY. THE LIFE YOU LEAD MAY BE YOUR OWN.

"What a beautiful morning, eh?" He had taken his place behind the steering wheel, on the left side of the car. "Where to? Are you going to pay the penalty?"

"How's that?"

"For last night, the penalty for last night." (Wink.) "Or will it be a hair of the dog?"

"Actually, I thought we might drive to the next town."

"Which?"

"What *is* the next town?"

"This is just a local service, you know. But I could take you to the beach."

"Take me to the police."

"Don't take offence, mister. Can't a fellow make a joke?"

"It has nothing to do with you. I simply want to ask them a few questions."

"You're the boss."

They drove, on the right side of the road, past Grocer, Druggist and Meat. There the concrete, encountering green grass, split in two and they took the ONE WAY left, between an ornamental, unpopulated park and coy, numbered cottages of gingerbread and vanilla fudge, wee nightmares of inexorable charm.

"Tell me," he said, in a tone of cautious indifference, "how do you *pronounce* the name of this town?"

The driver scratched his head. "Well, you know . . . it isn't really big enough to be called a *town*."

"More of a village, I suppose you'd say."

The driver, without slowing, turned around. A big, big smile. "You took the words out of my mouth."

He settled back into the plasticine and gave the streets of the Village the same serious attention one must give to a sore tooth. In the park quincunxes of clipped trees alternated with beds of late drooping tulips and fresh poppies. The residences that looked across to this allegory of dullness tried to compensate for its civic stolidity with a kind of metronomic whimsy, as though in each of these die-stamped witch's cottages there lived a banker in a party hat. Chance and individual enterprise could not, unassisted, have created an atmosphere so uniformly oppressive; this village was the conception, surely, of a single, and slightly monstrous, mind, some sinister Disney set loose upon the world of daily life.

The question was – had this vast stage set been inhabited yet? Where were the elves and gnomes and fairies, the village maidens and the village youths, the old old women in white linen wimples and bombazeen skirts, the old men sucking the enormous pipes on which they had carved their own grotesque and wrinkled effigies? For the little taxi had not passed by another vehicle, and the pavements on the left were as empty as the gravel paths on the right. He had seen, at a distance, a single gardener, crawling through a tulip bed. There had been, moreover, the waitress, and there was now this taxi driver, but neither of them seemed large enough, somehow, for the great godawfulness of the Place. They were not much better than toy soldiers four inches tall while the set demanded figures at least half life-size.

The park eventually grew bored with itself, at which point a church had grown up in the middle of the road. It almost seemed real.

He said, "Stop." It stopped.

He got out. He walked towards the church. He mounted the first, the second, the third step. There were many, many more and then a door.

"Cremona?" he wondered.

No, not Cremona. Somewhere else.

"Bergamo?"

Not Bergamo either. But *someplace*, certainly.

"Now that *is* a pretty church." The miniature taxi driver had come out of his miniature taxi. His approval encompassed church, park, the beautiful morning, the universe, without, for all that, coming right out in favour of anything. It was possible, after all, that it was *not* a pretty church. What do taxi drivers know about churches?

"You religious?" he asked.

Was he religious?

"I was thinking," he said (it was not an answer, but then what answers had *he* got this morning?) "that I've been here before."

"Lots of people get that feeling. Here."

"In front of the church?"

"In the Village, generally. It seems to do that. You know what I think it is?"

"What?"

"I think it *represents* something." He stroked his small, square chin, savouring the plum of *represents*. "People come here from other places. Like you. And they see our Village, and they get the feeling that something has always been *missing* from their lives."

"And the Village represents that, the thing that is missing from their lives?"

"It was only my idea," the taxi driver demurred. Clearly, it was doubtful whether taxi drivers ought to have ideas.

"And this thing that's missing – what is it?"

Startled, the taxi driver looked for it on the steps, up in the steeple, admonishing, Italianate, in the cirrus clouds.

"Something good? Or—"

"Oh, certainly! Something like ... I don't know ..." He turned to his taxi for help. "Like being contented!" Triumphantly.

"With?"

"With?"

"What is it like being contented with?"

The taxi driver shrugged. "This kind of life. The kind of life that the Village represents."

"The way it contents *you*?"

"Oh my god! Jesus! Of course! Say, what is this? Where are you going?"

"Don't you remember? To the police."

"Yeah. Well then, let's go there."

The police station (it lay not more than fifty yards from the church) occupied the grey stone building that would have been, in the usual scheme of things, the episcopal residence. A mansard roof peered out over the top of adolescent elms, each one protected from the world by its own individualised prison of wrought-iron spikes that dissembled their ferocity as fleurs-de-lis.

He approached the door (it was the kind of door that insists upon ceremony, like a rich relative who had only condescended to visit this house after many misgivings) slowly, gravely, as though he might shame some kind of justice out of this Village by his own stern gaze and conscious dignity.

He pushed the bronze handle of the door. He pulled.

He read the card in the small glass frame above the bell. Its brief message was printed in florid script, like a wedding invitation:

> Police
>
> Closed

With a wonderful sense of appropriateness, the taxi driver chose just that moment to make his break for it. He had left the two Knocabouts on the curb.

He walked through a bed of marigolds to stand beneath the window just left of the Door. He looked into what appeared to be the waiting room of a very fashionable dentist. The armchairs were decorated with antimacassars of yellowed lace, the end tables with copies of *Vogue* and *Bazaar*. A framed document (the dentist's diploma?) punctuated the rhythm, mild as Mantovani, of the wallpaper. The room was empty.

He walked, with less mercy now for marigolds, to the next window. This was the dentist's office, where, at a Danish teakwood desk, his stenographer took dictation in the morning, where, twice a week, his cleaning lady dusted the shelves, where it was demonstrated to clients that there was no need to be afraid, it wouldn't hurt at all.

At all the other windows, the blinds were drawn and the curtains lowered. There was no way to know therefore, whether things went quite as smoothly for the dentist's patients as they had been led to hope. Probably he used gas. Or might it be that he had taken such good care of *everyone's* teeth that he had simply put himself out of business?

Abandoning the marigolds to a lingering death he returned to his bags. Fortunately Hartmann luggage is designed for people who have no patience with porters: his hands gripped the moulded leather as naturally as though he had picked up a pair of perfectly mated foils. He took his way west along a residential street that promised to take him more directly than the boulevard bounding the park back to the railway office.

He had not quite lost sight of the police station before he saw it ahead on the left, set back only a few feet from the pavement: his new home, the converted gatehouse he had leased through Chandler & Carr. There, at the corner of the steep tile roof, was the glided weathercock he had intended to take down as his first act of possession. There was that single dormer window, standing open now as it had stood open in all the photographs, like certain celebrated politicians who can command, during an entire career, only a single facial expression, which they wear, like a badge of office, to every function they attend. There (he stood directly before the gatehouse now) was the big red number torn living from a first-form workbook for arithmetic and screwed to the oak muntin of the door:

6

And there, with his hand resting on it, was the brass knob of that door.

The hand and the knob rotated clockwise ninety degrees.

The door swung open.

The furniture that he might have bought (could he have afforded it) yesterday in London – the chairs he had seen at Mallett's, the table from J. Cornelius, the Sirhaz carpet, the Riesener secretaire, even the three-legged, spiraling object that had amused him momentarily by its studious lack of any other purpose than that of standing, as now, upright against a wall – was disposed about the room, his living room, just as he might himself have disposed it. It was as though the usual gap between desire and necessity had been bridged during some freakish fit to absent-mindedness on the part of old Father Reality, temporarily indisposed with sunspots. His first sensation could not be anything except pleasure, for here were all his pumpkins turned into carriages with the gilt still fresh and the price tags in full view. But if one is not willing to believe in fairy godmothers, such pleasures burst at a finger's touch: they are not real.

What then, with any certainty, was?

He thought he recognised the answer in a mirror, until he noticed with chagrin, that his trouser-fly had been left unbuttoned.

By himself?

No. Though he *seemed* to remember, now, forgetting to do this.

The Village, this splendid room, the mirror in its frame of ormolu, and even the image in the mirror were not to be trusted. What, then, was?

His body, the body beneath these wrinkled evening clothes, that could be trusted.

And his mind.

Because these things could not be tampered with.

He could trust (as finally, we all must) himself.

Chapter Four

The Villagers

"Can I help you?" a woman's voice asked.

"Please. I am trying to reach a number in London–COVentry-6121."

"I'm sorry, there is no provision for me to accept long distance calls from a public telephone."

"And *I'm* sorry, but this is an urgent call. I have no telephone at my residence. I'm sure the party who answers will accept the charges."

"I'm sorry, there is no provision—"

"Then let me speak to your supervisor."

A click, a hum, two clicks, and a muted rattle. Then she said: "COVentry-6121?"

"Yes."

"I will see if there is a line free." Then, after a suitable interval: "I am sorry, but at present our outside lines are all engaged. If you would like to wait, I will call back as soon as—"

"I'll try and place the call later; thank you."

He left the glass booth, and the man with goitres who had been fretting outside the door all this while rushed in and began to speak excitedly into the telephone in a language that resembled Bulgarian. He had not bothered to dial.

He returned to his seat on the flagstone terrace, at the table farthest from the chirruping little orchestra. He looked out to the sea where, a brighter white amid the whiteness of the midday haze, a sailboat came about and made towards the northern limit of the bay. He took a small cigar from his leather case and lighted it, shielding the match against a salt breeze that puttered aimlessly about the terrace, fluttering the fringes of umbrellas, the pages of menus, the hems of skirts, moving now in from the sea and then a moment later moving out towards it, fitful as a child with nothing he can do and no one he can play with.

The waitress returned to his table and asked, in a voice as crisp as the black nylon of her uniform whether he had made up his mind.

"Coffee."

"Just coffee? Wouldn't you like to see the pastry cart?"

"No, just coffee."

"A sandwich perhaps?"

"Very well, a roast beef sandwich."

She shook her head. "We don't *do* roast beef, sir. When you've made up your mind, I'll come back." She remained standing by his table, looking westward to the obscured horizon. Her hand brushed a gauze of blonde hair from her eyes.

"It's a remarkable view," he said, "from up here."

"Yes, it must be. Everyone says so. And some days it's much better than this. You can see all the way out there."

"You must become quite busy here, this time of year."

"Never much busier than this, really, and never much quieter either."

"But the tourists . . . ?"

"Oh, tourists never find their way *here*. You're not a tourist, are you?"

"More or less. Unless, just by being here, I'm not."

She smiled morosely. "That's rather good – I'll have to remember that. But I'd better get your coffee now. And I'll see if we have any roast beef left." She hurried off towards the small brick building behind the platform where the orchestra of three old men was wending its weary way through Ziehrer's *Faschingskinder Waltz*.

A sparrow hopped from the flagstones up to the rough ledge of the escarpment, paused to estimate the drop, and flung itself over the edge. A moment later it was back, as though, even for sparrows, there were no passage down to that empty beach.

He watched the sea with the patience of a carved face staring out from a sandstone cliff. It was not that he lacked a plan of action. He had known from the moment of waking that he ought to depart this Village by any means available. If he lingered, it was a sign only that he did not yet doubt that means of some sort were available. He would leave whenever he determined to leave, but meanwhile each new increment of fact made him hungrier for the synthesis that would make of the scattered pieces a coherent picture. He had every reason to expect to dislike that picture, but he did want to *see* it.

That he was himself intended to form an element of that picture he could no more doubt than that the clothes he wore – the slacks, the turtleneck, the jacket fraying at its cuffs – had been tailored for just his frame and no other.

But when, exactly, had they (omitting the question of who "they" were) recruited *him* in their conspiracy against himself? Had he already been, in a sense, co-operating with them at the moment he had chosen to lease just that particular converted gatehouse in Pembroke? It was not a facsimile – he had assured himself of that: it tallied brick for brick and slate for slate with the photographs. As it was simpler to suppose that he had been *led* somehow to elect this choice than that the whole elaborate absurdity of the Village had been constructed suddenly about some building he had simply chanced to like, it followed that he had been tampered with, like a clock that has been set back to provide the murderer with a false alibi.

But if his choice had been less free than it had seemed, *how* had it been coerced? A question that was posed, more subtly, by the presence of the furniture, furniture that he had only, and in the idlest manner possible, *wished* for.

And what (this question, which concluded the series, had occurred to him within moments of entering the house) were they expecting of him now? Would not the first, the most natural reaction have been to run away? But he was not – and they must know this – likely to react with such Pavlovian simplicity.

And so, while he weighed this imponderable against that and pursued each question till it vanished into paradox, he had temporised. He had unpacked his suitcases and disposed their effects into closets and drawers, convinced, as he did so, that whatever they were expecting from him it would not be that. He had inspected the kitchen (the icebox was well stocked, and he helped himself to a lager and some cheddar cheese) and then the other rooms of the ground floor. He determined that there was no staircase leading to the floor above, either within or without, though there was space between his ceiling and the eaves for a suite of rooms not much smaller than his own. He attempted to enter the upper floor through the open dormer window and discovered, without surprise, a second wall, just behind the window, of solid ironplate. He dug out from his watch pocket the house-key Mr Chandler had handed him in ratification of the lease; there was no lock on any door to which this, or any, key might be fitted. He looked for a telephone and found none. He showered and changed into fresh clothes. He made himself at home.

It was not yet noon when he left the house, returning the way he'd come, past the retired police station, past the steps of the church, from which vantage he had seen the elephantine umbrellas of the terrace restaurant. There, though he were visible to them, *they* would become much less invisible to him. He could not imagine grounds for any greater uncertainty than these on which he stood, in which he sank, and so, on the theory that he could only get out of their hands by playing into them, he let himself be led to the reserved table.

As soon as the man with goitres left her, the tweedy woman in the Tyrolean hat gestured more emphatically for his attention. She was fiftyish, tailored, and stout in an agreeable, oaken way. Her hair was shingled and her face so carefully made up as to seem almost her own. Having caught his eye, she gave him a long, apparently significant, yet incomprehensible look. She rooted in the bottom of a swollen canvas satchel, not quite a purse and not quite a shopping bag, and with the stub of pencil she exhumed she began scribbling on a paper napkin. She had finished before the goitres came back.

Humouresque fell dying to the flagstones, and the elderly violinist bowed low in acknowledgement of his defeat. Raindrops of applause spattered the terrace. The tweedy woman lifted her pigskin fingers to pantomime her mildest approval, and the breeze whisked up the paper napkin thereby released and harried it from table to table until it lodged beside the metal leg of that adjoining his.

The clarinet hobbled into the *Swedish Rhapsody*. He stooped forward to retrieve the napkin, but the man with goitres had preceded him by an instant: "Allow *me*, please." He put the napkin in his pocket.

"That was very thoughtful of the gentleman," said the tweedy woman, who had followed the goitres to his table.

"And very careless of you, my dear. You must excuse my wife."

"It was no inconvenience."

The goitres quivered.

"None at all."

"You see, it was a sort of … sketch … a map I drew in order to explain to my husband—" A pigskin glove caught hold of the man's arm, so that there should be no doubt who was meant: this was her husband, *this* "—just how . . . the Prater is laid out. Have you been to the Prater, may I ask?"

"Yes, though not recently."

"Didn't I tell you, my dear, that he looked like a man who has travelled? I have always admired travellers. Travel is a kind of passion with me, but, alas . . ."

"Alas," her husband continued for her, "my wife's health does not permit her to travel."

She nodded. "My health does not permit me to travel."

They glared at one another, each stonily determined not to be the first to depart.

"Won't you share my table?" he suggested. "I'll have the waitress bring more coffee."

The woman thumped into a chair. "Thank you. We always enjoy—"

"My wife," the goitres announced, livid with courtesy, "does not—"

"—seeing a strange face. *Don't* we?"

"—*drink* coffee. The doctor forbids it."

She stared up at him. "So we must ask him to be kind enough to order lemonade for me!"

He seated himself, with ill grace, on the edge of the metal chair, which he did not trouble to draw towards the table.

"Perhaps now you can tell us," she said, rising to the alto register, "something about Vienna. Do you love the Opera?"

"I would have thought, actually, that you could tell me much more about Vienna than I could tell you."

Her laughter, mirthless and operatic, disrupted the gambols of the breathless clarinet. "Would you listen to him, my dear! He thinks that I . . . that *I* . . ."

"My wife," the goiters explained sullenly, "has never left this Village. Due to her unfortunate health."

"But surely before she came here . . . ?"

The clarinet resumed its rhapsody. The woman placed an expressive glove upon her tweed bosom. "I was born in this Village. Alas."

"Really."

"Do you find that surprising?"

"Yes, in one who has such a passion for travelling. Or unfortunate, to say the least."

"Passions are stronger for being unrequited," the goitres remarked, with evident satisfaction He even edged his chair some inches nearer.

She leaned forward intently until the feather in her cap was brushing his chin. "Have you been, as well, to Italy?"

The goiters stiffened. "Really, my dear!"

"If my questions offend him, he needn't answer, you know."

"What offence is there in asking that? Yes, I've seen quite a lot of Italy."

"Venice," she muttered balefully. "Florence. Rome."

"And to a number of the smaller towns. I'm very fond of Bergamo."

"Bergamo! Where they make those wonderful violins?"

"You're thinking of Cremona, my dear."

"Cremona, of course. We'll he's probably been there too. I read about Cremona in *The National Geographic*. Do you know that magazine? It's been the chief comfort of my life, excepting, needless to say, my husband. In fact, I am a Member of the Society!"

"You *used* to be," her husband amended.

"I used to be, yes."

"I'm afraid the waitress has gone into hiding," the goitres said, rising to his feet. "I shall have to go and seek her out."

When he was out of earshot, the tweedy woman caught hold of his hand. Despite her agitation, her grip seemed weak, almost languid. "You heard all of that!"

"Yes, but I'm afraid I understood very little."

"Isn't it clear? Isn't it obvious? *I am a prisoner!* They never let me out of their sight."

"Then what your husband said about your health . . ."

"Oh, him! He's one of them, you know. He helps them every way he can. Not that it makes a speck of difference to *them*! That's why I tried to give you that message – to warn you!"

"I'm afraid I still don't—"

"Oh good heavens, man – don't you see? It's staring you in the face. If *you* don't see it, then you're the only one here who doesn't."

"That I'm a prisoner, too, you mean?"

"Of course."

He shook his head.

She backed away, "Then . . . you are one of them!"

"I am neither."

She stood up, clutching her canvas bag to her stomach. "My husband is waiting for me. We're expected somewhere else. I'm sorry to have *disturbed* you."

"You needn't apologise. On the contrary, I owe you my thanks for your confidence. And for trying to help."

Her lips wavered between scorn and commiseration. Her eyes tried to meet his, but always it was the man with goitres fidgeting on the other side of the terrace who commanded her attention.

"So that's what it was I was trying to do, eh?"

"Weren't you? It's what you said."

Commiseration won out. "There you have it! That's just the special horror of this place – that you never *can* decide, when someone offers to help, what it is they have in mind. I would love to stay and talk, dear boy, but look at my husband – he's getting ready to murder me."

She patted his hand. "*Wiederseh'n.*"

"Goodbye."

"Hello?" He jiggled the hook. "Hello?"

Silence displaced the vague static; dead silence.

"This is the operator. Can I help you?"

"The number I've been trying to reach in London – it rang twice and there seemed to be an answer. And then the line went dead."

"Would you like me to try that number again?"

"If you would. COVentry-6121."

The operator performed veiled mysteries at her switchboard, and once again the receiver echoed a hopeful Bizz, Zim; a second; a third, still hopefully, and then:

"Hello?" A woman's voice.

"Hello, Liora?"

"This is Better Books. May I help you?"

"Is this COVentry-6121?"

A pause. "Well, almost. It's COVent Garden-6121. Same letters. Did you want Better Books?"

"No, but perhaps you *can* help me. I'm outside London, and I've had considerable difficulty getting through to that number. I know it exists. I reached someone there only yesterday. Do you have a London Directory on hand?"

"Somewhere."

"Would you look at the front, where the exchanges are listed, and find COVentry? Perhaps it's not among the central London exchanges."

"Is this some kind of a joke? Who is this?"

"Believe me, I'm perfectly serious. I wouldn't put you to the trouble if I could receive any kind of co-operation from the operators here."

"Well, just a second."

In fact, a minute forty-five seconds.

"I find no COVentry exchange. Just COVent Garden. It makes sense, doesn't it? They wouldn't have two exchanges with the same letters?"

"You looked down both lists? Central and Suburban?"

"Yes of course. Say, is this Lee Harwood?"

"No, I don't think so. Well, thank you. I'm sorry to put you to any trouble."

Better Books made a doubtful sound and hung up.

He stared for a while, with the receiver still in his hand, at the telephone dial. He replaced the receiver on its hook and stepped out of the booth.

He found himself looking directly into the kitchen that served the terrace restaurant. There, sitting on the chopping block beside a monumental double-sink, was the blonde waitress who had served him on the terrace. She was bent double, her knees pulled up to hide her face. The nylon uniform was bunched into her lap, exposing the sallow flesh of her thighs. Her sobbing followed the slow tiddle-tiddle-thump of the distant orchestra.

He stepped across the threshold on to slippery, garbage-strewn concrete. "What is it?" he asked quietly.

Fear glistened in the smudged eyes. Her mouth gaped, and clenched. Hands tugged the nylon down to her knees.

"Is there some way I can help?"

A small noise rose from her chest, strangled in her convulsing throat, as though at some far distance her twin had screamed and her own body had taken up, this faintly, the resonance.

"Go away," she whispered. "Leave me! Oh, leave me, leave this town. Why did you— Oh, stop *looking* at me, for God's sake, stop!"

Chapter Five

Something White

The old woman standing by the greeting card rack satisfied, better than anyone he had seen yet, his ideal conception of what a resident of this village ought to look like. The wispy white hair caught up in a bun, the silverpoint wrinkles, the knobby, venerable hands, the stooped shoulders and fallen bosom, the crepe falling in black folds to her ankles, allowing just a glimpse of what might even be button shoes: she was in herself a more perfect greeting card than any of those that, with many a low chuckle and many a nod and a smile, she read aloud to herself in a dry, slow, delighted drone.

The clerk, a middle-aged gentleman suitably dressed for a dinner party in Surbiton, appeared from beneath the counter. He held a feather duster rigidly in one hand, an allegory of his trade. "Can I—" His courtesy exploded into coughing; he covered his mouth discreetly with the feather duster, sneezed, sniffed.

"I'd like a newspaper," he said. "Any newspaper for today."

The clerk blinked back tears. "I'm so sorry." He touched the knot in his tie, the handkerchief in his breast pocket, trying, by as much as it lay in *his* power, to make this a better world. "You see, we don't . . ." He laughed self-deprecatingly. "You understand, surely, that it isn't me . . ."

"You're trying to tell me that you don't handle newspapers."

The clerk sighed. "Just so – we don't handle them."

"I wanted something to read on the train."

"On the . . . ? Yes, well! That's . . . There's . . ." He stabbed the air with the duster. ". . . lots of books. Do you like to read . . . books?"

"I'd prefer a magazine."

"Oh yes, magazines, those, yes. We keep the magazines over in that corner: *Country Life.* And *Hair-Do*, but no, you wouldn't . . . *Car and Driver? Analog?* Or that one there, on the top, with the greenish cover and that lovely what is it, some kind of, oh, that's for children, isn't it? *Muscular*

Development, mm? If you could give me ... some idea?"

"I'd like a *New Statesman.*"

"No, I don't think .. We don't receive much *demand,* you see, for—"

"*The Spectator*? *Newsweek*?"

"Not that sort of thing, really. That's all, how would you say, politics, isn't it? They say there's two things you should never discuss – politics and religion."

"Then perhaps you could tell me, at least, when the train departs?"

"Which train?"

"Any at all. Preferably one this afternoon. I've been to the station twice today. The ticket window is always closed, and no schedules are posted."

"Yes. Well. I think they're on the *summer* schedule now. But I'm not at all sure. If you asked at the station ..."

"I've just come from the station. There was no one there."

"Did you look around? They might have been somewhere else, you know, doing something."

"Where do you suggest I look?"

"Oh ... Oh, that's difficult. I'm not really qualified, am I? I mean, this is just a *book* store. People don't buy their train tickets at book stores, now do they? So unless there's something that ... ? You can see for yourself that there *are* other customers."

They both looked at the other customer, who glanced sideways at them, smiling, and jiggled an embossed and glittering birthday card, enticing them to share its message with her.

"Thank you for your help."

"Not at all. Think nothing of it. I try to do what I ...." And, his eyes seemed to express, if that wasn't very much, it wasn't *his* fault.

The sweeper, a thick suet pudding of a fellow, tackled his job with great zeal, conscientiously oblivious to the fact that his broom, this third time around, raised no dust, none, from the floorboards. It was his job to sweep, and so he swept on. Perhaps he was motivated less by a conception of duty than by an admiration for the tools of his craft. It was a wide and quite handsome broom, in perfect condition, the bristles still fresh, soft, and supple. No one could ask for a better broom than this. His uniform was no less handsome, of heavy black twill on which had been lavished all manner of pleats, pockets, buckles, zippers, snaps, and, on the back, in chartreuse script, the insignia *Department of Sanitation*. He was equipped, in addition, with a fine leather harness (black) that suggested immense utility, though, unless he were to be harnessed to a plough, it was hard to imagine any real use for it.

The broom bumped his shoe. The sweeper, encountering this unprecedented obstruction, stopped. The sweeper, temporarily deactivated, considered this obstruction and how best to deal with it.

The sweeper spoke. He said: "Hey! You. What are you doing here?"

"I'm waiting for a train."

"Huh? What train?"

"This is a railway waiting room. Outside there are tracks for trains. I arrived here this morning by train, and I'm waiting now for another in order to leave."

"Uh. But. It's closed."

"In that case how is it that the door is standing open?"

The sweeper looked at the open door. He looked at his broom. He looked at the face of the clock. The big hand was on XI; the little hand was on IV. He tapped the clock with a thick, segmented sausage of finger. He said: "Look at the time."

"I've been looking at it for hours. Perhaps you can tell me when the next train leaves?" A very far-out possibility, but he would mention it.

"Uh. You ask the ticket window man about that. I just sweep."

"There is no ticket window man to ask."

"That's because we're closed." It followed logically, it did!

"Since the waiting room is closed, I'll wait outside on the platform." Which he did.

In a few moments the sweeper had followed him out the door, trailing his fine broom in dejection. "Hey. You. It's closed."

"How can it be closed when there are still people waiting for a train?"

The sweeper stood on his two feet and confronted this question, as though it had been a wall erected just in front of him in the middle of the platform.

"Well. Anyhow." (Climbing over the wall.) "You can't sit there. I got to sweep."

He stood up. The sweeper swept. From the other end of the platform a third figure approached them. The sweeper stopped sweeping. He smiled. "You talk to him. Okay!"

The approaching figure was of the secular (as opposed to the official, and uniformed) order, a prodigy of good grooming, good taste, and good cheer. As a model he would have commanded the very highest rates: well-built but not *so* well-built that you could not imagine those same clothes looking almost as nice on you; bright, even teeth (his grin broadened as he grew nearer) that would have done credit to any toothpaste; a prominent bone structure that one might photograph from any angle. He could have worn the most implausible clothing and yet it would have seemed, on him, fashionable rather than peculiar. He approached, grinning, within three feet, within two, and then, with as much grace as efficiency, he swung his fist into the stomach of the man who had begun to ask, once more, about the trains.

Who was answered, as well, by the handle of the broom in the small of his back. Vertebrae crunched.

He doubled up.

Caught hold of the manicured hand chopping at his neck. Twisted, left, twisted, farther left. The buckled, square-toed shoes slipped.

The bristly end of the broom swept on a long arc towards that point in space his head had occupied only a second before; which now was occupied by the more photogenic head of the model.

The handle of the broom broke off at its base.

He had stopped. Now, taking leverage on the suddenly limp wrist, he lifted the well-built body up: up higher. And dumped it into the suet pudding. A buckle-shoe caught in the harness. The harness gave.

The sweeper looked unhappily at the body littering the platform. "You shouldn't," he said, in a tone more of disappointment than of disapproval.

"Neither, for that matter, should you."

He hit the sweeper in the stomach.

He hit the sweeper in the stomach a second time.

He hit the sweeper in the stomach a third time.

The sweeper lifted his arms in self-defence.

Sometimes his fists sank into the pudding, sometimes they were deflected. The sweeper stepped over the pile of litter. Grabbed for a blue lapel with white piping.

His fists battered at the blinking face. Seams strained, split. The sweeper got a better grip, beneath the swinging arms. He lifted, tightening his hold, oblivious, as a bear to bee stings, to the pelting hands, the kicking feet; hugging, more tightly still the small of that back.

Thinking: *Break, godammit, break!*

Then:

(The sweeper did not understand this, but he didn't let it distract him.)

They were on the platform, the other body tangled beneath their legs. They rolled, in each other's grasp, across the well-swept boards. The sweeper's head bumped the frame of the door. They rolled back. His head bumped the frame of the door, again. They rolled into the waiting room. His hands and arms and head concentrated on squeezing the small of that back.

He began to choke.

Eventually, his attention was distracted by this choking. The man he grasped was not hitting him any longer. Instead he was pulling at the broken straps of the harness. The straps were across his neck.

He understood everything now: the man was choking him with the harness straps.

He relaxed his hold to grab for . . .

To get . . .

But the straps were embedded too deeply in his flesh. Too tightly. He could not get . . .

He choked.

His head stopped thinking. His arms flopped.

He stood above the sweeper, listened to the wheeze from his welted throat. His own breath came irregularly. He looked at himself in the mirror of the gum machine. The left lapel had been torn from his coat. He removed his billfold from the breast pocket, dropped the coat in a wire basket, Property of the Village.

The movement of the sweeper's arms indicated his return to consciousness. He put his shoulder against the back of the gum machine and shoved. The machine crashed down on the sweeper, whose arms once more relaxed.

The body outside was still quiet.

He jumped from the platform down to the track and began walking east along the ties. He stopped at intervals to remove a cinder from his shoe, but on the whole he made good time.

He passed no houses. The station had been built at the easternmost limit of the Village. The track stretched on across a perfectly even and featureless plain, and so it was some time before he was out of sight of the station. A mile away Nature grew bolder and asserted herself with, here and there, a shrub of dogwood or a spindle tree. Saxifrage, iridescent as puddles of oil, squinted out from the cinder bed. Dandelions bred promiscuously amid the select gatherings of their betters – knapweed, butterbur and sneezewort yarrow.

There were no birds. There was nothing in all this landscape, except himself, that moved or made noises.

Two miles from the Village the tracks stopped, abruptly. The meadow continued, without the aid of perspective lines, to the horizon.

A white sphere stood at the horizon, or just before it. Its size could not be estimated with any exactness. Twelve feet? Fifteen feet? More?

The sphere approached, rolling smoothly and easily across the weeds, westward, away from its shadow.

He broke into a run.

The sphere swerved right, its silhouette warping momentarily with the torsion: it was soft.

It was very big.

He crouched, shielding his head in his arms. The sphere slammed into him, knocking him off his knees. He slid on his side several feet through the weeds. The sphere bounced high into the air, settled gelatinously, bounced, settled, quivered.

He stood up, nursing his right shoulder, which had taken the brunt of the collision. The sphere edged towards him, nudged; pushed. He pushed back at the yielding white skin, but the great bulk of it moved on, resistless as a bulldozer. He slithered, braced against the advancing sphere, across a mulch of crushed weeds and meadowgrass, until, his heel catching in soft earth, he could not slide. The straining muscles accordioned, he collapsed. The sphere moved back.

He stood, wincing at the pain. An ankle sprained. The sphere rolled forward, nudged. He stepped back. The sphere stopped. He walked slowly backward, facing the sphere.

He began angling to his left, still moving backward. The sphere, like an anxious collie, corrected his false trajectory.

He angled to the right, which the sphere permitted until he had returned to the tracks. Thereafter no deviation from the true path was allowed. The sphere insisted that he return to the station. It insisted that he walk along, between the rails, at a moderate pace, back to the Village. It did allow him to stop at intervals to remove a cinder from his shoe, but it would not tolerate indolence on any larger scale.

Chapter Six

Something Blue

Ashrill voice, but when it broke, which occurred at almost every point of emphasis, it became, quite evidently, a man's. When it was most strident it seemed to possess overtones beyond the range of human audibility, pitched, perhaps, for dogs or bats, It spoke:

"You!"

"Number 6!"

"Pay attention please." The clearing of . . . a throat? a microphone? "I am addressing *you*. Will you stop fussing over that pot and come into the living room?"

He placed the artichoke on the wire rack above the boiling water, placed the lid on the pot, set the timer at thirty-five minutes. Sliced the roll, set its halves beneath the broiler to toast. Folded his arms.

"I'm waiting. This obstinacy can only make matters more difficult for you, you know. For my own part, there are many other things I can do besides watching this cooking lesson. Are you listening to me, Number 6?

"Number 6?"

"My name is not Number 6. So, if it is me that you address, you would do well to use my name. If you don't know it, which I doubt, you might introduce yourself. Then, perhaps, I'll do as much for you."

"Oh, fuss and bother. *I* am Number 2. For administrative purposes, numbers are much more convenient than names, and more reasonable as well. In this Village there might be any number of people with the same first name as you, or, in your case, even the same surname. But there can only be *one* Number 6, Number 6."

"And only one Number 2?"

"Precisely. Numbers have the further advantage that they are meaningful. When I say that I am Number 2, that you are Number 6, that tells us something about our relationship. *Will* you stop buttering that roll and come into the living room?"

"I'd spoil my supper if I left off now. And in any case, I'd prefer to speak to Number 1. You may tell him that."

"For you even to suggest that shows how little you understand your position – or mine. I have full authority to handle your case, rest assured. What are you making there?"

He took the roll, brown crust bubbling with butter, turned the oven to a low heat, placed it inside to dry. Poured the egg yolks into the top of the double broiler: they swirled into the melted butter.

"Eggs Beaugency. This is the sauce."

"Well, leave it."

"Leave a Béarnaise sauce? You must be insane."

"You don't seem to realise your position here, Number 6. If you did, you wouldn't jeopardise those advantages you possess – such as my readiness to indulge you in this fantasy that you are free to oppose me."

"It's an uncomfortable position. And I intend to change it."

"You are a prisoner, Number 6. It is as simple as that."

"I doubt that even in this Village anything is as simple as that. I am not Number 6. I am not a prisoner. I am a free man."

"Ah, philosophy! I cherish philosophy, but of course in *your* situation it becomes downright necessary. There was a philosopher of ancient Rome, Horace (no doubt you've heard of him), who wrote. 'Who, then is free? The wise man who can govern himself.' Now that's philosophy all over!"

"More to the point, he said: *Hic murus aeneus esto, nil conscire sibi, nulla pallescere culpa.*"

"Don't your English public schools do wonderful things? There was never time, the way things went for me, to learn a classical language. I've always been kept going up and down, to and fro, *doing* things."

"You're American?"

"My accent? It's mid-Atlantic, actually. And in other ways, Number 6, you'll discover that I'm not *quite* what I seem." A chuckle.

Then: "It must be a burden for you, Number 6, to stand there stirring that Béarnaise sauce, when there must be so many questions that you want to ask."

"Not so difficult when my questions produce no answers."

"Always these suspicions, Number 6! Always this hostility, these frowns, this lack of mutuality!

"If all who hate would love us,
        And all our loves were true,
The stars that swing above us,
        Would brighten in the blue;
If cruel words were kisses,
        And every scowl a smile,
A better world than this is
        Would hardly be worth while.'"

"Not Horace again, surely?"

"No, an American philosopher – James Newton Matthews. But you meant that as a joke, didn't you? You're feeling a little better. I'm glad to see it. A sense of humour is an absolute necessity in situations like these."

"In prisons?"

"Oh, in general. Once you become accustomed to our life here, you'll find it isn't *that* much different from the world outside. What you might call a microcosm, in fact. We have our local, democratically-elected government."

"Its powers must be rather limited."

"Yes, somewhat. Were it any otherwise, how could I insist on our typicality? Further, our residents enjoy considerable affluence. Your kitchen, for instance – you find it well equipped?"

"It lacks a Mouli and a garlic press, and I don't have much use for tinned spices, unless they're all that's to be had. And for what I'm doing now I should have beef marrow, but that can't be helped."

"I'll make a note of that and speak to Number 84. Stocking your kitchen was her responsibility, and she'll have cause to regret her carelessness. You see, Number 6, no one is idle here. There is always work to do, and there is always someone to do it. *You* will not be required to take a job, but should you find your leisure becoming a problem—"

"The very least of them."

"A man of your vigour – and without any compulsion to *work?*"

"I am retired, you know."

"So I've been given to understand. And so young too! Thirty-eight?"

"Forty."

"You were born?"

"Yes. On 19 March 1928. Don't you have that in your dossier?"

"You can't expect me to keep track of all of that. You should see your dossier, Number 6 – it's very nearly the largest in our files."

"When the eggs are done, I'll take you up on that."

"That sauce isn't ready *yet*? It's rather impersonal to be discussing these matters at such a distance. I distrust a man who won't look me in the eyes."

"Always these suspicions, Number 2! If all who love would hate us, and all our hates were true—"

"You have a point. But as I was saying, about the organisation of the Village (forgive me dwelling on a theme so dear to my heart): we also possess excellent recreational facilities. There are clubs that cater to every possible interest: photography, the theatre, botany, folk singing. There are discussion groups on comparative religion, on political philosophy (I attend some of those myself), on almost anything that an educated man might want to talk about. We have some lively bridge tournaments, and if you play chess, we can boast three acknowledged masters of the game."

"Have you played against them?"

"Yes, and I've even known to win. Then, what else? Sports? Dear me, all the sportsmen here! We have no less than four elevens. There are soccer teams for both men and women. Tennis is very popular, and squash. Our older citizens amuse themselves at croquet, and the spryer among them badminton. What are your preferences, Number 6?"

"I've always preferred individual sport. But once again, that should be in my dossier."

"Yes, it said that you do quite a bit of boating. Sad to say, no one shows much interest in that here."

"And marksmanship?"

"Oh, Number 6!"

"Boxing, then? I sometimes like to box."

"For shame, Number 6 – that *you* should be the one to bring it up! Poor Number 83 is in hospital with concussions. You really didn't have to go that far."

"And the other one?"

"Number 189 is back at his job, sweeping, sweeping. He's quite resilient, that one. But even so, you must recognise how futile these violent outbursts are. Do you think that we'd be so naive as to base our security on a few pairs of fists? Our residents are always under surveillance, and those who are as important to us as you receive individual attention. Whenever you leave your house I'm kept informed of your whereabouts. Should you decide to take a walk into the country – and at this time of year, who can resist to? – you will be brought back to the Village, as you were today, whenever you overstep the boundaries."

"By your big white balls?"

"By a Guardian, yes. Though not all are white. Some are pink. Some are baby blue. A few are mint-green, and there is one – I pray to God that you should never encounter *it* – in fawn."

"And the boundaries, how are they marked?"

"We don't like to deface the natural beauty of the surrounding countryside with unsightly signs and ugly wire fences. If you're curious, you'll discover them soon enough. After all, wasn't it Wordsworth who said—"

"Stone walls do not a prison make nor iron bars a cage. No, it was Richard Lovelace. In a poem he wrote to his mistress from prison."

"It wasn't Wordsworth? I'm sure he said something, then, to the same effect. Perhaps I'm thinking of:

> 'This royal throne of kings, this sceptre'd isle,
> This earth of majesty, this seat of Mars,
> This other Eden, demi-prisonhouse . . .'"

"Whoever wrote them, they're beautiful lines."

"Stirring, stirring! Well, God bless Richard Lovelace! And how is the sauce Béarnaise coming?"

"You haven't been watching: it's done, and soon the artichoke will be."

"Can't one trust an artichoke to cook itself? Come into the living room a moment and talk seriously, do."

"Very well, but I must have answers then."

"You need only ask the proper questions, Number 6."

He went into the living room.

The damask curtains of the false window framed the smiling image of Number 2. He sat behind a circular blue desk; behind him, out of focus, hung heavy maroon drapes identical to the real ones framing the screen.

Unless his face was naturally blue-grey, the transmitting apparatus could not reproduce flesh tones with any accuracy, though in other respects the image was astonishingly clear.

The camera zoomed in slowly on the face until it occupied the greater part of the window frame; until, from the knobby blue chin to the faint citras-yellow curve (a strand of hair?) bounding the bald blue head, it measured fully four feet. It would have seemed, in other colours than these, a very friendly face. The general spareness of its features – the thin lips, the Draconian nose, the deep-set eyes (were they actually purple?) – could be accounted to age rather than to any sort of meanness. His smile seemed unforced and sincere, and his eyes, despite their dubious colour, shared in this good humour.

Fifty years old? Sixty? More?

In short, a nice old man; a bit of a Polonius perhaps, but then Polonius had been a nice old man too.

The four-foot head nodded.

"Now, isn't this much more intimate?"

The voice, imperfectly synchronised with the movement of the lips, lagged a split-second behind the image.

"Why don't you take a chair, Number 6? And we can have ourselves a heart-to-heart talk. Face-to-face. Man-to-man."

"First, my question. It's very simple: what do you want?"

The head showed its profile, as though to make certain that the object inquired after were still there. And turned back, smiling:

"Why, the world, of course. Who is really ever satisfied with less?"

"What do you want *from me*?"

"Information. Only that. Your friendship, though of inestimable worth, would be almost an embarrassment of riches."

"Go on."

"The information in your head is priceless, Number 6. I don't think you have a proper reckoning of its value."

"Didn't you—"

"Didn't I what?"

He would have to ask this; it was only a matter of time. He took the plunge: "Have I been here before? In this room? In this Village? When you said that just now, it seemed . . ."

"Ah-ha! Now *that* is a most pertinent question. Yes, Number 6, you have been here before. You remember nothing of it?"

"I—"

"Such a look, Number 6! Such a look! I've done nothing to deserve that. In fact, I've helped you. I answered your question candidly and truthfully. And I'll go on helping you, if you'll just tell me what other things you want to know."

"How long was I away?"

"Not very long. A month, a year – time is so subjective. May I say, parenthetically, that you seem suddenly much less sure of yourself?"

"I was in London."

"Were you?"

"I remember being there. I remember . . . some things. Other things are vague. And there are areas that are . . . blank."

"Very nicely put, Number 6. That, in a nutshell, is the process of memory. Since I can't very well ask you which things you've forgotten, may I inquire what you do remember?"

"Almost everything that doesn't interest *either* of us very much."

"And that which *would* interest us?"

"Is blank."

"How convenient for you!"

"Am I supposed to believe that this comes to you as a surprise?"

"We suspected that something of the sort had happened. Your behaviour today has tended to confirm that."

"And *you* have had no hand in it?"

"In your brainwashing? As a matter of fact, Number 6, no; we haven't. We're not even certain who did. Naturally, your former employers are prime suspects. But on the other hand, all kinds of people *might* have. The information you possess is, as I've said, priceless – and not only to those who, like ourselves, lack it, but equally for those with whom you share it. When you disappeared for your little holiday here, they must have grown quite worried, and when you returned . . . Well, put yourself in their place. You seem disgruntled."

"It strikes me that you're being extremely communicative. Which means either that you're lying, or that you have your own nasty reasons for telling the truth."

"The truth in this case is simply so much more interesting than any lie I might invent. I *had* considered suggesting, as an experiment, that you hadn't actually left the Village at all, that your little interlude in London was a hallucination induced in our laboratory. In theory that could have been done. With a competent surgeon and a few drugs, all things are possible. Life, as (I think it was) a *Spanish* philosopher said, is but a dream. Or else he said it's very short, I don't recall. One can make a case for either theory. But why should I want to confuse you more than you must be already? After all, *this* time, Number 6, we have a common cause. We both want to know what it is you've been made to forget – that is, if you *have* forgotten it and aren't just malingering cleverly."

"And if *you* don't already know."

"Well, if we did, then you need have no scruples about confiding in us and letting us help you remember the matter yourself. That would be a very altruistic undertaking."

"Yes. I had already discounted the possibility."

"Splendid. We understand each other now. And we can begin, just as soon as you like, to recover some of that lost time."

"What makes you believe it's still there to be recovered?"

"The fact that you're alive at all. Presumably, you're still considered useful. The surest way to have guaranteed your silence would have been to silence you. And the next surest way, though it would have left you alive, would have – how shall I say? – *reduced* you. The reason that *we* never tampered any more than we did (though we had *many* opportunities) is because, valuable though your information might prove, you, Number 6, are infinitely more valuable. What price can be set on the autonomy of the individual? Isn't that a fine phrase, by the way – 'the autonomy of the individual'? No, that information will still be there: it's just been swept under a rug, so to speak. We need only poke about here and there, peeking under the corners, to find it."

"And who is scheduled to perform this poking and peeking?"

"As Socrates once said, 'Know Thyself.' Or was that Hamlet?"

"You're thinking of 'To thine own self be true.'"

"Ahh 'And it must follow as the night the day, thou canst *then* be false to any man.' How Shakespeare understands the human heart! But to get back: no one but yourself can undertake to dive down into the deeper waters of your head. But we can offer you assistance, someone to handle the pump, as it were. Our Number 14 has helped other people who found themselves in your unfortunate situation."

"By what means?"

"By sympathy! At root it's the *only* means by which one human being can help another. Sympathy in conjunction with some form or other of animal magnetism."

"You'll find that I'm a poor hypnotic subject. I resist."

"Not always, apparently, or you wouldn't be in this bind now. I realised when I brought the matter up that you wouldn't rush into our arms. It's enough for now that you should know they're open."

A bell rang in the kitchen.

A blue finger reached up to pull at a blue ear lobe; the blue smile became a frown of deeper blue. "Now who in hell could that be? They *know* that I'm—"

"It's an artichoke," he said. "You'll have to excuse me. I must poach some eggs."

"By all means. Wasn't it Bismarck who said—"

"'You can't make an omelette without poaching eggs.' No, it was Jean Valjean."

"Number 6, you'll kill me."

"Not unless you grant me an interview in person, Number 2. Thoughts can't kill."

"And words can never hurt me. Robert Lowell?"

"Jean-Paul Sartre."

He lifted the artichoke gingerly off the rack, poured the sauce in a small pitcher which he placed above the still-steaming water. Selected two eggs, broke them, let them ease into melted butter.

"You do that nicely," the voice said from the living room. Dissociated from the face, it seemed suddenly younger, and at the same time less benevolent. "If you're serious about establishing a more personal relationship, perhaps I can invite myself to dinner. This Friday, say?"

"Sorry. My engagement calendar is filled for months ahead. I lead a full life."

"It does say in your dossier that you're hard to get to know. But I've always held that it's just such people who end up being most worth knowing."

"That's too bad. I feel I know *you* very well already."

"You're depressed, that's why you're like this. It's still your first day back at home, and it's been a busy, busy day. And then, finding out on top of everything else that someone's been diddling with your head, that's the kicker, that's the unkindest cut of all. You must try to remember the positive aspects of your situation, however."

"I'll bet a philosopher said that."

"Yes, Susan Coolidge. But you didn't give me a chance to say what it was she said. She might have written it just for you."

"Comfort me, then."

"It's called 'Begin Again' and it goes like this:

> 'Every day is a fresh beginning.
>> Every morn is the world made new;
> You are weary of sorrow and sinning,
>> Here is a beautiful hope for you –
>> A hope for me and a hope for you.'"

"Yes, well? The comfort?"

"That's it – that's the wonderful thing about your being back here: that everything that didn't quite work out the first time can be done over again. The way it should have been done *then*."

"Thanks for a glowing opportunity."

"Your eggs are ready."

"In forty seconds."

"I'll go now."

"Don't feel that you have to."

"Tomorrow is another day, Number 6."

"And tomorrow."

"And tomorrow. Toodle-oo."

In the living room the blue face winked and vanished; the speaker barked.

PART II ESCAPE AND CAPTIVE

"You've been only a few days in the Village and already you think
you know everything better than people who have spent their lives
here ... I don't deny that it's possible once in a while to achieve
something in the teeth of every rule and tradition. I've never
experienced anything of the kind myself, but I believe there are
precedents for it."

The Castle, Franz Kafka

Chapter Seven

The Delivery of the Keys

He memorised the Village: each winding street, the shops, the park and sporting grounds, the gravelled access-road to the beach, and the farthest limits he might advance through the outlying meadowland before the Guardians would roll forward to establish the invisible but undeviating boundaries of his microcosmic world.

He determined, as best he could, the locations of the cameras by which his Argus-eyed jailers surveyed the wide expanse of their bucolic jail; he discovered fifty – he might have missed as many more. He also located the various concealed speakers of the public address system, an easier task since Number 2 would at odd moments during these explorations (it made no difference where he might be) address some homely piece of wisdom to him, a stale poem or a grandfatherish admonition not to walk through *that* gate, not to try the handle of *this* door. When he did walk through the gate or try the door, he would find, as often as not, that Number 2 had been having a joke with him, that there was nothing beyond or within that merited special prohibition.

In that first week he had narrowed the range of his curiosity down to the Village's two chief points of "interest" (they were the most common subjects on the picture post cards sold at the Stationer's).

The first of these was beyond question the administrative centre of the Village. Once, as he had stood outside the heavy iron gates staring up at the great grey mass of the place, Number 2 had delivered over the PA system a long appreciation of this building – its functional beauty, its impregnable defences, the Minoan complexity of its corridors, and the warmth and simplicity of his own suite of offices at the heart of the labyrinth. The encircling fence was a formidable thing, its gates patrolled by armed guards and a beige sphere acting as Cerberus at the single entrance to the building proper. ("We call him 'Rover,'" Number 2 had explained. "He's unique among the Guardians in that his design allows him to – how shall I say? – *annihilate* whoever causes him undue aggravation.")

He decided that, for the time being at least, he would not try to breach these defences. Soon enough, Number 2 had assured him, he would be invited inside, and it was more than likely that even then his satisfied curiosity would not seem worth the price of entrance, whatever it might prove to be.

The second "point of interest" was the Village church. Twice during that first week he had entered the church in the routine course of his explorations, but though he had been somewhat taken aback to find the interior even more incongruously elegant, even more accurately Lombardic, than its facade, he had not paid it any more attention than he would have given, just then, to an altarpiece by Cosimo Tura (an example of which, unless it were a forgery, was displayed above the main altar; it was the same, possibly, that had been stolen from the Colleoni chapel in the last days of the war.) It was lavish, it was beautiful, and though it couldn't be authentic it was entirely convincing. But it was (it had seemed) altogether unimportant.

On both occasions the church had been empty.

Then (this had been on the afternoon of that second visit) he had been sitting at his usual table at the terrace restaurant. He had been coming here at four o'clock each day to observe and to be observed. He was not ready yet to approach strangers himself (he wanted to be able, first, to distinguish between the jailers and the jailed) but he was willing they should approach him. As yet the only person who would speak to him was the blonde waitress he had so unaccountably upset when he had found her crying in the kitchen. Of course, she had little choice in the matter – he was a customer who had to be served. The tweedy woman was never again at the restaurant, but her companion, the man with goitres, was often there. The goitres would leave his table just as promptly as he came to his, and on this particular afternoon, having nothing better to observe, he had watched the goitres making his way purposefully towards the steps of the church. Shortly after he had gone in at the door two other men, both as lacking in the external signs of piety as the goitres, followed him inside. After another brief interval three different men left the church. So much bustle in and out of a building that had been empty only minutes before suggested that something else was at issue here than could be accounted for by the combined attractions of Cosimo Tura and pious exercise. After he had finished his coffee he walked to the church himself.

He found it, as he had left it, empty: the nave empty, the transepts empty, the five small side-chapels of the ambulatory empty.

There were no other doors but the one he had come in at, which he had been watching constantly since the goitres and the two other men had entered.

From that afternoon he began to make more regular visits to the church. He bought a sketchpad at the Stationer's and made studies of architectural details: the Tuscan pilasters, the caissons of the arched vault, the fine mouldings (stone, not stucco), the gigantic festooned bucranium surmounting the door – and the three cameras mounted high on the cornice 10ft below the base of the vault and 50ft above the floor, inaccessible. Together they commanded a view of the whole interior of the church, except for the darkest recesses of the first and fifth sidechapels.

Though the cameras were out of harm's way, their cables had been strung along the cornice and down the west wall (concealed by some slovenly stucco work), where they disappeared at a point just above the bucranium.

It was reassuring to find them making such simple miscalculations. This, admittedly, was only a chink in their inner defences, but if he could discover their first error as easily as this, he would eventually find a way to breach the outer walls. He *would* escape.

In the meantime, there was this. A secondary mystery admittedly, but the unravelling of it would keep him in trim. The occasion came so soon and required so little effort that he was never able to decide, afterwards, whether *they* had not in fact, handed him the keys and written out the password.

Five o'clock of a heavily overcast day: he was watching from the terrace the high breakers curl in upon themselves with a distant roar, and rush, foaming, up the shingle beach. Two figures came on to the beach at a stumbling run, carrying an orange life-raft between them. As they reached the water, a klaxon sounded. The restaurant's clientele gathered at the edge of the terrace to watch. They pointed to other figures – guards clambering down the steep descent and cheered when, just as the two fugitives had wrested the bobbing raft to the seaward side of the breaking surf, a pastel sphere bounded into view on the access-road. Perhaps, after all, it was the fugitives they cheered – or (most likely) they were prepared to applaud pursued and pursuer indifferently, so long as either put on a good show.

The sphere hit the line of the surf at the wrong moment and was hurled back into the frothing undertow, where it spun wildly, a tyre trapped in a drift of snow. The two men were in the raft now, rowing out into the heavy sea.

The klaxon continued its alarms. Guards were arriving on the beach on foot and by car. More guards were scurrying down the rocky paths. Other rafts were being inflated. It was a grandstand show.

He counted them as they left the church: a pair of them within moments of the klaxon's first shriek, then after an interval, the goitres.

He left his table unobtrusively and walked directly towards the church, relying on the excitement of the escape to provide his camouflage. He approached the camera that eyed the entrance to the church, shinnied up the lamppost on which it was mounted. With the fountain pen from his breast pocket he squirted the camera's lens, then tamped a bit of paper napkin on the ink-damp glass.

He mounted the steps to the church three at a time, threw open the door, and leaped up to grasp the splayed horns of the garlanded ox-skull. The stone held his weight as he pulled himself up. Now, if the church were being monitored, he could be observed, but only for – he caught hold the cable above the bucranium, yanked – seconds.

He was, effectively, alone: the cameras defunct. For perhaps the first moment since his arrival he was unobserved.

Outside the klaxons still agonised. He wished the fugitives the best of luck – if not (for he was realistic) complete success, then at least a quarter-hour of sustained illusion.

The high, leaded windows filtered out most of what little sunlight the day offered. Somewhere he had noticed . . . Ah, there by the door, of course. He flicked the switch up, and a loudspeaker coughed:

"KRAUGF! Mmmmb. You have come here," purred a velvety voice from the vault, "seeking comfort. At these moments when the burdens of daily life grew too heavy to be borne alone."

He swore. No other switch in view. He should have thought of this before.

"—we look to a Higher Power for assistance, as children will turn trustingly towards their loving Father. We raise our eyes—"

To the front of the church, at a half-run. Lifted the altar cloth, rapped the marble facing of the altar: it *sounded* solid enough. So, the entrance to the crypt must be concealed elsewhere; they were subtler than he would have supposed.

Then, to the side-chapels, each resplendent with its own Old Master, so that the church was a kind of digest of the major art thefts of the last quarter-century: Bellini's *Massacre of the Innocents* from the Hermitage; one of Ribera's more graphic martyrdoms (a flaying); the missing panel from the Isenheim Altarpiece, representing the temptations of St Anthony; the Rouault "Judge" from New York, and ...

By a trick of light the fifth side-chapel was as dark as the entrance to a cavern, and by a trick of acoustics the recorded sermon here reverbed with such force that its meaning became lost in its own resonances, like the jabberwocky of a great railway terminal.

"—the perfect joy of this surrender (OR RENDER) for only by (or render) giving (FORLORNLY) up the illusion of a (UP THE HILL, forlornly) personal identity can we hope (ENTITY) to achieve real (WEEP, entity) *freedom*" (EDAM! EDAM!)—"

There was something disturbing, something out of plumb about the interior of this chapel. The enfouldered darkness gave it the illusion of being much deeper than the other chapels, while in fact (yes, a glance into the Rouault chapel confirmed his suspicion) it was two to three feet shallower. The placement of the huge, time-blackened canvas on the back wall reinforced this impression (in the other chapels the paintings hung, in the usual manner, on the side walls where the light was stronger), so that the murky recessions of the painting contributed a second false depth to the chapel.

He took out his pocket torch and played its faint light across the painting. In the upper left corner, the least darkened, an oblate circle was sliced into ochrous stripes by the bars of a tall, ornamented gate, which enclosed nothing more, apparently, than this sunset. The heavy gilt lock of the gate was placed so as to provide the chief focus of interest, while off in the lower right corner, dwarfed by the rocky landscape, two figures stood, two dark silhouettes. The first, with his foot planted awkwardly upon a sharp outcropping, seemed to be trying to push away the second, who stood facing away from the viewer, a hand lifted, admonishing. In the other hand he held a small golden object.

He stepped closer to the painting; the ellipse of light tightened to a circle and intensified. Now he could recognise the painter – it was a Rubens – if not the subject. The white-bearded man seemed to be Peter. And the other figure: Christ?

Yes, for there, resting in the palm of his hand, were the two keys that he was offering to the reluctant apostle.

The painting began to move to the side with a slight squeaking sound. The light of the torch had been intense enough to have registered on the photoelectric cell behind the keys (heavily retouched by another hand) and to trigger the release-mechanism.

He jumped on to the altar and stepped across the ormolu frame (copied from Boulle) on to the first iron tread of the narrow spiral staircase.

Here the light was bright as in an interrogation chamber. He poked his torch through the thick wire lattice, shattering the light bulb it guarded.

Five steps farther down, a second bulb, and twelve steps on, the third. Pitch-darkness, and he heard above him the whirr and squeak of the painting moving back into its frame, the last muffled words of the sermon:

"—within this new hierarchy (IRE) of values (key of) lies the key to (LIES) the sturdy edifice (lies, dead) of our moralit—"

Silence, and the darkness. He continued the descent.

Chapter Eight

Twice Six

Into:

A corridor:

A sequence of doors. Above, just out of reach, parallel tracks of neon insisted on the raw whiteness of the walls. Far off, where the corridors bent, a single element, six feet of glass-tubed gas, flickered mortally.

Locked. And locked. And locked. And locked. And locked.

The sixth door opened.

A room: metal files. An iron garden-table and three iron chairs flaked white paint on to the concrete floor. On the table: a mug of coffee, still lukewarm; a Martina ashtray brimming butts; a crumpled Senior Service package; a box of safety matches; a Japanese paperback (he could not read the characters); three Danish girlie magazines; a plastic box of transistor elements; a ring of keys numbered from 2 to 15.

The keys unlocked the files; the files contained canisters of film. Each canister was stenciled with a red numeral (from 2 to 15), followed by smaller black code-letters. There were seventeen canisters marked with a red 6. He opened, at random, 6-SCHIZ. Squinting, he studied frames of the film against the light.

His face? And from this angle, the same or another?

Then: moustached, hair darkened – him? Or only a good facsimile? His judgment oscillated between credence and doubt. Yes it was he / No it was not.

Without a projector it would take days to examine all the footage contained in these seventeen canisters. And he had . . . minutes?

There was a second door. Which opened to darkness and a voice said: "Negative."

There was a scream, piercing, a woman's. He eased the door back but did not, quite, close it; he listened at the crack:

The voice, a man's: "Shall we try that again? Necessity."

And hers, unsteady: "Inter—" A choking sound. "No, inven—"

"Please, Number 48. Just give the very first word that comes to you."

"Intervention?"

"That's better, much better. Now: pluck."

"Courage."

"Negative."

And her scream.

His voice: "Again, Number 48: pluck."

"Cour—"

"Negative."

The scream.

"Again? Pluck."

"I . . . eye . . . eyebrow."

"Very good! We're making progress today, Number 48."

Inchmeal, as this dialogue continued, he widened the crack: darkness, and still darkness, though with a faint flicker of bluish light, like the death-throes of neon. Neither speaker in the darkened room seemed to notice the intrusion.

"Now, Number 48: courage."

"I . . . no, can't!"

"Courage."

"C— Ca— Collage."

"Continue with the sequence, Number 48."

He recognised the woman (wires twined into the shingled red-dyed hair, thick body strapped to the chair) shown on the screen as his confidante of a week earlier, the tweedy companion (the wife?) of the goitred man. Had it been the goitres who had left the film to play on unwitnessed in this room? And for what purpose, other than his idle amusement, had he been watching the documentation of this woman's torture?

"Collage," she said. "Cabbage . . . Kale . . ." The camera moved in to a close close-up, then tightened to a shot of her wounded eyes, eyes that stared, dilated, into a flickering light.

"Curtain . . . Cur – cour – age . . . Cottage . . . Cottage." The words she spoke seemed to crumble into their component syllables as they left her lips.

The man's voice: "Courage? Please respond, Number 48! Courage."

"Curdle! Curdle . . . curd . . . el . . ."

"Go on: curd."

"Cord . . . Core . . . Ca—Ck-ck-ck—"

"Core?"

The camera backed away to show the flaccid red lips, the powdered flesh eroded by sweat and tears, the jaw chewing slowly on unspoken words, and in her staring eyes a vague lust for the end of this pain, for nonexistence.

Then, abruptly, a blackness across which a dotted yellow line graphed an optimistic ascent towards the upper right corner: beneath, in bold letters:

NUMBER 48

Day 4

Pre–Terminal Aphasic Therapy.

The film ended. The tag-end of the reel flapped in the projector's beam, and the screen blinked a semaphore of black / white / black until he found the switch, flicked it OFF.

And ON, the overhead light.

Beneath the empty canister for *Day 4* were six others; the last day – 7 – was labelled *Termination and Review*. He replaced the film in its container in the same manner he had once, years ago (he remembered this entire era of his life intact), prepared a package of the personal effects of a friend (gored by shrapnel) to send back to his widow in Châlons-sur-Marne.

Threading the film of 6-SCHIZ into the projector, he wondered if it had been only that brief exchange on the terrace, the message scribbled on a napkin, those few guarded words, that had convinced the jailers of this place to perform their macabre "therapy". Would other Villagers be asked to pay as high a price for his friendship – for even such a small gesture in that direction?

And, if they were, could *he*, in justice—

A point of ethics he would have to consider at some later time, for now the numbers flashed backward to zero on the screen, and he saw himself waking, walking to a mirror, and staring at the image it recorded with an expression of disbelief and, to a surprising degree, terror.

A wide face that could have been called (and often had been) Slavic, though anyone who has known the Midlands would recognise the type: the fine brown hair that a single day of sunlight could dull to ash-blond; the rough modelling of brow, cheeks and nose, sturdy Saxon craftsmanship but scarcely a work of art; the thinness of the upper lip that opposed the fullness and slight thrust of the lower; the swag of flesh at the back of his jaw, a detail that had been coded into his family's genes for generations. It was a serviceable face – nor especially noticeable until you noticed it, but (in his line of work) all the more serviceable for that reason. It could express, most easily, stubbornness (indeed, whatever else it might express, that stubbornness would remain, a permanent qualification), but never anything that could be called elegance. Fortunately he had never wanted to be called elegant.

Such was the face that, without paying particular attention to the matter, he was accustomed to. But *this* face, the face on the screen, was this his, too? And (cutting to another shot, in another room) *this* one?

In the first sequence all the details seemed correct. His hair was the right colour, he wore it so. The clothes fit his body, the smile fit his face. But the eyes . . . ? The eyes seemed, somehow, amiss. But of course we only know our image from a mirror, unspontaneously; perhaps our unrehearsed expressions are quite different.

The second face was less obviously his own. The hair was darker, parted on the left. This face wore a moustache, though with apparent discomfort, for his hand (his left hand) kept reaching up to touch it, to tug at it, to test its reality. Yet apart from these merely cosmetic differences it was (it seemed to be) his face, his own.

Then: a shot of himself (moustached) walking down a street of the Village – or was it merely *a* village? Though the candy cottages on each side of the street resembled those he knew here, there were subtle differences in the warp of the land, the silhouettes of trees, the angle of the light. A seasonal difference? Or could there be, for villages as for people, such elaborate facsimiles that only by these slight tokens could the original be distinguished from its reproduction?

The man walking down the street wore a badge on his lapel that identified him as Number 12. Well, if they had to choose a number for his double, it could only be that.

Two stills, side by side: this same "Number 12" in a barber's chair. First, moustached, his darker hair parted on the left; then, shaven, the hair lightened to its natural (or was it, in this case, natural?) colour, parted on the right.

Then: himself – one of these two selves – in a room of bland modernity, sprawled on a modular sofa, looking very much at home, or doing a fair job seeming so. His other self entered at the door.

"What the devil . . ." his other self said. Surely for *one* of them the surprise must have been feigned. He wished that he were not such a good actor, though of course it would be the double who would be required to act, his own reaction the "genuine" one. No?

They approached each other until the camera included both in a medium close-up. They wore on the lapels of their identical jacket badges with the numeral 6. He could not be certain, seeing them together, which of them had been shown as 12 in the earlier footage. Had he seen an episode like this in any more conventional theatre, were he not already convinced that *he* had been one of the principals, he would immediately have assumed that this was nothing but trick photography, an actor playing a double role.

The self who had just entered nodded, smiling a thin smile (his). "Oh, very good. Very, very good. One of Number 2's little ideas, I suppose. Where'd he get you – from Xerox? Or are you one of these double agents we hear so much about?"

His smile, and the voice his too.

The other replied (smiling the same smile, speaking in the same voice): "Since you've gone to so much trouble, the least I can do is offer you a drink."

"Scotch."

And (he thought) on the rocks, by preference.

The one who'd made the offer went to the wrong cabinet; his doppelganger, almost apologetically, corrected the mistake.

As they faced the bar, their faces turned from the camera, one of them said: "I take it I'm supposed to go all fuzzy around the edges and rush into the distance screaming 'Who am I?'"

Was *that* the way he talked? He hoped not but he wasn't sure.

"Ice?"

"Please. Oh, careful! Not from the kitchen, you know. That's an ice-bucket on the second shelf."

They toasted. Again their two opposing profiles filled the screen. Each man studied his mirror image.

"Do you know – I never realised I had a freckle on the side of my nose. Tell you what, when they film my life story, you get the part." He turned The camera followed him. "Cigar? Ah-ah! With the right hand, yes? Yes. And that wasn't what *I* would have chosen for myself. Most people find my taste too individual, so I carry those as a courtesy. Also, they made a slight mistake with your hair – it's a shade too light."

The other: "It's not going to work, you know. I have a particularly strong sense of identity."

Yes, he thought, he did/I do. Provisionally he accorded this one (the sprawler on the couch, the fumbler at the liquor cabinet) the distinction of being his True Self; the other must be, then, the Double.

The Double answered: "*You* have?" And laughed: in pitch, in timbre, in rhythm it was his laugh. "Oh yes, I forgot for a moment – you're supposed to be me. You're Number 6, the goodie, and I'm the baddie who's trying to break you down. Right?"

It might also be maintained against this Double that his dialogue was bad, but then his own reply was not much better:

"Right. Only there's no *suppose* about it."

"Another drink?"

And so they continued, in close-up and medium close-up, their war of wit, until one of them (he'd lost track, by then, which was which) proposed a more effective test: they would duel.

It developed into a minor pentathlon. In all the events the one he'd elected to be the True Self came in a poor second. His score on the electronic pistol range was six hits to the Double's perfect ten. When they fenced (not without appropriate reference to *Hamlet*, Act 5, scene 2), the True Self's movements were overwrought, rough, even desperate, while the Double executed each thrust and parry with consummate ease, as (he pointed this out himself) one would expect of a fencer on the Olympics team.

"If ever I challenge you to a duel in earnest," he said, the tip of his foil pressed against the other's throat, "your best chance would be battle axes in a dark cellar."

They raced, but of this the cameras had recorded only the finish: the Double's triumph, his own chagrin, the resulting fight – and his further chagrin. He was spared from a definitive defeat only by the arrival of one of the Guardians, which shepherded them towards the Village's administration centre.

Cut to:

The office of Number 2. Here the modernity was anything but bland; it was the nightmarish progeny of the union of the Ziegfield Follies and IBM. It assaulted the senses, attacked taste, made pageants of plastic and Day-Glo paint. Was this the "warmth and simplicity" that Number 2 had boasted of?

Was this, for that matter, Number 2? This stripling youth, in hornrim glasses, dithering on in that pure Oxonian accent that only a few Fulbright scholars ever master? So – since the events of this film there had been at least one shuffling of the staff. It was another evidence of their weakness, and he welcomed it.

Cut to:

Himself, or his double, strapped and wired into the chair (or its double) in which Number 48 had received her "aphasic therapy". Dilated irises reflected the blinking light.

The voice of (the anterior) Number 2: "Who are you?"

And he: "Would you mind switching that idiot light out? I'm getting cramps."

"Who" (very owl-like, his who) "are you?"

"You know who I am. I'm Number 6."

"Where do you come from?"

"You know that too."

"How did you get here?"

"Ah! Now there's something you'd know better than I. I was unconscious at the time, if you remember."

The irises flared with a brighter burst of light, and his lip curled back in pain.

"What was your purpose in coming here?"

More and more, he decided as he watched *this* Number 2 go on, he preferred his own. If nothing else, he was a better entertainer.

"I had none. I'll go away if you like."

This time, at the cue of light, he cried aloud.

"How did your people know that Number 6 was here?"

"What people?"

"How did they know enough about *him* to produce *you?*"

"I don't understand."

Number 2, mildly: "What were you doing in the recreation room?"

"Showing this synthetic twin of mine how to shoot and fence."

So: this was the one he had supposed was ersatz. Then why (again the light flared, and he writhed in an agony that could not have been faked) were they torturing *this* one?

"For the last time, what do you people want with Number 6?"

And, screaming: "*I'm* Number 6, you sadist! *I'm* Number 6, you know I'm Number 6. I'm Number 6, I'm Number 6, I'm Number 6, I'm Number 6." Until, mercifully, he fainted.

He checked his watch. It was now fifteen minutes since he'd seen the three guards leaving the church, the limit he had set to this investigation, and half the reel still remained. Would he be cautious, then, or curious?

There was this to be said for caution – that he could never, in any case, stay to see all seventeen instalments of the serial; even if he could, it might be that he would learn only so much from it as his jailers wished him to know. The film seemed carefully edited – but to what purpose, on whose behalf? There had been something (he had known this all along) too pat about this undertaking, as though it had all been prearranged – the false escape, the alarm, his discovery of the secret staircase, the open door to the film archives, the keys laid out on the table, the projector left running. But if they had *meant* him to see this, were they likely to interrupt him now?

Curiosity, on the other hand, did not need apologies. It had become by now his dominant passion. He resisted it only to the extent that he adjusted the Fr/Sc dial to MAX. A blur of images skittered across the screen: his face, his other face, their dialogue a jabber of chipmunks; a woman (to him unknown); the three of them careening about Number 2's office, bobbing up and down in chairs, gesturing, chirruping.

Then, a procession of geometric images almost too rapid to be seen singly – squares, circles, crosses, star, and three wavy lines. Rhine cards – the abbreviated Scripture of the ESP fanatics, though how *these* had come into it . . .

Abruptly (half an inch was left on the reel) the tone of the film altered. He reduced the speed, backtracked, and saw:

His two selves, standing silhouetted in a cottage doorway. About them the dead black of a moonless night. The camerawork, unlike that which had preceded it, was shaky, botched, as though this one scene had not been stage-managed for the benefit of a television crew.

One of the two figures broke from the doorway (had they been fighting?) and ran across the lawn for several yards.

And stopped.

Directly before him stood one of the spheres. The streetlamp made of it a crescent of beige ("Rover" therefore) above the great, shadowed, pulsing mass. It advanced on the man who had run from the cottage; who, with terror, addressed it:

"The Schizoid Man!"

Rover rolled to a halt.

The other man stepped from the doorway and addressed the same watchword, though with more assurance, to the sphere.

It swayed and quivered, rolling towards the man in front of the cottage, then back to the other, like a wolf that stands at an equal distance above two equally attractive sheepfolds, unable to choose. The first man chose for him – he broke. He ran.

The sphere, pursuing, hit a stone in its path, sailed a few feet into the air, settled with a quiver, and swerved down the same sidestreet where the man had disappeared. The camera held the shot of the deserted street: there was a scream.

The reel ended with a final still: a tabletop, and on it a beltbuckle, a keyring with two keys, some nails, a cigarette lighter, a few odd-shaped tiny lumps of silvery metal, and a small silver disc of the type that surgeons use in repairing fractured skulls. Presumably, but for these few artifacts, the other remnants had proved digestible.

Was it of any significance that he had never had a silver plate in his skull? (More precisely, that he did not *remember* anything of that sort?) Finally, could he ever *prove* he was who he believed himself to be? Finally, can anyone? Conviction is not a proof, for he was inclined to believe that it had been the Double they had tortured, not himself, and he (the Double) had certainly been persuaded that he was Number 6. It was just that, the strength of that conviction, that made him think the man was synthetic: for he did not think that he (himself) at root would *insist* on being a mere number.

But it made no difference, really, who he was, who he had been, what he remembered and what he had been made to forget: he was himself, and he knew the interior dimensions of that self. This was sufficient.

Once again he reversed the reel. Again he watched the sphere start off after its victim, hit the rock, bound up, and settle, quivering.

There – in those three seconds of film, and not in any vortex of speculation and ravelled deceit – lay the *significance* of the thing; even if they had set up this private screening for some involuted reason of their own, they had betrayed their hand.

It was enough to make him laugh.

It remained for him to cover his tracks. He returned to the outer room and replaced all but three of the canisters (6-SCHIZ, 6-MHR, 6-FIN) in their drawer. He removed other canisters from other drawers at random, opened them, and piled their reels of film in the middle of the floor. Threw the empty canisters into a corner, except for two (marked 2-POLIT and 14-LESB); in these he placed the reels from 6-MHR and 6-FIN. The film of 6-SCHIZ was placed at the top of the pyre.

Using the safety matches on the table, he set it alight. With luck and good ventilation the blaze might reach the file drawers he had left gaping open; it might even work through the walls and into other rooms or through the ceiling to the church With this in mind, he propped open the door to the corridor.

He remembered another time – when? Long ago, years and years – like this: a room of gutted files and the first flickering as the heaped documents began to catch; himself standing, as now, on the threshold to – where had that happened? Ostrava? Or that other town across the border, a suburb of Krakow: Skawina? Wadowice? Well, that was the past – eventually, even without assistance, one forgot the names, the dates, the faces. There were just a few bright images here and there, like the sweepings from an editing room floor.

He paused at the foot of the spiral staircase. A voice said: "What the hell?" And a second voice, the goitres': "Someone has smashed the damned *bulbs!*"

The squeak of the Rubens closing, and the slow clanking descent of the two men in darkness.

Carefully, distributing his weight among all four limbs, he twined his way up the spiral of the stairs, pressing close against the central support-pole. At the twelfth step he stopped: the footsteps were now very near, the voices only slightly farther away:

"Hey, do you smell—"

"Smoke!"

The footsteps quickened to a staccato. He reached up blindly, caught a trouser cuff, and pulled. There was almost no resistance. A scream, a thud. An obscenity silenced by a second thud, and the irregular cascade of limbs and torso down to the foot of the staircase. No, not to the foot: three more muffled bumps. There, he had reached the bottom.

"Eighty-Three?" the goitres called down into the well of darkness. "Are you ... did you trip?"

The air was tinged with smoke that tickled his nose and throat. His heart beat not much louder or faster than usual.

"Maybe I should ... go ... and warn ..." The tone conveyed, like a Reuters photograph coded into binary blacks and whites, the image of his leg lifted at the knee, hesitating whether to place the foot on the tread above or the tread below, poised between two fears.

The foot came down on the lower tread. The goitres was more afraid, at last, of the consequences of neglected duty. He moved down into the thickening smoke by fits and starts, still calling on Number 83, who, in reply, had begun to groan.

Either his eyes were now adjusting to the darkness or some faint glimmer from the fire was lighting the stairwell, for when the foot, shod in white buckskin, came into view he could just discern it.

The goitres had not developed momentum equal to his companion's: when his leg was pulled out from under him, he fell solidly on his behind. He caught hold of the central pole, resisting the hand that would pull him farther down. He began to scream.

The buckskin shoe came off in his hands. Throwing it aside, he clambered up the steps to the goitres' level. A hand clawed at his trousers.

The goitres' face was a grey oval above a lighter grey triangle of shirt-front. He struck him across the side of his head in a manner intended more to startle than to cause real pain. He felt no malice towards their pawns. God knew what kind of men they might have been once!

The body tumbled slowly, moaning, from tread to tread.

He raced to the top of the staircase, where the smoke with no egress, was thickest. He tried to push the painting to one side, but it stuck firmly in place. Regretfully, he kicked his way through the lower left-hand corner (the viewer's left as he faces it).

Squirmed out through this hole, hopped down from the altar to the diapered floor. He turned back to make certain he had not damaged any of the finer passages. No, the rip did not extend beyond the dark jumble of rocks. A competent restorer would have no great problem with that. From the newly-made fissure in these rocks smoke curled forth in black, baroque designs. He thought of the harrowing of hell and left the church, still unobserved, whistling a tune he hadn't remembered for years, another shard dislodged from the proper strata of memory, while inside the velveteen voice continued to promise some kind of salvation to anyone ("you") who would surrender his insignificant identity to a Higher Power, which remained unspecified.

Chapter Nine

In the Cage

According to the general report of the Villagers, the fugitives had succeeded in their escape – but by the expedient of suicide. When the sphere capsized their raft, they had been far enough from the shore so that their weighted bodies sank to a good depth; there was ample time to drown before the divers could recover them. Number 2 maintained that this was an entirely legendary account, that in fact the fugitives had been caught warm and struggling and were presently undergoing rehabilitation.

"That's too bad," he had said.

"You would have preferred for them to be dead?" Number 2 asked.

"No, I'm not a romantic, and I don't expect death to solve any problems. It's too bad that they didn't escape."

"I'm surprised that, being there for the beginning, you didn't stay to see the finish. Where did you go, by the way?"

"An escape is as private a matter as lovemaking. As I'm not a voyeur, I went home. You mean to say there are actually minutes of the day your cameras aren't watching me?"

"Oh, I have the report somewhere, but asking you is easier. It's tedious study, cataloguing your habits, Number 6. You rise at seven, put on water for tea, shower, dress, drink your tea. Then, at seven-fifteen, you run to the beach for a quarter-hour of callisthenics. Then – should I go on?"

"I'll admit it isn't an inspiring theme. Now, if I were living somewhere else, I might put on a better show, with more variety."

"Which reminds me – when are *you* going to attempt *your* escape?"

"Soon, Number 2, soon."

"This inaction isn't like you."

"On the other hand, I'm not impetuous. When I do make my break, I expect to get through to the other side."

"To freedom, eh?"

"To freedom."

Number 2 chuckled. "Ah, it's little moments like this that make it all seem worth the effort. Don't abandon your ideals too easily, Number 6. Hold them up proudly, and show your pluck."

He paused to study his listener's response to this key word from Number 48's therapy. "Doesn't that word . . . ring any bells for you?"

"Should it? Was it the theme of one of your recitations?"

Number 2 sighed. A stalemate. "No, not that I recall, Number 6, but I'll see if I can't dig something up."

He made the promised escape two weeks later, a month from the day of his arrival. It had been carefully planned, the detail-work accomplished during the hours of curfew and the necessary apparatus cached at the eastern perimeter of the beach. The sheer rockface that bounded the beach all along its length pressed forward here into the sea. One could continue beyond this point only by taking to the water (and he knew that the bay was well-patrolled, that any escape by this route was almost guaranteed to fail) or by scaling the rocks, an action certain to call oneself to the attention of the Guardian that shepherded that sector of the plateau above.

The advantage of this position was its isolation. Villagers seldom ventured here, for the water was rough, the shingle more than usually coarse, and the prospect seaward without any picturesque merit. It was also, because of the cul de sac formed by the cliff, the outermost point from the Village to which one could advance without being turned back by the Guardians.

He stood, that morning, at the base of the cliff, surveying for the last time the line of ascent he had marked out.

7:20 am.

The sea heaved and shattered against the cliff. The cliff's shadow slid eastward by imperceptible degrees across the wet shingle. A muck of oil that had been steadily encroaching on the beach these past two weeks (a freighter must have foundered nearby during the storm) writhed amorphously at the water's edge, prismed, bubbled.

He climbed quickly to the first ledge, unravelling as he advanced nylon cord from a thick spool. The other end of the cord was knotted about his bundle of equipment.

The second stage was the most dangerous, though it did not take him to any very dizzying height, for here he had to move out along rocks drenched by the breaking surf. Twice his shoes slipped on the wet sandstone, and twice as he sought for a handhold the projecting rock tore loose, like a child's rotted milk-tooth, to vanish into the white turbulence below.

At the next ledge, forty feet above the beach, he paused for breath and dried the soles of his shoes with a handkerchief.

A gull leaped from a cranny in the rocks below and rode the updraft on a long arc, wings taut. As it sliced the air inches from his face, it screamed. A flicker of sentient black beads. And gone.

He had never seen another gull along the beach, nor in the town any birds but sparrows and pigeons. Had he been a believer in omens, he would have supposed this a good one.

7:24.

Without a pause at the third ledge, he scrambled up the last ten feet to stand, panting, on the ratchel, in sunlight. Grass stretched on before him to the south and west, a pastoral vacancy that reverberated with the crash of the waves on the sea-wall.

Where the cliff's overhang allowed him to draw up his equipment without danger of snagging it in the rocks, he drew the cord tight, tighter. It accepted the strain (as it had in his earlier tests) and the bundle rose, with a slow pendulous swing, from the beach far below.

Then (7:31): it lay spread out before him in the grass – a sack of food, twenty-odd lengths of curved aluminium tubing, and an adjustable spanner. Still no sign of a Guardian. He needed five minutes to assemble the cage, five minutes, and then let them bowl their whole armada at him. If, that is, there was any truth in Euclid's geometry.

He grabbed the spanner and set to work.

The sphere (it was baby-blue with a few lavender spots of acne) stopped short some thirty feet ahead. Always before at its appearance he had headed back like an obedient sheep to the Village.

"Budge me," he said. "Just try."

The oblate hemisphere of the cage was planted in the earth four feet behind him; not much farther behind the cage – the cliff's edge.

He would allow the thing five minutes to make a charge. Then, if it proved too patient or too wise, he would set off without that particular satisfaction.

To taunt the sphere (did they have some kind of robotic – and woundable – ego programmed into them?) he cast small rocks at it, which bounced harmlessly off its hide. (Plastic? Probably.) The sphere quivered, just as (he hoped) a bull, its rage building, would paw at the dust.

He dashed to the right, to the left, without, however, straying more than a few feet from his cage at any time. (El Cordobes, clowning close beside the barriers.) The sphere echoed his movements uncertainly, approached to twenty feet, to fifteen feet. He flung the largest of the rocks. Where it struck another lavender blotch slowly spread across the baby-blue. Then, if it had been a bull, it would have bellowed; it charged. He threw himself behind the cage.

Too late, as though it realised its error, it tried to slow. Too late: it struck the cage broadside, deforming at the impact. (The cage held.) The sphere's momentum carried it up across the arched tubing and, cresting the small dome, still up, and out.

He turned on to his back to watch it sail forth, blue against blue, into the vacant air, and drop (had it been alive, it would have screamed) towards the roaring confrontation of sea and cliff, of sea and cliff, and, now, sphere.

There was an explosion. One could just trace its outlines amid the continuing tumult. So, the things were mortal. He hadn't expected that.

The assembled cage stood a bit over three feet high, with a diameter at its base of seven feet. The 35 pounds of tubing, pilfered from the terrace restaurant (they had supported the umbrellas over the tables, the awning above the bandstand), described lines of longitude and latitude with diagonal struts to reinforce major points of stress. Though not as sturdy as a geodesic dome, this design required fewer joints and was therefore easier to assemble. Even so, its construction had occupied four hours of each night for the last two weeks.

For easier carrying it could be disassembled into three pieces, but he could also carry it, as he did now, tortoise-fashion, on his shoulders. He walked at a steady pace, for the slightest break in his stride tended to make the carapace tilt and snag a foot in the grass. His arms ached from the cruciform attitude required to keep it balanced, but caution was to be preferred to comfort. The next sphere might appear in an hour or in the next minute: until he was certain he had reached safe ground (and he didn't know yet whether he could, whether the Village was established on the mainland), he could not afford to let down his defences.

It was noon before the second sphere evidenced itself. This one was beige.

"Hello there, Rover," he called out, quickening his pace. The sphere followed at a considerate distance, sometimes shooting out on a tangent from its direct course in a sudden burst of speed, at other times describing broad loops or bouncing. Its erratic, whimsical zigzagging reminded him of a puppy at play.

At one o'clock he chose a level of ground and pulled the cage down about him firmly. Then he opened his make-shift knapsack and took out the lunch he'd prepared – a roast beef sandwich, pickles, two deviled eggs, and a pop-top can of soda.

Rover rolled up to the edge of the cage. Tentatively, sphere pushed at hemisphere. Joints creaked. It pressed harder, and beige skin bulged in through the squares and triangles of the lattice. He sipped his soda and watched the sphere slowly mount the mound above him and roll to the other side.

Then, a second time, with a running start that carried it over the top and several feet into the air. It landed with the sound of a fat body unstuck from a bathtub.

The third time it tried to climb the lattice of the cage as slowly as possible. Halfway up, miscalculating the force required, it collapsed back to the ground.

The cage had withstood each test without any sign of weakening.

The sphere withdrew to a normal conversational distance, and a voice said:

"Well, Number 6, I have to give you credit. This is a splendid idea, splendidly executed."

He looked around, but there was no one, nothing visible but himself and the sphere amid all this green uniformity, yet it *had* been the voice of Number 2, and, as the sphere shook like a bowl full of beige jelly, his laugh.

"Haunted?" Number 2 asked.

"Oh, another advance in technology. Where do you put the speaker, if you don't mind my asking?"

"This whole thing is just a membrane, you know, and then, what with the miracle of transistors . . . I can take the volume up to something unbelievable – LIKE THIS:

THE THING THAT GOES THE FARTHEST
TOWARDS MAKING LIFE WORTHWHILE,
THAT COSTS THE LEAST AND DOES THE MOST,
IS JUST A PLEASANT SMILE . . .

"But," he went on, sniffing, much subdued, "I have to remember to adjust the audio pickup on this end when I do that. It's much worse for me, with these earphones, than for you out out there in the pasture with your picnic basket. I always seem to be interrupting your meals."

"It's your most excusable fault, Number 2."

"May I ask you a personal question, Number 6?"

"By all means! Let's have no secrets between *us*!"

"It's about Number 127, the young lady with whom you had arranged a tryst this morning. I was wondering what *lure* you used to persuade her to come to such a strange place, at such an odd hour."

"Ah, how is she?"

"*This* is a fine time to show your concern! After sending her out to the meadow – and heaven knows what you'd led her to expect – as your *decoy*. She's back, a little sadder and wiser, but none the worse for wear. In fact, I think . . . let me see which camera is . . . yes, she's already back at her job. The restaurant should take her mind off your betrayal for a little while, but I'm certain she will never trust you again."

"She probably will never see me again. But if you would like to apologise to her on my behalf, I would appreciate it."

"I already explained to her that you were only following our instructions. That seemed to cheer her up a little."

"If I could have come up with any other way to divert Boy-Blue's attention, I would never have—"

"Yes, yes, I know: ends and means. People are only pawns in your ruthless bid for power, eh, Number 6?"

"For freedom, rather. And far from being ruthless, I think I've shown great restraint."

"You call arson restraint?"

"Arson? Did I leave something heating on the stove?"

"And the wanton destruction of equipment worth . . . well, I won't say how much."

"Boy-Blue, you mean? It didn't show that much restraint about destroying my equipment, which is irreplaceable, after all. It was quite ready to herd *me* over the cliff."

"That was an error, however. It was on auto-pilot, and though its sensory apparatus et cetera would have sufficed in most circumstances, it was simply unaware of the drop-off. The Guardians can sense objects and discriminate shapes, even in the infra-red spectrum, but the *absence* of an object requires some larger degree of sophistication. It shouldn't have charged, of course, and had I been forced to choose between you and it I'd agree that you're less easy to replace and therefore more valuable."

"You flatter me."

"But that doesn't excuse your taunting the poor thing."

"Well, perhaps I am ruthless. I'll tell you what – when we come to the *next* cliff—"

The beige sphere emitted a dry chuckle. "Oh, we can't allow you to repeat your successes. Rover isn't on auto-pilot: I'm in charge now. And our engineers are already making modifications to insure against any future repetition of such an error. But why am I telling *you* all this? Really, I'm too candid with you, Number 6. You draw me out. What is the secret of your charm? It's unnatural of me, your jailer, to deal with you on terms approaching equality. Don't you agree?"

"That it's unnatural? Quite. But unnaturalness – I thought that was the whole point of the Village."

"You're being semantic again, Number 6. What I meant was quite simple, heart-warming even. I feel an *affinity* for you – I have from the first. And admit it, Number 6, don't you feel something of the same sort for me?"

He glanced up quizzically at the huge sphere, which rolled forward a few inches across the grass, as a dog will step nearer when it is expecting to be scratched. "Well, I can say this much – nothing human is alien to me."

The sphere breathed a sigh, a brief hiss of gas before the puncture sealed itself. "That rather begs the question, but I won't press the matter. As for me, I have always found *everything* human to be alien. But this is all philosophy, and though I enjoy a little philosophy just before I go to bed, it sorts ill with heroic endeavour. Have you finished your lunch? Are you ready to continue this doomed escape? I am. This is quite a holiday for me, you know. I've never run one of these contraptions before. The sensation can't be described."

Indescribably, the sphere bounced up and down in place.

"All right. Why don't you back up some twenty yards or so, and I will be able to walk on much more comfortably. If you come too near, I shall have to go along at a crouch."

"But our conversation"

"Just raise your volume."

The sphere backed away with evident reluctance. "Here?"

"A little farther, I think."

"HERE?"

"There, and now—" He glanced at his watch (1:36 pm), strapped on the pack, and lifted the aluminium cage from the ground. Balancing the cage on his shoulders, he set off to the southeast. "—freedom or bust."

The sphere followed at the agreed distance. Number 2 had switched the audio to the regular Muzak tape that was constantly broadcasted over the Village PA system. Unconsciously, the sphere bobbed and his feet marched to the varying tempos of Sigmund Romberg's *Desert Song*.

3:20.

Two horizons: the first, an ochrous line of scrub, marked the limit of the foreground, so near that he could distinguish even from here the few late blossoms on the branches of the gorse and the guelder rose; the second, above this, was a thin wavering stripe of ultramarine – a pine forest. How far ahead, or what might still lie before it, he did not stop to consider.

He did not stop. He walked, crouched, never raising the cage more than a foot off this rougher ground, pocked with holes, dotted with boulders, intent on just the few yards directly ahead of him, careful of his own and his cage's footing.

The sphere, taking advantage of the irregular terrain, followed him closely or moved ahead in order to deflect him towards the rockier patches of ground, ready to rush against the cage whenever the lay of the land might make it the least bit vulnerable. It need not overturn the cage to succeed; it was enough, by attrition, to disable it, to bear down on it when some dip in the earth or spine of rock prevented an equal distribution of the load.

Cripples are easy prey.

And so he did not notice when the simple green horizon behind him generated the first telltale dot, the merest whirring gnat; did not notice even the gnat grown, at ten o'clock before its zenith, to a hawk's stature. Only when the shadow of its segmented body lay, flickering, in the dry grass ahead did he pay it any heed.

The helicopter hovered, describing a slow conical helix that narrowed and lowered towards him with gentle persuasiveness.

To the right the warp and wrinkle of the ground that arched up to the ochre horizon was less pronounced. The sphere, as he angled towards this smoother passage, darted ahead and planted its bulk before him. He veered left. The sphere rolled closer, pressed itself against the bars of the cage with force enough to bring them both to a stop but not so much that it would be propelled up and across the dome of the cage. It had learned the precise balance of thrust and counterthrust required to achieve equilibrium.

Little by little, he sidled the cage about the sphere, a small gear circling about a larger. Eventually the sphere had to concede another few yards of ground, but, so long as it persisted, never much more. Again it would station itself in his path, again he would be forced to revolve the cage's cogs about the base of the sphere. The sphere could not finally prevent his progress, but it could, and did, reduce the speed of his advance to a glacial crawl.

The helicopter depended directly overhead, deafening. Its rotors sliced at the molecules of the air, a sword-dance above the tiny, struggling Damocles below.

Again the sphere approached, and just as it would have pressed itself against the cage, he shifted the bars sideways. The sphere skimmed over one side, plopped into a boulder, bounced, and rolled several feet down the slope before it recovered its wits. He had gained a dozen yards meanwhile. He reversed his course, and the sphere bounded over the crown of the cage, landed with a damp smack, bounced high, and bobbed even farther down the slope. A gain, this time, of almost twenty yards.

Growing cautious, the sphere circled some distance ahead and bore down on him slowly until again sphere and cage were locked in their abstract embrace and again he had to begin the laboursome business of revolving the cage inch by inch across the resisting grass, the gouged earth: though he made certain at regular intervals that the joints were tight, he knew the aluminium latticework could not hold out against this kind of strain.

At 4:30 pm he was still fifty feet from the crest of the slope. It had taken an hour and ten minutes to cover 300 yards of ground (half that distance discounting the diversions and false starts that the terrain and the sphere had forced on him).

But now Rover seemed to undergo a sudden change of heart. It sailed up the hill on a smooth arc, its great beige bulk all atremble from the unequalness of the land. It topped the ridge, dropped from sight, then rose on a high skyward bounce, a swift beige idea of a flower, fell behind the ridge, rose again; though to a lesser height, and called out in a tenor voice that rivalled the bass of the helicopter:

"BRAVO!"

And, on the third bounce, lower, louder:

"MOLTO BRAVO!"

And finally, with just one hemisphere rising over the hilltop:

"WELL DONE, NUMBER 6! WELL DONE !"

At the top of the hill he thought of Moses on the bank of Jordan. He stood at a brink no tortoise could ever negotiate, a drop of twenty feet to the rocky ground, not sheer but steep enough to make the cage worse than useless.

The sphere bounced itself out, diminuendo of a Japanese drum.

"No, no, no!" it grumbled at a sane decibel level. "Not *now*, Number 19! Fly away home, and I'll whistle when I need you. Can't you see he's still full of *hope*?"

The helicopter canted left and rose to vanish at the horizon that had engendered it.

"And now, Number 6 – how do you intend to get down *here* without being tipped out of that shell of yours? Eh? Eh?"

"I'm thinking."

"The fault extends to your left for a good mile and for longer than that on your right. Of course, you *could* try and take your chances here."

"No, I'll take your word instead." He set off towards the left.

"You mean it – you really *are* taking my word! Oh, you sly fox! Do you know what I'm going to do just for that? What nice reward? I'll move off *way* down over there (oh, I keep forgetting I can't point – there, towards those hills) and let you lower your shell by its cord and climb down after it. In perfect safety, undisturbed. Isn't that big of me?"

"Number 2, you're a peach."

The sphere laughed uncertainly.

"I'm waiting for my reward."

It bounded off, beige on tawny green, towards the pine slopes, a mile across the intervening plain.

He lowered the cage by the nylon cord, eyeing the sphere carefully meanwhile to see whether it would swoop to the bait.

From the distance a tiny voice called to him: "YOU HAVE MY WORD."

The cage settled upside-down. He threw the cord after it and scrambled down the incline at breakneck speed. At the bottom he quickly set the cage upright, safely enturtled once again.

The sphere had not stirred. Its tiny voice called out: "READY?"

He started off in the direction of the pines. Two miles? Three?

"READY OR NOT!" The sphere rolled towards him, but preserved a comfortable distance, although the ground here was as uneven as it had been on the other side of the fault.

"Not so much as a thank-you?" Number 2 asked.

"Does the mouse thank the cat?"

"Perhaps a very clever mouse would."

"Clever mice – do they taste better?"

The sphere reproduced, highly amplified, a sound of smacking lips.

5:30 pm.

The hills were tantalisingly near. He cursed the long midsummer day, which he had been thankful for till now. Until darkness offered him an equivalent defence, he hadn't wanted to abandon the cage.

Number 2, who had been mumbling something to himself for the last mile about the Lake Poets (he seemed to have it in mind to bring them to the Village for rehabilitation), suddenly stepped up his volume and gargled for his attention.

"I hope you're beginning to get some idea, at last, of the futility of this adventure of yours."

"I thought it was the other kind of attitude you wanted to encourage in me, Number 2 – my idealism, my resolution, my optimism."

"Oh, those things are fine to talk about, and the entertainment industry would be ruined without them. But there are times one must be serious and despair. Not of everything, of course, but of these treacherous, abstract ideas. Freedom! As though we weren't all determinists these days! Where, in this vastly overpopulated world, is there even *room* to be free? No, Number 6, though you may clang your bells for freedom, the best that you can escape to is some more camouflaged form of imprisonment than we provide, though we do try to be unobtrusive. Freedom? Perhaps there was a time long ago, a Golden Age, when men were free, but I see as little sign of that utopia in the past as in the future."

"So much philosophy, Number 2. It must be close to your bedtime."

"Philosophy? Psychology rather, or literature. My arguments aren't based on reason but on the particular situation you find yourself in at this moment, sustaining, with ever-increasing difficulty, the illusion that you are escaping."

"If I can sustain the illusion long enough, it would be as good as a reality. That's Bishop Berkeley. I should think that jailers must experience a larger degree of futility than even the most degraded prisoner. A prisoner can take refuge in the consciousness of the injustice done him, and for him there are at least *fantasies* of freedom. But the jailer is sentenced to his jail for life: he and his jail form an identity. Every one of his prisoners might escape, but *he* would still be left, a jailer in a jail, the prisoner of a tautology. The very best he can hope for is to make his jail perfect – that is to say, escape-proof – but the manacles he loads with iron are locked to his own wrists. No, if it's a question of futility, I'd rather be a prisoner any day."

"All that you say, Number 6, is half true. Mine is not an enviable lot. It is, indeed, futile at times, but a little futility never hurt anyone. It's homeopathic medicine for the larger futility of Life with a capital L. However, there are *some* advantages in my situation. There is pleasure in the exercise of power, and more pleasure in the exercise of more power. I can hope not only to perfect my prison – our prison, I should say – but also to fill it with more and more and more prisoners, until finally – but it would not be modest to say that."

"Until finally you have made the whole world a single prison."

"It almost makes me sound like an idealist, doesn't it? My intention was only to demonstrate that even jailers have their dreams, and a jailer's dreams are, in a practical sense, more realisable than a prisoner's. The moral of that, Number 6, you may draw yourself."

"An offer of employment?"

"Possibly. Your qualifications are evident: you have initiative, intelligence, experience of the world. You lack only acceptable character references, but that could be worked on. If your interest is sincere, what better moment to demonstrate it than now, you are still, putatively, escaping?"

"Speaking of my escape – look: we've almost reached the woods."

"Yes, I was about to mention that myself. It means that I shall have to press you for a reply. You are still free to return, free to join us."

"Thanks, but if it's all the same, I'd rather be free to be free."

"You intend to return, then, to London?"

"Not then – now."

"And there, what will you do?"

"Contact the authorities."

"You see, immediately you leave our jail, you fly to theirs! I'm sorry, Number 6, but I really cannot allow that."

The beige sphere made a sudden rush.

Squatting, he pulled the cage down about him. The sphere swerved and interposed itself between the cage and the woods, pressed itself against the bars.

"We've been all through this, Number 2. The woods aren't fifty yards away. You've lost."

The beige sphere began to pulse at a rapid tempo. Its south pole depressed and darkened to chocolate-brown

"You won't reconsider, Number 6?"

"Not even if you threaten to turn to Golden Syrup and candy me. Sorry, pal."

"Well then, adieu," said the sphere, and shot high, high into the air.

"Finally," he muttered. He slipped the three false joints from the carefully sharpened poles and swung them on their hinges. Then, as the sphere reached the apogee of its ascent, he slipped out from the cage and begun running to the woods. He had not gone twenty yards when the sphere smashed into the cage with a loud metallic groan (the cage collapsing) and a plastic burp (the sphere punctured).

He turned to see the sphere gradually metamorphose into an ellipsoid, as it writhed, impaled, on the three spikes. It flopped softly to its side, and shook the wreckage of the cage from its wrinkling hide. Half its surface now was lavender, with scarlet pox-marks where the spikes had entered.

The hissing changed to a bubbling whistle, a flute clogged with spittle. Rather, a trio of flutes, which one by one abandoned their shrill, monotonous song. The damned things were self-sealing!

He started running, for his life.

The sphere bellowed at him: "FUM BLOOM EH SCHPUSH UFH! SHUH BEPPEP!" and lumbered liquidly after. Even half-deflated, it could slop along at a fair clip, but he reached the woods with yards to spare and stood once more encaged by the gigantic bars of the pines.

The sphere somehow was managing to re-inflate itself. It addressed him earnestly: "WABE, NUBBER SHES! WABE A MINNUB!"

He wabed, and in a minubb the sphere had reassumed its earlier, Euclidean proportions, though all but a little patch at the top was lavender now.

"Thank you," Number 2 said. "I wanted, before you went off, to extend my congratulations and—"

"If that's all, then I really must—"

"*And* to say that I've found that poem you asked me to dig up. So if you will wait just a moment . . ."

"Why not send a copy to my address in London?"

"Because it's very apposite to the present occasion. If I may?"

"Is it long?"

"Just six lines. It's called 'Pluck Wins.' Listen:

'Pluck wins! It always wins! though days be slow
And nights be dark 'twixt days that come and go.
Still pluck will win; its average is sure,
He gains the prize who will the most endure,
Who faces issues; he who never shirks,
Who waits and watches, and who always works.'"

At the northern horizon he saw the gnat that would become the hawk that would become the helicopter.

"That was nice, Number 2, but now I really must say goodbye."

"I understand. Goodbye, then, and I do hope you'll come back soon. I'll miss you, Number 6. You're my very favourite prisoner, you know. Give my regards to—"

Was he gone now? A regular rabbit, that fellow, when he had the chance.

"To my friend, Mr Thorpe," Number 2 continued quietly, "if by any chance you should meet him in London."

Chapter Ten

At the Office

"I'm sorry, sir," the receptionist said, "but Mr Thorpe *is* engaged. If you care to wait until—"

"I've waited, already, three days."

"I understand there's a *crisis* somewhere." Having spoken this most magical of words, she thumped a fat fashion magazine on the glass desk, nodded at the neat rows of people behind the glass wall. "You can see that you're not the only one who's had to wait. The crisis—"

"There's always a crisis *somewhere*. Thorpe knows me. He knows I wouldn't bother him unless I had a crisis, too. For that matter, *you* know me."

Though she wavered at "crisis," she could resist any personal appeal. "If you say so, sir. I am only following Mr Thorpe's instructions, and his instructions were that he is not to be interrupted on any account."

"I won't be put off any longer by these rituals. I *must* speak to him!"

The receptionist caressed one of the photographs, as though his anger threatened not herself but the glossy image on the paper. Once or twice a year there would be one like this, one who simply would not leave her alone. As though there were anything *she* could do for them! It was the whole purpose of her being placed here, at this glass desk, overlooking the glass-walled waiting room, that she should signify to those who waited that nothing *could* be done for them, that they might stew there for days, weeks, months, and no attention would be paid to them, no one would listen, that they were, in an official sense, invisible.

"He knows that, sir. A memo was taken to him on Wednesday afternoon, when you arrived, and again yesterday, and again this morning."

"If he knew I'm here, he'd see me."

Well, if he just refused to understand, then she would too! She stared intently at the vibrant new nomad fashion mix, flurries of red fox about a wool tweed vest, a lace-stippled linen blouse, brown kidskin knickers, cataracts of heavy gold chain, and boots by Herbert Levine.

"I'll be back tomorrow morning."

"Just as you like, sir." She smiled with the go-native Nomad Look from Ultima II, a melange of terrific tawny shades: pinks, ambers, opals, amethysts. "Tomorrow is Saturday, however, and Mr Thorpe *golfs* on Saturdays."

"Then I'll see him at his club."

She nodded, clinking her necklaces, bobbing her curls, pressing the button that opened the glass wall. As he left (without a single pleasant word) she thought how, if it weren't for people like him, her job would have been almost perfectly ideal.

She buzzed the wall shut, and the pages of *Bazaar* opened, like creamy petals, to swallow the frail butterfly of her mind.

"I'm sorry, sir," said the clerk, as he entered the camera shop, "but your projector isn't ready yet."

"It was promised for yesterday."

"We hadn't realised the problems involved, sir. If the film were an ordinary size . . ."

"If I'd thought it would cost me all this trouble, I would have done the work myself."

"And if *we'd* realised that, sir, we would have been pleased to let you."

"When will I have it?"

"Tomorrow, sir. Our man is working on it now."

"Tomorrow is Saturday. You'll be closed."

"I'll be coming in just on your account, sir."

"Will you look at that, Jeremy?" the clerk said to the man behind the curtain as soon as they were alone. "Have you ever seen such *incivility*?"

"But Mr Plath, I told you I had his projector ready."

"You never seem to remember what I try to teach you about *psychology*. Do you think he'd appreciate the effort you've gone to if it were ready for him when it was promised? Of course not. The more times he has to phone up or come back, the more he'll realise how hard he's made us work, and the more we can charge him for it."

"And you'll be coming in on a Saturday just for psychology, Mr Plath?"

"No, that was psychology too. The shop will open on Monday at the usual hour."

"And won't the gentleman be angry?"

"Naturally, Jeremy. That's the *point*. When they're furious, they'll pay any price just for the pleasure of throwing the bills on the counter and slamming the door. Why, once I got a customer to hit me starting off with no more than a simple black-and-white enlargement. He'd been coming here daily for three weeks. His attorney settled with mine for five hundred pounds – no, guineas it was. The best piece of work I've ever done. A triumph, Jeremy, an absolute triumph of psychology!"

"I'm sorry, sir," said the man behind the bar with a tactful frown. "You're quite correct in saying that this is Mr Thorpe's club, but—"

"*And* mine."

"Yes, sir, and yours, as you say. We've missed you recently. *But*, as I said, sir, this is Saturday. Mr Thorpe detests the course on Saturdays. It's so crowded, you know. Will you have another gin-and-tonic, sir?"

"I'm drinking Scotch."

"Of course, sir. You always drink Scotch, don't you? I don't know what's wrong with me today." As though to emphasise his malfunction, he dropped the glass he'd been drying for ten minutes into the sink: a starbust of crystal across the stainless steel.

The Muzak carpeted the air with *Humoresque*. He remembered having joined the club, but he could not remember his reasons.

"I'm sorry, sir," the old woman said with a pleased look, "but the Colonel is spending the weekend in the country."

"With whom, please? It's essential that I reach him at once."

"No doubt it is, sir. Everything that concerns the Colonel is essential. But—" She jingled the ring of keys chained to her waist. "—I'm not at liberty . . ."

"Then who would be at liberty?"

The housekeeper shook her head, as though he'd asked a question that was at once meaningless and faintly immoral, an invitation to indulge in a physiologically impossible act. "*You* ought to know that better than *me*, sir."

With that careful flaw of grammar she had as much as slammed the door in his face. Servants, it implied, do not converse with gentlemen, ever. Then, realising what she had implied, she did, in fact, slam the door in his face.

"I'm sorry, sir," said the operator, "but that number has been disconnected."

"In that case, perhaps you would do me a favour?" The receiver fizzed noncommittally. "Perhaps you would tell me *whose* number it was. Or the address, rather."

"What number did you say, sir?"

"COVentry-6121. Or COVent Garden. I'm not sure about the exchange."

"We're not allowed to give out that information over the phone, sir. I'm very sorry."

"Then why in hell did you ask the number?"

"I was *trying* to be helpful, sir," she answered aggrievedly.

He slammed the receiver into the cradle. His sixpence returned. He wanted to swear at someone, to their face, but there was only the telephone to swear at, an old black plastic telephone with halitosis, and you could see by its scars how often already it had been abused for the faults of its betters. Even so, he swore at it.

It couldn't be a plot. Not all of it. Not everywhere. Not every one of them, the clerks in stores, the secretaries in offices, bartenders, servants, telephone operators.

It grew increasingly difficult to remember that the world had *always* been like this.

The glass wall slid open. He stepped through. Already, as the receptionist lifted up her smile to him, he heard the inevitable though still unspoken words, in the way an astronomer anticipates, before the sky darkens, the exact position of Saturn in the constellation of Scorpio.

"Good morning, sir. Mr Thorpe would like to see you right away."

"He . . . would?" (As though the planet had vanished!)

"Yes, sir. No, not that way, sir. He's upstairs, with Colonel Schjeldahl. Suite P, on 7. Do you know the way?"

"I can find it."

"You won't find it if you use *those* elevators, sir. They're for the public.

Let me buzz a guard. He'll take you." She buzzed a guard. Before he'd been led away she remembered to ask: "Did you have a nice weekend, sir?" (That's the question you ask on Monday.)

He said, "Yes."

And even, "Thank you."

And even, "Did you?"

"I had a *super* weekend, just super!"

How nice of him to have asked, she thought. *He's actually a lot of fun when you get to know him.*

"My dear fellow," said the Colonel, "before you go off the deep end, let us explain! In our position you would have done exactly the same thing. Wouldn't he, Dobbin?"

"Yes, Colonel," Thorpe replied, "he would."

"We want to help you, but we have a problem. Tell him our problem, Dobbin."

Thorpe tapped the mural world-map with an electric pointer, citing with each tap a city and an aspect of the problem. "You resign. You disappear. You return to us with a yarn that Hans Christian Andersen would reject for a fairytale."

The Colonel, who had some notion of who Hans Christian Andersen was, chuckled and made a note on his memo-pad so that when he described this scene later at his club he would remember his assistant's joke. A regular wasp of a fellow, this Thorpe!

"We must be sure," Thorpe continued, speaking quite slowly for the Colonel's benefit. "People do defect. An unhappy thought, but a fact of life. They defect, from one side to the other . . ."

"I also have a problem," he said. "I'm not sure which side runs this Village."

"And we're not sure that this Village even exists. It's highly improbable."

"I've shown you the pictures."

"Postcards and pencil sketches of a holiday resort."

"I have other documentation."

"We would like to see it," said the Colonel agreeably, having caught the drift again. "Wouldn't we, Dobbin?"

"Absolutely, Colonel! Anything he can produce even slightly more concrete. Names, for instance."

"As I explained, the residents are given numbers. One seldom knows, even, which are the prisoners and which are the guards. However, if I could look over photos of suspected defectors – covering, say, the last ten or even twenty years – I would probably recognise several faces."

"*That*, old man," Thorpe said, touching him with the pointer, "is exactly what we're afraid of."

"Then you won't help me?"

"The Colonel and I will carry the matter higher up. In the meantime, if you'd bring in this other documentation . . . ? Tomorrow, shall we say, at eleven?"

"After lunch would be better, Dobbin," the Colonel said. "I'm always tied up in the morning. Let's make it two o'clock. If we should need to get in touch with you before that, perhaps you'd tell my secretary where you can be reached."

"At the moment I'm between hotels. I'll be here tomorrow at two. I want to see Taggert then. The receptionist tells me he doesn't exist."

"Dobbin and I will be discussing this with him today."

"I would have preferred to be present when you talk to him. I have somewhat more confidence in his listening to me."

"A ladder," Thorpe said, "must be mounted rung by rung. Before you *retired*" – as he pronounced it, the word might have meant anything else except *retired* – "you could omit the lower rungs. In *those* days, it was you who stood between Taggert and me."

"You're enjoying this, aren't you, Thorpe?"

"Mildly, old man. Mildly."

The bedsheet was pinned across the drapes of the hotel room to form a screen. A small cigar smoked, forgotten, in the empty canister marked 14-LESB. The film was threaded into the modified Bell & Howell projector, for which he'd been charged thirty guineas above the list price. He had only to touch the switch and the past that had been stolen from him would unwind itself, at the rate of thirty-two frames per second, into his possession, restoring the shadow of a memory if not the memory itself.

Why this reluctance, then? Why did his hand hesitate? Wasn't the crucial thing, now, to recover what had been stolen? Until he did, his escape would be the hollowest kind of victory, for they would still hold his past hostage, in the prison files, like the leg a wolf leaves behind in the steel jaws of a trap.

He touched the machine that held his memory – and was shown:

A glass wall. Behind it, the people, waiting. Some thumbed through the familiar magazines with the same skilful inattention with which a pianist in a cocktail bar might whip through *Mood Indigo* for the tenth time in a single evening. Others, less practised in patience, stared wistfully at the clockface above them like spurned lovers who are still allowed to be *present* so long as they never declare their love.

The *same* people. He knew them. In this film they were a little younger, their clothes a bit fresher, their eyes not quite so dull – but the same. He had sat in that room with them hours at a time. He could not be mistaken.

Then, a medium close-up of Thorpe, dressed for golf. Behind him, indistinctly, the Colonel was poking about in the sandtrap next to the fourth hole.

"We must be sure," Thorpe said. "People do defect. An unhappy thought, but a fact of life. They defect, from one side to the other ..."

The camera panned to his own face, zoomed in artfully to reveal the resentment that underlay the frustration, the stubbornness behind the resentment, and behind the stubbornness, the suspicion he had not permitted himself, consciously, either then or now.

"I have a problem too," he'd said. "I'm not certain which side runs the Village."

While the camera held its close-up on his face, the Colonel spoke: "A mutual problem."

"Which I'm going to solve."

"Quite," the Colonel said.

"If not here, then elsewhere."

There was no point in watching more of it. He switched it OFF, and in the darkness and the silence he caught the first whiff of the gas. The flickering.

He tried to stand amidst the sliding forms, on the warping carpet, above the roar.

The locked door was opening.

He knew that he had been captured long before he had escaped.

Chapter Eleven

On the Retina

"Where is he, Number 14? What is he doing?"

The woman in the white gown frowned, touching her closed eyelids gently with the tips of her fingers, touching then her temple where the white wires of the electrodes tangled in white hair. "Still at the gate, Number 2. Still at the gate."

"If you fed another image to him—" His voice entered the operating theatre through six loudspeakers, an entire campanile of consonants and vowels, as though the disembodied speaker had converted his physical substance into pure sound.

"Until the fantasy begins to develop autonomously, there is no point in that. The subject's still in shock. I trust you observed the scene he made here, *despite* sedation. That he should dream at all in his present condition is astonishing to me. Let me remind you, Number 2, that rapport is difficult enough to maintain without these purposeless interruptions. Are you so possessed by the vice of conversation that you can't restrain your tongue's lust for half an hour?"

"Number 14, if you think because you're wearing your white smock that—"

"Each word you say, Number 2, is a wedge between his mind and mine. Quiet now – he's moving! He's trying to . . . get in."

"To get *in*!"

"Or out, I can't be sure. Such a vacant place. Just bars, stretching up out of sight. Orangy-yellow light, no shadows. But a fine colour sense. I think I'll *like* this one's dreams. He's begun to subvocalise. Simple rhyming associations – they're not worth repeating. I think we can flash an image to him now. Number 96, is the beam adjusted?"

The technical nurse gave one last tug at the subject's head: clamped within the mould of tailored steel, it didn't budge. She took a reading from the chrome Behemoth positioned above his supine body. "Yes,

Number 14, the image should be clear as crystal."

"Number 28, I want just a silhouette, at ten milliseconds, until I've seen how long he holds the afterimage. I suggest that we begin with a key, Number 2. It should take him past those bars."

"I leave the matter in your fair white hands, Number 14. Entirely."

"Number 28: a key."

In an adjacent room a young man sorted through a file of slides, selected one, inserted it into the cybernetic idolon he served, which coded the celluloid image into the minimum series of retinal cues necessary to produce that image. This code was then transmitted to the Behemoth (a laser) positioned above the sedated subject. The infinitesimally brief image of a key was etched on to the retina of his left eye.

The woman winced as the wires twined in her white hair conveyed to her eyes the same dazzling image.

"*Ah!* Cut that to five milliseconds next time. It's far too bright. No, three. He's ... How fast!"

"Yes?" the loudspeakers bellowed curiously. "*Well?*"

"I'm .. he's in a church. The gate is an altar screen. I'm—"

"What of the key?"

Her laughter was warm, but such a little warmth was soon lost in the vast whiteness of this place, like a single germ struggling to survive in a vat of disinfectant. "What indeed! Tell me, Number 2, if the image of a key were blurred, what would it become?"

"Don't be a tease, woman! Just tell me what you ... what *he* sees."

"An executioner's axe, and it's a whopping big one."

The priest mounted the pulpit, a rude wooden platform that creaked beneath his weight. He wore a simple alb over a black surplice and a black hood of imitation leather. Reaching the platform he stooped to pry the crescent-bladed axe from the wooden block. The unseen congregation spattered tepid applause. The priest lifted the axe, signalling for silence.

"Dearly beloved," he said, the orotund tones muffled by his hood, which had not been provided with a hole for the mouth, "and you especially, Number 6." Again applause, again the lifted axe.

"We are gathered here today to surrender, or render unto seizers the things that are gauds. We must axe ourselves who we really are, and let the sleeping

doggerel that is within us lie. This is the first stone, and upon this stone we will spill our dirt, in order that these lies shall not have been dyed with the blood of our veins."

He turned to the wispy, wrinkled, white-haired woman next to him and inquired of her the name of this preacher. Smiling, she pressed a senile finger to her withered lips, a finger that resembled the numeral 1.

The preacher placed a large book upon the wooden block and read to the congregation "The Crime of the Ancient Mariner," chopping off the stanzas that displeased him. Soon the pulpit was brimming with the lopped heads of seagulls, but he continued to read the dismembered poem, while the congregation reverently filed up the aisle to receive, each, his own severed head.

"This is accomplishing nothing," Number 2 burst out through his six speakers, after listening to the doctor chant the first thirty stanzas of the "The Rime of the Ancient Mariner." "We have learned only that at some point in his schooldays he was required to memorise Coleridge's stupid ballad, and that he now associates that memory with prisons. We must establish whether or not it was *he* who broke into the archives and set that fire. That should be easy enough to find out. Then, we shall explore his more interesting recesses."

"You had told me," the doctor said, 'that there was no doubt he'd done it. The two films taken from his file, one of which was found in his possession in London. His fingerprints on everything. Any court could indict with evidence that strong – *legally*!"

"That's why a doubt lingers. He isn't a bungler. It might well be that the film we found him watching was mailed to him, as he claims, in London. As for the fingerprints, they would have been available to any of us."

"Of us? Surely you don't think . . . ?"

"Everyone, including myself, would like to see certain of those records destroyed. Why did *you* first come to work for us, Number 14, eh? Not purely from your dedication to science. 3, likewise, would prefer to forget that unhappy incident in Poland. 4 might well wish for some final discontinuity with his 1952-model face. 6 – his motives are different but even more compelling. 7? 7 is always whining that he wants to be back in London frying literature in a cork-lined cell."

"We both know, Number 2, that my brother is *incapable* of such derring-do. He's a dear boy, but *quite* incapable."

"Personally, I have a higher regard for the boy's capabilities, but that's not at issue."

"I would have thought you'd take more satisfaction in accusing *me*."

"Not accusing, Number 14 – suspecting. None of us were continually before the cameras or with witnesses during that afternoon. Any of us *could* have used the tunnel to get to the Archives and back. Except 8, of course. He was in *your* care at the time, wasn't he. But 9, 10, 11, 12, 13, any of *them*, in any combination."

"It all sounds very baroque to me."

"Rococo, if you like. It isn't *my* idea in any case – it's Number 1's."

For the first time during this exchange, she opened her eyes: they were of different colours, one milky blue, one hazel-brown. "Damn!" She closed them quickly, covered her face with her hands. The high pale brow furrowed with concentration.

"Did you lose rapport?" Number 2 asked anxiously.

"No I'm still ... the priest is still chopping up seagulls."

"And the vocal?"

"This one's a strong subvocaliser, so that's no problem. I do wish you wouldn't say things to startle me like that. I *could* have lost touch. Now, what image do you suggest in order to lead him back to the scene of the crime?"

"Why not a photograph of the room?"

"Too complicated. The laser would burn his eyeballs out before enough identifying detail could be established. It has to be something readily gestalted."

"Could you suggest a descent down a spiral staircase?"

"Number 28," she called out, "do we have anything like that?"

"Just regular staircases," the young man replied from the next room. "There's a code classified as 'Vertigo.' Would that do?"

"Possibly. Space out the cues, and it should be almost the same sensation."

"Right."

Number 14 gasped. "*Slower!* It's—Oh! oh, this is awful, I can't—Slower!"

"If I space the cues out much more," he complained, "the programme will run to five minutes before it's completed."

"Then cancel it. The resemblance to a stairway of any kind is nil."

After a long pause Number 2 asked: "Where is he? In the crypt?"

"Not there, no. I don't recognise the place. We'll just have to let him make his way around, until I can tell. We can't feed more cues to him for five minutes at least. That "Vertigo" sequence was murderous. Number 28, make a note to modify the code for "Vertigo." Strange ... I'd swear I've seen a place exactly like this, but for the life of me ..."

He was in hell. The parks were planted with beds of tulips and marigolds. Muzak played in the busy streets. It was a holiday. CLOSED sign hung in all the windows. The signs in the grass said SMILE.

He asked the taxi driver what the place was called, but the taxi driver said he wasn't allowed to be there. Like all the other damned souls, the driver was very small, almost a miniature.

The old woman he had sat next to in church got in the back seat and sat next to him in the taxi.

"Are you going to vote today?" she asked, smiling.

"Who is there to vote for?" A rhetorical question.

She tisked. "There's always Someone to vote for, Number 6. Here—" She dug into her purse and took out a large gilt button, which she pinned to the lapel of his jacket. It said:

GUILT

"That's some kind of progress anyhow," Number 2 grumbled. "It shows that his attitude is maturing."

"No, wait—She's getting out. He took the button off the minute she was gone, put it in the ashtray. He wore it from courtesy rather than conviction. Now he's getting out. There's a large hill. And there's Rover. This must have something to do with his escape. Now he's pushing Rover up the hill."

"An allusion to Sisyphus, my dear. Number 6 has a classical education."

"Rover's talking to him. Do you want to hear what—"

"Of course, woman! It isn't *Rover* talking to him, it's *me*. He's dreaming about *me!*"

She let the patient's unspoken words, the dream's faint resonance in his larynx, be amplified by her own mouth, shaped by her own lips. The voice Number 2 heard was neither hers nor his, but theirs together:

> "But tell me, tell me! speak again,
> Thy soft response renewing—
> What makes that ship drive on so fast?
> What is the ocean doing?"

"Oh hell, hell, hell, hell, hell, hell," the six loudspeakers chorused. But Number 2 knew better than to interrupt again, so, while Sisyphus/6 struggled at his task and the Ancient Mariner jingled interminably towards redemption, he waited, daydreaming of his own hells, the ones he had already made, the better hells to come.

Hell is filled with The Sound of Music. *Forlornly, he pushes the great beige stone up the hill; forlornly, it rolls down again. How many times? How many more? Forlornly, up the hill; forlornly down. He has read this myth, he knows the story, but he was caught within the role and his contract required him to stay with the show for its entire run, and already it was threatening the record set by* The Mousetrap.

"No, Number 2, the only vocal I get now is just those songs. I get the impression that he's thinking too, but I don't get a glimmer what about."

"Nonsense, nobody *thinks* in their dreams! That's the wonderful thing about the id, that it doesn't have to think. But I shouldn't lecture you in your own speciality. While you were warbling, I thought of an image certain to prove whether or not he was down there. The one film of him that had been put on the bonfire concerned an earlier contretemps with a double we provided for his amusement way back when. What was left on the reel showed that it was reversed, as though it had recently been played through quickly and not rewound. Let's flash the image of his own face on to his retina. Surely, if he saw that film, there'll be some indication in his dream."

"There's one drawback in that. I've done the same thing with other subjects, usually in the routine course of charting libidinal structures. Seeing oneself tends to bring one nearer consciousness, especially when there is a strong narcissistic component."

"If he starts to rise to the surface, we can drag him back under with a big heavy archetype."

"All right. Let's have a photograph of Number 6."

"Here it is," Number 28 called into the amphitheatre.

"28, you oaf! That was a profile! I wanted him full-face. No one ever sees himself in *profile*. Damn! It's too late."

Outnumbered, he continued to struggle. The guards forced him down on the operating table. The surgeon appeared, all in white. Even her hair, though she was no older than himself, was white, spun glass, luminous. Though of different colours, her two eyes showed a distinct resemblance one to the other. In her own analytical way, she seemed to be admiring him.

"Number 28, hand me the new identity, please."

The young man handed the surgeon a wide, somewhat Slavic face. She examined the profile, touched the moustache tentatively, ran a comb through the dark hair, changing the part from the right to the left.

"Hold still, please, Number 6. This won't hurt."

She grafted the face to his, tugging at the seams when she had finished to make certain it would not come off under pressure.

"Excellent! Now bring me that other body, Number 28, the one from the freezer. Once we've locked him in that, he'll be no trouble at all. There's no sturdier cage than a hundredweight or two of good solid flesh."

"This other face, what does it look like, Number 14?"

"Like his, of course."

"In the film, at one point, he was shown with a moustache and his hair darkened. If the face in the dream—"

"No, Number 2. The new face is *exactly* the same." (And, she added with silent spite, *you* can go to hell. Her lie was not a matter of protecting the subject so much as it was a way of getting at *him*.)

The loudspeakers soughed a sigh. "Of course, that doesn't prove it *wasn't* Number 6."

"Unfortunately, though, it won't convince Number 1 that it couldn't have been one of us. For my own part, I'm convinced it was 6. Shall we keep trying?"

"How much time have we left?"

"Ten minutes at most. Beyond that there's a danger of personality disintegration – for either of us or both. Also a possibility of reversal, which is harmless but a waste of time. That is, if I try to channel the dream too often where I want it to go, he may start dreaming *my* dream. Or else – I'm not sure just how it does happen – I lose an objective sense of what his dream is about, like critics who find their own theories in everyone else's books."

"I can see you're under a strain, Number 14. You never start to lecture me until you're tired. So, with the time left, I'd like— Oh, what is he doing now, by the way? Still strapped down?"

"In effect. He seems to regard the second body as a kind of straitjacket."

(*The way he stares at me, she thought. I wish he wouldn't.*)

"We must learn something about the interval he spent away from us. Not his little jaunt last week to London, but the longer absence when he was not observed. Once we know who was involved in his brainwashing, we'll have a fair idea of what techniques were used. I suggest, therefore, that you begin with the photograph of Number 41."

Liora!

He tried to approach her, but though the straps had been removed, his imprisoning flesh was adamantine, unyielding.

He tried to speak, but his mouth would not form the syllables of her name.

Her name – Liora. And her eyes.

Her eyes!

"What fantasies now, eh?" If loudspeakers could wink . . .

"Nothing."

"Nothing? But I thought they were in love!"

"Wait. Her eyes—"

"Only her *eyes?*"

"—are glowing. The strangest thing."

"That's as good as nothing. I think you should chart *his* libidinal structure."

"Incredibly, incredibly bright. I—I—Oh, it's—"

"Try and get a *real* response out of the lout, Number 14. Let's flash him a weapon, or something *positive*."

"So bright. My God, Number 2 – it's beautiful! I've never seen a thing so beautiful. And he's—Why does she—"

She screamed.

"Number 14?"

She had fainted. As she slumped forward, the electrodes tore loose from her temples, unravelled from the white hair, and at the same moment, her patient woke smiling amid the collapse of his dream.

PART III NUMBER GAMES

"Thus, albeit straitly confined in a small enough cage, Fabrizio led a fully occupied life; it was entirely devoted to seeking the solution of this important problem: 'Does she love me?' The result of thousands of observations, incessantly repeated, but also incessantly subjected to doubt, was as follows: 'All her deliberate gestures say no, but what is involuntarily in the movement of her eyes seems to admit that she is forming an affection for me.'"

Stendhal, *The Charterhouse of Parma*

Chapter Twelve

The Nomination Committee

The fat woman ascended from the sofa, like a giant squid rising out of the sea, in a froth of pink chiffon. "May we congratulate you," she burbled, "on your *swift* recovery?" His hand still on the knob, he stared with glum astonishment at the crowd assembled in his living room. Three ... four ...

Seven of them.

"Budgie, my dear," said the fat man, also rising (the teak creaked relief), "*shouldn't* we apologise first? We have, you know, rather invited ourselves."

"But, dear darling sweet, it would hardly have been a *surprise* if *he'd* invited us!" She smiled with a Gargantuan coquettishness, inviting him to share her amusement at dear darling sweet's inanity.

"You should, at the very least then, *introduce* us." He shrugged bloated shoulders, as though to say: *Our Budgie is incorrigible, but we must love her just the same.*

"I was just *about* to, my pigeon, before you interrupted. Be assured, Number 6," she said, her hand fluttering forward to roost on his, clenched about the doorknob, "that we would never have taken this liberty" – she tittered, as though, she had risked a slightly off-coloured remark "without Number 14's assurance—"

The doctor nodded to him with the very smallest smile. Not half an hour ago, he had left her in her ceremonial white smock at the hospital. Now she wore a summer dress of silky pastel flowers. A cluster of fresh-cut roses was pinned to the white wide-brimmed straw hat that framed the whiter hair.

"—that you would be *delighted*—"

"Thrilled!" the pigeon added, his head bobbing up and down excitedly.

"—by the news we've brought you."

"The offer, so to speak," the pigeon explained. "The opportunity."

"I am, or rather I have been, the Mayoress of this Village, and *this* is my husband."

The pigeon blushed to have his distinction so publicly proclaimed. "Number 34," he murmured modestly.

"Yes," the ex-Mayoress continued, "he is Number 34 and now I have no other wish *myself* than to become, once more, Number 33, a private citizen, a mere equine among equines. Your other guests constitute, with us, the Nomination Committee in its entirety. You are already acquainted with Number 14."

"Number 6 and I are almost old friends by now," the doctor said.

"Have you met her brother too? Number 7, one of our youngest citizens, but not by any means the least."

The young man who bounded forward to shake his hand looked to be in his mid-twenties. If her brother, then distinctly a kid brother. He shared the doctor's idiosyncratic good looks: the fine hair was cut down to a nap of blond cornsilk; lively eyes of a stark, ingenuous blue; a wide, dimpled chin; a wide, dimpling smile; a nose just pleasantly out of plumb; clothes of calculating modesty.

"I've looked forward so much to meeting you, sir," he said, earnestly, gripping his hand with convulsive strength. "My sister's always talking about you. Everybody talks about you. I think—"

Then, stage-struck, words failed. He smiled dismally at imagined spotlights and dropped his hand. The blue eyes stared at the splendid, unobtrusive, hand-sewn cordovans from Maxwell's, Dover Street.

The fat man led Number 7 back to stand beside his sister, who took the dangling, defeated hand fondly between hers.

"We're all very *fond* of Number 7," the fat woman confided loudly, "but he does have an enormous sensibility sometimes. It only lasts a moment, and then he'll be himself again, if we just ignore him. Now, let me see, who's left? Do you know Number 83?"

The man indicated stood apart from the other Committee members, slouched against the damask curtains of the false window, waiting to be photographed. His arm was in a bright Madras sling.

"I ran into Number 6 at the railway station the day he arrived – but we were never formally introduced."

"Well, well," the pigeon cooed, "numbers aren't that important, are they? With some of my best friends I can't remember their numbers from one minute to the next."

The fat woman shrieked agreement. The pigeon, rewarded, tried to repeat his success. "I'll lay odds that old Granny here doesn't even know her own number. I'm sure that none of *us* do, anyhow."

Granny (there could be no doubt which one of them was "Granny") gave a dry chuckle. Sitting all folded up on one of the Chippendale chairs, she seemed more than ever to be a greeting card come, just barely and for only a little while, to life.

"Pigeon-poo," the ex-Mayoress chided, "what a *terrible* truth for you to say! Of course she knows her number. We all do. She's . . . she's . . ."

"Number 18," said Number 7.

"Number 42," said Number 14.

"Number *60*," said the fat woman, resolving their discord with a sum. Isn't that so, Granny dear?"

"Yes, thank you," said the old woman. "With a wee bit of milk, please, and one lump of sugar."

The pigeon sniggered. The fat woman sighed. She patted the aged hands with the expert condescension of a Practical Nurse. "In just a minute, Granny. We haven't *actually* been invited to stay."

He remained grimly silent. It was clear now why he'd been released from the hospital while he was still reeling from the sodium pentathol.

The pigeon pouted his lips and rolled his eyes in a dumb-show of social distress, as though his wife had just spilled the imaginary cup of tea on the Sirhaz carpet.

"We call her Granny, you see," the ex-Mayoress twittered on imperturbably, "because she's been here in the Village longer than any of the rest of us can remember. And she's *such* a darling that you can't help feeling that she *is* your grandmother. Especially since there is such, how would I put it—" The face frowned itself into a cluster of pink grapes.

"A scarcity," the doctor suggested, with a squeeze of her brother's hand, "of more authentic family relationships?"

"Ah, doctor, you are blunt, blunt, but your mind cuts like a knife! That's just what was never so well expressed. Now, is that all of us?"

"Me?" asked the seventh committee member, pressing his Homburg into his lap.

"Oh yes, last but not—" She coughed. "Number 98. If you've been into the Stationer's, Number 6, you might remember him." (Or, her tone implied, you might not.)

The Stationer's clerk rose from his chair and approached his unwilling host. "We've had the pleasure, that is to say, I've had it, when this gentleman . . . The uh, sketchpad, if you . . . ?"

He lifted his hand meekly, not so much offering it to be shaken as to question its suitability for that purpose, or any other. His host did nothing to relieve him of the responsibility for this decision, and he retired, with his questionable hand, to the chair, where his Homburg was able to offer him some degree of reassurance.

"There now!" the fat woman said contentedly. "We're all *friends.*"

The Nomination Committee looked at him, each member smiling his or her characteristic smile, each refusing to acknowledge the obvious message of his determined silence and the door he held wide open.

At last he conceded defeat: "In that case, would you do me the courtesy of explaining your friendly visit?"

"*You* tell him, Budgie," Number 34 insisted.

"It's hardly for *me* to do that! *You* tell him, pigeon."

"But I can't! Don't you remember – I'm on the *Election* Committee. It wouldn't do!"

Finally it was Number 14 who, with no attempt to conceal her amused disdain for the idea, broke the news to him: "The Nomination Committee has decided to nominate you, Number 6, to succeed Number 33 as Mayor of the Village."

"The Nomination Committee would have saved themselves a lot of trouble if they'd asked me first. I refuse to be considered."

"Didn't I tell you, Budgie," the pigeon burst out angrily. "Didn't I *predict?*"

"Your refusal doesn't affect the nominating procedures, I'm afraid. In fact, the ballots are already printed, and the election is tomorrow."

"My thanks, then, for having informed me. Now, I suppose, you must be anxious to fly away and tell the other candidates the same good news."

"There are no other candidates, Number 6. You were our unanimous choice."

"Unanimous," they murmured in chorus. Even Granny's lips seemed to approximate the right syllables.

"So," the fat woman said, "in effect, you are already our new Mayor. May I be the first to offer you my sincere congratulations?"

"All right then, elect me Mayor. Proclaim me president, proconsul, anything you like. But don't expect me to act my part in the farce."

"As for that," the doctor said, "you needn't worry. The Mayor has no duties whatever."

The ex-Mayoress puffed up indignantly, and the pigeon rallied to her defence: "I'm amazed at you, Number 14 – to say such a thing! Why, the Mayor of this Village has *unbelievable* duties!"

"*Utterly* unbelievable," she echoed. "Not to *mention* all the paper-work involved."

Granny's hands, which till now had been resting in her lap emblematic of the peace that passeth understanding, seemed to have sensed (independently of her face, which still wore the same serene smile) the discord growing about them, for they were wandering in agitation all about the crepe of her dress, plucking at folds and tugging at buttons.

It was Number 98, the Stationer's clerk, who first noticed these symptoms of distress. He rushed across the room and knelt beside the old woman, trying to soothe the troubled hands, whispering to them and petting them.

He looked up imploringly at his host. "She really should have a cup of tea, sir. All this dissension, it's bad for . . ." One of the hands escaped from him, grabbed for his ear. ". . . her heart!"

"Very well," he said. "We don't want to make more work for Number 14. Darjeeling or Earl Gray?"

"Earl Gray. But don't you trouble yourself, sir – I can make it. It will only take me a . . . a . . ." He looked for the word on the carpet.

"An *hour* at the very most," Number 14 said, helpfully. "And I'll take lemon with mine, if you have one that's fresh."

The pigeon and his wife plumped down with one accord on to the brave little sofa. "Budgie would prefer cream to milk," he called out to Number 98, who had run into the kitchen.

"And my little pigeon likes *his* just as sweet as sweet can be, doesn't he?"

Her little pigeon gave his big Budgie a little peck.

"Now, Number 6," the doctor said, tapping a sharp almond nail on the arm of the Chippendale the clerk had vacated, "why don't you sit down and make yourself at home?"

"I hope you don't mind my staying on this late," said the doctor's younger brother, helping himself to another Scotch. "But it was important I speak to you *alone*. What time is it, by the way?"

"Mm! What? Oh, yes." He opened his eyes, studied his unwound watch. "Nearly six. P.M., that is."

Every surface of the room was covered with dirty cups and saucers, plates of biscuits, ashtrays, and glasses half full of watery liquor.

"They all just insisted on staying. I was getting desperate," Number 7 said.

"They did, yes, and so was I. When you say that we're alone, though, you forget—" He gestured to the corner where the numberless old woman, noticed, twinkled benignly and chinked cup against saucer, as though to say: What a very *nice* party!

"Oh, but that's just Grandmother Bug. No one worries about *her*."

"Bug? Isn't that unkind?"

"It doesn't bother *her*! does it, Granny?" He flashed a triply-dimpled smile at the old woman, and she gave another chink of recognition: What a fine time we're *all* having!

"There's a theory, I don't say that I believe it, that she isn't altogether, how do you say, *alive*. Just a kind of machine. A mechanical person, like in *The Tales of Hoffmann*. To my mind, extreme senility amounts to the same thing – one is reduced to the condition of a machine. Of course, age only makes it more obvious."

"Makes what more obvious? Excuse me, I was dozing."

"I mean, with the sort of thing my sister does at the hospital you don't need to make *machines* to do that sort of thing."

"What sort of thing?"

"Well, anything. In her case, bugging. Which is why it makes no difference if Granny stays on. This cottage must be bugged in any case. Do you have access to the floor above this?"

"No."

"That's the standard design. There should be four cameras here in the living room – I see one of them just above the mirror – and three in the kitchen, four again in the bedroom, and one in the W.C."

"Two."

"Ah, you have a shower. I only have a tub."

Once more the young man braked to a sudden silence. Stirring his drink morosely, he resumed at a safer speed. "You'll probably think this is ridiculous, but I felt I had to tell you that I admire what you've been doing. Terribly much." As though recoiling from his own confession, or perhaps simply unaccustomed to this much Scotch, he collapsed on to a Chippendale.

"What have I been doing?"

"Your escape! You don't think anyone is taken in by the story that you spent this whole week in the hospital—? My sister told me all the details. *She* was terribly impressed too. We both think you're wonderful. Do you . . . I mean, my sister, does she . . . ?"

"She tried to brainwash me, if that's what you're getting at."

"Oh, no! I mean, of course she did, that's her *job*, but she didn't do anything like what she *might* have. You have a very strong ego structure."

"Thank you."

"It's a fact. She says it's almost impregnable. But what I meant to say, before, was – are you . . . fond of her?"

He laughed, and Grandmother Bug laughed with him, a little uncertainly, for she'd been caught unawares. If they were telling jokes now, she would have to pay closer attention.

One could not tell if the young man's sigh was one of relief or disappointment.

"Perhaps you think that she's . . . cold? Women doctors generally give the wrong impression that way, you know. Even before she was brought here, it was always painful for me to see how people reacted to her. Actually, she's a very *warm* person."

"One of the warmest in the Village, I've no doubt."

"Oh, but you can't blame her for being here, any more than you can blame yourself. We're all *victims*, you know. She was blackmailed into coming. Three months after she arrived, they got to me. I was *kidnapped!* It was the most exciting thing that ever happened to me."

"What do you do for them?"

"Me? I've never done anything for anyone, except keep them company. My sister says I'm a dilettante, but that makes it sound more *professional* that it really is. I imagine they thought it would improve her morale if I were around. I imagine it has. We've been awfully close to each other since we were this big." His fingers measured a smallish embryo. "Also, I write. Poetry." He made it sound like one of the least fashionable diseases.

"But then anyone who doesn't have anything better to do *writes*. Do you write? No, of course not, not *you*. That's just why I admire you so, because you do do things. And what I want to suggest is – well, you'll probably think this is absurd—"

"That's beside the point."

"I'd like, if you'd let me, to *help* you."

"To help me do what?"

"To escape, obviously. I mean, when one is in prison, isn't that what a person like yourself *ought* to do?"

"You consider yourself a likely ally?"

This time it was Number 7's turn to laugh, and again Grandmother Bug was taken by surprise. These two certainly did have the strangest way of telling jokes.

The laughter expired bubbling into the Scotch. "Don't, please take offence, Number 6, but it wasn't at all the sort of response I would have expected from *you*. I mean, it was almost, if you'll excuse my saying so, naive. The whole point of the way this place is organised is so that you can never trust anyone. Any of us could be one of *them*. You could be, for all I know, and my sister could be too."

"Your sister is."

"Not at root. At root she's on our side."

"Then isn't it unwise of you to say so?"

"Not if they already suspect it themselves. Besides, if she is one of them, then she's all the more valuable to them if she were to seem, in a way, not to be. That's why *you* would make such a splendid agent for their cause, because you appear to be such a thorough-going rebel. It's like psychoanalysis that way – if a thing is true, then its opposite is also true – or if it isn't, it's at least much more probable. You're making such faces, Number 6, but I'm only saying what everyone in the Village takes for granted, the By-Laws, as it were. I'm surprised you hadn't figured all that out yourself. Or are you only annoyed at the rest of us for having figured it out too? It's not that we're all such sly foxes – but what else is there to *think* about here? In any case, the upshot of it is that I'm just as likely a candidate to be of service to you as anyone. I might, of course, be Number 1 himself, incognito—" He chuckled self-deprecatingly.

Grandmother Bug, recognizing her cue and having prepared herself, produced her very best laugh, a soprano cackling that modulated into helpless tears, a shaking head, and a dying fall of "Lord! O Lordie! Lord!"

"Or I might be, as I'd like you to believe, perfectly sincere in making the offer. The only way you'll ever know is to try me. You're shuffling your feet. You want me to leave now, don't you?"

"Hospitality has limits, and with that glass you've pretty well exhausted them. Unless you want to switch to gin. Also, I don't think Granny ought to be sent home without an escort."

"I'm going right this minute. There's just one last thing, which may not seem that important to you, though it is to me. Do you have any idea why you should have been given that number? Why 6?"

"I never thought to question it. Six of one, half a dozen of the other."

"You think it's that simple? *We're* all inclined to think there's some significance, perhaps even a crucial one, in our numbers. For instance, Number 1 and Number 2 are just what one would expect of a 1 and a 2."

"I wouldn't know. I've never seen or heard the first, and I know the second only through the media, so to speak."

"But ought not a Number 1, if he wants to play God, preserve something like God's silence and invisibility? One is an *absolute* idea, and reality never measures up to absolutes. As for Number 2, you'll probably be granted an audience soon enough. Dictators are usually queasy about exposing themselves to the dictated. Understandably."

"Have you met him? Off the screen, that is."

"'Met' would be too strong a word. I've *seen* him. Which is more than my sister can claim. They're not friends, but I don't hold that against him. My sister is hard to get to know. But to return to my theory: take her number as a for-instance. She's Number 14, which is twice seven. And *I'm* Number 7!"

"Are you twins?"

"No, but there are nearly seven years between us."

"And seven deadly sins."

"And *sixth* columns. I know all this symbolism is silly, but I do have the feeling that there must be some sort of what would you call it? Not link."

"Affinity?"

"Yes! An affinity between us, seeing that you're Number 6 and I'm Number 7. At least it's true of me and Number 8. We're tremendous friends. At least, we were."

"What happened? Did you try and help him escape?"

"Oh no! 8 was very much the company man. What happened is he went around the twist. Paranoia, *soaring* paranoia. It's the people who are loyalest to the Village who are the most susceptible. They begin to think everyone is betraying the cause but themselves. And Number 1, of course – no one ever doubts *his* loyalty. Which is another good reason he should be invisible. No one doubts what he can't see."

"But they do doubt Number 2's loyalty?"

"Especially his."

"Speak of the devil," said a voice from behind the damask curtains, "and I appear."

Grandmother Bug crumbled out of her chair with a nervous squeak, dropping cup and saucer on the carpet. The cold untasted tea formed a dark oval that overlapped the interlocking pears.

"We'd better be going now," Number 7 shouted, wrestling the old woman back to her feet. "It's how late I hadn't realised and—"

"It was a pleasure," he said, opening the door for them.

"The pleasure was mine," Grandmother Bug chirruped, remembering her party manners. "I don't know *when* I've had such a lovely little pleasure." Her hand fluttered about the high collar of her dress, in search of the button of the coat she had not worn these last thirty years.

Number 7 pulled her out the door roughly. "We *both* don't know," he said to the closing door. "And thanks a lot."

He faced the drawn drapes which were speckled by the cold flickering light of the television.

"Thank you, Number 2. You accomplished that very economically. I hope you're not looking for company, too."

"No. I thought I'd take the opportunity to offer you my congratulations on your new honour. Congratulations! And to tell you that your first mayoral duty should arrive at your doorstep any minute."

"It can sleep there if it wishes, but it won't be let in. I promised the voters that I'd never perform the duties of my office, and one must keep faith with the electorate."

"That would be unkind. You see, this is her first day out in the Village, and she's still extremely disorientated. It's the Mayor who explains to newcomers our little customs and mores."

"She? Who?"

"Number 41. But I see—"

The doorbell rang.

"—that she's arrived. So I'll leave the two of you alone. Do try and be some comfort to her, Number 6. The poor thing doesn't know where to turn at this point." The faint glow faded behind the damask.

He went to the door. Even now, despite the suspicion Number 2 had awakened (the hope, as well?), he might have bolted it. If there had been a bolt.

He opened the door.

"Liora!"

She took a step backwards, staring at him, with that ill-feigned unconcern one pays to lunatics and freaks.

"Pardon me, but I was told that this was the residence of the Mayor. Are you ..." She looked at the scrap of paper in her hand. "... Number 6?"

Chapter Thirteen

Number 41

He twisted the dial its clockwise limit; the living room became a glare of incandescence in which they examined each other – to confirm that this was indeed Liora, she as though she were encountering for the first time and without protection the chief suspect in a notorious murder trial, in the very room where the corpse had been discovered.

She was, unquestionably, Liora. Her appearance had not been modified even by such little changes of emphasis as one expects to encounter in a woman of fashion after a two-months' absence. The brown suit was familiar to him, the bracelet disguising a watch, the emerald pendant. Her modish Sassoon haircut had grown out to an unmodish length, and he remembered her telling him, during their dinner at the Connaught, that she'd decided to let it grow long again. By all the signatures of identity – her carriage, her speech, the small transitions between two almost identical expressions – she declared herself to be Liora.

"Do you find the light better in here?" he asked.

"The implication being that I should recognize you? I don't, of course, but I expect you'll want to carry on with whatever little masque you've gotten up for the occasion."

Even that "gotten" was hers, a declaration of her origins as convincing as any stamped on a passport. (In her case, he recalled, even more convincing, for she had travelled usually as a citizen of a long-defunct banana republic.)

"Is this a game, Liora, and if so whose side have you taken? Or am I being punished for having declined your recentest proposal?"

"Shouldn't you offer me a seat before you open the script? Evidently, the plot is elaborate. And I *am* tired, as you know."

"By all means, sit where you like. I'm sorry I can't offer you a Scotch. The last two members of the committee that was here to inform me of my mayoralty left just before you arrived. You can see from the debris that they were thorough." He lifted the empty green bottle to the light.

"I never drink Scotch."

"There's gin."

"Gin-and-ginger. Thank you."

"When I was in London last week," he said, uncapping a Schweppes, "I tried to call you. Your line had been disconnected. A month before that I reached a bookshop when I dialled the number. Where have you been this month?"

"So, for all your mummery, this is only to be *another* interrogation?"

He handed the drink to her. "You think I'm one of them?"

"The alternative would seem to be that I am. Or that I'm unhinged."

He considered other possibilities.

"Or," he added after a long pause, "that *I* am. Unhinged, that is. They do tamper with people's heads."

"If it's to be this complicated, I shall need pencil and paper to keep it all straight. Let us, for the sake of proper exposition, define our presumptive identities. First, my name is not Liora, it's Lorna. I've been told that so long as I'm detained here that I'm to answer to the name of Number 41, though if you care to tell me now that I'm another number entirely I won't protest that. I was abducted on the seventh of July, from my flat in Bayswater. It was done with something like ether, I suppose, unless there's some more contemporary drug that accomplishes the same thing. I don't know how long I was kept unconscious. I woke in the hospital here, feeling unaccountably weak and quite accountably confused. At first I thought I'd had an accident. I've always been terrified that some day I'd injure my brain. A woman doctor with unmatched eyes ran me through an interminable battery of tests. I co-operated for some time, since the tests gave me a sense of security, of being undamaged. Then the hospital staff became inquisitive about things that ought not to interest hospitals, and I stopped co-operating. Some imbecile of a male nurse released me this morning. Of course I immediately tried to get out of the Village. When it had been demonstrated that one does not *leave* this Village, that one must *escape* from it, I went to the local restaurant and enjoyed the view from the Tarpeian Rock. The imbecile from the hospital found me there and gave me a slip of paper with your name – your number, rather – and a sketch of how I was to find your house. And there you have it, everything I know. Now lay down *your* cards and let's see if you have a canasta."

"Do you know the Connaught in London!"

"A hotel?"

"And a restaurant. Near the American Embassy. You're still an American, aren't you, in your new identity?"

"It's a relief to know you're not going to try and persuade me I'm actually Turkish. As for the Connaught, I'm certain I've never done more than walk past it, if that. The only hotel I know in London is the Savoy, and that was ages ago."

"Then let me begin my story by telling you about the dinner we ate at the Connaught on the evening of June 6th."

"And then," she said, ending his tale for him, "the door-bell rang, and it was me, the girl of your dreams."

"Was it? I'm still trying to decide. You'll admit that my story is no more improbable than yours?"

"Only somewhat more ornamented. It remains, however, a story. You, on your side of the mirror, will claim the same thing. It was a long way to go to reach the same impasse. Again we see that either I am lying or you are lying."

"Or neither," he added.

"Or we are both Cretans, but we can't consider that possibility with any pretence to consistency, though dramatically it would be the most appealing."

"If I'm lying, it would mean that you're of interest to our jailers on your own account. Are you?"

"Hopefully, I'm interesting to all kinds of people. Contrariwise, if *I'm* lying, my arrival would be part of the general plot against your sanity, yes?"

"Yes. And if neither of us is lying, it's a plot against both our sanities."

"It's a nice theory," she said, "if only on account of all the *machinery* that would have to be involved. If one of us is lying, then we must act out a simple melodrama of innocence pitted against iniquity. While, if we're both perfectly *sincere* in contradicting each other, then it's a matter of *our* much larger innocence and *their* enormous iniquity. There would be ambiguities in every glance and clues buried in every commonplace. So if we're to continue in our roles, stagecraft as well as etiquette seems to demand that we assume *that* to be the case Do you agree?"

"For the time being."

"So it stands thus – that we both think we're telling the truth. Now, Mr Pirandello, resolve that."

"Either I did know you and you are Liora, or I didn't and you aren't. If the second case obtains, then I've been brainwashed into thinking otherwise, and the brainwashing would have to have been done *before* I was brought here, since I tried to call you within hours of my arrival."

"Possibly while those other memories were being amputated, these were being grafted on."

"Possibly," he said. "But I'm inclined to believe that it wasn't anyone connected with the Village who arranged my amnesia. If they had, why would they be bothering with me now? They'd have what they wanted."

"Perhaps they want you to work for them." A tinselly laugh underlined her irony.

"Then why set me loose after they'd ordered my brain to their liking? Simply so we could dine at the Connaught?"

"Let's grant that Occam's razor won't slice that, though we're already *miles* from the simplest solution. You think we must posit another set of *theys* to account for your amnesia?"

"I think so. If there is someone who is desperate to obtain information, there must also be someone equally desperate to keep it to themselves. Couldn't you imagine your own people doing the same thing, if they thought there was a likelihood of your telling their secrets to, for instance, our jailers?"

"I can imagine it all too easily. So, I'll allow you both sets of *theys*. The problem then arises, why would these other *theys* want to make you believe you knew me? After all, it was these *theys*, here in the Village, who have arranged our meeting."

"And it's a problem I have no solution for. Unless both theys have interlocking Boards of Directors."

"The mind boggles."

"That's what they're hoping, Liora – that the mind will boggle."

"Lorna, please."

"There's one other reason why I don't think the manufacturers of my amnesia could also be the engineers of the presumed 'false memory' –

and that is the clear recollection I have of our dinner. They could have inserted false memories into our past, but how could they have dibbled with my future? That dinner took place *after* they'd done their work, and immediately after the dinner I set off from Paddington. The next morning – or to be precise, the next time I woke – I was here."

"This dinner that you harp on – just how distinctly *do* you recall it? Most of the dinners in *my* memory are jumbled into one big stewpot of leftover scraps."

"I remember what the waiter looked like, the ring on his hand, the wax on his moustache. It was you, in fact, who pointed out those two details. I remember the bouquet on our table, a single rose in a silver vase. I remember how you looked and things you said. I remember the *taste* of each dish, the wines that accompanied each course. With the bisque we had a Solera, Verdalho Madeira, 1872. With the salmon, Coindreu—"

"I'm certain if I *had* had dinner with you and you'd played the wine-snob so grossly, I would have laughed in a most memorable way."

"My snobbery took me in the other direction: I didn't *mention* the wines then. But, as the dinner set me back almost fifty pounds, I do recall the vintages quite well."

"It strikes me that this scene is *unnaturally* clear. Especially since the backdrop to it, your whole past *before* that, is as misty as the moors in November. Didn't it bother you *then* that there were these blank spots?"

"My entire past isn't gone, just key areas, and I can only say that I didn't notice their absence then. One doesn't miss something, after all, until one begins looking for it. Possibly I'd been specifically instructed not to go delving where they had excavated. By . . ." He smiled wryly. "I've blocked the word."

"By post-hypnotic suggestion?" she suggested.

He nodded, saying no more.

"Yes. Yes, there would have had to have been something like that, if your story is to make any sense. Even so, I'm still suspicious about that evening. The focus is too sharp, and the colours are too clear. It's like a good Hollywood movie where everything is more real than reality. What I would suggest is this – that the whole thing, all that you think you remember about me, including the dinner, was fashioned right here in this Village, either on the day you arrived (for you admit to waking in the station without quite knowing how you'd got there), or else you never left the Village *at all.* The whole interlude in London was a dream, an illusion *they* manufactured. You'll notice that my theory doesn't require two sets of *theys.*"

"Why stop there? An even simpler theory would be that my entire life has been a dream."

"And mine as well. Or we may both be figures in some larger dream, though that won't solve our problems, for surely the dreamer dreaming us will require us to solve his conundrums as though we were real. But whimsy aside, I'm serious in suggesting that the false memories were grafted *here.*"

"To what end?" he asked.

"We'd have to know to what larger end we are their means in order to answer that. Perhaps it's enough that we should be asking ourselves questions like these. What is real? Who am I? Do I wake or dream? Then, when we're hopelessly muddled, they'll tell us the answers they've already prepared."

"All right, that takes care of my case. I'll agree that if my memory of you is false, it was falsified here. *Now,* what if it is your memories that have been remodelled?"

"In principle it would amount to the same thing. There's no problem, in my case, as to when they could have gone to work on me, since I did wake up in the hospital. However, with me they'd have had to revise a lifetime's memories; for you they need only insert a chapter entitled 'Liora' here and there. How important *was* she to you? Were you in love?"

"In and out. We see-sawed very skilfully, so that we seldom were both in at the same time, or out."

"That much sounds like me, at least. What particulars can you tell me about her? For instance, was she married or single?"

"We tried not to be inquisitive. When we were alone, we would pretend that our lives were uncomplicated. I believed you were single."

"I'm divorced, twice over. When did you meet her? What things did you do together?"

"I remember our first meeting quite well. But I should remind you that we probably have listeners. There are more bugs in this cottage than in an embassy in Washington. It must have been in order that one of us should start answering such questions that this interview was arranged. I can answer indirectly by asking you a question: have you ever been in Bergamo?"

"Bergamo . . . I was *through* Lombardy at different times, but eventually all those churches and palaces and piazzas, they blur. Isn't it likely that we were all in Bergamo at one time or another?"

"We?"

"People in our line of work."

"Then you admit that much at least."

It was as though he'd seen across these endless mists of speculation a single, real, hard-edged object, a bicycle with a dented fender, a kiosk papered with the morning's headlines.

"It's a trifling admission. You – or they – had to have *some* reason for abducting me. Even if my charms rivalled Helen's, I could have been raped without all this *equipment.*"

"Then there's nothing in my story that relates to the world *you* know? If you're Liora, they can't have reshaped your entire past. The easiest thing would have been for them to chop out the scenes where I appear and fill up any cracks with putty. But they can't have filled all the cracks. Life, even when it seems fragmented, is too much of a piece to allow such operations not to leave scars."

She sighed. "We have to do this, don't we? God, if I'd thought when I began my life of sin, that I'd be spending an evening like this some day, hearing the whole thing played back at the wrong speed, I'd have stayed at the University and taught courses in Pound and Eliot. Well, if we must we must, but do try and act more like the bewitched, bewildered lover you claim to be and bring me another drink, that's a mercy."

He described, for Lorna, the Liora he remembered: her flat on Chandos Place, and its furnishings; the names and characters of maids she had employed; her preferences in art and music. He recounted the day, years before, that he had accompanied her to the V & A to have a teapot identified: she'd been told it was New Hall and quite valuable.

"That *couldn't* be me," she protested. "I know nothing about porcelain and care less."

"And cathedrals? You were always driving off to the cathedral towns."

She shrugged. "I go into any great pile of masonry when it's put in my path, but I wouldn't drive ten miles out of my way for St Peter's itself."

"You don't know Salisbury? Or Winchester? Or Wells?"

"I know Americans used to be hot for such cultural plums, but that was a *century* ago. This Liora of yours sounds like a heroine in Henry James."

"Liora couldn't read James. She said he was antiquated."

"And I've read *all* of him. Also, I gather from your account of the dinner that she fancied herself a gourmet. While my friends have been known to say behind my back that *I* have a wooden palate. But continue with your portrait: eventually you'll have to see it doesn't represent me."

He inventoried, as best he could, clothes he'd seen Liora wearing, and Lorna contradicted each blouse, slip, and scarf on his list.

"And," she added, "the most damning evidence, as I see it, is that you say you're familiar with everything I'm wearing *now*. I'm reminded of the way ducklings learn to know their mother. There's a crucial moment just after they hatch when their brains are *printed* with the image of any large moving thing about them, and that thing, whatever it may be, becomes Mother. I'm beginning to believe that there was a Liora, once, somewhere. Your description is too circumstantial to be entirely fanciful. What *they've* done is to erase the face in the portrait; then, when I arrived, they triggered the *printing* mechanism, so that my face, the physical me including the mannerisms and tricks of speech you say are hers, became your new definition of 'Liora'. They might have selected me on account of some point of resemblance, or, as I'd prefer to think, they rummaged in your past for the woman who most resembled *me*. I have enough vanity to want to be the focus of their scheming, rather than a convenient rack to hang your memories on."

"I'll admit that the evidence, as it piles up—"

"As it doesn't," she corrected.

"I'll admit it looks damning," he went on. "But who does it damn? *I* don't know."

"You really do want to find a way out for both of us, don't you? You don't *want* to think ill of me."

"Yes, I'm that big a fool. I like you too much, even—" He turned away from her angrily, though his anger was not with her.

She caught hold of his hand. "Even as Lorna?"

The hands tightened about each other.

"So. You like me too much. And love . . . does that come into it? No, don't answer, just let me see your eyes."

Once more they stared at each other in the incandescent glare, and this time each of them supposed he saw, behind the masks, a kind of truthfulness, the real face of the other person.

"Yes," she said, lowering her eyes, "*something* registers. Not a memory, though. Only a kind of sadness. I wish, I really do, that I *could* remember you. I wish . . . if we could just *ignore* the past. No, I see we can't."

"Isn't *this* a kind of proof?" he insisted. "You don't strike me, even doubly divorced, as someone who falls headlong in love."

"A proof? Even if I let myself believe your story, Number 6, I'd have to doubt your intentions. Lovers can commit treason. Especially lovers."

Her hand had grown slack in his. He placed it on the arm of her chair.

"They can," he admitted. "I've seen it happen."

"Though even then, a kind of love survives. Judas, for instance, might have felt a terrible tenderness at the moment of that kiss."

"He might have. Though he forfeited, with the same kiss, any claim to have its sincerity believed."

"Belief! All my life I've wanted to *believe* things. Knowledge always gets in the way. I want to believe you knew me, that we were in love. I want to believe I was the princess you described, with my own – what kind of teapot was it?"

"New Hall. You found it on Portobello Road for just ten pounds."

"How clever of the person I wish I'd been. I want to have had a posh flat just off the Strand, and a number that isn't listed in the Directory. What was it, by the way? It's details like that will make me really believe in your Liora."

"COVentry-6121 ."

The hands tensed; fingers knotted about the slender bowed mahogany. Her face froze into a sudden mask of disinterested curiosity; terror swirled beneath the brittle surface, "You called me at that number . . . often?"

"Often, off and on."

"When was the last time you rang it?"

"When I was in London last Friday. It had been disconnected."

"But you said, before, something about a wrong number. You talked to someone at a bookshop. What did they say to you?"

"Only that I had a wrong number." The memory rested, invisible, on a high shelf: by stretching, his fingertips could brush its edges.

"What bookshop? Who spoke to you?"

It tumbled off the shelf and shattered: a stain spread across the carpet. "A woman. And it wasn't a wrong number, exactly. The first three letters of the exchange were the same, but I'd given it a different name. It was you?"

"It was me. I'd completely forgotten that. I only remember how you made me go to some sort of trouble. You said you were calling from out of town."

"From here. It was the day I arrived. But – why did you pretend to be a bookclerk?"

"I *was* at Better Books. Look in the directory – that's its number."

"But you're *not* a bookclerk!"

"A friend of mine was to give a reading there that evening, a poet. He'd gone into the basement with the manager and left me to look after the counter. The shop was empty. That's how I *happened* to answer the phone. My God, I can remember almost every word of it now! I thought it was some tedious practical joke. You made me look down the list of exchanges to make certain there wasn't a COVentry exchange somewhere in the suburbs."

"How long were you in the shop, altogether?"

"Not five minutes. That was the only call I answered. How did you pick just that moment to call?"

"It was completely spontaneous. Completely, Liora. I'd been sitting at the—"

"Damn it, don't call me Liora!"

"But this means you are Liora. It's the link we were looking for. It's the one crack they forgot to putty."

"It's nothing of the sort. My presence in the shop was just as unpremeditated. We'd been up and down Charing Cross all that afternoon, and we only stopped in to pick up posters for the reading. I didn't even return that evening. Only someone who'd followed me would have known I was there. *When you called.*"

"It's not possible. We couldn't both just *happen* to—"

"No, we couldn't. It's certain that one of us is lying. It's certain."

"But why would either of us tell such a foolish lie? Why would I have mentioned making the call, if I'm lying? Just to be proven a liar?"

"No, I *won't* go through all this again. I refuse to. I'm very tired. I was told that you'd show me where I'm supposed to stay. Needless to say, I can't accept the offer of your *private* hospitality."

"Liora, or Lorna if you prefer – I *believe* you now. That is—"

"That is, you believe I'm sincere in my delusions. And you want to help me become my old self again. And when you've restored me to my former glory, what then, eh? How do you intend to *use* me?"

"Believe me, I—"

"Believe you? I understand that if you torture a person long enough, you can make them believe anything. We don't call it torture now, though. What is the pleasanter term they've adopted? Behaviour therapy. I suggest you try that."

"I want to help you. I'll do anything I can help you. I can't be plainer than that."

"There's one thing you can do to help me, Number 6 – set me free."

"I'm not your jailer, Liora. I am . . . a prisoner."

He had refused, before, to say this in just so many words. Now, the proposition seemed inarguable: he *was* a prisoner. He could not set another free when he was not free himself.

And he was not free.

"Then," she said scornfully, "if you're determined to keep up your role of 'prisoner' help me to escape. You say you've managed one escape for yourself. Manage one for me."

"Yes, I'll do that. We can't discuss it, here, for the reason I explained. But I have another notion, and we should be able to bring it off. With a little help."

"Not *we*, my would-be-darling – *me*. You'll help me escape, all by myself. If I left here with you, how would I ever know I'd escaped?"

"I'll go that far too. I'll help you escape by yourself."

"And, if you do, and you succeed, I might even come to believe you. Eventually."

"When, later on, I get out of here myself . . ."

She shook her head sadly. "A rendezvous?" As she spoke it, the word took on an almost tangible quality, as though what he'd offered her as a diamond she'd handed back to him in an envelope, a powder of paste.

"Not immediately," he assured her. "We could let a year go by."

"An entire year? And where should we celebrate the anniversary of my escape? At the terrace restaurant? In the hospital? Then we might invite the pretty white-haired doctor."

"All right, we'll make no plans. It may come about by chance."

"I don't know, after this evening, if I'll ever believe in chance again. Enough! Take me to my hotel now. I'm sure the warden is beginning to worry about me."

She rose from the chair. They stood beside each other, close enough to embrace, without embracing, yet without moving apart.

"I'll have to call one of their taxis," he said. "We aren't permitted to walk the streets after curfew. The patrols are not friendly."

But he did not go towards the telephone, nor did she seem to expect him to.

"You'll have your memories, at least," she said, in a softer voice. "I'll have nothing. Not even my own identity, if what you say is true."

"You'll have your freedom. You want it, don't you?"

"Yes." She smiled bittersweetly, touching the emerald pendant on her throat. "And at any price."

He remembered, after she had left, her words that evening at the Connaught: *If you can't trust me, you'll never be able to trust anyone.* It summed up the situation nicely.

Had she, that long ago, meant it to?

Chapter Fourteen

Number 14

"Come in, Number 6," the doctor said, snapping shut her compact, "and take off your clothes. Thank you for being so punctual."

"Thank the guards who brought me."

"You're *looking* very well," she said, handing him a hanger for his trousers.

"Shouldn't I? Was I infected with something the last time I was here?"

"So far as I know this hospital has never had a single case of staph infection, if that's what you mean. This is only a routine examination. Let me see your tongue."

He stuck out his tongue. She wrote something on the card clipped to her board.

"What did you write on the card?" he asked, once his tongue was back in his mouth.

"That it's pink. You show no *symptoms* of any kind?"

"None."

"Palpitations? Giddiness? Shortness of breath? *Tension?*"

"Not a trace."

"Your dreams?"

"Exhibit neither sex nor violence. The entire family could be allowed to see them."

She tossed back waves of white hair to plug a stethoscope in her ears for auscultation. He breathed slowly or rapidly as she required.

"I hear so much from my brother," she chattered, as though his internal processes were of interest to her only as background music, "about the lively process you've set in motion. I've never seen him work so hard at anything before. And not only my brother – everyone seems to be catching fever from it. Now breathe quickly. Yes, like that. What I couldn't understand is why *you* should have become, all of a sudden, so civic-minded. When I last saw you, at your cottage, you showed something bordering on contempt for the greatness we were thrusting on you. Now, cough."

He coughed.

"And again. Good. You can talk now." She scribbled numbers on the card.

"Can I get dressed?"

"No, there are still your reflexes to be tested. Sit up there where your feet can dangle, and tell me about your change of heart."

"It's no change of heart. I'm doing this for myself, not for the Village. Ever since college, where I did a bit of acting, I've wanted to direct this play. There was seldom opportunity and never time. Here, there is plenty of time, and your brother, by arranging all the business of permits, rehearsal space and the rest of that, has provided the opportunity. It was his idea more than mine."

"Not to hear him speak of it. I must say you've rewarded him handsomely enough: the *two* best parts in the play."

"Your brother is a born actor."

"The cast is complete now?"

"Very nearly. I had to take the Duke's part myself. No one else would audition for it."

"My brother says it's an awful role – hundreds of lines and every one pure lead. The Duke, by his account, just goes around during the whole play, dressed up like a monk, doing nice things and *saying* nice things. Whereas Angelo is a *monster* of wickedness and hypocrisy."

"Is that your interpretation or your brother's?"

"Not mine – I never interpret anything but dreams. Is it a wrong interpretation? I read Shakespeare so long ago that all the plays are muddled together, the comedies especially. I remember that everyone sings a lot and runs around disguised as someone of the opposite sex, and that in the last act they're all obliged to get married. *Measure for Measure* – isn't that the one in the Forest of Arden?"

"No, Vienna. Half the action is set in the city prison. It's the darkest of the comedies. In fact, the chief thing that makes it a comedy is that everyone *is* obliged to get married in the last act."

"In a prison! Then it's meant to be *edifying*! A kind of protest, in fact?" She tapped his kneecap with a ballpen hammer. His foot jerked reflexively.

"There are correspondences to the world we know. In Shakespeare there always are. But I won't underline them. The play speaks for itself."

"The people in this prison, *ought* they to be there? That will be crucial, if it's to be effective propaganda. In my own experience, I've never found anyone in prison who doesn't really belong there. Sometimes, as in your case, they must go to the most extraordinary lengths to get in, but once they've made it you can see they were always meant to be prisoners. Would Shakespeare agree?"

"On anything concerned with the problem of authority, Shakespeare has two opinions. In this case, everyone in the prison has done something to deserve to be there, but—"

"Then I'm surprised you've chosen this play. The way you keep harping on this matter of *your* innocence and *our* injustice—"

"—*but* its central theme is the gross injustice of the person in charge of the prison."

"My brother?"

"Angelo, yes. There is, as well, a heroine of unimpeachable innocence, whom this Angelo abuses in the worst way."

"Don't tell me – he seduces her."

"He tries his damnedest. She has come to him, from the convent where she's a novitiate, to plead for her brother's life. Angelo has condemned him to death."

"That's the other part my brother's playing, the condemned brother?"

"Yes, Claudio and Angelo are never on the stage together until the very end of the last act, when neither of them has much to say. I thought there was a certain fitness in having the same actor play both the judge and the condemned man particularly as Claudio's crime is the same as Angelo's."

"Claudio was . . . concupiscent?"

"That, and carelessness."

"Playwrights always take these matters so much more seriously than the rest of us." Meditatively, she tapped his other knee with her hammer. The foot jounced. "Well, perhaps they have to, if they're to go on writing plays. Surely, the sensible thing for Claudio and his girlfriend to have done, even in Shakespeare's day, was to get married."

"Claudio offers to, the girl is more than willing, and Isabella also tries to convince Angelo of this, when she pleads her brother's case."

"And *that's* when Angelo tries to seduce her. Oh, he is wicked! The story seems to be coming back to me now. Angelo promises to spare Claudio's life on condition that Isabella surrenders her virtue to him, and when she goes to the dungeon to tell her brother about it, *he* tries to persuade her to *do* it. But does she? I remember it both ways – she does and she doesn't."

"You'll have to come and see the play."

"I suppose your new friend – or your old friend, whichever turns out to be the case – the lady with the black hair, has been handed the plum of Isabella."

"She read for the part, but she doesn't have the voice for the grand Shakespearean manner. She'll be Mariana, and even in that role she'll be straining."

"So the most important part in the play is still open?"

"It's gaping."

"Good! That's what my brother told me, and I just wanted to be sure. You can put your pants on now. That was the *real* reason I had you brought in. I have a copy in the desk drawer, and I want to audition. Now."

"Would you have time, with your professional duties—"

"I have time, in this Village, for anything, and to spare. If it came to that, I'd rather pretend to be an actress than to go on being a doctor in real life. I love theatricals, however amateur. When we were little, my brother and I did hundreds of plays together for our parents. Besides, if he's to be Claudio, it's only proper that his sister should play Isabella."

"Perhaps. But when he's Angelo . . ."

"That's no problem. Even when we had other children in our productions, Poppa insisted that if there were any scenes that threatened propriety, my brother and I had to act them, since there could not be question, between us, of anything indiscreet. Isabella doesn't end up marrying Angelo, does she? That wouldn't be a happy ending."

"No, she marries the Duke."

"Then I must have the part. I'd *love* to marry you."

"Doesn't taste forbid that a doctor propose so shortly after a medical examination?"

"What taste forbids, Number 6, appetite excuses. Seriously, although I'll admit it's hard to be serious about a thing like marriage, I like you. Even something a bit more than that. Didn't my brother *tell* you? I told him to."

"No. He must have been too embarrassed."

"Is it so impossible to credit? That little waitress is still in love with you, as you must know, despite the way you abused her confidence when you escaped. You've given *her* a part in the play, haven't you? And Number 41 is Mariana, even though you'll have to teach her how to pronounce the words. Make me Isabella, and you'll have every female in the cast in love with you. Isn't that the principle most directors go by?"

"There's still Mistress Overdone, and I don't think our ex-Mayoress has any designs on me."

"The way she flirted with you at your open house? Her husband was giddy with jealousy. Every other time I've seen Number 34, the man's been as taciturn as granite, and though she can be talkative enough, it's usually with other mathematicians about the problems of higher mathematics, trigonometry and such."

"*She's* a mathematician?"

"I'm told she's brilliant. But with you she becomes a giggling schoolgirl. You have that effect on women. You can't pretend you didn't know that, not the way you exploit it."

"How have I exploited it in your case?"

"By assuming that I'll go on keeping your secret."

"Which is?"

"That you *were* the one who set fire to the films in the church crypt. Number 2 has been worried silly trying to establish that fact."

"I'm afraid I don't follow you."

"You needn't be disingenuous with me. You knew I was auditing your dreams that day, and you understood how we were directing them. Surely you must have figured out by now *where* we were directing them."

"As a matter of fact I wasn't able to. Whether or not I did in fact set a fire where you say, Number 2 never seemed to doubt that I did."

"Number 2 doesn't doubt it, but Number 1 apparently is unconvinced. I gather that Number 2 thinks Number 1 thinks he did it."

"Is that what you think?"

She smiled, pressing the ballpen hammer to her lips. "I don't have to think – I *know*. But, as I was beginning to fall in love with you even then, I didn't tell. You still don't believe me; why is that?"

"Because if it were a 'secret', you would want to keep it. You wouldn't be speaking of it now, in front of the bugs."

"Oh, that! That's one of the advantages of having a trustworthy staff. My Number 28 can perform wonders with electronics. When I need privacy, I can get it. You don't think I'd declare my passion to you on television! It would destroy the reputation I've been so long building."

"You would if you were told to. In any case, as declarations of passion go, it's a rather tepid thing."

"I got your clothes off, Number 6. To have gone any further without your co-operation would have exceeded a woman's strength. If *this* was tepid, your rencontre with Number 41 was quick-frozen. Yet you seemed willing enough to credit what she said, and most of what she only implied."

"I know Liora."

"You *think* you know her."

"All right then, as you claim to be speaking to me in confidence, tell me – *do* I know her? Ought I to believe, if not in her story, in her candour?"

"On principle you should never believe in a woman's candour. As to whether she's who you think she is or who she says she is, anything I told you would only add to the confusion. Even assuming you would believe in *my* candour (and remember, I'm a woman with a woman's best motive for deceiving you), how can we be sure that I know the truth in this case? I'm told only as much as *they* want me to know, and that often includes a great quantity of falsehood. I could read you the list of *names* in her dossier. Or I could—"

"Just answer this one question – why did I call that bookshop? Why was *that* number in my head?"

"I didn't put it there. I had nothing to do with your case till you were brought back from London two weeks ago. Beyond that, it's all speculation, fog, and upset stomach. You shouldn't take these things so seriously, Number 6 – what is true, what isn't true. Doubt, as I've seen it noted in your dossier, is your Achilles' heel. Choose a truth that suits you and stick with it."

"Truth, then, should be whatever is most agreeable?"

"Has it ever been anything else? In this case, haven't you given Number 41 the benefit of your doubt, and wasn't it agreeable to do so?

You love her, and you're determined to believe she loves you. I love you, and I've managed to persuade myself, against every evidence, that *at root* you must love me in return, or at least that the seeds are there. After all, look how long we've been talking together, and you haven't even started putting your shoes on. That must mean something. I entertain you. God knows, I *try* to entertain you."

"Since you're part of the establishment, I can afford to let myself be entertained by you; I could never afford to trust you."

"Did I ask you to? Trust isn't a precondition of love. In fact, in most cases, the opposite is true. I'm sure I wouldn't have grown so fond of *you*, if I weren't terribly jealous of Number 41. Do you trust *her*? You trust her even less than you do me for the sound reason that with me you know where you stand. I'm one of *them*, and the fact that I'm *not* one of them makes no difference, since you'll never be convinced of it. But you needn't let that stand in the way of affection. You're putting your shoes on. You no longer are entertained. Is that because I've finally convinced you that I mean what I say?"

"It means I'm hungry. Your guards didn't give me time for lunch."

"But my audition! At least let me try out for Isabella."

"You won't have to. I think you're a great actress, and you have the part. Start learning your lines. We rehearse the first two acts tonight."

"I've already learned them, Number 6." She kissed the tip of the hammer and waved it at him. "Bye-bye. I'll see you at eight."

"*Now, sister, what's the comfort?*" Number 7 asked, entering the examination room a moment later by a second door.

"*Why, as all comforts are: most good, most good indeed.*" Then, since Isabella's next lines strayed from topicality: "The play goes on, and I'm to be the leading lady."

"Have you ever been anything else? Between the two of us, there's scarcely a scene in the whole play that we can't steal. And even behind the scenes . . ."

"Will everything be ready when the curtain rises? There I mean – on the set behind the scenes?"

"I've been busy with it all day. The hardest part is accomplished. I got the remains of the sphere (Thank God for Number 2's niggardliness!) out of the storeroom and up to the roof of the theatre. Your Number 28 has already knit up the major damage, but there are still fifty little rips to be mended where it was abraded by the cliff after it had burst. We won't know for certain, of course, till everyone is in the theatre and we can inflate it. You won't be afraid?" he asked in a concerned and brotherly way, a Claudio to her Isabella.

"My blood is saturated with adrenalin, but I don't know if it's fear or the excitement. I'll feel no more afraid, certainly, at the ascent than when I have to go on as Isabella:

And have you nuns no farther privileges?"

He replied, falsetto:

"Are not these large enough?"

And she, rolling up her blue eye and her brown, ethereally:

"Yes, truly. I speak not as desiring more,
But rather wishing a more strict restraint
Upon the sisterhood, the votarists of Saint Clare."

He hopped gleefully atop the examining table. *"Then, Isabel, live chaste—"*

And she tapped out the iambs on his kneecap:

"—and, brother, die:
More than our brother is our chastity."

Wresting the hammer from her, he adopted a graver tone, judicial, sober, sanctimonious, without dimples. He became Angelo. "Did the prisoner, when he was here, exhibit any signs of *suspicion?*"

"Indeed, milord. He suspects everything, except the truth."

"He suspects *me*, in that case?"

"Not of setting this up on your own behalf, but I think he's worried that you'll betray him to Number 2. After all, have you presented him with any better motive for your helping him than altruism?"

"That's the motive he expects *me* to believe. He's going to all this trouble he explained, for *her* sake, for Mata Hari."

"But if he's saying *that*, how can you be helping him for *his* sake?"

"I said right out that I didn't believe him, that I wasn't that naive. As soon as I explained my *real* reason for wanting him out of the Village, he admitted that they were *both* escaping, but that he couldn't tell *her*, because he'd promised her he wasn't coming."

"Do you think he does intend to take her with him?"

"We'll never know, will we?"

"And what was your *real* reason?" she asked.

"I want him far away from you, jealous, possessive brother that I am."

"And so you are."

"And, when you've left him behind, I'll have accomplished that purpose too: you will be far away from him."

"And from you. Aren't you going to miss me?"

"Terribly. You know that."

"Then why *don't* you come along?"

"Me? Why, I get dizzy just climbing a ladder. I'd die of terror in that thing. It will be bad enough to think of you sailing off like another Phaeton, or Icarus, or Medea. In any case, once you're gone they'll probably have no more use for me. I'll promise never to tattle on them, and they'll send me back to London, and we'll live happily ever after. Yes?"

She gave him a sisterly kiss. "I hope so."

He patted her hand. "You can stake your blue eyes on it. Within two weeks we'll be back together. I don't suppose you'll be returning to your old flat, not right away. Shall we set a time and place?"

"For our rendezvous? Yes – somewhere sentimental."

"The Tower of London?" he suggested.

"Another prison? That's not the sort of sentiment I had in mind. Besides, it's so big, and if the weather is nice I'd rather wait outdoors. Let's make it Westminster Bridge, on the side by Big Ben. If this were a movie, we'd *have* to meet there. So that even Americans could tell it was London."

"Once a week?"

"On Saturdays."

"At one o'clock in the afternoon."

"It's a date."

Chapter Fifteen

Measure for Measure

"My beard! Is it on straight?" Number 7 asked earnestly.

"Yes, but you've forgotten this." He reached forward and removed from the young man's hand the signet that he had, as the Duke, just entrusted to Angelo. "You're Claudio now. Remember to whine."

"The theatre's full? I've been up on the roof, with 28."

"All the seats are filled, except the two we had predicted: Numbers 1 and 2 declined their invitations. What of the balloon?"

Number 7 edged towards the wings. The brothel scene had opened, and Mistress Overdone (Number 33) was entering, swathed in an entire rummage sale of tattered indelicacies. "It's inflating," he said absently.

"The wind?"

"Is seaward." As his tongue licked nervously at the horsehair fringe pasted beneath his nose, he reviewed with abbreviated gestures the blocking of his next scene. In proportion as he neared the stage, the play's success concerned him more than the progress of the escape.

In the brothel the First Gentleman asked Mistress Overdone: *"How now! Which of your hips has the most profound sciatica?"*

And Number 33: *"Well, well; there's one yonder arrested and carried to prison was worth five thousand of you all."*

"Who's that, I pray thee?"

"Marry, sir, that's Claudio, Signior Claudio."

"Claudio to prison? Tis not so."

"Nay," she replied, fluttering scraps of lingerie at the spotlight, *"but I know tis so. I saw him arrested, saw him carried away, and, which is more, within these three days his head to be chopped off."*

Number 7, having added the whiskers and stripped to the tights that made him Claudio, smiled just such a smile as the condemned dandy, overhearing this, might have smiled, an expression at once bright and miserable, compounded of insatiable vanity and a dying, desperate faith in the power of his own boyish charm still to prevent the worst. In the first scene, as Angelo, Number 7 had had to act; to portray Claudio nothing more seemed to be needed than that he remember to be himself.

The red beacon winked its patient message of on and off, on and off, from the spire of the church, a spike of blackness thrust against the lesser blackness of the hazed night sky. Farther away, squatting on its artificial hill, the unfenestrated mass of the administration building glowed in a perpetual twilight of mercury vapour lamps. The Village streets wove serpentine patterns of light across the nether blackness of the earth, but the cottages along these streets were uniformly dark. Even in the neutralising darkness and from this altitude, he could not regard the place as the picture postcard it tried so hard to be: it remained the same inimical caricature he'd seen on that first taxi ride through its streets.

Behind him on the gravelled roof, the blue plastic, filling with helium, bulged and popped and lurched towards its one-time sphericity under the attentive supervision of Number 28.

On the ledge a makeshift speaker crackled the pentameters of Act III, Scene 1, a prison in Vienna.

A figure emerged from behind the swelling balloon and approached him. Shimmers of dark rayon in the darkness, slither of rayon on gravel.

"I came up to see how the work was progressing," he said. "It occurred to me that you might be here too."

"It's progressing," she said, "and I am here."

"All this time? People were beginning to worry."

"Since the start of Act II. I told Isabella – the doctor – that I was feeling queasy. She said I needed air. Once I was here I couldn't tear myself away. It's a kind of torture to watch it. Growing so slowly. I can't believe it will be all round and floating in the air in time."

"If I'd paced the first two acts any slower, the audience would never have stayed in their seats. There's not one archaic pun or proofreader's error cut from the script."

"Yes, you've done wonders drawing it out. It just goes on and on and on."

Her voice trailed off into a vacancy, which was filled by Number 14's – Isabella now – thin, wavering declamation:

"There spake my brother: there my father's grave
Did utter forth a voice. Yes, thou must die:
Thou art too noble to . . ."

"And on," he said. "At least no one can accuse me of having done this
for art's sake."

"For mine then? I'm grateful. Did I say before that I was grateful?"

"No, you didn't."

"Because I didn't believe, till now, that it wasn't all an elaborate trap.
I've been waiting each day for the bite of its teeth. I shouldn't let myself
believe it *now*. I look at this absurd plastic beast, and try to imagine
myself lifted up by it, and carried off, and it's like . . ."

The speaker: ". . . *a pond as deep as hell* . . ."

"It's like the first time my mother explained to me where babies come
from. I couldn't believe that such elaborate machinery was needed to
produce such a simple-seeming result. Being brought here between
sleeping and waking, then leaving like *this* – I shall never believe, if I do
get away, that I was here at all. And you . . ." She took one of his hands
between hers, lifted it, like a housewife trying to estimate whether the
weight stamped on a package was to be credited: was this *really* a full
pound and a half of hamburger?

"You find *me* no more probable than the rest of this?"

"If anything, Number 6, somewhat less. I've always suspected that there
were dragons in the world, but to discover, after I've been chained to the
dragon's rock, that there is a Perseus as well – it's too providential. I owe
you—" She paused, still weighing his hand in hers, doing calculations,
reluctant to name the exact sum of her debt.

Fifty feet below, Isabella, in the chaste passion of her indignation, shook
the bars of her brother's cell, a sound reduced by the speaker to the
merest rattling of a die.

"Dost thou think, Claudio,
If I would yield him my virginity,
Thou mightest be freed."

Claudio, answering, had difficulty concealing the hope that surges
beneath his pious protest:

"O heavens! it cannot be."

And Isabella:

"Yes, he would give't thee, from this rank offence,
So to offend him still. This night's the time
That I should do what I abhor to name,
Or else thou diest tomorrow."

"Isn't it time you returned to them?" she asked. The sudden thaw was, as suddenly, starred with frost. "If the Duke is to enter on cue."

"There's a moment yet, and I'd rather spend it here. We won't be alone again, you and I, except for an instant on stage, for . . ."

"For ever. Isn't that what I said? And what you've agreed to? I don't remember now how that came about. What my reasons could have been. It seemed logical then. Wouldn't *you* feel, if you were to run into me again, out there, as if this prison had breathed on you? All my talk about *distrust* – you must, if you've not been trying to deceive me, feel just the same thing towards me. The same distrust. The same reluctance."

"That's true," he said.

"Yet you would be willing, despite that—"

"To see you again, out there. Yes. I'd *want* to."

She turned away from him to look across the darkened Village at the grey, gleaming planes of the administration building. "Where?"

"Wherever you like."

"Westminster Bridge?"

"That's as good a place as any."

"On the side by Big Ben. I'll go there once a week. What day?"

"Saturday, or any other."

"Saturday, then, at one o'clock in the afternoon. Do you believe me when I say I really hope you'll be there?"

"We must try to stop asking each other, Liora, how much we believe of what we say to each other. Soon enough, *that* will be put to the test. And for now—" He opened the door to the stairwell.

They listened, attentively, to Claudio, as he sank terror-stricken into a new vice.

"Sweet sister, let me live.
What sin you do to save a brother's life,
Nature dispenses with the deed so far

That it becomes a virtue."

"Now the god must run downstairs to tend his machine, I know. Oh! one last thing, Number 6."

He turned, silhouetted by the fluorescence streaming from the stairwell, the hooded figure of a Franciscan monk.

"What I tried to say before, what it is I owe you." Again she hesitated at the sum, and he had time to notice that her face, in this peculiar incidence of light, with its heavy theatrical makeup, was not a face he would easily have recognised. Even the self-defeated smile belonged more to Mariana than to either the Liora he remembered or the Lorna she claimed to be.

She averted her eyes. "An apology," she said.

"Don't mention it."

He raced down the stairs, taking each flight at two bounds, the friar's robe bundled about his waist. He paused two beats outside the exit to let the robe fall into place and reached the wings at Claudio's cue:

"O hear me, Isabella,"

As he stepped into the light (the judgement chamber of the second act had become, by adding indigo filters to the overhead spots and modifying their amperage, by replacing doors with grates, by scattering a bit of straw about, the dungeon of Act III), he reminded himself that he was no longer who he had been a moment before: he was now a Duke who is impersonating a friar; who pretends to encounter as though by chance a beautiful young nun in the condemned cell of a Viennese prison; who, bending his head, says to her in a near whisper:

"Vouchsafe a word, young sister, but one word."

Tears trembled at the corners of the brown eye and the blue, but she allowed no pain to be audible in her cold, conventionally reverent reply: *"What is your will?"*

(This fleeting thought: She *is* an actress!)

Then, he was inside the play again, he was the Duke devising Machiavellian schemes to honour clandestine virtue and expose guilts veiled by fair appearance. Till the curtain went down on the third act he could think no thought of his own. Mariana's cottage was being wheeled into position for the opening of Act IV.

The lighting now (and throughout the play) bore out his contention that this was the blackest of Shakespeare's comedies. The audience would have difficulty, from more than a few rows back, to distinguish this crumb of decayed gingerbread from the dark prison walls just visible behind it.

He felt a hand in his and gave a reassuring squeeze before he realised it was the Doctor Isabella – Number 14.

"How am I doing?" she asked.

He mustered a smile. "Innocence was never threatened so magnificently." And let go of her hand.

Another hand: on his shoulder: Number 7, wearing scraps of the elegance Claudio had preened at his entrance in Act I. He whispered into the monk's cowl: "It sprang a leak."

This was (he thought) the instant of treachery he had been waiting for all this time. His fist clenched (he did not think) around the golden tatters.

"It's fixed!" Number 7 cried aloud. "For God's sake, don't *hit* me."

The stage manager, in the wings opposite them, made frantic hand-signals: The curtain? The curtain?

"Where is Liora?" he demanded.

"*Number 41* is on the set – waiting, like all the rest of us, for the *curtain* to go up," he answered reproachfully. "The intermission has lasted fifteen minutes. If you hold things up much longer, you'll have the entire theatre *wondering*. I've never seen you like this, Number 6."

He signalled back to the stage manager. As the curtain rose, a snare drum trembled in the pit; then, in unison, tenor recorder and horn d'amour, in their lowest registers, sounded the slow triads of Mariana's song. The simple melody swelled, ebbed, faded back into the knife-edge rolling of the drum, across which Liora's piercing, flawed soprano traced the same mournful pattern:

> "Take, O take those lips away,
> That so sweetly were forsworn . . ."

His hand still gripped the ragged collar, and he shook Number 7 back and forth to the rhythm of his words, the rhythm of Mariana's song: "Now tell me, again, and coherently, what *happened* up there?"

"Nothing. Really. A false alarm." He writhed and grovelled, whined and smiled, never departing from the character of Claudio. "Number 28 is fixing it now. He's *finished* fixing it. Just a *little* leak. The balloon's already in the *air*."

"How long a delay will this mean?"

"And those eyes, the break of day,
Lights that do mislead the morn . . ."

"Five minutes at most, he says. But it will be ready at the curtain call, and you can't go up to the roof till then, in any case. It doesn't change a thing."

"It means that she'll panic."

"So? You needn't tell her. It's not the delay that upsets you, is it? You thought I'd sabotaged your project. Admit it."

"Damn." And, on reconsideration: "Damn!"

At the refrain, recorder and horn again joined the song, moving first in opposition to the soprano's ascending melody, then, as though she could not resist their downward impulse, uniting with it in a slow decline to silence:

"But my kisses bring again, bring again,
Seals of love, but seal'd in vain, seal'd in vain."

"That's your cue," Number 7 said.
It was. It was his cue.

"What was *that* all about?" the doctor asked her brother, as soon as the Duke had begun to deliver his lines.

"A little game, a bit of amusement."

"We shouldn't go out of our way, you know, to worry him," she said, worriedly. "*Did* it have a leak?"

"Of course not."

"Then why on earth—"

"Don't raise your voice," he said loudly. (With his sister he seemed to prefer to take the role of Angelo.) "He'll hear you."

"It will only make him more *anxious* to get up there the minute the curtain comes down – and that much harder for *me*."

"I've told you that that's already taken care of. Don't, don't, don't *fret!*

Stop acting like yourself, and act like Isabella. You're *on*, in seconds. Good lord, you can't collapse *now*. This is the crucial moment of our own little play, symbolically: this is where it's arranged for you and Mariana to exchange places. Get out there, darling – and break your leg. *Now!*"

The doctor stumbled in the wings; Isabella walked gravely on to the stage, a symbolic moment that was, after all, only one among many.

Shortly afterwards, it was another woman who stood with Number 7.

"Can they see us from where they are?" he asked.

"No. I tried to all through my song. You were so *loud* – you nearly ruined it."

"Does that matter? *We* won't be here to read the reviews."

She stood on tiptoes, waiting.

"You're *sure* they can't see us?" he asked teasingly.

"I wish they *could*."

He kissed her: the exchange had been completed.

"Do you love me?" he asked.

"Love *you?*" she asked incredulously. "Don't be silly – I love him."

"Then shouldn't you save your kisses, my dear Judas, for him?"

"I save a special kind for him. Do *you* love *me?*"

"Don't be silly," he said. "I love . . ." He had to stop and consider.

Meanwhile, before the painted door of the canvas cottage, Isabella was explaining, to the disguised Duke, the arrangement she had made for her night in Angelo's bed, an appointment which the Duke would then have to persuade Mariana (who had been, years before, compromised and abandoned by that same villain, when her dowry had been lost at sea) to keep in her stead. By such devious means (the false friar assured her) would virtue emerge not only triumphant but unscathed.

Reluctantly, as though she still were not fully persuaded that virtue could be so oblique, she repeated Angelo's instructions:

> "He hath a garden circummur'd with brick,
> Whose western side is with a vineyard back'd;
> And to that vineyard is a planched gate,
> That makes his opening with this bigger key.
> This other doth command a little door
> Which from the vineyard to the garden leads.

There have I made my promise,
Upon the heavy middle of the night,
To call upon him."

Chapter Sixteen

Act V, and After

Isabella has made her accusations against Angelo, Mariana has confirmed them, and the Duke has revealed himself to have been the Friar who arranged the details of Mariana's assignation.

Only the denouement remains.

"*Sir,*" he said to Angelo, "*by your leave,*" He paused to gather fresh thunderbolts, while the guilty deputy, revealed, disgraced, curled into a heap of abasement at his feet.

> "*Hast thou or word, or wit, or impudence*
> *That yet can do thee office? If thou hast,*
> *Rely upon it till my tale be heard,*
> *And hold no longer out.*"

Angelo's sternness, turning against itself, became the cringing of Claudio:

> "*O my dread lord!*
> *I should be guiltier than my guiltiness*
> *To think I can be undiscernible,*
> *When I perceive your Grace, like power divine,*
> *Hath looked upon my passes. Then, good Prince,*
> *No longer session hold upon my shame,*
> *But let my trial be my own confession.*
> *Immediate sentence, then, and sequent death*
> *Is all the grace I beg.*"

He gestured sternly to Liora. "*Come hither, Mariana.*"

Reluctantly she released the Doctor's hand to step forward a pace, two. She seemed acutely sensible of her own guilt in creating this scene, as though not justice but revenge had been her motive in helping to bring Angelo this low.

"*Say,*" the Duke demanded of Angelo, "*wast thou ere contracted to this woman?*"

Angelo, in the fury of his penitence, had knocked his eyeglasses to the stage. Squinting, he moved towards her on his knees.

Liora – Lorna – Number 41 – Mariana took a third step forward.

"I was, my lord."
"Go and take her hence, and marry her instantly.
Do you the office, Friar – which consummate,
Return him here again. Go with him Provost."

Exeunt Number 7 and Liora, flanked by a monk and the prison warden.

He stepped down from the rude wooden platform erected on this make-believe highway that looked remarkably like a brothel, a judgement chamber and a prison.

At the Duke's first step towards Isabella these multi-valent walls were to begin their slow evaporation, while the lights would mount towards an afternoon brightness. He waited for the man at the light box to pick up his cue.

In the expectant silence he could hear, off-stage, the opening and closing of a door.

At his next step the light dimmed. The small crowd of Officers, Citizens and Attendants assembled on the stage shifted uneasily.

There was no help for it: he began the brief scene in which the Duke, not done dissembling, condoles with Isabella for the death of her brother (who isn't dead). By his last line – "*Make it your comfort, so happy is your brother.*" – thick night had palled the stage in the dunnest smoke of hell. A single feeble spot picked out the faces of the Duke and Isabella.

Angelo and Mariana returned (bound in wedlock), a black shimmer of velveteen, a sheen of black rayon. Contrary to his own blocking, he approached the pair of them as he pronounced the sentence (which he would, a moment later, revoke): '"*An Angelo for Claudio, death for death!*"' Angelo collapsed, throwing his arms over his head (another departure from the acting script), while Mariana backed away from him along the edge of the apron until her long gown had snagged in the extinguished footlights.

He repeated her cue: "*Away with him!*"

"*O, my most gracious lord!*" the blonde waitress cried, with genuine terror. "*I hope you will not mock me . . . with a husband.*"

The Duke's pause exceeded Mariana's in its unreasonableness. Even the most tolerant members of the audience were beginning to think this an eccentric interpretation to judge by the sudden epidemic of coughing from the orchestra and balcony.

Recalling that the balloon would not be ready to ascend before the curtain fell, he decided to continue to be the Duke. The play was near its end, in any case. The few moments' head-start she'd won by having Number 127 stand in for her would not, probably, prove to be decisive.

When the Duke began speaking again, his delivery was more eccentric than his sudden, unaccountable silence. It was almost as hard to distinguish the words rushing past as it was to make out the faces of the actors on the darkened stage, and even when the words could be sorted out their sense could not be, for he was omitting phrases, lines, entire speeches seemingly at random. When Isabella and Mariana tried to plead in Angelo's behalf, he interrupted at their first pause for breath. He dispatched the Provost off-stage to resurrect Claudio, and a full minute before he had returned (barely in time for the end) he addressed the darkness as though it already contained Claudio (as, for all anyone in the audience could tell, it might have).

With a final admonition to Angelo to love his wife (omitting the final scene with Lucio, as he had skipped past Escalus already), he began the Duke's concluding speech. It went by, like a racing car, in a single blur of blank verse, braking only as he reached the last six lines of the play. This much, a few seconds, he was willing to sacrifice for art's sake:

> "*Dear Isabel,*
> *I have a motion much imports your good,*
> *Whereto if you'll a willing ear incline,*
> *What's mine is yours, and what is yours is mine.*
> *So, bring us to your palace, where we'll show*
> *What's yet behind, that's meet you all should know.*"

By sticking out the play to its end he had lost, at most, two and a half minutes. Now, as soon as the curtain dropped . . .

Instead, in floods of light, the audience rose, as though it had often rehearsed this moment, clapping and cheering, and the cast surrounded him. Hands wrapped about his arms and legs, lifted him into the air, placed him on the shoulders of the Provost and Lucio, who carried him forward in triumph to the foot of the stage. The applause swelled. Flowers arced upward, fell to the stage and into the pit. The last row of the balcony began stamping its communal feet, and soon the entire theatre had taken up the steady, stupefying rhythm.

Not till Angelo had stepped forward for his second standcall did he notice that it was not Number 7 in Angelo's velveteen robes, but the doctor's assistant, Number 28, who had prepared the balloon for its ascent. Likewise (as 7's double role had required), it was another actor who received the applause for Claudio.

This was a possibility he had never once imagined, and what he found so astonishing now was not their collusion but his own guilelessness: never *once*!

When he had stopped trying to squirm down off their shoulders, they lowered him of their own accord. Hand in hand with the leading lady, he took several calls. She was presented with an enormous bouquet of roses, white and red together as at a funeral. He was given a plaque, with his number etched on the gilt plate beneath two masks, one that smiled and one that frowned.

The ovation went on for fifteen minutes before the curtain was allowed to come down.

Number 14 regarded the bouquet in her arms with a look of aversion. She seemed about to fling it to the floor. Then, with a more considered contempt, she let it drop.

They had been left alone on the stage. The cast and stage hands had gone downstairs to their party, while on the other side of the curtains the audience squeezed itself out in a thick human paste through the exits into the lobby and the night streets.

"There's no point, is there, going up there?"

He shook his head. "They've gone."

"And I'm here, and you're here, like two punchlines without their jokes."

"Am I to believe, now, that you—"

"Believe whatever you care to, Number 6." She laughed, almost lightheartedly. "You know, he must regret that he's missing *this*. It's the sort of thing that would tickle him." Wearily she zipped open her costume, pulled it over her head. She was wearing, beneath the novitiate's habit, slacks and a heavy wool shirt.

"This?"

"Us, now, here. Oh, for pity's sake, can't you see – they foxed me *too*. He'd made me think it would be *my* escape, just the way he led you along the whole long way he wanted you to go. You haven't really been doing all this on *her* account, have you? You wouldn't look so chagrined, if that were so. The balloon was supposed to be for *you*, wasn't it?"

"I—" He could see the explanation stretching on to the horizon and decided that an answer would be simpler. "Yes."

"Alone?"

"I don't know. Up to the last minute I couldn't decide. Earlier tonight when I saw her on the roof, I almost let myself believe—"

"No doubt she felt sorry for you then."

"I wonder," he began (an entire chorus of alluring Possibilities waved scarves at him from that horizon). But a glance at the doctor's eyes fixed on him, measuring him like calipers, made him break off.

"You wonder," she continued for him, "whether *they* were escaping. Or if this was just another play-within-a-play. I don't think we can ever be sure. If a play, I fail to get the point, but that happens to me at most plays."

"But if it were genuine, a *real* escape, how did he arrange all *this* on his own?" His gesture indicated only the painted prison walls, but she understood what else his words encompassed: the collusion of Number 28, of the waitress, of the cast, the stage hands, even the audience, whose enthusiasm had far exceeded anything the play might have merited on its own.

"That's so," she said. "He couldn't have done all that."

From the wings Number 98, the Stationer's clerk, approached them, still in the costume of Elbow, the foolish constable. "Number 6?" he called out hesitantly. "There was a . . ." He held it out at arm's length to show that there actually *was*. "One of the guards brought this . . . this, uh . . . I told him you were probably still . . . And I was right! "

"It will be from *him*, I expect," the doctor said. "A Parthian shot."

Number 98 handed him the sealed envelope, then turned to the doctor. "And there's this for you, Number 14." A second envelope.

Elbow waited between them, meekly curious. "A note of congratulations? I think everyone thinks that we've had a ... tremendous ... Although the ending ... I can't imagine how the man at the light box could have ... But even so, it was ... I mean, the *audience* ... Don't you think so?" His eyes darted back and forth between Number 6 and Number 14, Number 14 and Number 6. His smile withered.

"I suppose," he said, repeating the lesson life had taught him in so many forms, "that you'd like to be alone now." Neither would contradict this, and he returned to the party below, shaking his head and marvelling once again at the coolness of the truly great even in the very furnace of success.

She finished reading her letter first.

"It's what I expected. He jeers sincere apologies. Passion, he must confess, overwhelmed him. Is yours the same? Or did *she* write to you?"

"I don't know. Here, read it." He handed her the first page, while he continued with the second. The letter read:

My dear Number 6,

There is very little I can offer in extenuation of my conduct. That I have systematically deceived you, all the while protesting my friendship and good intentions, I cannot deny. Yet I would still protest that that friendship is real, that my intentions remain good, and that my actions were dictated by an impersonal Necessity. Isn't it true that I've taken from you no more than you would have taken from me? That is to say, the means of escape.

In my position, under a surveillance stricter than any you have known, there was no way *I* could escape unless I seemed to be playing one of the standard variations on our theme of cat-and-mouse. Do you know de L'Isle-Adam's *The Torture of Hope*? Its premise is that nothing is so conducive to despair as to allow an escape to succeed up to the very moment the prisoner breathes his first mouthful of freedom – then to spring the trap-door under his feet. That was the principle behind your "escape" to London, and it was the *stated* principle, in my official reports, behind tonight's affair, though of course in *this* case I would hesitate to trace each sub-plot to its ultimate literary source. In any case, while it must be admitted that our lives imitate art, I like to think that sometimes we may invent some little twist all our own before the novelists think of it. If not this time, perhaps the next. (My *credo*.)

You may recall having debated with me, some time ago, concerning the relative advantages enjoyed by the prisoner and his jailer. I was obliged then to present the case for the prosecution. Now, though my opinions haven't changed, my *position* has, and I am forced to concede (in my own defence) that, yes indeed, the jailer *is* less free than the prisoner, that the warden's office is also a cell of maximum security. The very fact that I must *escape* proves that I have been, like you, a prisoner – without even your solace of being able to blame someone else. (Though I have always been able to find *excuses*.) Ah, this is all philosophy, and I know how we both recoil from *that!*

Some facts, then, and a bit of explanation:

All that stuff above (the philosophy) would never have occurred to me – would never, at least, have *affected* me – without your adventure in the archives. *I* know you set that fire, *you* know you set that fire, but Number 1, whose imagination at rare moments can equal yours or mine, was not to be persuaded it was as simple as all that. There were films concerning myself destroyed then that had been used to secure my . . . (Would "allegiance" be the right word?) . . . to this Village (and *that* is not the right word either). Though I pointed out to Number 1 that my "allegiance" had since been secured with links of guilt (which is, I'm afraid, exactly the right word) far stronger than the trifling scandals documented in those films, Number 1 remained suspicious. After all, when the mood hits him, whom does he have to be suspicious of, except for me? Lesser suspicions can be delegated.

I could measure day by day the growing pressure, the spread of insubordination, and the steady fraying of the cord that held the sword above my head. Had I not succeeded at *this* escape, I would have had to take the advice you offered, as the Duke, and "be absolute for death." That much of an absolutist I am not.

Goodbye then. Let me express the sincere hope that we may meet again. Perhaps by then the wheel of Fortune will have turned 180 degrees, and you may enjoy (would you?) the sensation of playing

Warden to my Prisoner.

Best regards,
Number 2

P.S. Concerning the technology of deception (I hope you take an interest in these details, retrospectively): My persona as a cracker-barrel philosopher was all done with electrons and a 1901 anthology called *Heart Throbs*. A character actor was hired and photographed through the entire gamut of what his face could do. This repertoire was coded into a computer. Whenever 'Number 2' appeared on television, there was always a live camera on me. My expressions were translated, by the computer, into his, just as my voice was changed to his by the same method. One of my few regrets in leaving the Village is that I can't take the old duffer along. I'd become quite fond of him. Hadn't you?

P.P.S A last word of good counsel from *Heart Throbs'* endless store:

> Should you feel inclined to censure
> Faults you may in others view,
> Ask your own heart ere you venture,
> If that has not failings, too.
>
> Do not form opinions blindly,
> Hastiness to trouble tends;
> Those of whom we thought unkindly
> Oft become our warmest friends.

"Then it was an escape, after all," she said, handing the letter back to him. "My brother couldn't have arranged a conspiracy on as large a scale as this evening's, but Number 2 could have accomplished it with three or four memoes. If irony is any comfort to you, there's this: it was the two of us, together, who put him on the skids. The fire *you* set; the betraying detail in your dream, which *I* kept back."

"You're certain it was your brother who wrote this letter?"

"Of course. You don't think . . ."

"That it was from her? Is there any evidence, in the letter, to prove it couldn't be? There isn't."

"Look more closely. There must a lapse, somewhere – some way of standing a sentence on its head, a pet word, something that's characteristic of only one of them."

"Give Number 2, whoever he is, credit for subtlety. Anything we might point to as 'characteristic' could have been planted in the letter just for us to point to. The only certain proof would be if one of us had carried on a dialogue with Number 2 while either your brother or Liora was present in the same room. I haven't. Have you?"

"No. But doesn't that make my brother the likelier suspect, in view of all the times I've been with him and all the times that Number 2 has intruded on me, at my cottage, in the lab, on the street? The coincidence seems mountainous."

"On the other hand, isn't this the best explanation of the paradoxes and impossibilities in *her* story?"

"Perhaps – but say what you will, until it's *proven* one way or the other, I'll be convinced it was him. It all seems, in hindsight, so in keeping with his *character.*"

"And I'll remain convinced it was her. I imagine all of this has been devised with some care just so each of us would reach the conclusions we have."

She smiled wistfully, as though remembering a pleasant weekend spent, some years before, on a country estate subsequently destroyed in the blitz. "He *would* have enjoyed this so much.

"Or," she added politely, "*she* would have."

The last performers entered on to the stage, a six-man squad of night patrolmen. After a flourish of jackboots, the leader of the chorus (or squad) stepped forward and saluted the couple at centre stage. He seemed to be waiting for orders to carry off the dead bodies. Would he believe that this had only been a comedy?

"Yes?" the doctor said.

"You are Number 14?" the squad leader asked.

"Apparently. As of this moment."

"We have orders to arrest Number 2."

"I'm afraid you've arrived well past the nick of time. Number 2 escaped, with a friend, in a helium balloon, some minutes ago."

The squad leader consulted with the members of his squad. After stomping them back to attention, he again addressed the doctor: "There appears to be a misunderstanding here, Number 14. We have orders to arrest the man standing beside you." He pointed to Number 6, standing beside her.

"You very well may have orders to arrest him, but *this* man is Number 6."

The squad leader smiled with tolerant amusement at Woman's ability to misunderstand whatever she needs to. "As of *this* moment, ma'am, that man is Number 2."

She turned to him, wavering between hilarity and bewilderment. "Have *you* been ... All this time? No. No, not you."

She turned back to the squad leader. "May I ask what your orders are, once Number ... 2 has been *arrested*?"

"He's to be locked up, pending further orders."

"From Number 1 ?"

"Our instructions, Number 14, are that we'll receive orders from you."

They looked at each other and, with better timing than in any earlier scene in the play, began to laugh. They grew helpless with laughter. Each time either of them tried to talk, nothing came out but a few sputtered syllables and then more, and more helpless, laughter.

"Pardon me, Number 14," the squad leader interposed. "Pardon me! Please, if you will, ma'am, *pardon* me!"

"Yes?" Still stifling giggles.

"We'd like to be told what we're to do with the prisoner. Where shall we take him?"

"Why – to prison, of course."

"Yes, Number 14. But—"He hunched his shoulders, as though to say: But there are so *many* prisons.

"Is there any particular prison you'd prefer, Number 6? Number 2, rather."

"One's as bad as another, it seems to me."

"Very well then – you will keep the prisoner confined to this prison until I've issued further orders."

The guard looked about suspiciously. At last, despite the pain of having to show his naïveté before a superior, he had to ask outright: "Which prison is ... this?"

She pointed to the painted canvas. "A prison in Vienna," she explained. "See that he doesn't escape."

PART IV COUNTDOWN

"In the dream of the man who was dreaming, the dreamt man awoke."

Jorge Luis Borges, *The Circular Ruins*

Chapter Seventeen

The Conversion

" I trust," Number 14 said, "that you can hear me, though if you can't, it's of no importance. What I say is addressed to Number 6, a person who will soon no longer exist, and who, if he can hear me, probably wishes that he could not. So I don't know why I bother saying this. Another apology? You've heard too many already, from all of us. 'I am doing,' we each say, 'what Necessity requires.' It has always seemed to me that that is rather worse than crimes committed out of a pure zest for evil. No, I'll offer no excuses.

"An explanation, that's all it is. When the worst happens, I've always thought it would be a small comfort to be informed of its exact dimensions. It's that, my faith in mere *measurements*, more than any special competence or knowledge, that makes me a scientist. Perhaps it's a faith you wouldn't share, and if this were *my* earthquake, I don't know whether I would be that interested in the seismograph readings. Perhaps in the labyrinth of my motives what I am offering in the name of charity – this explanation – is only a new twist of the old thumbscrew. Perhaps, perhaps, perhaps – the word multiplies itself as wantonly as an amoeba. I won't say it again.

"When I outlined this project, it was then an abstracter kind of crime. The prospectus was completed before I knew that *you* existed, months before you were brought back to the Village. I did wonder, later on, whether their decision to retrieve you had been determined by the parameters I'd drawn up for selecting an optimum subject. (Subject! there's a lovely euphemism. We psychologists have invented a richer treasure of cant than all the gentlewomen of the 19th Century together.) If that *was* their purpose, then they took long enough getting around to it. Perhaps – oh, I've said it! – perhaps Number 2 *was* your friend, insofar as it must have been he (or she) who kept you from this day for ... how long? Over two months. Surely it's significant that the order to set to work should be issued immediately Number 2 had escaped, departed, whatever.

"I keep saying 'they.' What I mean, of course, is Number 1. Number 1 has never been able to find a lieutenant exactly to his taste. Either they have been enterprising and imaginative in performing their duties, in which case they have invariably shown an imperfect loyalty, a tendency to place their individual interests above the interests of the Village and of Number 1. (An orthodox faith would not distinguish between the two.) *Or* he would be a man of unquestionable loyalty who proved, at a moment of crisis, to be a nincompoop. Once, Number 1 discovered a subordinate who combined both failings – he was a disloyal nincompoop – but he's never found someone who was at once fanatically loyal and a brilliant administrator. Few dictators ever have had that good luck, with the possible exception of those four paragons of the Golden Age of Authority, the '30's and '40's.

"For a dictator nothing is impossible: that is the first tenet of orthodoxy. Number 1 decided that since he could not find an ideal 2, he would have one made to order. I was brought here expressly to design a model of this superveep and to work out a method by which that model could be converted from graphs and equations into flesh and blood. Since science hasn't yet advanced to the stage where it can create a true homunculus from raw scraps of DNA, it was clear that something like a metamorphosis was called for. It was also clear that it would be more feasible to graft loyalty to an already existing imagination than the other way round.

"Which is not all as easy as you may think. Though it would take at most 48 hours to transform you, or someone of your sort, into a perfectly loyal minion, such a transformation would virtually destroy those qualities that would make your loyalty worth having: initiative, creativity, and all those other vague words that are lumped under the heading of (that vaguest word of all) Spirit. The usual techniques of brainwashing affect these virtues the way ordinary laundering affects the more perishable kinds of clothing: at worst they are demolished, like laces, and at best they shrink, like argyle socks. The merit of *my* programme is that those useful qualities will be preserved, while your loyalty is shifted, ever so gradually, from its present locus to where Number 1 would like to see it, revolving in a worshipful orbit about the sun of that exalted idea: One, Oneness, Number 1. Since your present loyalty is centered not on any particular nation, institution, or surrogate father, but about a pantheon of *ideas* – Truth, Justice, Freedom, and the rest of the Platonic tribe – its transfer to this new orbit will be relatively easy, for the idea of One is no less abstract, vague and exalted than, for instance, the idea of Freedom.

"In fact, even as I talk to you now, even as you listen, the process has begun. Like Ishtar disrobing on her progress through the seven gates, you, in the amniotic void of that tank, have surrendered your senses, one by one, till now it is only the sound of my voice that ties you to reality. When my voice ceases you will exist in an elemental state. You have read, I'm sure, about these experiments, and you know how people, under sensory deprivation, become malleable as refined gold. The mind cannot tolerate a vacuum, and when the senses no longer are pumping data in, it begins to fill up from the springs of its own unconscious. Fantasy takes over, but not the fantasy of dreaming, for there is no distinction now between dreaming and waking. It is the conscious mind that dreams, the ego. And it is, at these moments, intensely suggestible.

"A picture is worth a thousand words, so let me illustrate my lecture with a slide or two. We need not bother, today, with lasers and such as that. Your own imagination, starving for images, will do our work for us.

"What shall it be? Since this is not yet the metamorphosis proper, let's choose something pretty. A marble egg. There was a marble egg on the desk in the study of your London flat. It was rose-coloured. It rested in an egg-cup of white china. You can see it now, that marble egg, the swirling veins of grey, the mottled rose that shifts, as you turn it in your hand, to pink, to a deeper rose, with here and there an arabesque of milky white. That egg has sat on your desk for years, growing steadily more invisible as it grew more customary, but now you see it, don't you, more clearly than you've ever seen it before? It is more *real* now than it has ever been, even though you *know*, because I'm telling you, that it is only an *imaginary* egg of unreal marble that rests in an entirely subjective egg-cup. When we set to work in earnest, I will no longer be able to remind you of that paradox.

"Now, to demonstrate the final, and crucial, mechanism. Hold the marble egg up to the light. Its loveliness increases. A little higher, and the light will be ideal.

"You did, didn't you? You held it up, because that is something you would have done without compunction back here, in the real world. The action did not contradict any principle or taste. But now, observe: Put the egg in your mouth. Do as I say, Number 2, *put it in your mouth.*

"Did you do that? Unless you have a peculiar taste for sucking marble, you did not. Such an action lies outside your character, the range of what you allow yourself to *be.* You'd be amazed at how easily that range can be moved back and forth.

"We humans are, at root, Number 2, very simple creatures. Like the computers we've fashioned in our image, we operate on a binary code of pleasure and pain, a switch marked ON and another marked OFF. Finally, everything can be reduced to one or the other, everything we've learned, everything we loathe or love, everything that forms our image of what and who we are.

"At this moment, Number 2, we have control of those switches. There are two wires fixed to your scalp, one for pain, unimaginable pain, and one for pleasure, unspeakable pleasure.

"Observe, now, what these switches do. Again I will insist that you put the marble egg in your mouth. Again you refuse. Again I insist – *put the egg in your mouth.* I do more than insist, I threaten.

"Put the egg in your mouth!

"You have not, and so I touch, gently, the switch of pain.

"I release it, and suggest, only *suggest* that you would *like* to put the marble egg in your mouth. It is, after all, in keeping with your character to do so.

"Can you feel it there now, the larger end lodged in the soft flesh beneath the tongue, the smaller end touching the roof of your mouth, a small cold ovoid of marble, in your mouth? You do feel it there, and now I touch, briefly, this switch for pleasure.

"And, oh the bliss! You realise that it is *good* to have that marble egg just where it is, in your mouth. Can you feel the goodness of it there? Can you? And I touch, again, the switch.

"If I should touch it once or twice more, you would never again be able to look at, or even imagine, a marble egg without a maniacal craving to place it in your mouth.

"That is how the human machine works. What it can be made to do depends on where we decide to drive it. The bulk of my work has consisted in drawing up that road-map. The transformation from 6 to 2 will be so imperceptible that you will never, I think, be able to detect a single bend in the road, but by the time you have arrived at your final destination, at complete Twoness, you would not be able to recognise yourself in what you have become, any more than that new self, that perfect figure 2, will be able to see himself in you, the 'you' who hears this.

"And it will be a terrible loss, I think. Because I did love you. I loved the person that you are and that you will so soon cease to be. I doubt very much that I could love the person you're going to become. For though I know that you don't love me now, you *might* some day, and this other person we are forming from your clay will not be able to love anything but One, the idea of One's Oneness. You, who listen to me and whom I love, will have been lost to me, and to yourself.

"Goodbye, Number 6. Forgive me for my part in this. If I'd refused to play it out to the end, they would have sent an understudy on in my place. Like every other traitor, I am a coward and a pragmatist. If you were able to understand what it means to be like this, you wouldn't be here now, and I would never have loved you.

"The light is blinking above the monitor. Number 1 is impatient with my speech-making, and no doubt you are, too. We will have to begin in earnest. You can, while there is still a moment, remove the marble egg from your mouth."

Chapter Eighteen

The Marble Egg

He looked at the imaginary marble egg. It was rose-coloured and streaked with greys and whites. His own fingers had lent it the warmth of their flesh.

Never once had he put the marble egg in his mouth, nor, though he had steeled himself against both, had he felt the least tingle of pleasure, the slightest twinge of pain.

He understood what she had done for him, and she had explained, in great detail, what he would now have to do for himself.

It was autumn, a brisk, tangy, delightful autumn day, and he was strolling through the park. He nodded in a cordial, absent-minded way to Number 189, the former sweeper at the railway station, who was working now for the Department of Parks. He had promoted him just last week to his new position. Number 189 acknowledged this gesture with shy, solemn respect, then returned to his work weeding hawkbit from the ordered files of the chrysanthemums.

He stopped beside the bench where the old woman was bent over her embroidery hoop. "Good *afternoon*, Granny."

She heard him the very first time and looked up with twinkles from her eyes and from the wire-frame spectacles. "Why, good afternoon, Number 2!"

"Hard at *work*, I see."

"Work? Oh yes, there's never a free moment for me!" With a little chuckle at her own little joke, she held the hoop up so that he might admire her handiwork.

"That's very *handsome*," he said, stooping to study the meticulously stitched orchids. "And very true to life."

"Thank you! I do love roses so – don't you?"

"Roses, well ... yes. Do you ever embroider ... other kinds of flowers?"

"No, just roses, Number 2. Roses have always been my favourite flower, since I was just a little snip of a thing. Red roses and white roses. I can never decide which I like better."

"It's very expert work that you do, Granny. This stitch here, for example." He pointed to one of the writhing tendrils.

"That's a scroll stitch," she confided in a low voice. "And this" – touching the dark mauve of the corolla with the tip of the needle "is a dorando stitch."

"A dorando stitch, well, well, well." In a tone that implied that this piece of information had appreciably expanded his intellectual horizon. Patting the veined, knobby hand that held the hoop, he doled out some further sugar lumps of approbation, until all the wrinkles of her face had been brought into play by a grin of proud, senile accomplishment.

It was *clammy*, he thought, leaving her. He rubbed his fingertips against the palm of his hand, as though that brief touch had drawn away all the warmth of his own flesh.

At the terrace restaurant he chose a seat at the table where Number 83, the male model, was playing dominoes with Number 29, the man with the goitres.

"How's it going, men?" he asked cordially.

"Great!" said the male model, with a smile that would have made anyone ready to buy the same toothpaste. "Just great, Number 2!"

"Pretty well," the goitres grumbled.

He shot one of his own smiles back at Number 83, not so broad but more confidential. "It's not hard to tell which of you is winning."

Even Number 29 had to laugh at that.

He watched their game for ten minutes, offering comments on the weather, kibbitzing when it was the goitres' turn, analysing Number 83's performance, last Wednesday afternoon, at the big soccer match.

The waitress who brought his coffee was the red-faced woman who'd been working at the cafe by the railway station the day he'd arrived.

"Where is Number 127?" he asked with some concern.

"Oh, her! " the waitress said, with an ant's scorn for the grasshoppers of this world. "She's *sick* again."

"Has she been sick often?"

"For the last three days. It's the *flu*, she says." As she pronounced the word, "flu" became a synonym for malingering.

"Give her my regards, would you, the next time she calls in? Tell her how much we all look forward to her recovery."

The waitress sighed her consent and returned to a sink of dirty pots, feeling somehow enriched. "It's amazing," she told herself, as she rolled up her sleeves, "how you can *always* tell a gentlemen." There was an element of sadness in this thought, for she knew that in the ordinary scheme of things such gentlemen were not for the likes of her, but even so, as long as she could bring him his cup of coffee in the afternoon, as long as there was one smile that he smiled just for her, there was some comfort to be had, there was a *point* in scrubbing all these pots.

The game of dominoes ended, and Numbers 83 and 29 rose from the table.

"Four o'clock already!" he said.

He stood to shake their hands, a handshake that made each of them realise his own special importance to the Village and to Number 2, and to what they represented. With a bemused smile, like a proud father seeing his sons set off to their work in the mines, he watched them go towards the church.

He took a deep breath of the salt air, swinging his arms up and out to stretch his tensed pectorals. His fourth set, and already he'd built up a good sweat. He took a straddle-legged position on the shingle for his next exercise. Despite all his new responsibilities, he always found the time for his morning workout and a mile's run along the beach.

At the eastern end of the crescent of shingle, near the cliff he'd scaled on that other morning (how long ago!) he saw a figure emerge out of the rocks of the cliff. A woman dressed for swimming. It was proscribed to swim at that end of the beach, where the currents were dangerous, and it was uncommon to see anyone swimming at all this late in the year or this early in the morning.

"Hallo!" he called to her.

Instead of replying by word or gesture, she ran into the dark, cliff-shadowed water.

He pressed the alarm signal on his wrist-band.

"Wait." Sprinting across the wet, shifting pebbles. "Wait a moment!

Stop!"

The woman, out to thigh-depth, veered right, towards where the cliff thrust out from the shore to meet the ocean head-on. At the moment he entered the water himself, the undertow pulled her down, dragging her – and several tons of crushed stone – towards the whitecaps. He caught a glimpse of blonde hair (and it was, as he had thought, the waitress, Number 127, who had been calling in ill with "flu") ten feet farther out, which vanished behind the curl of a breaking wave. He sighted her again, past the line of the surf, swimming towards the deadly roiling beauty of the cliff. He struck out in pursuit, breasting the line of the surf, gaining quickly at first, until, nearer the cliff, the varying currents mocked both their efforts, flinging them towards each other, and tearing them apart.

He caught hold of an arm. She jerked free of his grip with a convulsive strength. Screamed: "Go—" Gagged by the salt water.

A handful, then, of the blonde hair. Towing her by this rope, he swam seaward against the current drawing them towards the cliff. Twisting around, she wrapped her arms about his kicking legs. They sank, interlocked, beneath the frothing surface into the stronger and stranger eddies below. Her arms were a vice of rigid, hysterical strength.

His first blow was not forceful enough. With the second she went limp.

He towed her unbuoyant body upward and surfaced, gasping. By luck the nether currents had carried them farther from the face of the cliff, and he could swim back towards the shore, even disadvantaged by the dead weight of her body, without being drawn back into the area of danger.

The patrol was inflating a life raft as he pulled her up on to the beach. He lay on his stomach; while the gentler water of the shore played about his ankles, he watched a medical aide administer artificial respiration to Number 127. The guards waited respectfully until he had recovered his breath.

"Is she all right?" he asked.

"She will be," the aide assured him, drawing his lips away from hers to speak.

"Send out all the launches," he said, to the leader of the patrol.

"That's been done sir." He nodded distastefully at the woman. A mixture of vomit and brine spilled from her unconscious lips. "Was she swimming out to meet someone?"

"Possibly. Any boat that attempted to enter the bay would be dealt with in the usual way. What I suspect is that the crew of one of our own patrol boats has been—"

He was interrupted by the scream of the medical aide. He had leaped back from his patient, scrabbling across the loose stones. Blood streamed from the deep cut in his lower lip.

The waitress was struggling up to her elbows. Threads of vomit still clung to the corners of her mouth and trembled as she spoke: "You needn't . . . bother . . . Number 2. I wasn't . . . swimming out . . . to meet . . . anyone."

"What were you doing, Number 127?"

But she did not have to answer him, for their eyes had already completed the conversation. Hers had said: *Suicide* – and his replied that he had known. Hers said: *If I had the strength, I'd try and kill you again* – his told her that she'd had her chance, and failed.

"You *pig!*" she said aloud, though her eyes had said this too, and with even more force. She tried to smooth back the bedraggled hair, but the hand was smeared with her vomit. She began to cry.

"Number 2?" the medical aide asked.

"Bring her to the hospital. Number 14 will look after her now. It's all in a day's work." He turned away.

"Number 6!" she screamed, forgetting in her pain that he was no longer Number 6. "You were the *only* one, and you—" She choked as more brine welled up into her throat. By the time she had emptied herself on the wet rocks, she had realised the hopelessness of what she had been about to say.

"Sir, you don't have to walk back to the Village. Take our jeep."

"Thank you, Number 263, but I haven't had my morning run yet. Be careful with that woman. She'll probably attempt some kind of violence."

He began to trot westward, following the long shadow that glided ahead of him across the glistening pebbles, the lumps of tar, the strands of kelp, the quaking, clustered foam.

Behind him he heard her final, and definitive, curse, then her screams as she struggled with the guards.

He ran on, concentrating on his breathing. It was shallow, even, relaxed.

Entering his cottage, he found yesterday's domino-players, Numbers 83 and 29, sprawled in the Chippendale chairs, half-asleep. Automatically his hand switched on the Muzak control, and the room filled with the waltzing ghosts of a thousand animated cartoons. The goitres snorted himself to alertness, and the male model stretched himself, cat-like, and produced a very sleepy smile that would never have sold anything.

"An unexpected pleasure, gentlemen," he said.

In unison: "Good morning, Number 2."

"Tea? Coffee?"

"We've had our breakfast, thank you," said Number 29.

"You'll excuse me if I go into my bedroom to change out of these wet clothes. I won't be a minute. Here – I'll leave the door open, and you can tell me what it is that brings you to me at this unusual hour. There's no serious trouble, I hope . . . ?"

"No sir."

"Did you hear about my little adventure at the beach this morning?"

The two men exchanged a look. The younger answered. "Yes, we did, Number 2."

"Quite a stroke of luck that I was on the spot. I think the poor girl thought she was going to *swim* away!" From the bedroom, a hearty laugh. Then, as though contritely: "Of course, it's not a laughing matter. Even if it turns out that no one else was involved, an incident like this should be a lesson to all of us. If she'd gone into the water just a few minutes later, who would have seen her? Who would have brought her back? No one! Do you realise what that would have meant?"

"That she would have drowned," Number 83 said, affecting to yawn.

"Does that seem such a light matter to you?" he asked sharply, entering the living room in his everyday costume of slacks, turtleneck and jacket. "Gentlemen, an attempted suicide is a graver threat to this Village than an attempted escape. A fugitive can be brought back; a corpse cannot be."

He took a seat beside the Riesener secretaire and studied the faces of his two visitors as they chewed on this concept.

"Number 2 is right," the goitres announced, having swallowed the concept, digested it, and transported it by blood corpuscles to his brain, where it was shelved in the bulging files of Orthodox Views. In the next month he would often take the opportunity to retrieve it from the files and read it to his fellow numerals in the service of the Village – the very words addressed to *him* by Number 2.

"But how can suicide be prevented?" Number 83 asked. He did not seem to have the same digestive capacity as the goitres.

"A good question, Number 83."

Number 29 began chewing on this good question. It was going to be a full morning.

"The answer is to be found in almost every aspect of our lives here in the Village. Tell me, Number 83, are *you* happy with your life here? Does it seem *big* enough? Is it active, exciting, stimulating? Is your work as agreeable as your leisure hours?"

"Oh, *yes* sir! There's nothing that—" He raised his empty hands as a sign of his plenteous fulfillment.

"Nothing!" the goitres echoed emphatically.

"Nothing that either of you could wish for in addition to what you already have been given," he summed up for them. "In short, the Village is a kind of utopia for you, and most of us here would have to say the same thing. There is comfort and affluence. Our work is scaled to our individual capacities, and our leisure is filled to bursting with meaningful and self-improving activities. But that represents only the material aspect of the Village. There is also a spiritual aspect, which can be summed up in a single word – Oneness. The idea of Oneness should inform our every action throughout the day. It should ... But I'm getting carried away. I know that both of you, in your own ways, treasure that idea in your inmost hearts. It's just this – the idea of Oneness – that makes our life so very much worth living that for people like *us* the notion of escape, much less of suicide, is literally unthinkable."

After a reverent silence, the goitres asked, "But in that case, Number 2, I don't understand! Why would anyone ... ?"

"Unfortunately, Number 29, there are a *few* people in this Village – and I must confess, to my sorrow, that I used to be the worst of them – a few people who will not accept that idea, or rather – who haven't been able to *understand* it. Often the more intelligent they are, the more difficult it seems to be for them to grasp the notion of Oneness. In that respect a man like Number 189, though he may be a little slower than we are, is one of the happiest, and most *loyal*, citizens of our Village. Faith is not a problem for Number 189. Of course, with the right education, faith would not be a problem for any of us. Disloyalty is only a form of *ignorance*. Always bear that in mind, gentlemen."

Loyally, the goitres filed this in the less crowded file reserved for the Eternal Truths, while Number 83 assumed his gravest expression, suitable for advertising the Great Books or an encyclopaedia.

Confident that they would be occupied by these lofty thoughts for a few minutes, he turned his chair around to face the papers spread out on the secretaire.

He froze, without knowing why, as though he'd glimpsed, with his peripheral vision, a glint of the blade above his head. His conscious mind sought for what his unconscious had already sensed.

It stood in the far left-hand corner of his desk, behind the report from the Employment Advisory Board: a marble egg, rose-coloured, in a white egg-cup. A film of dust obscured the mottled grain.

My God! he thought. How *long has it been there?*

Then he recalled that last night, when he'd been working on his security recommendations, he had placed a cup of tea on the same spot, that he had left the cup and saucer there when he had gone to bed.

He spread open the folder of cost and maintenance figures of the Guardians. Reaching across the desk with apparent casualness, as an addicted smoker might reach for the cigarette he has left burning in an ashtray, he took the egg from the eggcup. He weighed it a moment in the palm of his hand, then, without seeming to notice what he did, he placed the dusty marble egg in his mouth.

Number 83 rose to his feet. "Number 2!" he said.

"Mmm?" Turning to confront him with a look of mild annoyance.

The goitres also rose, realising from Number 83's meaningful glance towards the empty eggcup, that the purpose of their visit had been accomplished while he'd been napping among the Eternal Truths.

Apologetically he let the egg slide out into his cupped hand. "Yes, Number 83, what is it?"

"We have instructions to accompany you to the administration building. Number 1 wishes to speak to you."

"*Number 1!*" he said, with an expression of transported delight that would have convinced the assembled saints in heaven that this was the real article, a bonafide Beatific Vision. "My God, why did you take all this time to *tell* me?"

"We were following our orders," the goitres explained primly. Of all the Scriptures in all his files, he liked this one the very best.

"*Number 1,*" he repeated reverently.
And thought: *It's about time!*

Chapter Nineteen

The White Room

"Come in, Number 2," another speaker said, as he waited before another door.

The last door unlocked itself and purred upwards in its steel frame, like the blade of a guillotine lifted for its next piece of work. He stepped into the white room.

Into a dazzling void, as though the lips of Reality had parted to show one last tremendous grin.

In a white alcove of this white room sat Number 1. She tilted her head sideways (a strand of white hair fell across white skin) and asked, with conscious coyness: "Are you surprised?"

"You're Number 1? *You?*"

She pursed her lips, nodded once. "You never guessed?"

"Never once. Though I always had the feeling that there was something ... a-bit-too-much about you. But I've felt that way about everyone here."

"Come," she said. "Share this window-seat with me. We'll be friends now, you and me. As we always *should* have been."

Slowly, across the white floor, darkened not even by his own shadows, he walked towards her. He no longer kept up a pretence of holy awe, but neither did he feel inclined to rush through these concluding lines as he had done when he'd played the Duke. He had expected to feel rage at this moment, for surely rage had been mounting in him these many weeks.

Instead, he felt ... what? Not curiosity: though he might still ask many questions, he knew better than to trust any answers, especially now that he'd made his way to the very source of all these lies. Not caution: caution had seen him as far as it could, and now, having forced the stakes to the limit, he was willing to risk everything on a single hand.

Did he suspect that this was only the penultimate imposture, not the centre of labyrinth but only its antechamber? The thought had passed his mind, but to have reached even so far as the antechamber was a good second-best when he had seen no more than an outer courtyard up to now.

Was the explanation for his reticence as simple as this – that he'd been schooled, from his earliest years, to show Respect for the Aged, to whisper and to walk with a softer step in the presence of antique flesh?

Possibly. These tokens that we pay to the very old are the same that we accord to the dying. Beyond a certain point, age and death are indistinguishable. And he did not want to cheat even Number 1 of the solemnity that should attend the moment of death.

He sat apart from her on the moulded plastic bench of the alcove, trying not to stare at her. Seen against this whiteness, in this sourceless, glaring light, each component of her physical being presented itself to him with unnatural clarity: the series of tiny metal spheres buttoning up the cracked black leather of her high shoes; the folds of the crepe, the crisp little puckers where it was gathered at the neck and shoulders, the flounces drooping at the ends of the long sleeves; the thin strands of white hair falling across her waxen forehead; the yellow tint of her fingers, whitening where age had drawn the flesh taut across the bones; the wrinkled face.

The wrinkles: these above all. Her face had become a pretext for these wrinkles. Unless he made a special effort, all the rest – eyes, mouth, nose, etc. – would blur and varnish into the generality, to become mere special instances of Wrinkliness.

"You have been waiting for this moment a long time, Number 2." Her manner towards him was at once warm and distant, as though beneath each simple cordial banality there lurked depths of significance which it were better most of the world should remain in ignorance of, but which she would reveal to him.

"Yes, a long time," he said, safely.

"Perhaps you'd even given up hope." A statement, not a question, but spoken in such an ineffable tone that it might have meant anything. He was to infer that she lived in those lofty regions where all opposites are resolved into Oneness.

He refused to make the inference, and replied to her statement as though it had been a question. "No. In fact, it was more than just a hope.

I always knew this moment was inevitable for us."

"For us!" He seemed not to understand that this was to have been his moment, not theirs, the moment of his fulfilment, a gift from the infinite One to the finite Two.

"Us, certainly. Here we are, after all this time, actually confronting each other, face to face." He stared directly into the wrinkles, where one thin line amid the calligraphic maze formed what on another face would have been a smile.

"Such a strange way you have, Number 2, of putting it – a confrontation!"

"Yes, that's the sort of thing I'd have said before my conversion."

"Exactly what I had thought."

"Why *am* I here?"

"Should you have to *ask*, Number 2? Isn't it enough to *be* here?"

"Here – in this room?"

"Here, with me. Why all these questions? Can it be so hard to look at old Granny in this new light?"

He ignored her question to ask his own: "Do you *live* here, in this room?"

She ignored his to ask *her* own: "Do you like it?" She waved a regal hand at the bright void before them, quite as though it contained a boutique's worth of particulars for his admiration and applause: bouquets of hair-flowers under glass bells, a collection of her finest red and white embroidered roses, albums of photographs, a cast-iron chandelier.

"It's very plain," he said noncommittally.

"But it's a plainness that *suits* me."

"Oh yes," he agreed, "it does that."

"One grows tired of ostentation more quickly than of plainness." She employed "One" not as an impersonal pronoun but as a monarch would refer to himself as "We."

"In principle I agree, though in practice I think that plainness can be carried too far."

The old woman rose from the "window-seat," wringing her hands in agitation. She followed a zig-zagging path across the room, as though for her there were obstacles everywhere. She looked all about, focusing on one particular point in this void after another. "I wish," she said (becoming; for the nonce, helpless, vague old Grandmother Bug), "you'd *tell* me what it is! These *hints* will drive me out of my mind. If there's something you don't like, then for pity's sake, say what it is, and I'll have them take it *away!*" She removed from one ruffled sleeve a lace handkerchief, in case she found herself obliged to cry.

He could not decide if the Empress really believed herself to be clothed. "There's no one thing I could point to," he said carefully. "It's a more general impression. Perhaps it's only that I'm not *used* to it."

This seemed to satisfy her, for she tucked the handkerchief back up her sleeve.

"Oh, but you will *grow* used to it," she assured him sweetly, and it was then, for the first time, for the only time, that he experienced true terror, the terror he had glimpsed in other Villagers, that had been occasioned, for them too, by something as disproportionate, as ludicrously mild as these few words, spoken so warmly, with such a gentle refinement. "Oh, but you will *grow* used to it."

"No. I won't."

One could not doubt his conviction. "No?" she asked, without a doubt.

"It just isn't to my *taste.*"

"Really?" She returned to the alcove, as the crow flies, straight at him. "Am *I* to your taste, then?" she insisted, thrusting the crumpled parchment of her face into his smooth vellum.

A smell of musk issued from the wrinkles.

By an effort of the will he did not draw back, nor could anything more be read on the vellum than a certain bland befuddlement. "In what *sense*, Number 1?"

She withdrew the parchment. His mere utterance of her number seemed to reassure her. Remembering to be Granny, she seated herself, folded her venerable hands in her lap, smoothed out the parchment to show that it had actually been a generous Bequest, to which she now added, as a kind of codicil, a smile, while her eyes, unsmiling, preserved a clause of *in terro rem*.

"Dear, dear Number 2," old Granny said, leaving no doubt that dear, dear Number 2 was expected to reply in kind. When he did not, she added a second log to this blaze of affection: "I wish there were *something* I could do for *you.*"

He *should* have said: "It's enough that you allow me to serve your cause." And further rhapsodies on that theme.

He *did* say: "There is. You could answer some questions that have been troubling me for quite some time."

The hands awoke in her lap and disarranged themselves. "Questions! Oh dear. Are you sure you want to ask them of *me*? I'm very bad at questions."

"There's no one else who can answer the questions I have in mind."

"That's very likely," she said. "But even *so*!"

"What is the purpose of this Village, Number 1?"

"Purpose? Village? Such an odd question. Villages don't have purposes – they have *people*."

"The purpose of this organisation, then."

Again Granny rose and walked to the middle of the white room, as though, being far-sighted, she could only observe him closely from this distance. "Organisation is *such* an ugly word. Though I suppose it's to the point. What is the purpose of *any* organisation, Number 2? To grow. And to exist. We want to grow as much as we can, to exist as long as we can. And, though it's not for *me* to say so, I think we can be proud of ourselves, of all that we've done so far in these two respects. Though we can't slacken *now*."

"How long has the Village been here? When did the organisation begin to *exist*?"

She tapped her lips with a bony index finger, frowning. And sighed. "I'm sorry, but I have such a terrible head for dates. I hope that wasn't one of the *important* questions."

"Did you come to this Village? Or did you make it?"

"I made it." With a modest smile, as though she had been praised once again for her wonderful pineapple upside-down cake.

"You – who *are* you?"

"But you can *see* me, Number 2! I am what I appear to be, neither more nor less." She shook her head at the absurdity of having to explain anything so obvious: "I'm Number 1."

A memory, from the farthest darkness of his past: of riding in a school-bus at night, sitting alone in a double seat. While he stared at the hypnotic flicker of the white lines on the highway, the other boys had sung an endless refrain of: "We're here because we're here because we're here because . . ."

He wondered if, after all, there was no other explanation for the Village than that: because it was here. Possibly at one time it had possessed a purpose, but over the years that purpose had been forgotten, or lost. Indeed, Number 1, as she threaded her way through the private labyrinth of the empty white room, seemed to be pantomiming some kind of search: she lifted cushions, peeked behind clocks, examined dusty shelves, looking for something she was certain she'd misplaced, though she had forgotten what that had been. Her spectacles perhaps? Her embroidery hoop? Her teeth?

And then – of course! – she found it in the pocket of her dress: her platinum buttonhook!

"You can answer this much, at least," he demanded. "Who *runs* the Village? Who makes its laws? Who judges us?"

"*I* do, Number 2," she said sternly. "Your questions become less and less necessary."

"Bear with me – I don't have many more. *How* do you do it?"

She stared at the notched tip of the buttonhook, frowning the wrinkles into a pattern of vexation. "By delegating authority, Number 2. By delegating it to *you*."

"*Why?* Why me? Why did you want *me* to become Number 2?"

"I didn't *want* it. You *are* Number 2. Now – have you *finished* with these silly questions, and may *I* say something to *you*?"

Was he ready to admit defeat? He had not in any case expected to win this part of the contest. It was time, therefore, to proceed to the second part, which (he smiled grimly) he *would* win.

Number 1, interpreting the smile as his consent, began to shake the platinum buttonhook at him energetically. "Number 2, I must say that I have been very disappointed with you today, very disappointed *indeed!* Your attitude suggests to me that your conversion has been anything but—"

She saw the tensing of the thigh, the shift of his torso. She raised the buttonhook to her mouth and bit down firmly on the notched end.

But not, by a nanosecond, soon enough. He had already sprung forward from the bench, out of the alcove, when the sound wave of the implosion crashed about the room.

He raised himself from the white, unshadowed floor, blinked sight back into his eyes. Number 1 stood by the far wall of the room, fondling the buttonhook.

Behind him, where the alcove had been, a perfect rectangle of blackness negated the middle third of the wall.

"I should like to know, Number 2, what it is you think you're doing?"

"And I'd like to know what you did."

"Stay away from me! Stay away, or I'll do it again!" She raised the buttonhook threateningly, but his step did not falter. There were no more alcoves now, and she would not spring the jaws of any trap in which she might be caught as well.

"Wall!" she shouted. "*Wall!*" She beat soundlessly with the end of the buttonhook against the unyielding white plane. Then, without a flicker of transition, the four walls, the ceiling, the floor, everything but the rectangle of blackness that had replaced the alcove, was transformed into something stranger than emptiness. Beneath him there was no longer the level floor but a rolling trembling mass of pinks and violets, veined with writhing tendrils of grey, flecked, like the ocean, with milkwhite clusters of foam, that burst, that bubbled up afresh. The walls and ceiling too had metamorphosed into the same composite of animal and vegetable forms – vastly enlarged inner organs that slid among even vaster petals. Yet his feet, for all that they seemed set upon nothing but this heaving pink stew, gripped the floor as securely as before.

An illusion, as usual.

Number 1 continued to pound soundlessly upon the soundless swarm of shapes, continued to call out, hysterically: "Wall! Wall!"

He caught hold of the hand that grasped the buttonhook. Her struggles were feeble as a child's. She glared at him with the swift, all-engulfing hatred of an infant powerless despite the conviction of his own omnipotence.

"Don't you *dare!*" she screamed at him. "Don't you—"

With a dry snap her hand broke off at the wrist. Her mouth gaped, and she uttered a cry, a quick inward gasp, of horror and outraged modesty. She ceased, in any way, to struggle.

At once the pulsing images about them receded, condensing into vivid squares, like single marble tiles set in the middle of each white plane.

The hand on the white floor slowly spread open its fingers They could both see, where the skin had been frayed at the knuckles by the buttonhook, the tangle of tubes and wires that had made it work.

Her wrist, where the hand had broken off, gave out a buzz that resembled the "engaged" signal a telephone makes, but higher-pitched, a humming, like the humming of a children's chorus, a great mass of voices, heard from a great distance, that rose, by swift octaves, out of the audible range.

Chapter Twenty

Much Adieus

Granny held up the stump of her wrist and looked at it curiously. "For heaven's sake!" she said. "Did you *ever?*"

A second rectangle of blackness had formed opposite the first: the guillotine had been raised to admit a squad, two squads of guards. They entered with great purposefulness, but the scene that confronted them in the white room did not suggest any definite course of action. They coagulated in a circle about the detached hand, one finger of which still twitched erratically.

One guard bent over and picked up the platinum buttonhook. He offered it first to Number 2, who declined it with a shake of his head, then to the old woman, who reached out for it, unthinkingly, with the same arm from which hand and buttonhook had just been removed.

She tisked, bethought herself, accepted the buttonhook with the hand left to her, and placed it in her pocket, where it belonged.

"Oh dear," she said. "Oh, dear, it *is* a nuisance. And just when everything had been going so *nicely.* I do hope you will *excuse—*" She tried to indicate the unmentionable object on the floor without in any crude way *pointing* to it.

"I'm certain I don't know *who* . . . In all this confusion—"

She turned imploringly to the one man in the room who seemed to be a gentleman: "If you'd be so kind as to bring me that *chair?* My legs, you know, are not all that they were."

The guards, gathering courage, had picked up the hand from the floor, and were passing it about their circle.

The doctor appeared at the threshold of the room, a white figure framed by the blackness, a painting on velvet. "That will be *quite* enough!" she said to the startled guards. Had she shaken a caduceus at them, she could not have presented a more fearful image of the authority of Medical Science. She pointed to the hand. "Put that back where you found it, and then leave this room so that we can ..." Her powers of improvisation flagging, she looked to him for help.

"So that we can discuss what must be *done* now," he said, with an authority (viceregal) to equal hers. "Quickly, please, this is a crisis!"

When they were by themselves, it was the old woman who spoke first. "Would ... a cup of tea ... be too much trouble?" With the loss of her hand, she seemed to have reverted completely from her character as Number 1 to the less demanding role of Grandmother Bug. "With just a *drop* ... of milk ... and one lump."

"What happened?" Number 14 asked, trying to catch a look at the stump, which was veiled discreetly by a flounce of crepe.

"A malfunction, it seems."

"Oh, but she's not—" The doctor placed her hand above Granny's sagging bosom, to be sure. "She has a *heart*," she said surely.

"Or something."

"You can *feel* it, beating."

"I'd rather not."

Granny, whimpering, sought to retain the interest of this pretty lady with white hair. "My dear, if you would just lend me your *arm* a minute ... it isn't very far at all. And I'm feeling so—" She shook her head. "And, in short, my dear, not at all *myself*."

"In a moment, Granny, we'll have you in a nice warm bed."

"Will we?" he asked doubtfully.

"Do you have another suggestion?"

He looked at Granny, at the hand that the guard had replaced on the floor, at the doctor, at Granny. Even if she *were* a robot, she commanded a degree of sympathy in her reduced state, and the doctor seemed persuaded that she was (at least partially) human.

A voice in a peculiar bass register, as enough a tape were being played at too slow a speed, addressed them from the whiteness all around: "I wish to announce that in the event of the demise" (slowing still more, to the croaking of a giant frog) "of Nummboor Onnne thaat mmmeaszhoorz haave" (and speeding, rising quickly from frog, to bass, to tenor, to soprano) "been taken to assure the certain annihilation of this Village and of—" It ended in a squeal of slate, a squeak of flute.

"That seems to decide it." Number 14 stooped, with a sigh, to retrieve the hand on the floor. "I had better see if I can reassemble this. Damn! Now you'll have to run off before we've had a single moment to ourselves."

"I will? As quickly as all that?"

"We wouldn't want the world, or whatever, to blow up on *our* account."

"The old girl is still on her feet. She seems to be in no *immediate* danger of dying."

"Well, until I know how she's been ... put together, *I* wouldn't give a prognosis. Besides, she could come out of shock at any moment, and you should be gone before she starts feeling 'like herself' again. That funny little mute servant of yours is waiting outside with your car."

"Quicker and quicker."

"Oh, I've had him on hand since you were decanted from the tank."

"I must thank you for that, you know."

"I was waiting to be thanked."

"Thank you, Number 14, for your sabotage."

"You're welcome. Do you know, this whole last month while you've been Number 2 – and such a dreadful scout-master of a Number 2 you were! – I was horribly afraid that I hadn't disconnected the right wires. In the past I was always able to rely on Number 28 for such things. I feared that you had metamorphosed in earnest. Your acting was that good that I could never be certain."

"And I was never certain at what point I'd been taken from the tank. Those dreams were every bit as real as you said they would be. Much realer than *this*."

She regarded the nothingness about them thoughtfully. "Who's to say this is real? It doesn't have the *earmarks* of reality. I'm sure that so long as you remain in the Village, you'll remain in some doubt. But once you've been in London a week or so everything will begin to look firmer and more trustworthy."

"Including yourself?"

"I won't be there, Number ... I don't know what number to call you any more!"

"Then why—"

"Do favours for you, if I won't be there to reap a benefit? Because, as I've said so often, I *love* you. But I know you don't believe that, even now. Leave the Village. Prove to yourself that you're *free*. Then, if for any reason you should *want* to see me again, I'll still be here. Waiting."

"Like bait in a trap?"

"You forget that you're still Number 2, officially. You can come and go as you like."

"Not once Granny's been restored to her old self."

"Well, it has to be done. I believe what that recording said. It's altogether feasible. A trigger of that kind, that's released by death, can be installed these days, at any large hospital, as easily as a car radio. If it were only a matter of the Village, I might say to hell with it, but Number 1 would have wanted a much larger blaze of glory than that. I feel I should do what I can. But as to Granny's wanting to be revenged on you, I think I've had enough practice fiddling the dials in people's heads that I can persuade her that things happened somewhat differently than they did. She'll believe that she's sent you off on some nebulous but absolutely essential *mission*. So, if you *do* begin to feel nostalgic. . ."

"*If* I do, I'll come back. But it's a damned small *if* to rest any hope on."

"Then I'll have learned not to gamble so recklessly next time. You do think better of me now, don't you, than you did at first? Allow me that much."

"Oh, I'd allow a lot more than that. Even then, though, the problem remains just how much you may have fiddled my dials."

"It can't be helped, my dear. That problem always remains, once you start this kind of thing going. Dr Johnson had the best solution: go kick a stone, and let the stone prove to your foot that they're *both* real."

She turned over Granny's hand palm-upwards and ran her fingernail across the exposed tubes and wires. "At least in *most* cases that's the best solution," she added with a small sad smile that was intended only for herself. She steered the old woman by one bony rudder of shoulder towards the black threshold.

Granny turned around in the doorway, a spark of intelligence rekindling in her eyes. "I remember now! I remember what it was I had to say!"

Neither of them would ask her what it was she had remembered.

"Young man," she said, in her loftiest voice, "you make a *wretched* cup of tea!"

Who is Number Two?

SECTION I

Drake woke. Automatically, naturally, without an alarm, he came to consciousness. London muttered outside his windows in the bright morning as he stretched, slowly, luxuriously, fitting every joint comfortably into place, feeling his body from the bones outward to the soft rumpled ridges of the sheets against his skin.

It was a matter of thirty seconds before he finished flushing his lungs with a yawn, and then he was out of bed, padding barefoot to the bathroom and pulling on a robe. His shower was brief and brisk, scouring the last of sleep's residue from his skin and followed by a great rough shaggy towel which wrapped him while he shaved.

Outside the tall front windows his hand-built pet, his long low lovely green KAR 1260, crouched in the 8.00 a.m. sunshine of Upper Berkeley Mews. Such an exceptionally fine day as this deserved to be driven through. *Bristol?* he asked himself as he switched on the heat under a kettle of water and removed three eggs from the refrigerator. *King's Lynn?*

He started a pan of water heating and returned to his room. He dressed casually, in layers, with the possibility in mind that it might actually get warm later. Over a V-necked sweater he chose to wear a jacket.

He picked one from his cupboard where it hung with the rest – a nicely-cut navy-blue blazer with white piping and a few nearly imperceptible pinholes in the left lapel. He slipped it from the hanger where it waited his pleasure.

This badgeless blazer was his reminder; though he wore no number, a few hundred forgotten men and women did. But for today, it was not a flag of revolution but a comfortable coat for a drive to Cheltenham or Lincoln.

His kettle spluttered wetly for a moment, chirped, twittered, and began to build to a piercing whistle before he came in to remove it from the fire and pour from it into a waiting cup. He sluiced the water around the inside of the china bowl, then dumped it thriftily back in the pot. The tea-strainer lay filled and ready; he dropped it into the heated cup and poured the seething water over it.

A long keen knife divided a lemon from the refrigerator; half was dropped into the cup to steep with the tea and half was pressed into a plastic film which would preserve its freshness for half an hour.

He glanced at his wrist-chronometer as he slipped the three eggs into the pan of bubbling water and reduced the heat, then plucked three lumps of sugar from a bowl on the first shelf and dropped them into the darkening tea.

Satisfied with its colour, he lifted out the tea-strainer and the steaming lemon and carried the cup with him back into the sitting-room. He sipped at it as he sorted happily through a stack of ordnance survey maps, considering a day's drive to Coventry, or a night at St. Ives.

Another glance at his wristwatch sent him back to start two slices of bread toasting while his plate warmed under the same electric coils for two minutes. When the unit switched off, he had thirty seconds before his eggs were ready – just long enough to arrange the toast tastefully and pass a light coat of butter across it.

While his eggs, opened, approached eating temperature, he made a second cup of tea. Then he dusted the firm, opaque whites and glossy liquid yolks with a sprinkling of salt and a few twists of white pepper from the grinder. He used the second lemon half, dropped in two lumps of sugar and sat down to breakfast.

It was well past the half-hour when he put the last of his utensils away, secured the kitchen and prepared to leave. A hat, a driving scarf, his gloves, his blazer and the map of Norfolk. His currency case and his keys. Then down the short, carpeted front hall to the outside door, past the closed and silent doors of two adjoining flats, to the heavy metal knob which turned beneath his hand and which he drew towards him as he had done every morning he'd been home for the last five years. Outside, a short flight of cement steps led down to the narrow pavement and his car, and faceless blocks of flats stretched to both ends of the street.

But this morning they didn't.

Outside his door, of his flat, in London, the ground was level with a single step to the doorsill, and a neatly bordered path with flowering rows ran along the front of his solitary building. The air was crisp and salty. Across green lawns early-blooming beds of spring flowers were a riot of glorious colour, and low rough-stone walls behind them held back a grassy slope decorated with cosily quaint buildings. Above them all rose a more massive structure with an eye-catching green dome.

He looked down. About waist height, just to the left of his door, so mounted as to be easily seen from either direction, a sign hung from a white post with a posy of nearly-fresh flowers nodding from the planter in its top.

The sign said simply, "6".

He started from the impossible and worked his way back. The outside of the door itself was the right colour, and the latch was correct. There was no lock. He tried the door of the first apartment – the knob spun loosely, but the wooden panel affixed to the wall like an imitation door (non-practical) in a stage set had neither hinges, jamb, nor any room behind it.

He stood in the hall a moment, then looked back into his flat. It was the same – it was his London flat, where he had gone to sleep last night, where he had awakened this morning, breakfasted on eggs he had bought yesterday in Covent Garden, and through the windows of which he had just looked at the street and his KAR.

He returned to the windows and stared through them at the same scene. The street was still there, and his green racing car still waited at the kerb below. And yet, somehow, with the image of grass and flowers, and gravelled walks and a shining green dome still in his mind's eye as he examined the scene, some quality, almost imperceptibly, seemed to be missing from it. The street seemed uncommonly still, and was there a trace of unsteadiness about that walking figure . . . ?

An eerie silence spread from nowhere, as if a giant hand were wrapping sheets of cottonwool around the entire flat. The almost-unheard noises of the city faded, and were gone. In the sudden dense stillness, a voice spoke behind him.

"It's a holographic projection, Number Six. Rather nice, don't you think?" The voice was unfamiliar – a sharp, grating voice with a raucous edge to it.

Slowly he turned. The screen of his television receiver, a commonplace commercial model, was aglow. As he watched, the face of a stranger appeared on the screen, with intent eyes and a quick, glittering smile.

"Welcome back, Number Six. Can you see me all right now? Good."

"Who are you?"

"The new Number Two. I'm afraid the Village just couldn't get along without you when you walked off the job, so you have regretfully been removed from your position of responsibility and restored to your old status. I was asked to replace you. In view of the revised situation, I suggest you consider the words of the great English poet who wrote, 'Now that I'm Six, I'm as clever as clever – so I think I'll be Six for ever and ever'."

He walked to the television controls and switched to BBC-2. The picture did not change.

"Sorry, Number Six; you'll find I'm on all the channels. Your brief tenure as Number Two was certainly one of the most ... active on record, but it did very little towards ensuring the mutuality of the Village. And this, after all, is the first responsibility of Number Two.

"Now," he continued, "there are probably a number of things you haven't really understood. If you have any questions. . . ?"

"Could I believe your answers?"

"You are welcome to – in fact, you are invited to. Let me see ... your predecessor as Number Two had 'Granny Bug' designed and programmed – an exquisite job – not exactly robotic, she was more in the nature of a cyborg, if you know the term. In fact, she was human, as far as she went. But after you left us she proved not to be worth repairing and was salvaged for parts, since a good deal of expense had gone into her in the first place."

"All that just to fool me! I'm retroactively honoured."

"Not all for you, Number Six. You're important, but not *that* important. No, Granny's main duty was observation. That particular Number Two had a deep inner drive for covertitude, if I may coin a term – one which I do not share. All this hiding around corners, spying on one's friends and fellow-Villagers – it's distasteful to me."

Slowly and deliberately, the man who was now called Number 6 walked back across the room and sat down. As an afterthought, he removed the map of Norfolk from his pocket and tossed it on the table. His eyes flicked around the room – *his* room – back to the unfamiliar gentleman on the telly – into the kitchenette – out the window to the tops of (*nonexistent?*) blocks of flats across the street – searching for something he'd missed that could have warned him of the miraculous transportation that had taken place while he slept. As he looked, the background track faded quietly up to its natural level, and with the sound of distant traffic he was almost back in London. Now he was aware of the difference that had completely escaped him. It didn't smell like London – but he hadn't noticed.

"You seem to have gone to some expense redecorating while I was away."

"We wanted you to feel at home, Number Six. You are a valuable individual; your well-being is of very real concern to us. This careful reconstruction of your natural habitat has been provided for your personal comfort. It took quite a while to prepare, too. The efforts of many people have gone into making this home-from-home ready for you."

"So I'm an individual now. But my name is not 'Number Six'."

"Number Six, the Village exists only to serve you – and others like you. Our facilities are sophisticated, but not unlimited. We have enough work to do that clumsy, irregular things like names only serve to get in the way. One can handle people so much more efficiently by numbers, and thereby do more for more people. After all, isn't one set of symbols as good as another for representing yourself as long as everyone is agreed it's you?"

"Not to me. I want to decide my own arbitrary set of symbols, not be forced to accept someone else's."

"Come now. Your parents named you – you didn't choose your name."

"I could have."

"You argue like a Scot. I will not be drawn into a debate with you. I hate debates – they turn a conversation into a contest." Number 2 looked off to one side and nodded, then smiled brightly out of the screen. "Now you see what happens when I let you monopolise the conversation – your welcome isn't even completed yet."

Just outside the back door of the flat, a door which opened from a small porch beyond the kitchenette into a dingy airshaft which connected to an alley through a narrow passageway, an electric starter whined briefly and a powerful internal combustion engine fired, coughed, fired again and caught, then speeded up to a stuttering roar filled with misfires for several seconds before slowing to an idle.

"If you will look outside your back door, I think you will find a most pleasant surprise."

Reluctantly, Number 6 rose from his chair and walked back through the dining area, through the kitchenette, and through the porch.

Outside the back door it was spring. Bright sunshine dappled warmly over tall flowers on either side of the door, and a single cement step lay between the doorsill and the bare dirt floor of a simple open-ended lean-to shelter which stood against the side of the building. From the outside, the main structure didn't look any different from the Basic Cottage Unit he had occupied during what he liked to think of as his previous visits to the Village. Which meant only the interior had been modified, and since the room plan was different, this left a fair amount of space here and there between outer and inner walls. Doubtless it had not been allowed to go to waste; he filed the observation.

The three walls of the shed bore waist-high workbenches, electric sockets and assorted shelves. Two or three doors were artfully ajar, and he could see tools neatly arrayed behind them – likely his own personally collected, carefully selected set, or another so similar he would be unable to tell the difference.

And in the centre of the shed, nearly filling it, stood KAR 1260; idling, and missing badly. The key stood from the ignition lock, waiting for him to accept the reality before him.

"It sounds as if it needs a little work, Number Six. You've been away from it for quite a while, you know." Number 2's cheerful face looked down at him from a standard Village monitor above the shelves to his right.

The engine needed tuning at least, and something was odd about the fuel flow – it would need work, as Number 2 said. So they were not only willing to give him special consideration to the extent of a custom-built dwelling, but they were giving him something to occupy his idle time. If he was willing to accept it.

Not only that, but it could be expected to serve as a hostage. The machine mattered more to him than any living human – and would be harder to take with him in another escape attempt.

Someone else had started it – he could refuse to accept the responsibility for it, leaving it to idle here for a few hours until it ran out of fuel and stopped naturally, and then avoiding the use of his back door entirely until they tired of the game and took it away. He could. He looked at it for a minute and more, listening to the uncomfortable sound of an engine which needed work – his engine.

Finally, resolutely, he reached forward and shut off the ignition. It was still his car, and even here in the Village he was glad to have it with him. He touched the wheel lightly with his fingertips and ran his eyes over the shining instrumentation and the deep curve of the leather driver's seat. This wasn't a duplicate – not even a perfect duplicate. There was something of himself in this machine, and he could sense it. This was his.

"It's a lovely car," said Number 2's faintly raucous voice. "I don't wonder that you missed it while you were here before before – it's almost an extension of yourself."

They seemed to be intent on making his existence satisfactory here, and it was annoying to realise they were making progress. But for the fact that what he demanded most was the one thing they could not give him, he was almost ready to admit (but only to himself) that they might succeed.

"Why, who knows, Number Six! You might even come to like it here."

"As the Bishop said to the Actress. I don't recall seeing a source of petrol around the Village – has that been changed as well?"

"That may prove a difficulty," said Number 2 regretfully. "We could have adapted your car to a nuclear-fusion engine, but that would hardly allow you much tinkering. They can be monstrously tricky. Still, we can doubtless find you a few gallons from time to time; either the chemist's or the ironmonger's might carry the necessary forms. There may be a scarcity – I suggest you look upon it as an incentive to improve your carburation.

"There have been those around me who have disapproved of allowing you to have access to tools, by the way – they feel you are not to be trusted under any circumstances. I really hope you won't bear them out."

"It would be too much to ask for a road to drive on."

"My dear Number Six! This long-ton of metal was brought here with great difficulty, at tremendous expense, and by helicopter – a truly impressive sight, I must say – especially for you. I quite understand the frustrations such a situation must engender, but you must appreciate the limited space with which we have to work. The impossible is simple; the inconceivable may take some thinking. You'd best see to that engine before you think about racing. I expect you'll find the altitude necessitates careful tuning and adjustment." He paused. "Then if you have no more questions at the moment, you may have some later. After you're re-oriented to the Village, perhaps you would join me for lunch tomorrow, if you're free."

"I don't expect to be called away suddenly."

"Quite right. We try to avoid such emergencies in the Village. Be seeing you."

The screen faded, and in the silence he could hear the familiar sound of breakers stroking a sandy beach just beyond the cliff edge. Back inside the cottage was his flat in London, as real and cosy and warm as he had formed it around his own tastes, prejudices and idiosyncrasies over five years. He had his own home, fitted around his personality like a well-worn shoe; he had his own creation, KAR 1260; he had his tools. And in the inviolate privacy of his own mind, he admitted Number 2's advisers were correct. He couldn't be trusted with tools, and his only remaining uncertainty was how far away he would be before this truth was acknowledged by Number 2.

Far behind his lips he smiled the slow secret smile of confidence challenged, and prepared to begin.

SECTION II: *Allegro*

He walked whistling up the front steps to the big bronze doors at the foot of the green-domed building on the hill. If anyone recognised the melody, they made no sign.

> *Singing toorali – oorali – annie,*
> *Singing toorali – ooraliay;*
> *Singing toorali – oorali– annie,*
> *And I'll see you in Botany Bay!*

That was how the refrain would have run if anyone had cared to sing it at this time, in this place; it was a song of ancient and dishonourable heritage, its wryly cheerful melody wrought by men a century dead, imprisoned and exiled.

The bronze doors gave back before him as he set foot on the porch and entered an elegantly empty hall. The sunlight and quiet sounds of the Village damped behind him as the outer doors closed silently and the inner doors opened into what could have been a film set for an imaginative control centre. A round room, like a planetarium dome with a sunken floor, panelled with moving images realistic and abstract, flickering like an electron shell around the circular instrumented desk and the spherical, rotating chair – the nucleus of this gigantic atom into which, like some unnamed particle with no particular charge or mass and undetermined potential energy, he had wandered.

At the focus of this concentration of power, in the cradle of the chair, sat Number 2. He was slighter of build than he had seemed on television, with black hair and eyes that pierced like his voice. He looked up as his guest entered and a chair by the desk rose smoothly from the floor for him.

"You're not wearing your pin, Number Six. Don't you want people to know who you are?"

"Not particularly, since I don't particularly care to know who they are. If I want to know I can ask."

"But consider – suppose a fellow-Villager wanted to invite you for a glass of wine, but didn't know how to introduce you to his friend, the waiter. It would be socially embarrassing for him."

"I don't usually drink with strangers."

"You do when it suits your purpose," Number 2 said blithely. "But fortunately, you and I know each other. Hence I have invited you for lunch – and you have accepted."

Two bowls of soup rose from a sliding panel in the desk between them, complete with napkins and spoons, as Number 2 continued to press his point. "If I saw a tree falling towards you, what would I shout to warn you? More practically, if it is your turn to be helped in a shop, isn't it simpler if the clerk can say, 'You're next, Number Six,' instead of 'You without the pin'."

"Since you brought that up, Number Two – just whom do I see about petrol?"

"Is your engine retuned already? It sounded as if restoring it to operative efficiency would be quite a lengthy affair."

"From what you'd implied, I'd gathered it might take a while to find something to run it on. So I thought to start searching. Where should I enquire?"

"I'm not really sure what department that would be under. It's sure to be listed somewhere, but I was waiting until you were ready to detail your requirements. What kind of fuel did you want, and how much? More than a few gallons will require special shipment, so we may as well ask for the best."

"Any lead-free anti-knock motor petrol with an octane rating around one hundred and thirty would be more than satisfactory. I'll want at least twenty gallons for the adjustment work – I can't very well tune an engine that won't run."

"Well, let's see, Number Six. The chemist could probably help you with a litre or two – the art supply shop might carry something similar as well, come to think of it. The ironmonger might be able to order some – he has the proper storage facilities as well. I suppose I'll have to look this up somewhere. Could we table this for a day?"

"It's in your hands."

"Yes – everything is. It's really tiresome, sometimes. I see you enjoyed the soup. Do have a lamb sandwich. . . . Suppose I had a butler. He wouldn't know how to introduce you, since calling cards are out of fashion."

"So are butlers – even short silent ones."

"Seriously, Number Six, I'm trying to explain why it is important you wear your Number. Be proud of your identity. Or do you prefer the notoriety of being known as The Man Without A Pin?"

"As long as I'm the only one around and it's perfectly clear who they're referring to, it's as good a name as any other. It may be a little long, but it's my own name, earned and not assigned. Besides, I shouldn't like seeing my name constantly repeated in telephone numbers and lorry licences."

"Your parents named you arbitrarily, Number Six – we have only re-named you as part of our family. We covered this particular chain of argument yesterday. Suppose more people started going around without Numbers – then no one could be sure who *the man without a pin* was.

What would you do then? Carry a walking stick? Wear a red coat, or a flower? Cultivate a moustache? Don't you see that it is in everyone's best interests that we all agree on who we are in such a way that there is a minimum possibility of confusion? Any symbols could be picked and ordered, but they must be specific. Numbers are the easiest to handle, the most efficient. That's all. I don't want you to start arguing relative morality now – we simply cannot change the entire Village to suit your whim. You may call yourself what you like, but your accounts are kept as Number Six, your medical and credit information as well; and to us in the Village you will always be known, simply, as Number Six.

"Now why not wear your pin, like a good fellow? I certainly hope I won't have occasion to bring this up again. Now, the Village Entertainment Committee has organised a small group doing Gilbert and Sullivan –"

"*Yeomen Of The Guard?*"

"Your favourite? No – I believe the production will be more appropriate. *Patience.* They've found a most talented soprano and an acceptable organist. Or do your tastes run more to Shakespeare and the Greeks? You should involve yourself in lighter things, Number Six. Take up a hobby. Don't just pace up and down your cage."

Some three hours past his own breakfast the following morning, Number 6 called at the small ironmongery store in the Village. As the bell above the door tinkled to announce his entry, the sturdy shopkeeper looked up behind the counter.

"Good morning, Number – ah . . ."

"Good morning, Number Twenty-six. I was wondering if you might have a few gallons of petrol about the place. Number Two suggested I ask here."

"Oh, Number Six!" He put down a sheaf of stapled pages and rose. "Yes, of course. Number Two told me you might be coming in."

He seemed so willing to help that his customer was taken slightly aback. Was it possible that it could be this simple? Of course not.

"You'll need three copies of Form 739/H-F – that's *hydrocarbon, fuel,* I think. There isn't anything that needs to be approved, though – no red tape to worry about. Just for the records."

"How much can I get?"

Number 26 shrugged. "I wouldn't have a guess. We usually stock the forms, but nobody's ever asked for more than a gallon at a time. It'd depend on how much was available, I suppose. How much did you plan on asking for?"

"I could easily use fifty gallons, and one hundred would not be too much."

"My word! Where would you keep all that petrol? And what on earth would you do with it?"

"Didn't Number Two tell you? I have an eight-cylinder engine to feed. As for storage, I was hoping you could tell me."

"Well, it's not a problem that's come up before. I suppose you'll want a tank of some kind, probably with a hose. The Safety Committee will want to approve the arrangement anyway – they'll be happy to help you in whatever way they can. Don't want your home to burn down in the middle of the night, after all." He paused and scratched his head. "You'll probably want to file an 8704/S – that's clearance for storage of dangerous materials. I think we've got one around here somewhere. . . ."

He turned to a pigeon-holed desk and riffled through a few stacks of paper, then shook his head. "Or maybe not. There may be some in the back room."

"What about the other one – 739/H-F?"

"No, we're out of those. I had to look round when Number Two called to tell me you might be by. He said you deserved all the help I could give you, but I just don't think we have those forms."

"Who would?"

"Stationery generally carries a full line of everything in print locally. Across the plaza, left at the bandstand and down the steps."

"739/H-F and 8704/S. Any others?"

"Not that I think of. Now, if you ever want to burn anything big with it, you'll want Form 2246 – that requires a couple of days notice so the Fire Brigade can help you with the job."

"If I ever want to burn anything large, I'll be sure the Fire Brigade is fully informed. But I only want to burn this a little at a time, in enclosed spaces. I don't suppose you have any petrol here?"

"Just a bit in the back room I use for cleaning up. If a pint or two would help, you might see the Chemist's – that's around on the far side of the Green Dome, under that big flowering tree."

"The dogwood."

"I suppose. Anyway, they'd have some there. It'd only be in a bottle, y'know – not a tin."

"I know. I could always use it around the workshop – for cleaning up. Do you have grease? Motor oil?"

"Oil, but no grease. And it's a rather light oil."

"Where would the Maintenance Staff get grease? Those electric carts have grease nipples on the axle bearings."

"Why, I never thought. You might ask them if they could spare some, or where they ordered it."

"I think I will. Thank you for your help, Number Twenty-six. Be seeing you."

Number 48 returned from the back of the Stationery Shop and shook her pretty head. "I'm awfully sorry, Number Six, but we just don't seem to have any copies of Form 739/H-F at all. There's a memo in the file to the effect that they were requisitioned from the Village Hall nearly a month ago, but I guess we haven't heard anything of it. Perhaps if you went to see Number Eleven up there, he could help you. Anyway, now you'll want one of these 8704/S's to go to Housing, and one to Safety, and you'll probably want a copy to keep for reference while you're preparing the storage area. Oh – and if you do go to see Number Eleven, you might ask about the requisition we sent in. We're out of half a dozen other things there's very little call for."

Number 35 measured the golden pint into a bottle plastered with a red FLAMMABLE label. "There you are, Number Six. We really don't have much use for motor petrol in the Village – it's a *clean* place. One of the things I've always liked about it."

He stoppered the bottle carefully and handed it over the counter to Number 6. "Use it sparingly – I've got less than a gallon left in stock now. I'd re-order, but I haven't been able to find the proper forms. Keep it well stopped up, and it won't evaporate."

Number 11 wasn't in, and hadn't been in all day. His personal secretary, Number 18, thought he had gone to the Printer's to ask after several jobs that hadn't been completed, and he'd had a luncheon appointment with Number 2 to which he might have gone directly.

"It's just on twelve," Number 6 pointed out. "May I use your telephone? It's a local call."

"Why certainly," she said, extending him a gracefully shaped handful of plastic.

"Number Two, please," he said to it. And, after a moment's pause, he addressed himself identically to the answering party. . . . "I'm sure he won't mind being disturbed. Tell him it's the man with the green car. . . . Yes, that's right. Thank you."

He shifted the phone and focused a calculating smile on Number 18. "Inasmuch as it is lunchtime, and your boss is away, will you be held in bondage here with a cold sandwich sent in or would you have . . ."

"*Good afternoon, Number Six,*" said a cheerful raucous voice in his ear. "*If you're calling in regard to those troublesome forms, let me assure you that I am personally investigating the situation. Number Eleven is here at the moment; he spent the morning tracking down an embarrassingly simple production problem and assures me that the forms will be available very soon. In the interim, I may be able to do something — ah — unofficially to ease your privation, at least to the extent of a gallon or two. Sorry I can't pause to chat at the moment, but you aren't the only man in the Village, after all. Be seeing you.*"

The disconnection tapped his eardrum and he looked up to see Number 18 standing with her sporty little cap in her hand. "I take it you got your party," she said with a twinkle as he replaced the hand set on the desk. "In answer to your last question, I have an hour for lunch starting at twelve. And I usually eat on the Terrace when the weather is nice."

"It's lovely today," he said. "I eat there myself — when I'm in town." He smiled at her with his eyes to see if she would respond. When she did, he added, "And over lunch I'd like to see what else we have in common."

He found her a passable companion, amicable without being demanding, and a mine of information on Village politics and staff-level sentiment. If he was to play their game, knowledge of the field was essential. As his self imposed daily schedule, a trained-in habit pattern keyed by the Village environment and designed to keep him at his peak condition and as fully informed as was possible, took shape again in the following weeks, he found luncheon on the Terrace with Number 18 becoming part of it – a harmless lightly sexual spice with lunch and no more, as he discovered in her nothing to interest him personally beyond her conversational capabilities.

He rose within five minutes either way of 7.30, took a brisk run before breakfast and a long walk around the Village after, followed by a few hours work-out, a quick shower, and lunch. After lunch he would attend to business around the Village, listen to a concert by the Village Band or sun himself on the seawall for an hour. On days when summer had the upper hand, he might go for a swim in the mid-afternoon or play a few rounds of chess on the Terrace. Leisure he had never found a problem, and with the challenge of a project like his KAR 1260 to occupy his attention, his evenings were never empty. He would usually lay down his tools and straighten the workshop when the eleven o'clock bell tolled over the Village from the tower on the hill. Then, drawing on his coat against the mists that rose from the sea and stole through the cobbled streets, he would make one last walking tour of the Village, silent and sleeping, to return to his London flat shortly after the twelve strokes of midnight and retire near 12.30.

He weekly cultivated an acquaintance with Number 40, proprietrix of the Artist's Shoppe, who incidentally supplied him with small quantities of paint-thinner which he used to clean his hands and tools. This allowed him to hoard the begged pints of petrol in his workshop, where he fed them to his engine by a siphon directly to the carburettor.

Afternoons when the weather was less halcyon, he would tinker with the machine. It would not stay properly tuned, and he had not been able to establish contributing factors. When running without a load at six thousand rpm exhausted a week's fuel supply in ninety seconds, sustained testing was out of the question.

One such afternoon, shortly before three, when this routine had evolved through a full cycle of the moon and more, he was checking the spark-plugs for signs of fouling or corrosion caused by the irregular quantity of fuel, which he suspected. Outside the open end of the flower-covered car-port, sunlight began to dapple through the threatening clouds and a warm breeze sprang up.

When next he chanced to glance in that direction, it was to see a mature, apparently tame, black cat wander around the corner of the

Basic Cottage Unit and stand regarding him appraisingly. He regarded it back, and after several seconds it deliberately sat down, closed its eyes, and turned its head some sixty degrees away from him. Considering, he returned to his work. As long as the animal didn't blunder into something, it was welcome to investigate. He had nothing to hide – yet – and didn't care who knew it.

He remembered noticing the cat here and there, now and then, about the Village, but he had never accorded it any particular interest; no more than it had shown in him – until now.

A minute or two later, the front door sounded its cheerful chime. He set the plugs gently on the workbench and went through the back door into his kitchenette as the chimes rang again.

At the front door was one of the little electric carts used for general transportation around the Village, with its red-striped fringed awning and its straw-hatted and blazered driver. Under the awning stood eight five-gallon cans with sealed caps and diagonal red and yellow striping. In the hand of the driver, who leaned casually against the doorpost, was a plastic clipboard with several pages attached and a ball-point pen on a chain.

"Number Six?" he asked, straightening. "If you'll sign these three copies in the box at the bottom, I've got forty gallons of hydrocarbon fuel for you. There's a data sheet stuck to one of the cans listing chemical content or something – I expect you'll know what it means."

Forty gallons! Dazzled by his good fortune and with pictures of half-mile runs along the hard-packed beach sands at low tide in his mind, he initialled the three forms while Number 94 unloaded the heavy cans in pairs from the back of the little truck to the path.

Number 6 hoisted the first pair as the truck purred off, and bore them back through his sitting-room, observing the black cat nosing about in the kitchenette as he passed through to the workshop. After three more round trips his fuel was safely stored, and he returned to find the cat sitting in the middle of the carpet, fastidiously preening its shoulder.

He left it to its own interests and sat down, spark-plugs postponed, to consider the largesse which had so miraculously been bestowed upon him. Forty gallons! The temptation to use it too quickly was recognised and quelled – at least half of it would go into storage somewhere until he could arrange a practical hiding place. And yet, to suddenly have forty gallons of top quality petrol after nursing a thirsty engine on drops and counting cubic centimetres like a miser! Fine; they couldn't guess at any remotely consistent rate of consumption through that much, and he would be able to run out twice as fast without arousing a whisper of suspicion.

What he would do with it was another problem. The KAR would barely fit through the narrow cobbled streets of the Village, and there was nowhere to go in any case.

Time would bring data to inspire ideas, and circumstances to take advantage of could only be recognised, seldom arranged. . . .

The black cat stood up deliberately and stalked across the carpeted floor to stand before his knees, looking up at him. He looked back, really becoming aware of the animal for the first time. Its eyes were a deep gem-stone green, and they looked into his grey ones for several seconds without blinking. He shifted his weight slightly. The cat glanced down, then crouched, looked up and sprang lightly into his lap. There it rose straight-legged and formal and turned to study his face doubtfully.

He returned its scrutiny. The exact quality of the eyes, the pink maze within the ears, the texture and growth pattern of the fur, the delicate tips of nacreous claws retracted between velvet pads, all seemed realistically detailed – but he had uncertain memories of mechanical devices in the guise of living things, guided to work secretly against him. He recognised the thought, dispassionately labelled it *paranoid*, and tagged it specifically to the Village environment. Insanity can be a necessity for survival.

This seemed to be a real cat – but it had behaved in an inexplicable and unprecedented manner. By his limited acquaintance with cats it had done nothing outside the wide range of normal feline behaviour, except for its sudden interest in him. So he examined it closely for seams or subtler clues to indicate a mechanical construction. A socially acceptable animal like this would make an ideal design for a robot surveillance device – and, all things considered, that made as likely an explanation as any for why it had come into his workshop for the first time and decided to stay.

Expressionless, with just a touch of the respect due to a potential bomb, he gathered it gently in his arms. It stiffened slightly at this uninvited intimacy, then relaxed; the musculature was absolutely convincing. He rubbed it behind the ears and around the side of the neck, fingers probing gently into the warm, sliding skin as it lifted its head and started to purr. Even the purr felt right.

He shifted his weight by way of warning and felt the furry body stiffen instantly. He gathered it closer to him and stood up, holding it to his chest, and stroked its head until the tension drained out and the legs relaxed their pressure against his body. Slowly, still petting it, he rolled the cat over in his arms so that its legs were up, green eyes lidded to gleaming slits. Then, suddenly and without warning, he dropped it.

A galvanised tangle of tail and legs scrambled frantically in mid-air for a quarter of a second before the cat landed flat-footed, fur abristle and looking around for an enemy. Then abruptly it sat down and began to wash itself.

He stood looking down at it for some time, then stepped over it and went into the kitchen. In the refrigerator, a piece of fish he had brought home for dinner surrendered half an ounce to his fingers. It smelled fresh – and he closed the insulated door and took it to the front room.

The cat stood up as he entered, stretched, and wandered curiously toward the bedroom. He squatted and clucked his tongue, extended the sliver of fish to the animal. It turned and looked at the sound, then wandered back to sniff cautiously at the offering from a few inches away. It made a tiny sound like a refined snort, then turned and stalked into the bedroom.

He watched it out of sight around the door, its tail a ten-inch question mark. Then he looked back at the fish in his hand. He mashed it lightly and sniffed at it – nothing wrong. He bit off a corner and crushed it between his front teeth, studying texture and taste. Nothing sensible wrong with it. He laid the questioned piece of fish on a paper in a corner and temporarily assigned the cat the status of Probably Real. Then he returned to his workshop, leaving the back door partly open.

An hour later, when the daylight began to fail, he went back inside to find the paper clean and the cat asleep in a corner of the sofa. It slept there while he prepared and ate dinner.

Two days later, about 10.30 in the morning, Number 6 jingled the bell beside a cold-case displaying a few moderately appetising cuts of meat, and cheerful Number 61 came out of the back, wiping bloody hands on a piece of waste, to help him.

"Lovely morning, Number Six. Fortunate you dropped in – I have some very fine veal which just arrived, and some lamb kidneys. If you'd like to take a look . . ." He pulled out a steel tray with a gesture which implied a black velvet case and a proffered loupe. The veal was white, with the slightly greenish tinge which proved proper feeding.

"So I see. Yes, very nice. It might be a bit dry, but a touch of Marsala should do it. Let me have a pound of each. And a half-pound of your less prepossessing liver – I seem to have a house guest."

"Staying long?" Number 61 threw the veal knuckle across his block and began knocking off a pair of fine-fibred fillets.

"I have no idea. Do you recall seeing a black cat wandering about the Village? Have you any idea who owns it?"

"Nobody ever owned a cat, Number Six. I've seen him from time to time, but I've no idea where he came from or where he sleeps."

"Nobody is responsible for feeding him?"

"No – guess he just fends for himself. It's a good thing for me people can't do that or I'd be out of business." He weighed the meat and wrapped it, then counted kidneys on to the scale until the pointer hovered just under a pound. He dropped one more and wrapped the small pile. Then a half-pound of liver was sliced and weighed. As he worked, Number 61 offered, "By the by, I have a bit of haddock left over from yesterday. I was about to throw it away, but he might like it. I'll make him a present of it."

"Thanks on his behalf. Be seeing you."

Shortly past two the following day, his front door chimed and a moment later Number 2 walked in. Number 6 looked up from his notes and said, "I don't believe I heard anyone invite you in."

"Don't be rude to your most loyal admirer, Number Six. I can allow you to be terse, but incivility, if you recall de Quincey, is the first step on the –"

"The last. 'If once – a man indulges himself in Murder, very soon he comes to robbing; and from robbing to drinking and from that to incivility and procrastination.' It's from *Murder As A Fine Art*. I've always understood he was referring to the social preferences of the crimes."

"It was foolish of me to venture on to such familiar ground with you, Number Six. You were quite a professional in murder for some time, as I recall."

The pencil did not break in his hand. After the slightest pause he said, "And you were chiding *me* for a social crime, Number Two! Since you have brought the forbidden subject up, let me suggest you re-examine my dossier and compare it against the crimes in your own career. Or have you been a bureaucrat all your life?"

"Number Six, Number Six, now you see why I seldom call on you. I honestly walked in here with the best of intentions, and in less than a minute you have me on the defensive." He sat down on the sofa, and the black cat lifted its head to gaze sleepily at him before returning to its nap. Number 2 noticed it with a nod.

"You seem to have found one friend in the Village, at any rate."

"Merely a passing acquaintance," said the unwilling host. "It walked in a few days ago and hasn't walked out yet."

"Have you named her?"

It was on the tip of his tongue to say the animal was not his to name, but he tapped the pencil lightly on the desk a moment, and then said, "Oh, I was thinking of calling it Number One."

"Really, Number Six, you must stop these witty sallies. I came here to take you for a short ride; if you continue to bait me so masterfully, the daylight will be gone and my surprise for you will fall flat. Besides, I expect you'll want to play with it yet today." He stood and beckoned Number 6 impatiently after him.

Reluctantly, intrigued, he put down his pencil and rose from the desk. Outside an awninged electric cart waited to carry them, humming, with Number 2 at the tiller, through half a mile or more of narrow, winding, bordered lanes out of the central part of the Village and among wind-wrought native trees to a cleared patch. A rough shelter some ten by fifteen feet stood by what looked like a fairly good hard-dirt track which bent out of sight a short distance away in either direction.

Number 2 parked the cart by the shelter, and both got out. "Well, Number Six, what do you think of it?"

"Out of context? I'd hate to spend the winter in it. Or is it a tram stop?"

"It's only meant to keep wind and rain and dust and sunlight off you and your car. If you wish a furnished *pied-à-terre* you'll have to build it yourself. But we thought you might like something simple and handy to the track."

They now stood beside the building under question. It was about the size of the workshop behind his flat, but bare-walled and unflowered.

"You mean . . . ?" He gestured with his arm.

"Yes; I've got you a place to drive. I must say it took a bit of work clearing and tamping, but you couldn't very well be expected to put as much devotion as you do into that lovely machine without any opportunity to take it out for a run." He walked to the middle of the track and looked around. "It's a half-mile more or less oval and fairly flat. The hills, and the seacliff to the left, limited us."

"It's a bit far from town. How do I get my car here – disassemble it and transport it piece by piece?"

"It should be possible to drive here. In bottom gear, of course, and with the greatest of care, you might be able to fit through the streets between here and there. We would have to warn pedestrians and electric carts out of the way, of course –"

"Perhaps a man could walk ahead of me waving a red flag."

Number 2 nodded seriously. "That is most likely what we shall have to do."

"Speaking of electric carts – I shall need a few pounds of grease and a few quarts of oil."

"Oil? I thought you got oil at the ironmonger's."

"Only light and medium machine oil, which breaks down at engine temperatures. I'll probably need a requisition form for the oil, but I haven't been able to find anyone who knows."

"What have you been using for oil?"

"My KAR had a full crankcase of nearly-new oil when it came here. I haven't had any occasion to put it to heavy use. But I shall want a change shortly if I'm actually to have a place to drive. As for grease, I imagine you'll have some spare close by."

"Grease? Me?"

"You as a personification of the Village –"

"I'm honoured."

"– maintain these electric carts, on which I observe standard grease nipples. Since axles and bearings require the same care regardless of motive power, there is a source of grease convenient to you."

"My word! Indeed there must! I never considered the carts in terms of machinery, and all this sort of thing is left to my staff. Why, if you'd asked me about grease, I wouldn't have had the least idea beyond a Special Requisition, and they're never heard from again. How fortunate you thought of it."

"It was elementary."

"But you will be able to drive for a little while, won't you?" Number 2 paced idly back and forth across the track, his face showing concern. "I mean, you won't be delayed while we find you grease and oil. You have air for your tyres, distilled water for your battery."

"Yes."

"And petrol – I spent some time making a fuss on your behalf, by the way – has your petrol arrived yet? I'd been meaning to ask."

"It arrived three days ago. Forty gallons, and top quality."

"Well, you should have petrol to burn, then. I hope it will prove adequate for a few weeks."

"It would go farther if I had a larger track – I shan't be able to get into top gear if this is only a quarter-mile on a side, and petrol consumption skyrockets at low speeds."

"I'd read somewhere that the most efficient operation was generally obtained at around thirty miles an hour."

"In stock automobiles. They're designed to operate in that range. But KAR 1260 is made to my own personal tastes, and a little less . . . conservative."

"Really! With all your insistence on the superiority of the individual over the group, I would have thought you the archest of conservatives."

"I thought we had agreed not to bring politics into the conversation again." He looked around the track, then squinted at the sun. "If you could arrange for that man you mentioned with a red flag to come by my flat, I will be ready to drive here in half an hour. And incidentally, what are the possibilities of having electricity laid on?"

He was at the track before four o'clock. Number 213 sat down in the shade of the shelter and propped his red flag against the wall. "Will you be long, Number Six?"

"I may be here until dark. Would you like to go and come back with a red lantern?"

"Number Two suggested I have one ready." He pulled a flat battery pack from his jacket pocket. "If you decide to leave the car here overnight and walk back, I'll be happy to keep you company on the way. And when you want to bring the car back, you can call me."

"I won't drive back this afternoon. Why don't you just take the rest of the day off?"

Number 213 grinned up at him. "Thanks, but I'd like to stay and watch for a little while. I've always liked cars. That's why Number Two asked me to do this for you. They always try to give people the jobs they most enjoy. You don't mind if I just sit here for a while, do you?"

He tapped his index finger on the polished steering wheel for a second or so. He wanted to walk once around the track, checking the surface texture and lay-out – he didn't even know how the putative half-mile course was shaped, since most of it was hidden by trees and irregularities in the infield. But he hesitated to walk off and leave his machine alone with this grinning imbecile who burbled happily of liking cars. Perhaps his company was preferable to the uncertainty of leaving him behind.

He killed the engine and stepped out. "I thought I'd look over the track once on foot before I tried to drive it. Want to come along?" Number 213 rose from his seat against the wall, nodding happily like an eager dog invited for a walk, and padded after him.

The track proved short indeed, being barely five hundred double paces around the centreline, but adequately surfaced. It was an eccentric oval, with the longest straightaway being about two hundred and fifty yards. The track was about fifteen feet wide, and trees had been cut back from it for another fifteen feet. The centre of the oval was a grove of tangled Mediterranean pines and cypresses like the surrounding woods, which would serve to shield this eyesore from the Village proper and absorb most of the noise he would be generating.

Then, since he was here and ready, and had waited so long, he started the KAR and drove a few leisurely circuits of the track, feeling out the remembered controls, listening keenly to the sound of the engine and every moving part, sensing the subtle vibrations of the suspension, reawakening the dormant reflexes which made him a part of his machine. Gradually he took the right-hand curves faster, gearing down for torque and accelerating until the approaching corner forced him to slow before throwing a skid and risking damage against the trees or wearing more rubber off the precious (and probably irreplaceable) tyres.

Eventually Number 213 lost interest in watching him go round and round and wandered away with a wave which he hardly noticed. It was nearly impossible to reach a speed greater than fifty miles per hour, and that only with the full – and uncomfortably brief and intermittent – effort of the eight pulsing cylinders under the lean green hood. He couldn't maintain an average over thirty-five, and that only between twenty-five in the corners and hitting forty in the straights. He could give the engine a more even high-speed workout in the lower gears, but that became a strain on the transmission, and forging gears was still beyond his technical capability.

When he returned the car to its shelter on the Village side of the South Turn by the light of long-cold headlamps, he made a mental note to drive anti-clockwise next time, and alternate to keep the steering gear and tyre wear balanced He was surprised to note how late it was when he returned, on foot, to his London flat to share an improvised supper with his black-furred guest.

In the next twelve days Number 6 grew to know and hate every tree, every bush, every stone, every leaf lining the track. At thirty-five miles per hour he passed them twenty times a day, sometimes from one side and sometimes from the other, which helped, but not much.

At last one afternoon when he came out to the track, he passed the KAR where it stood in the shelter with scarcely a glance and walked on down the track past the north end of the oval. He had surveyed that barren area beyond the last line of trees cursorily in the process of checking the track for security – he had found two wide-angled pickup cameras covering the track from convenient trees, one with a clear view into the open end of the shelter. Now it was time for a more thorough study of the ground between the North Bend of the track and the sheer cliff another half-mile away.

Beyond the trees it sloped roughly, steeper to the left than to the right. Near where the smooth wall of granite rode two hundred feet from the narrow end of the beach, the sea-cliff slanted down to the sand to meet it at a point where a stream must have run ten thousand years before. A furlong to the right the barren ground came level with the end of the track, and above that, sparsely, the trees began again.

Bounded by sea, stone and trees, the area in the middle was a rugged, ragged wilderness of boulders, gullies, scrub brush and bare dirt. He spent the full afternoon exploring it, nosing uphill as far as the trees to the east before the bobbing pastel spheres of Guardians came whiffling through the woods ahead of him. He stood his ground and spoke to them gently; since his track had been kept so free of them, he expected no interference here. They paused at the edge of the trees and flobbed menacingly, but made no further advance.

Not willing to press the confrontation, Number 6 withdrew and carried his survey downhill to the sea. When he had finished, he returned home and spent the evening sketching things in a large notebook.

As the tower bell rang the hour of 4.00, he came up the steps to the Green Dome. Doors opened silently before him until he stood before the tall white double panels with a tasteful "2" in bronze at eye-level. He paused, knowing his arrival had not been unobserved, and waited until these too swung inward.

Number 2 looked up from a flickering panel set in his desk with an acceptable imitation of surprise. "Why, Number Six! I was just wondering about you. Can you stay for tea? You seem to be in quite a hurry."

"I may grant you the pleasure of my company – I thought you might know where I could pick up another set of petrol requisitions and help me push them through."

"More petrol? Already? When Number Two-Thirteen mentioned you spent all day going around and around that track, I must admit I was gratified. But I seem to recall you said it would last you a month."

"I would never have made so specific an estimate. I have less than five gallons left, and that won't last another week. And while we're on the subject, I haven't heard anything about the motor oil either. I'll need at least ten litres, thirtyweight, non-detergent."

"I shall see to it. Did you get the grease from Maintenance? Oh, please don't stand –" He pressed a button to produce a chair into which Number 6 sank and crossed his legs.

"Yes – a couple of pounds. Quite satisfactory. Number Ninety-nine was good enough to bring a gun and give me a free mechanical inspection. She was quite impressed."

"I should imagine. Tea?"

"Thank you."

Number 2 generated a beautiful porcelain cup made of insulating plastic and filled with steaming Earl Gray as Number 6 continued.

"Now about the length of the track – I appreciate the fact that I have a place to drive at all, but it's simply not big enough. There is open space to the north to extend it; how do I go about getting this done?"

"But that is park land, Number Six. It's supposed to be for the use of the whole Village. You already have three or four acres all your very own."

"You can't play soccer on a chess board. I have seen no one else making use of that part of the grounds. Most of my present four acres is still available for picnics – the infield is maintained as a wilderness area. All I need is room to extend the track, down that barren slope into the rill."

"Well, I really don't know, Number Six. The subject could be brought up at the Village Council, but I expect they would feel that enough of our limited land has already been placed at your personal disposal."

"I doubt they would notice if the track was extended. The natural contour conceals it from the Village and would deflect the sound as well as the trees block it now. How the good Villagers would react to it, as you very well know, depends on how it is presented to them. What if they were to discover, without any fanfare, that the track was there and in use, causing no particular inconvenience to anyone?"

"Your attitude is shocking, Number Six – shocking! I could have no part in such an ... such an *unmutual* deception."

"You needn't. Tea?"

"Thank you. I must warn you against assuming responsibilities you have no right to."

"A man has the right to any responsibility he can handle. Whereas you feel that the fewer responsibilities a man has, the better."

"It's certainly easier to consolidate them in trustworthy hands. Leaves so much more time and effort free for other things. More efficient, more practical. Why should everyone make their own shoes? Hunt their own food? Till their own fields? You delegate responsibility for your health to a doctor; for your welfare to a lawyer, for your nourishment to total strangers – I don't believe I've seen you smile before, Number Six."

"I find little to amuse me here."

"Your own personal nourishment, I am aware, is a matter of

considerable concern on your part; I was speaking in a much larger sense. But you take advantage of professionally prepared food – when it is a matter of convenience. Even you have heated cans of soup during your wide experience. The median man survives largely by the efforts of others while he pursues his own individual goals as best he can. Why, I don't even know the Number of my own cook."

"*The median man*. The expression interests me – the statistical excuse for your actions?"

"That's an oversimplification."

"But an accurate one."

Number 2 shrugged. "Relative accuracy," he said, dismissing the subject with his tone of voice. "The median man is the statistical individual for whom the greatest amount of effort produces maximal results. The social equivalent of the physical measurements used in designing automobiles, theatre seats and beds. For that matter, as the distance between bookshelves is designed to fit the 'median book'."

"A non-professional acquaintance of mine claimed to have been connected with the St Lawrence Seaway construction project, and he swore that the engineering facility in charge of bridging operations took careful measurements of all vessels capable of negotiating the Seaway and built all the bridges with five feet of clearance for the average funnel height. I never believed him, myself."

"Number Six, your parables astound me. Have we been knocking your funnels off? I myself have been – in several senses – moving heaven and earth to build a series of bypass canals, drawbridges, locks and tunnels so you can drive your car, fuel your car and tinker with your car to your heart's content!"

"Out of the boundless charity you feel towards all living creatures."

"My job here is to make you happy – but it includes seeing that you don't bother other people any more than is absolutely necessary. This was a happy Village until you came here, Number Six, and I must say frankly that I look upon you as a challenge in this matter. Is dissatisfaction so deeply bred into your personality that you can never be happy anywhere?"

"Make me happy. Get me that motor oil and fifty gallons of the same mixture as before. Your man can come around for the seven empty cans at his leisure."

"You are so single-minded, Number Six. Of course I shall do all I can to expedite your petrol requisition, though it may take a fortnight. The oil should come with it. I do appreciate your bridge parable, honestly; what you mean is that we don't allow enough for exceptions. We really do all we can, but our motto has never been able to reach beyond *The Greatest Good For The Greatest Number.*

"Any quantity of individuals can be effectively handled in statistical form – the same formulae can tell how many people are watching a given television broadcast or how many will die in a given holiday weekend. These mathematical models are of demonstrable accuracy and are identical to those which predict natural radioactive decay in a mass of unstable atoms. The behaviour of individuals is of no statistical consequence – whether five hundred people or five hundred and one are killed by motor accidents in Bank Holiday traffic matters not the slightest except to the personal acquaintances and intimates of the five-hundred-and-first; the social impact, the public outcry for safer streets would not be substantially altered by one death, or a dozen. A hundred more or less would barely gain recognition as a significant factor."

"Unless the five-hundred-and-first is a politician or a film star."

"That only enlarges the effective circle of acquaintances. There again you have tried to make an exception destroy a generality. Exceptions are to generalities what holes are to a sponge. A few more or less don't matter – statistically."

"But if the sponge had no holes at all, it wouldn't hold water."

"And if pigs had wings they'd be pigeons! Honestly, Number Six, I had promised myself I would not be drawn into argument with you again. Do go away and let me get back to my work – you'll have your petrol."

"Thank you, Number Two. Be seeing you."

For the next two days Number 6 walked around the barren area north of the track, pacing off distances, sighting past large rocks, trees and major irregularities in the ground, poking at the dirt here and there like a prospective builder looking over a site.

The black cat followed him there the first day, wandering along behind him, beside him, in front of him, stopping at will or disappearing to reappear later, as if bound entirely on business of its own, and while he surveyed, the cat prowled around the rugged field, hunting its own game.

That same afternoon he had the opportunity to observe an educational confrontation, and was pleased with what he learned: fortune placed him at the side of a thickly gnarled bush twice his height when a moving white shape caught his eye and he froze against the bush to watch a Guardian bounding lugubriously towards him.

As he watched, it swerved towards a darting black shape in the scrubby grass and picked up speed. The cat sped across an open space, tail a-bristle; the spheroid took to the air in fourteen-foot leaps, quivering like a berserk custard ball. The cat doubled on its tracks and shot through the shadow of the Guardian in mid-leap, dodging out of sight down a gully in a few seconds.

Number 6 ducked back around the bush as the sphere fought its momentum to turn and follow its quarry; by the time it rolled vaguely off in the direction the cat had taken, the trail was cold. The uncanny thing hesitated, searched blindly for a minute or so, then trundled off absentmindedly in the general direction of the Village.

When it was gone, Number 6 came out. He had probably had no real reason to hide from the thing – it wasn't one of the dangerous ones, and he had every right to be here. Well, nearly every right.

The cat was sitting beside the back door washing itself when Number 6 returned to his flat a few hours later, and seemed satisfied with the chicken giblets supplied by the good butcher that morning (as they were two days old).

After another day of study he had determined the optimum layout for the projected extension of his track. The following morning he set out on his regular tour of the Village, and encountered, after two-thirds of a casually meticulous search of the town, three men in overalls riding in an electric cart. He hailed them.

"Where are you going?"

"Reseeding the South Walk."

"Ah, then you're the ones I was looking for. The reseeding job can wait – you're to come with me. Number Fifty-five, can you fetch that small bulldozer I saw shoving around debris on the beach after the storm last month?"

"Uh, certainly, Number – uh . . ."

"Good. Does it have a roller or a grader attachment of some sort?"

"Well, it's got the scraper blade. There's a power roller, but it's working out on Seaview Point all day."

"Reserve it for next week." He climbed into the fourth seat of the cart, next to Number 92. "We'll go back to pick up the 'dozer with the scraper blade. Are you checked out on it?"

"Yeah –"

"Fine. Then you'll follow us to the job site. You'll be working with me."

It was ten o'clock when they stopped at the top of the uneven slope, and Number 6 spent the next forty-five minutes establishing the nature of the job to be done. He indicated the placement, direction and width of the lane he wanted scraped in the wild terrain, then joined with Numbers 84 and 92 in cutting down one tree and rooting out a number of rocks before lunch. They met again at two o'clock and worked until dusk.

At half-past-nine that evening, Number 2 greeted him from his television, which he had unplugged. "Number Six, what is this I hear about you kidnapping three workmen this morning?"

"I used no particular coercion; I caused no particular trouble."

"How long did you plan to keep them from their proper jobs? That reseeding was part of our entire spring schedule – if part of the Village fails to bloom this summer, yours will be the blame."

"I'll give you back Number Eighty-four, but I'd like to keep Number Ninety-two and the bulldozer for a week. Then you can have him back too, and I'll trade the bulldozer for the heavy roller. But I want to keep Number Fifty-five."

"Number Six, this is intolerable! This is uncountenanceable! This is impossible! This is insane! These men have their own responsibilities, their own jobs to do. I cannot possibly agree to so monstrous a bargain!"

"Thank you. I'll tell Number Eighty-four not to mention it to anyone when he goes back to reseeding tomorrow. He'll remember. He's not too bright, but he's honest and trustworthy."

"I've always felt it a pity that those qualities correlated so closely."

"Oh? I've generally found it the other way round. An intelligent man knows that trust is worth having."

"Yes, and is more likely to find some opportune time to betray it."

"And less likely to betray it at some inopportune time, or by an error of judgement. An intelligent man, a man who reacts rationally, is easier to predict than a man who reacts randomly."

"And here we return to our basic difference of opinion, Number Six. A large group of individuals reacting randomly is the easiest thing in the world to predict. Fortunately, the overwhelming majority does react randomly – the human race is a natural phenomenon. A statistical population of intelligent, self-determining individuals would be almost impossible to handle on any but the most basic, physical grounds."

"Has it occurred to you that they might not need – or want – to be 'handled'?"

"Don't bandy semantics with me, Number Six – they will want to be fed, and clothed, and transported, and entertained and sheltered. If that particular term offends you, let us say *served*, even though the euphemistic loading that word has acquired offends me."

"Why must they be served statistically rather than individually?"

"You have no concept of numbers over a few hundred! It would be humanly impossible to serve a million people individually – it is impossible to serve a thousand with any efficiency. Your petrol is an individual service, and represents a great deal more effort on our part than you seem to appreciate."

"I *do* appreciate it, Number Two. I feel indebted to you for all you have done to make my stay here a busy one. And I will send your gardener back to his beds the first thing in the morning."

"Thank you, Number Six. Be seeing you."

"Be seeing you."

Now Number 6 abandoned his self-imposed schedule to fill his days with physical labour and his nights with retuning the car's engine. It took a week to scrape a strip of roughly cleared dirt between ten and fifteen feet wide and somewhat over a mile long. He directed the bulldozer over the course he had paced out, levelling minor irregularities in the ground to a point where his KAR could take them without undue strain on the suspension.

Then the roller was brought by a long and indirect service road maintained around the Village for that purpose, and the rubble left by the bulldozer was packed down into a passably firm surface. Number 92 was released as soon as the heavy work was done, and Number 6 worked on with the roller and Number 55 for some days more, carving a passable road out of the wilderness. They spoke seldom, sharing little but the interest in doing a job well.

Number 92 came back to help on his days off, and even the weather remained amiable. Through the whole period of work as well, they were never bothered by Guardians. Number 6 took this to mean tacit approval, and proceeded with an untroubled conscience.

At last, one afternoon, they stopped work and studied the last square yards of solidly packed earth. Number 6 nodded. "That's good," he said, and looked at Number 55 seated on the quietly humming tractor. "How would you like a ride all the way around?" he asked.

Number 55 shifted to the right. "I'll carry you back up to the shed."

The north end of the irregular oval had touched the edge of the last row of pines – now, kinked in like a hairpin to a figure-of-eight, the track extended another half mile down the hill and back, veering here and there to take the contours and avoid major obstacles, but with the landward leg so angled as to allow of just over a half-mile straightaway, running downhill to the north and including a straight side of the original track.

The curve at the bottom was banked and turned inland uphill for seventy yards to the rising wall of rock that stood as stark cyclorama to the whole Village, then made a sharp 180-degree to the left for a long downhill all the way to the edge of the beach, straight and smooth for a hundred and twenty yards, gently sloping to level at the bottom. At the fringe of sand, it turned left again, angled around an ancient, wave-hurled boulder half again his own height, made a long curve around two trees, cut right directly up a twenty-five degree grade through a cut which had cost them two days of sweat and aching muscles though it was only sixty feet long, then left up a tyre-wearing grade with half-a-dozen irregular switch-backs evading trees and bushes all the way to the top, where it dodged slightly left and became the landward half of the original oval, around the south end of the track back to the shelter. It would give him enough of a workout and enough opportunity to open halfway in top gear; parts of it might need a little more spade-work, but he had always intended to put the final touches on the course himself. All in all, as he said to Numbers 55 and 92 over a small private celebration that evening, it was a job to be proud of – though he had in mind certain aspects of which his guests and co-workers were hopefully unaware.

Two weeks of physical labour had not distracted him from his KAR 1260; though he had driven less than a thousand miles his oil needed changing and he had less than a gallon of fuel outside his inviolable cache. He took it around the track half a dozen times before reluctantly creeping back to his garage with faithful Number 213 waving the red flag before him, grimly hoping to be spared the embarrassment of running stone dry in the streets and having to be pushed home.

He had about fifteen gallons cached from the forty he'd got most of a month ago – five gallons less than he'd hoped to save, but his fuel consumption figures simply could not be padded by more than 60 per cent and remain remotely acceptable to Number 2. Besides, the volatile fluid had proved a problem to store securely; something would have to be done about that before he could put away much more.

The motor oil arrived four days after his track was finished – the full ten quarts he had requested. But he had to return to the Chemist's Shop for two pints of petrol to warm his engine again when he changed the oil.

Number 2 assured him regularly that his petrol should arrive any day. On the days when it didn't, Number 6 contented himself with walking around the enlarged track once every afternoon in addition to his other regular peripatetic exercises. Evenings he would polish the chromework or buff another coat of wax into the instrument panel. When this palled, he busied himself with pencil and paper, roughing out notes and sketches of sleekly streamlined shapes, doodling airflow lines around them, estimating cross-sections, plugging arbitrary values into arcane formulae while the black cat dozed on the hearthrug before the unlit electric fire.

The arrival of thirty gallons of fuel was as unheralded as the previous delivery; his doorbell chimed one evening at half-past seven and Number 94 straightened from an identical slouch against his doorpost to extend a clipboard with the forms. This time there were only six of the red-and-yellow tins, and line 8 had "30" instead of "40" written on it – it would be worse than useless to question the messenger, since if something was wrong with the order, it obviously shouldn't be delivered. Again he initialled the forms in the space left for his Number – they'd accepted it last time without a murmur.

But did this mean they were going to reduce his supply? Had they kept closer track of his fuel consumption than he'd allowed for? It took him ten minutes to get the six cans stowed neatly beneath the workbench, and as he worked he calculated odds. All factors considered, he saw no reason to abandon his primary plan – which called for him to do nothing unusual for another fortnight. He would have to drive with caution and economy at all times, since his primary plan included at least fifty gallons of petrol.

His face registered none of the grim purpose in his mind, and when he returned to the sitting-room he cleared his conscious mind of all secret thoughts and dwelt upon the delight of having petrol to burn again. He telephoned Number 213 to request his services at nine o'clock next morning, then poured himself a glass of dry sherry, inspected his small collection of records which had been duplicated or transported with him, and settled back to surround himself with the crystalline structures of electronically synthesised Bach.

Some time later he became aware of a light warmth against his hand, and looked down to find the cat curled up beside him. When he returned from turning the record over, the animal lifted its black head to be petted as he sat down beside it. He refilled his glass and leaned back in his chair. As the patterns of the music interwove about him, he felt a gradual easing of the tensions within him – almost for the first time in the Village he was beginning to feel at ease.

The cat purred soundlessly under his caressing fingers, and as his eyes closed it suddenly occurred to him that he could say, considering, that at this point Number 2's expressed desire had been fulfilled; he was happy. But since the core of this joy was the relentless progression of his own secret goals as opposed to – or even parallel to – those goals proposed by Number 2, he felt fully justified in seeming satisfied with the present situation. In fact, it was important to his covert expectations that he must continue to appear at least as satisfied and cooperative as he did. He did not resent the fact that assuming the appearance was presently far from difficult.

He maintained it well for the week he had determined on, and then he went to see Number 2 again early one afternoon.

"You're early for tea, Number Six. Don't you ever think of ringing up before you call?"

"I see no reason to duplicate effort – you know where I am every minute anyway."

"Do you think this entire Village is run for your benefit alone? And even if it were, do you think I am so desperate for diversion that I would spend every waking moment studying you like a jealous lover?"

"Like an entomologist, perhaps. I expect you, personally, have other things to do than watch over me day and night, but then I seldom consider you, personally. You are the personification of the Village. You probably deserve the Royal Plural in your address, as such. A pity Modern English lacks a specific second plural."

"You flatter me. Don't tell me you need more fuel already?"

"I shall shortly. Have you inspected the recent extension of –"

"I don't want to hear about it. Number Six, I was humiliated – *humiliated!* – in council session when Number Four brought up the matter of a hundred and nine unauthorised man-hours expended on that ... that *project* of yours! Not to mention machine-hours and energy expended, schedules thrown off for weeks in half-a-dozen departments ... You certainly created a pretty mess."

"I trust no permanent damage was done."

"No – the Village will bloom more or less as scheduled, though perhaps not quite as fully flowered as it might have been. I only hope you're satisfied now."

"It will hold me for a while. But now that I have further to drive, I'll need more petrol. There is no point in continuing these monthly dumb-shows – I shall continue to need fifty gallons a month to drive as I wish."

"That is utterly out of the question, Number Six! With a degree of regularity, we might be able to arrange for twenty or even twenty-five gallons on a monthly basis, depending on your actual consumption, of course."

"Two litres of oil monthly."

"One."

"Impossible."

"You should be able to drive two thousand miles on a change of oil. At fifteen miles to the gallon, that would take one hundred and thirty-five gallons of petrol, perhaps one hundred and fifty. At twenty-five gallons a month, that's one oil change every six months ..."

"At ten litres per change, allowing another litre every three months for loss and margin, that comes to two litres a month."

"So it does. Very well, in addition to the regular litre each month, we can arrange for six litres when you want a change."

"Very well. But my fuel consumption has been closer to ten or twelve miles to the gallon. Keep that in mind when you're calculating my ration."

"Ten or twelve? I should have thought you would be squeezing twenty miles per gallon, with all the care you seem to take."

"Performance can always use improvement. I hadn't even hoped to get better than fifteen, and I think considering the displacement I've done fairly well."

"Mechanical devices are not my forte, Number Six. I shall be delighted to help you whenever possible, but don't attempt to communicate with me on a technical level. I'm more of a theoretician, I'm afraid."

"Most people who want to run other people's lives for them are theoreticians."

"Is your chief hobby automobiles or debating? I shan't invite you to stay to tea today – I have several important people coming on business which, as you may or may not believe, actually has nothing at all to do with you."

"I intend to remind you daily until my petrol arrives."

"Then I will not be in. Good afternoon, Number Six – you have all the promises you are going to get from me this time."

"Then good afternoon. Be seeing you."

Miraculously, twenty gallons of petrol arrived within a week. His driving schedule increased to the putative limits of his fuel supply, and after another fortnight he called one morning on Number 40 at the Artist's Shoppe just off the Village green. She displayed an introductory kit for leatherworking, and he asked about the materials and techniques of moulding and sculpting in fibreglass.

He found sheets of glass fibre were formed and impregnated with an epoxy cement which supplied the toughness and resilience which the glass alone would lack, while the glass itself lent the essential structural strength. As Number 40 described casting various small objects, then lining the moulds with glass cloth, she located a colourfully lithographed box which contained a Fibreglass Starter Kit.

"Here we are, Number Six. This includes complete instructions for two projects which will familiarise you with the techniques. If you've never worked with it before, you may find it a bit sticky at first."

"Perhaps I'd better take that. But I had something larger in mind – too large to mould, actually. Can I form this over a framework?"

"I should think so. . . . Just how large were you thinking of?"

"I should like to cover about seventy-five square feet with a three-eighths-inch thickness – or a centimetre."

"Seventy-five square *feet*? What are you planning on building – an addition to your cottage?"

"As a matter of fact, I was thinking of designing a racing fairing of some kind for my automobile. Perhaps I might even try replacing the entire coachwork with a fibreglass body of my own design and construction."

"That's an ambitious project. I hope we can help you – I don't think we've ever had a call for that much all at once. I'm not even sure the same techniques would apply to something that had to be . . . well, really *practical*. I mean, I thought you wanted to use it for a work of art!"

"Can't art be useful?"

"Oh, of course, I mean, it's nice if useful things can be artistically designed, but they have to be made – more sturdy, don't they, and there's bound to be a certain sacrifice to practicality. I was really thinking more of 'Art For Art's Sake'. Or something. But you might be able to find out about what you want in the Village library – there are lots of books on handicrafts and things. And there's a bibliography in the pamphlet that comes with the Fibreglass Starter Kit."

"You don't have any idea how long it would take to get the larger sheets."

"I don't even know how much they'd weigh, or how they would be shipped. I'm not even sure they could be brought here. I'll see about ordering them as soon as you know how much you want and what kind. But you had best be prepared to follow up the orders yourself."

A discreet tapping at the open end of his ersatz garage brought his head up from under the bonnet to find Number 2 leaning against the corner, lit by the lowering golden sunlight from the west.

"I thought I would take the opportunity to drop in on you

unannounced, Number Six. Your car looks lovely."

"Thank you. Having disposed of the social niceties, would you care for a tour of inspection? I have nothing to hide."

"I should love to look around at another time – but there is one point of curiosity which I should like to get out of the way first. I hear you've found a new hobby."

"Word seems to get around."

"In my position, I pick up most of the rumours."

"They're remarkably vague rumours. I didn't expect to have to bother you with it, knowing how busy you are – just a sort of decorating project."

"You must be decorating something very large. Since one of my responsibilities is the aesthetic unity of the Village, I'd like to know where you intend to display seventy-five square feet of fibreglass."

"It will be a good deal smaller when I finish with it – I intend to design a racing fairing for my KAR. I feel that the operating efficiency I've been able to achieve could be increased materially if not significantly by the addition of a lightweight, streamlined shell. In fact, I've been considering replacing the heavy coachwork entirely." He leaned back against the bumper and crossed his ankles.

"It'll keep the KAR out of operation for a couple of weeks," he continued cheerfully, "but I never have enough petrol anyway. I can save up a little while I'm working on this new project."

"Number Six, it honestly does my heart good to see you taking so much interest in things. Idle hands are the devil's playground. I'm sure we can find you what you want. After all, our goal here is to keep you happy, and any reasonable service towards that end is our duty."

"Your solicitude touches me deeply, Number Two."

"But it is difficult to keep up with you much of the time. Why couldn't you have had a passion for crewel work, or badminton, or the bagpipes?"

"I might have taken up parachuting, or speedboat racing. Or amateur radio. My tastes are not especially exotic – I consider myself an easy man to please."

"Not noticeably. But I pride myself that within our limited facilities you are kept reasonably satisfied. You shall have your fibreglass in a few weeks – until then I suggest you concentrate on refining those rough designs you have sketched out. Be seeing you."

He straightened from the doorpost and was gone. Number 6 looked after him in the gathering twilight, and was bold enough to permit himself a smile.

SECTION III: *Andante Captibile*

"You're going to let him have the fibreglass?"

"I see no reason not to. After all, we're watching him every minute he's at work. Anything he does will be noted and anything he makes ready will be prepared for."

"Don't you think he *knows* we're watching? Don't you think he has made allowances for that as he has every time in the past?"

"*Not* every time, Number Four – far from it. Only once has he actually committed a totally unsupervised escape."

"We've been lucky. Several times we haven't found out until –"

"Nonsense! Luck is a loser's excuse. We are simply on top of him every minute. Nothing he does escapes us."

"He moves fast. And you can't follow his mind."

"So you expect him to leave us, 'sweating and swearing, a mile and a half behind'? If his mind wants to escape by itself, let it. There's five million words of escape fiction in the Village library. He can lose himself from Erech to Barsoom to Coventry. *Die Gedanken sind frei.* But if he makes the least attempt to take his body with him, we can stop it. When he learns to teleport himself, we shall be defeated. I am willing to wait."

"Mmm. Number Two, how far from the north end of the track is our nearest Rescue Unit stationed?"

"About a mile and a half. But an amphibious Guardian is posted in the rocks at the north end of the beach less than fifty metres from the spot where the track touches the sand, and two heavy-duties are permanently stationed among the trees at the top of the rill. I don't see any way he could make it up the lowest part of the rock face in less than ten minutes, and we can gas him into a net before he's halfway to the top."

"He's beaten the Guardians before – at least, he believes he has, which is how his behaviour will be predicated."

"Well, what he doesn't know, in this case, will be very careful not to hurt him."

"I still say you should never have given him tools. Any tool magnifies his ability to do things. And One knows we've nearly had problems with that in this subject before. He does enough bare-handed . . ."

"Number Four, what he *does* is all we *can* monitor. The less he does, the more I would worry. The more he does, the happier I am. For over a year, in the Village, he brooded upon his fancied 'captivity' and built up a head of emotional steam which drove him to continue his attempts to escape.

"You see, he has never had any reason to want to stay here. The Village is a beautiful place. It is – beautilitarian. It is restful, peaceful and tranquil. It is Shangri-La by the seashore. But a certain personality type, with nothing to do, nothing to occupy his mind and hands, will go to amazing lengths to find a direction for his energies. What I have done is channel this *drive* into paths which are readily observable. Otherwise, how could we possibly tell what he might do if left entirely to his own devices?"

"All I'm saying is that he has too many devices. He should not have been given tools. And that engine, in the most basic terms, is a source of energy. With tools and energy people like him have been conquering the universe. Who do you think we are?"

"Do you expect him to beat his mudguards into rotor blades and depart from our midst in a fibreglass helicopter? Really, Number Four . . ."

"I don't expect anything – or more precisely, I *do* expect anything. Don't underestimate him, Number Two. And don't overestimate yourself. He has only one thought in his mind, day and night – escape."

"That may have been true a few months ago. But now there are, at least occasionally, moments when he thinks about his car –"

"Only in terms of escape."

"– and the cat is definitely, observably, becoming a part of his life. I shouldn't doubt he has considered taking the cat with him when he makes his next escape attempt."

"Then you admit . . ."

". . . Only that *currently* – or recently – he is thinking about escaping. These thoughts will gradually, imperceptibly, fade over the period of another six months through procrastination to oblivion. I felt from the very beginning that if we could just keep him here and happy for a little while, his life would come to centre around the Village. His life outside was not an especially happy one."

"He hasn't done much towards making friends."

"Compared to his previous record, he has been remarkably sociable. He is on nodding acquaintance with Number 40 of the Artist's Shoppe, the Chemist, the Ironmonger, the Butcher . . ."

" . . . The Baker and the Candlestick-Maker. And those workmen who helped him build the track. All right, he's on a comfortable social footing in the Village. He's done that before."

"He has never allowed anything of ours to become part of his life before."

"The cat? All right, I'm willing to admit you did a good job on the cat. Wasn't that your conditioning apparatus?"

"Yes. Its effects are more predictable on less advanced mechanisms. We gave the animal fifteen minutes of moderate pleasure stimulation combined with Number Six's personal effluvium and voice. We could easily have driven it to react to him as to catnip, but Number Six is far too perceptive to let pass something as unlikely as a strange cat which suddenly demonstrates a passionate attraction for him. Even with the gentle predilection we programmed, he was unduly suspicious for some time. Fortunately, his ego permits him to think the animal could desire to stay with him. His remarkably perceptive examination of the animal was only physical – like us, he can observe only what happens. The mind is still a locked box, Number Four, and opening it from the outside tends to affect the contents, even under laboratory conditions."

"Precisely why I object to your giving him tools. How do you know what he's thinking about doing with them?"

"Because I can – and do – influence what he thinks about. Until recently there has been nothing in the Village that *mattered* to him. He will not make friends among the Villagers – he is capable of conscious effort to avoid it, in fact – but his atrophied social instincts are at least being stimulated by the presence of the cat. Besides, at least subconsciously, he may tend to feel it's 'good luck'."

"*Good luck*, Number Six?"

"I never implied he thinks of the cat as a lucky charm. But if you recall, we brought them together shortly before the delivery of his first large shipment of petrol. The learning mechanism of the brain is designed to link, at least tentatively, any unusual incidents in close temporal proximity. *That* particular mechanism is far older than the human race."

"But he would never begin to believe ..."

"I sincerely hope he doesn't. If he ever becomes consciously aware of it, he'll discard it automatically simply because it happened in the Village. I re-stimulated the pattern by giving him his short track just after he'd brought something delicate home from the butcher's for the cat. He seems more willing to let it live in his home than he was at first. And after all, this man is possessed of a fantastic psychological resistance. I shall probably reinforce the cat by letting it stay away for several days when Number Six must suffer some setback or another, and then returning it when we do him a favour. These things take time, Number Four – *time*. You would hardly expect him to rush out and join a Fraternal Organisation."

"Unless it was important to some goal of his own."

"That goes without saying. But you will admit that he is becoming more a part of the Village."

"He has only worn his Number once – that time he wore it upside down and passed as Number Nine for hours until a clerk noticed that the Ordinary behind the digit was standing on its handlebars."

"Ah well, Number Six has a nearly infinite capacity for painful whimsy. Still, though he is slow to adopt our ways, he is participating willingly in them more and more. He fills in our forms and follows our official procedures – anyone, no matter how stubborn, will run a maze if they see the right reward at the end. He is willing to play our game, by our rules, on our time, in order to get his precious petrol."

"He didn't go through your channels to build that extension to his track."

"There were no available channels for that; I expected him to do something typically audacious, and he did. It was lovely. He used every erg and calory of energy – physical, mental, and especially emotional – in carving that highway out of the wilderness. Now it represents a personal investment in the Village. He *made* it, and he is the only person to have driven on it. In his peculiar but predictable mental set, that establishes it as his 'territory', and it is a precious thing to him because of this."

"An area of ground? How primitive!"

"Not as an area *per se* – an emotional quality surrounding this area which links it with him. Related to anthropomorphic Nature Religions in various cultures. Bear in mind that in order to predict his reactions you must recognise the causes behind his action patterns. The reconstruction of his flat, for instance. He feels comfortable there, even though he knows consciously he is in the Village, because it is 'his own'. His personality is written all over it, and was perfectly simple to forge. It is as soothing to him as a roomful of mirrors to a narcissist. Consider how much of his life has been spent keeping his own company. You've studied his dossier – you know he's never been prone to form warm, normal human relationships. He hasn't had a pet since childhood."

"Your cat took to him, Number Two, but I don't think you can say he's accorded it the status of a *pet*. He contributes just less than half the animal's nourishment – it sleeps under his roof about two-thirds of the time – it seems to prefer his company, and he doesn't object to it, but I don't think you could honestly call it a pet."

"A free companion, then. But he shares his territory. And he is occasionally even affectionate towards the cat."

"I can't imagine that adjective ever being applied to Number Six."

"I have a videotape of it. Would you like to see it?"

"I'm not sure. What does it consist of?"

"Not a great deal, actually. Here, I can punch it up for you in a moment. There it is."

"I shouldn't say 'affectionate', Number Two. The cat curled up against him in the chair, and put its head under his free hand – stroking it would be an instinctive reaction. Even scratching it around the neck and behind the ears."

"Of course it's instinctive, you ninny! We cannot approach this man on a conscious level – how often must I explain this to you? It's instinctive, indeed – but it's an instinct he has not used before. It is the most stabilising, enervating, tranquillising instinct known. He has buried it under the callouses of years of bitter experiences. Awakened now, at our will, it will put him completely within our parameters in – oh, conservatively, another year. And without any damage to the essential BGR patterning."

"If it's awakened. Look at him. That manual action is as idle and void of emotion as drumming his fingers on a tabletop."

"No. Look. The cat is purring. There's a frame coming up I want to hold for you – just when he glances down at. . . . There it is. Perfectly clear. He is smiling. And it's not that damned canary-swallowing smirk he affects around me – it is an honest, sincere smile of content and pleasure. Pleasure in his *companion*, Number Four. The cat may eat and sleep where it pleases. Our concern is with Number Six, and his peace of mind. The fact that he *can* and has, even if only once, even if only for a moment, smiled like that, proves my entire case. He has been happy here for one second; therefore he can be made happy. If he can be made happy, he can be *kept* happy."

"You cannot have the argument both ways, Number Two. If the prisoner is happy, why lock him in? If he is not, why pretend that he is?"

"Bernard Shaw was writing of marriage, Number Four, and I hardly think the quotation is apt. Our relationship is on nothing remotely approaching an equal footing – it is far more that of the parent to the child, educating and guiding, even though it may be against the momentary will of the child, for his and society's greater good. He will thank us for it, eventually."

His inexpensive but practical ten-scale slide rule was in the left-hand waist-level drawer of the Georgian tallboy beside his broad work-table. It had told him how much fibreglass would be needed to surround KAR 1260 in an aerodynamically contoured housing, but it wasn't able to tell him what the contours should be

Pages and pages of notes and sketches, any and all of which could bear suspicious examination, detailed the framework and bracing and mounts to the chassis of the KAR. Other, rougher, sketches had been doodled in smooth dirt with the end of a stick as a temporary aid to visualisation of certain problems in mechanical linkages which could have had nothing to do with a streamlined hull, and had been erased with a smooth shoe-sole as soon as the problem involved had been worked out. The finished drafts of these he carried in his head.

He didn't really expect the fibreglass – it would be too simple. But they'd been expecting him to ask for things, even encouraging him by being so improbably obliging. His most overt actions so far had been met with no more than mild reproof. They were obviously building him up for something. Fine. Since he couldn't guess what they were trying to do, worry about it was pointless. Instead, he would keep them busy guessing what *he* was doing.

They couldn't have bought that story about a racing fairing – Number 2 was not a complete idiot – but they had swallowed it whole with a perfectly straight face. Since he hadn't had any better ideas, he would continue until something better turned up. He was willing to play their game as long as he won his own points; if it meant playing Stirling Moss for their television cameras he was far from loath to drive around a few hours a day and cache a third of the fuel they gave him towards his unexpressed needs.

They had helped him in so many ways already – could they now be coaxed just a little farther? As nearly as he had been able to fathom Number 2's character, it might even be possible. As long as he gave every evidence of being *nearly* satisfied, he might, like the cold camel in the fable, eventually take everything he wanted.

As long as Number 2 insisted on attempting to make him happy within limits, the least he could do was offer his benefactor every opportunity to pass those limits in a series of short, easy steps from one little favour to another – increments which could conceivably end with Number 2 offering him a ticket to freedom, open return – if not literally, at least practically.

In fact, the fibreglass was such a ticket – it had been reserved, even if not confirmed. With nearly thirty gallons of fuel and some oil put away he already had a feeling of accomplishment; what he needed now was something to put it in. Only some work on the transmission and assorted unlikely mechanical connections remained to be accomplished in his shop, though several of his sub-assemblies might suffer from the inability to fit certain parts together in plain sight, and several mounting holes which would need to be vertically symmetrical to within a fraction of a millimetre could never be tested before the omnipresent cameras without betraying his intentions. Only surreptitious and momentary comparisons would be possible until the actual moment of necessity – after which time no mistakes could be rectified.

But since he was playing the game to the hilt, as he always would, he needed technical assistance which only Number 2 could give him. If his "racing fairing" were to be aerodynamically perfect, he could request the use of a computer terminal for his calculations. He couldn't claim to understand the equations in the textbooks, but he could plug in values and apply the results. After all, Number 2 would be in an ideal position to monitor his calculations, which would keep *him* interested in analysing them. And except for interface problems, which might be disguised as ground turbulence, everything would have to do with pressure flows over a dynamic surface and would guide the complex three-dimensional pattern which would form his hypothetical fibreglass.

He spent a week working on the framework of rod which would support his imaginary coachwork, bearing bags of bolts home from the ironmonger's along with parcels of groceries and occasional scraps from the butcher for the cat.

Number 18 asked him about it one afternoon following luncheon on the Terrace, which they now shared two or three times a week. "What is this mechanical thing you're doing?" was her exact wording; to her partner's quizzically amused expression she enlarged, "All those nuts and bolts you carry around with you. Are you building something?"

"Not exactly. I'm modifying something."

"What?"

"My motorcar. You remember my motorcar – when I was first looking for Number Eleven some months ago, it was in regard to –"

"Oh yes. The 739/H-F forms. I remember. You mentioned your car then. Do you still have it?"

"Yes – and I'm putting a new body on it."

"What colour?"

"I hadn't thought, actually. It'll probably be a sort of off-white."

"That's not right for a racing car. It should be – not red; not for you. Blue. A dark blue."

"What about a dark green?"

"That would be nice. Yes, I think a dark green. With one bronze stripe along it."

"What makes you think it's a racing car? There isn't much room in the Village for a racing car."

"Oh, Number Six – everybody was talking about your facing down Number Two and extending your track. Oh, not out in the open, of course, but everybody in the office knew about it. And then when you mentioned your car just now, it reminded me." She twinkled innocently at him. "Besides, I can't see *you* driving anything but a racing car. Do you ever give people rides?"

"Very rarely. Besides, it's out of operation at the moment."

"Did something go wrong?"

"No – I can't get any petrol, and the engine's out of tune."

"You got your forms without any problem, I hope."

"Yes; I filled them in and passed them on to Number Eight personally a week ago."

"And while you're waiting, you're building a new body."

"Only a frame for it. I'm also waiting for the fibreglass from which I can form the coachwork."

"Oh, I see. And the fibreglass is sort of off-white?"

"I think so. I doubt if it's dark green."

"They should make it in different colours. Can you change your order?"

"I shouldn't like to try to change anything now – it would only confuse matters and delay it another six months."

"There must be paints for it. Have you tried the Artist's Shoppe? Oh, I'd just *love* to help you paint it!"

"We can discuss that when the time comes. I'm interested now in what else everybody in your office knows about me, since my triumph over Number Two seems to have been common knowledge."

"Well, you're sort of the 'Mystery Man' of the Village. You keep to yourself so much, and nobody seems to know much about you – except Number Two, I suppose, since he knows everything, but ... well ..." She lowered her voice conspiratorially. "I heard you'd tried to leave here." She looked away from him in embarrassment.

He cleared his throat. "I'm afraid it's true," he admitted. "But I hope that won't offend you. I promise not to try to take you with me the next time."

She blushed furiously. "Number Six!" she said. "You have always behaved like a gentleman before. I'm sorry I brought the subject up, and I really wish it could be dropped at this point."

"I'm sorry," he said. "I trust it may never come up between us again."

"Very well. Now about painting your car –"

"A number of enquiries will have to be made," he said. "The Artist's Shoppe will be one place to ask, but I don't know enough about the subject to say whether help would be advisable. It calls for research, among other things. But you shouldn't roll up your trousers before you come to the river, as they say – after all, I haven't even designed it yet."

"The new body?"

"It'll be like a shell, actually. And it has to be properly streamlined so as not to interfere with the airflow."

"Oh. Like a boat."

"Yes. Or an aeroplane. Or a racing car, for that matter."

"Can you really go fast enough on that track for this airflow business to be important?"

"Enough that it could make a measurable difference That's why I'm doing it. I've really become interested in improving my performance."

"What an exciting way to pass the time! Would you take me for a ride some time when it's all together?"

He smiled. "Perhaps. We shall have to see what modifications will need to be made. When I get it all together again I'll let you know."

One afternoon when his mountings were nearly completed, he was deep in concentration beneath the bonnet readjusting his ignition timing. Somehow the tiny variables in his engine kept slipping out of tune and demanded nearly constant attention. He faintly heard a footstep outside his garage, and elected not to react.

"Good afternoon," said Number 2's cheerful, raucous voice at the door. "I wasn't sure where to knock, but I don't want to come upon you unannounced." When this overture was not answered hostilely, he followed it into the shelter, around the stripped chassis of the car to the tool bench where the mechanic stood silently wiping his hands on a piece of waste and looking at him expectantly.

"I just thought I'd stop by and see how you were getting along. When you don't come by my office to complain about something for a full week, I begin to worry about your health."

"I'm feeling well, thanks. Except for a constant slight headache."

"Not sinus?"

"No – eyestrain. Naturally, I'm interested in doing the best possible job on this fairing, so I've been swotting up on aerodynamics. But the equations on the curves are quite a bit beyond my mathematical ability. I've been slogging through them by slide rule, but it's not remotely satisfactory. In short, I wonder if I could borrow a goodsized calculator for a few weeks."

"As I believe you know, we have a central computer facility here; all we could offer you would be access to a time-sharing terminal. There might be a security problem, of course."

"I'm sure you could find some way to trust me. I'm expecting my fibreglass any day now, and it would be most frustrating not to be able to get directly to work."

"I quite understand, Number Six. In point of fact, one reason I stopped by was to say that I hadn't had any word yet on your fibreglass order. But I can see about having a terminal brought into your ... Where would you like it connected?"

"How big is it?"

"About as big as a breadbin."

"My work-table. You can probably hook it to one of the television lines."

"Have you any idea how long you'll want it?"

"No – at least a week. Will I get a short course in operating it?"

"You will be given a programmed text which will teach you in half an hour enough to let the computer teach you itself from there on. I learned from one, though it took me almost two hours. You are familiar with the basic principles involved?"

"Fundamentally. If your computer can do the work of a million competent clerks, you hire them out a score each to fifty thousand people, each of whom pays only one ten-thousandth of the cost for the whole computer's time."

"You also have access to the machine immediately whenever you want it – never too busy to work for you. You'd want one with a visual display, I shouldn't wonder – and a light-pen. That would do wonders for your designs, Number Six. You can make a rough sketch directly on the face of a cathode-ray tube, order the computer to correct every line to precisely the mathematical curve you wish either directly or by equation, and see it done at once. With another hour's practice, in fact, you might be able to run a complete three-dimensional simulation of airflow over any shape you would care to specify. I think you would find this capability a help. Unless you object to its being an artificial replacement for something."

"My object is an optimum design for my fairings. I use a torch to cut metal – I don't break it in my bare hands. I'll be happy to use your computer. Just as long as your computer doesn't try to use me."

"Superstitious nonsense, Number Six. No tool is independent of the hand behind it. You would be accusing me or my staff of conspiring against you. That couldn't have been your intent, after all we've done for you."

"Perish the thought, Number Two. I would be overjoyed to have the use of a score of your clerks for a while – especially if they're so artistic."

"Now, I haven't said I could get you one. In fact, I don't believe I even suggested it. Well, perhaps I did suggest it. I really don't know whether it would be feasible, in view of your record – and the assorted technical problems involved. This type of unit is still very new, and they aren't really in volume production yet. But if I can arrange for one for you, I certainly shall.

"Now I may as well not cut into your afternoon any longer. I shall look into your fibreglass and test the feasibility of this terminal arrangement. I can let you know in a few days. And by the by – thank you for not starting debates with me this time."

"My pleasure. Be seeing you."

The braces which would support his (still hypothetical) fairing were sturdy aluminum angle irons, with half-inch primary frame members and quarter-inch secondary braces. If it seemed over sturdy for what should be no more than a couple of hundredweight of fibreglass, he didn't think Number 2 would be unduly concerned even if he noticed. They were intricately joined, and included a few holes which served no apparent purpose. There were wing nuts on a few of the bolts which held major sub-assemblies together, but they were all inside the frame and well out of sight. A couple of small eyes where pulleys could hang were unnoticeable amid the neat jumble of raw metal. Jutting ends remained untrimmed, awaiting the final pattern which would be carefully developed and extensively tested for microseconds, then reassembled and retested repeatedly until it achieved theoretical perfection before it was given physical reality in the graceful curves of formed fibreglass.

The computer terminal arrived within the week, and he spent seven consecutive hours familiarising himself with its operation and capabilities. When he finally leaned back, switched it off and went out to the kitchen to make a much-belated supper, he felt fairly familiar with the device and its limitations. Apparently he could not use it to gain access to any data he had not put into it, which was to have been expected; his clerks didn't discuss their other jobs. On the other hand, it should prove more than adequate to the job at hand. To both jobs at hand, for that matter – the ostensible racing fairing and the secondary form it should be expected to take.

In the course of a long, intent afternoon he had started his second level in Terminal Operation, Visual, with the light-pen, a plastic stylus with a long cord to the unit and a microswitch beneath his index finger. He had used it to leave glowing marks on the cathode ray tube, then modified them by computer into exactly defined curves and finished by drawing a rough freehand circle on the CRT, making it into a mathematically perfect circle and bouncing it in slow motion with specified acceleration, mass and elasticity against a base line.

The next day he was able to sketch a skeleton cube and make it rotate about any axis. Before he stopped he had included centrifugal distortion and gyroscopic inertia in his spinning cube, specifying physical constants and combining axial rotations. He had discovered most of the *Handbook of Chemistry and Physics* was available from a whole reference section which was open to him after all, along with an omnilingual range of dictionaries, the *Encyclopedia Britannica* (five years out of date) and several screensful of titles he could have scanned at his leisure.

Now he was ready to start work. His mornings were still spent out and around in the Village, and among his recent acquisitions were two rolls of metal screening, so heavy an electric van had been engaged to haul them to his workshop, along with a coil of steel ribbon two inches wide and sixty feet long.

The first roll of screen was a wide-gauge net of welded wires, the type known as "hardware cloth". With the bracing structure mounted in place on the chassis of his KAR, he began to form a close-fitting, roughly curved covering of this heavy screen around it, yet unattached to it. In a dozen places, then, he cut slits in the screening and pushed through sturdy steel T-brackets, their tongues eyed for mounting bolts and their bases behind the screen, and he soldered them temporarily in place.

By this time he knew roughly what the contours of his imaginary shell should be, and he prodded and levered and bent and pushed at the resistive screen until its curves approached his approximations. Then he unrolled the ribbon of steel and ran lengths of it around the heavy wire mesh shell, riveting it to the T-brackets and drawing it tight, strapping vertically and laterally around the shell to reinforce it. Then he covered the entire affair with a full wrapping of the second roll's fine-mesh windowscreen.

That was, all told, the work of twelve afternoons. He saw no reason to prolong his labours unnecessarily when he could be pressing Number 2 for further favours. His evenings were now spent chiefly with the computer terminal, animating airflows over small sections of complex curves, varying rates of flow and viscosity and adding an unlabelled factor which involved cavitation potential but could pass for air friction in the context he used it in.

And then his fibreglass arrived, like great bolts of cloth wrapped in heavy brown paper. The tall rolls stood against the wall of his workshop for two days, spurring him to finish the last set of calculations on the camber of his suddenly possible rear deck, and run a final simulation of this last modification under several hypothetical conditions. Then, with carefully traced and measured templates, he set to work building the hull itself.

Over the fine screening, with gloves on his hands against the brittle glass-cloth, he drew sheets of it in irregular patches which he tacked in place and covered with penetrating pungent epoxy resins. The brownish liquid soaked into each layer of matting and hardened there slowly, fixing every fibre in a tough, resilient bond. Flows of resin dripped through the fine wire mesh to dry into lumps, stalactites, ridges and strings; some he could chip off later, the rest he could ignore.

Five layers of whitish, burlap-textured matting were laid down, and five layers of cement soaked through them to cure to final hardness in the graceful unbroken curves of unit construction.

Sanding the surface took longer than laying it down. An electric buffer among his tools adapted well to coarse sandpaper, and carried him through progressively finer grades until the whole fairing was smooth to the touch. Then dark gray-green enamel went on, and dried to a colour like a cloudy sea. It took him, from start to finish, nearly three weeks.

And then the last coat of enamel was dry, the oil had been changed and the fuel tank filled. With proper ceremony, he summoned Number 213 and together they carefully loaded the shell, sectioned for transportation to the track, on to the car. Since the Village paths were too narrow to pass the vehicle with its fairing mounted, the segments were carried like pieces of a display sign tied together on the car, while Number 213 walked importantly ahead with his red flag, clearing the way of staring pedestrians.

Once at the track, together they lifted the unwieldy slabs and untied the bundles of braces which hung like fasces along both sides. Number 6 bolted them into place on the coachwork while Number 213 watched, fascinated, only coming forward to help him lift sections of the fairing into place. Then Number 6 crawled about under the car tightening the mounting bolts. They would hold as long as he needed them to hold.

With the last bolts in place, he eased himself into the driver's seat and started the engine. He drove one full circuit of the track under thirty while the eight pulsing cylinders warmed and circulated the oil, then picked up speed. Number 213 sat on the ground by the shed watching him go by every two minutes for a while, and then was gone without waving his usual *Be seeing you.*

Number 6 studied the height of the sun above the smooth and nameless sea which was one wall of his prison. The light would not begin to fail for another hour. He'd expected Number 213 to wait longer, especially since Number 2 must be most interested in what was going on now that this vast project approached its penultimate moments. No sense in wasting more petrol; he completed one more lap, then pulled into his pit stop.

With the bulk of the car shielding him from the distant television camera, he loaded a number of well-wrapped parcels into the boot of the car, crawled underneath to check a couple of connections and connect a number of small pulleys, and then topped off his fuel tank from the last can sitting in the row along one wall. The last drops went into a plastic sack concealed under the rear deck and nearly full of fifty gallons of petrol. The sack had been tucked, empty, into the space as the first layer of fibreglass went on, and into it he had transferred his hoard. Then he had spread it beneath the hardening shell and anchored it into the framework, leakproof and electrically grounded to one long trailing cable. Now it held his long-distance fuel.

The sun had passed behind a curtain of golden clouds which were already darkening to rose and lavender as he started the engine again and purred out on to the track in the gathering dusk.

Out from among the trees and down the long grade he rolled, shifting for the turn at the bottom and cutting hard right up the hill, slowing to twenty on the hairpin curve at the top, then roaring down the track along the base of the sheer granite wall towards the lowest point of the course at the edge of the beach. The tide was approaching flood, and the sand was packed hard just beyond where the track swung left up the slope through the irregular zig-zags and cuts of the return leg of the course.

He cut the lights of the car as he drove on to the sand just at the edge of the tide, stopped the engine and climbed out. He was now in range of no camera he had found, and his best estimates gave him fifteen minutes to complete his modifications.

He got out, reaching under the shell to release three wing nuts on each side, and then rolled the sections back from the braces. These he loosened and swung to new angles, then tightened. The quarter-inch aluminum angle-irons swung out and slanted downward around the upper part of the car, bristling a dozen diagonally-cut points at thirty degree intervals.

The fibreglass segments slid into a new configuration, still like the racing shell, but now upside down. The stern was open; he climbed back into the car, started the engine, shifted into bottom gear and eased forward into the hull.

It rocked as the weight came into it, settling into the sand. The rear wheels dug into the hard sand and pushed the shell to the edge of the water until he felt it lifted free by the wash of a wave. The next surge swung his hull a few inches to one side, then swept around the open stern and swirled about his tyres. He climbed out again to hoist the rear panels of the hull into place, fit their snug joints together and bolt them securely.

A soft glooping sound brought his head around, instantly alert. A giant soft spheroid, a Guardian, pale in the twilight, was flobbing towards him with definite intent to investigate and interfere. He jumped back into the car and picked up one of the two spare braces he had held out for this situation. Six feet long, diagonally cut on one end, it would be sharp enough to puncture the tough protoplastic hide of the thing if it pushed very hard.

It came wobbling across the beach as if blown by a gust of wind, rolling and bounding. He set the brace quickly against an inner angle of the chassis, and ducked in the seat as the eight-foot sphere sensed the spear before it and vaulted more than its own height to clear the car.

The leap carried it past the line of foaming breakers on the sand and brought it down in the surf a car-length beyond the ungainly craft which was now bobbing and swaying unsteadily as shallow waves lapped about it. Number 6 swung his single line of defence to face seaward as the great bubble somehow found traction in the water and skidded towards him with a draught of no more than three inches. He thrust at it with his pole and it veered sharply to bounce against the bow of his still-grounded craft.

The impact shook him from his unsteady stance in the seat. He staggered, flourishing the pole to regain his balance, until the edge of the door caught him behind his knees and he fell backward, twisting like a cat to land on his hands. The jolt knocked the wind out of him for a moment, but the Guardian's momentum had already carried it far up the beach beyond the car. Before it could slow and return, he was almost on his feet again, brushing sand from his burning palms.

The pole had fallen near him and he scrambled to pick it up as the ungainly thing lurched towards him. His conscious thoughts were mostly for the tide, which was rising with every minute spent and would begin to float his craft without him if the Guardian detained him long enough. He braced his spear in the sand like a pygmy faced with a charging lion, and held his ground as the blundering behemoth lumbered towards him.

As it approached, it slowed. As it slowed, he pulled the spear back to a new foothold and retreated a step towards the boat behind him. The sphere hesitated, then rolled swiftly and smoothly to his landward side. There it began moving forward, slowly, inexorably, until it just touched the tip of his brace.

Holding it tentatively at bay, he clambered back into the seat on the car. The Guardian was almost behind him now. He prodded at it, standing on the seat, then dropped the pole into the hull and turned to slide down into the seat and kick the engine to life again as the Guardian lunged ferociously at the rear of the craft and bumped it forward into the rising surf with two ramming attacks.

He gunned the engine and felt the power transmission to the rigged screw begin to push against the water under his keel. His heart began to pound in rhythm with the racing pistons as he felt his boat begin to move; he glanced back to see the great sphere, pale in the twilight, charge at him and bounce again off the transom – then he felt the stern drag clear of the sand and the surging freedom of the sea was his.

The engine rumbled and roared as he shifted pressure to his foot throttle and felt the speed increase. Looking back one more time, he saw the slow-turning spheroid floating after him, falling farther behind by the minute. He took a deep breath of the exhilarating air of freedom and then almost jumped as something landed on the passenger seat to his left.

He looked down. There, already rubbing up against him, was the black cat. And there was something unusual about it – there was a harness of some kind strapped about its body, holding a small box mounted between its shoulder-blades. A signalling device? He slipped it free and examined it in the light of the instrument panel lamps. The cat had been sent to follow him – but to what result? Since this device was probably still transmitting . . . He threw it towards shore as hard as he could, and gained a momentary pleasure in seeing it bounce off the outdistanced Guardian, harmless though the impact was.

Nevertheless the exhilaration of his escape was now allayed by an awful suspicion of betrayal. The cat was incontrovertibly there, and it had brought an unidentifiable and unexpected device to him. Yet his reaction in throwing the box away had been the obvious response – how could they have expected to track him after the cat found him? Something was not . . .

A sound very like a muffled groan seemed to come from behind him, and he twisted to look in his rear-vision mirror. The Guardian was a hundred yards behind him, a dim bobbing dot in the distance; the lights of the Village twinkled around the short rocky headland which already blocked the right half (in his mirror) from view. The sound was repeated and enlarged upon, and his hearing now placed it nearby – in the stern.

Something shifted weight, and scraping, struggling sounds from the parcel-packed bilge astern held Number 6 staring with a horrible fascination into his mirror in an effort to see around the end of his car, only glancing momentarily into the darkness ahead.

Then a silhouette rose in the mirror, obscuring the lights astern, and the throbbing craft rocked slightly as a figure stood up unsteadily, holding on to the gunwale and the car's rear mudguard. Over the muffled purr of the engine and the slapping of waves against the hull rose a familiar harsh and faintly raucous voice.

"Number Six, just what do you think you're doing?"

It could only be Number 2. The driver smiled. "Escaping," he said.

"Well, stop it at once! I was hoping to catch you in time to dissuade you from this rash act, but I had no idea you were prepared to add kidnapping to your list of antisocial actions." Heeding the pitching of the craft he crawled forward over the rear deck towards the passenger seat. The cat scrambled out of the way as Number 2 threw a leg over the door and started to climb in.

"I hope you don't expect to force me to turn around now," the driver said. "I shouldn't like to throw you overboard."

"Dear me, no! In dealing with a professional killer such as yourself I would always exercise the greatest care. I am an administrator, not a fighter." He settled into the other seat, holding his free hand to his head. He took it down and looked at the smeared palm. "Oh dear – I seem to have cut myself. I don't suppose you have a clean rag?"

"What are you doing here?"

"Being kidnapped, I believe."

"You stowed away in my boat and remained hidden all the time I was trying to launch it? And adding ten stones to the weight, while you were at it. I don't intend to feed you for a week either, by the way."

"I did not stow away, Number Six; I acted entirely out of concern for you. You had started down the track and failed to return. You could have been lying in a flaming tangle of metal at the foot of some grade. I came down with the cat, and sent it ahead to look for you. When I came out on the beach, I saw you were engaged in combat with the Guardian. As I think I said, I am not a fighter – I stayed on the far side of this . . . ah . . . boat and came up just as you were thrown from it. Then I thought – well, I must admit I thought I might be able to prevent your hasty, thoughtless departure from us until I could beg for another chance to redress whatever wrongs you may feel you have suffered.

"Then, as I started to climb in over that side, the Guardian or you jostled the thing. Or it may have been a wave. But I fell, and I think I hit my head on something down there. And when I was able to sit up again, we were already well away from the shore. And here we are."

There was silence for several seconds over the ceaseless sweeping sounds of their passage. "Do you expect me to believe that?"

"There it is – your belief or disbelief will not alter the facts a whit. And the fact remains that I am being carried away from the Village against my will."

"And mine. But under the circumstances, you may understand my reluctance to put about. I assure you, I intend to set you ashore at the earliest opportunity."

"Surely, Number Six, you can't expect to succeed in this mad adventure!"

"*The scheme is rash and well may fail, but ours are not the hearts that quail, the hands that shrink, the cheeks that pale in hours of need,*" he sang. "And you can stop calling me Number Six now – we're past the three-mile limit. You know my name – what's yours?"

"Number Six, this is insane. I insist –"

The engine died. Easily, quietly, and with one feeble kick, the engine died. The boat lurched as it lost way, and veered slightly to port with the breeze from land.

Number 6 pressed the starter, and the electric motor under the bonnet whined and strained, but the engine did not fire. It was as though the ignition were switched off. He kept trying to start, varying manipulation of the foot throttle and choke until they were dead in the water, drifting gently with the ebbing tide, and the great silence of the sea rose around them.

Even Number 2's rasping voice seemed somehow hushed, if none the less indignant. "Now look what you've got us into! And you don't even have a radio in this thing – how will anyone find us?"

"At least you admit they're looking. You should also know better than I how they will find us. Infrared seems most likely, though I imagine the metal of the car would stand out to radar."

"You continually assume that I know everything. There is a great deal of ocean, Number Six – we shall probably have to spend at least one night and day in this cockleshell before we're rescued. I trust your hospitality will extend over that period, especially considering the consequences if you are found without me."

"You're an important figure, Number Two – surely the Village will not let you spend an unsheltered night at sea with a homicidal madman."

"Come, come – you're putting words into my mouth. I never implied that you killed thoughtlessly or needlessly – merely professionally. You seem to have a great deal of guilt concealed around that subject, you know – really far too much. And the feeling is perfectly normal for someone with an upbringing like yours – the conflicting concepts of your ingrained moral ethos telling you your patriotic duty and your human responsibilities were irreconcilably opposed, and you opted for the easy path, the selfish path. And you kept it up as long as you could, knowing it was wrong, hating yourself more with every death on your conscience. Because only the first two were really hard. The third was almost easy, and the fourth was meaningless. It seemed strange how casually you could become accustomed to snuffing out human life." Number 2's voice remained cool and clinical. He did not look at his subject.

"But of course, you couldn't keep it up forever – no one could and still remain remotely sane. You have a remarkable instinct for self-preservation; your resignation came just before you were to have been ordered to Argentina."

"I would really rather hear *your* life story, Number Two – I know my own fairly well. Up until last summer, I should say; portions since then have been somewhat confused. But you could tell me about that, too, couldn't you. You may as well – if you'll pardon my saying so, we're in the same boat and likely to remain so for several hours at least. I don't play cards, I am not fond of word games, riddles, or ghost stories. But I dote on detailed reminiscences. Tell me your life story, Number Two, since you already know mine. What has brought you to this place, at this time?"

"This is really –"

"Start at the beginning. Leave nothing out. No, you can omit your primary schooling – it's written all over you."

"My school, it may interest you to know, took your school at rugger three years out of four while I was there."

"Ah. So you were three years ahead of me."

"No – five. Look! Over there!"

Sweeping spotlights fanned out from a distant power launch bearing towards them, and the stutter of the diesels carried faintly over the intervening waves.

"*At least a night and a day*, I believe you said? Really, Number Two, you underestimate your own minions. Why, it's hardly been half an hour. You've been marvellous at helping pass the time, but I'm afraid I can't afford to wait. . . ." He stood up on the seat. "You can keep the car – there's land about a mile away, and I intend to try for it."

"Against the tide? You'd never make it. I'm almost embarrassed to have to curtail your dramatic gesture, but I feel I should point out there is a Guardian directly beneath you, and whichever way you swim, it will bring you back here and keep you here until the Rescue Unit arrives. So why not leave your shoes on and save yourself a useless drenching?"

The glare of the searchlight splayed him against the darkness like a projected image before he dropped back into the seat and heaved an almost inaudible sigh.

Nothing further was said until the launch pulled alongside them and dropped a ladder. An amplified voice echoed over them: "*Stand by to be taken in tow. Would you care to come aboard?*" A rope sailed over the side in a flying coil to drape ten slack feet across the bonnet and the far gunwale. "*Make it fast,*" the voice advised, and Number 2 scrambled over the windscreen to obey.

Number 6 stood, and looked over the side of his captured boat. The black waters could have concealed a fleet of submarines, and very likely did hold at least one animate spheroid, but he had little to lose. He rose to his feet as Number 2 stooped out of sight to secure the hawser to his front bumper, braced his hands on the edge of the door and took two deep breaths.

As he lifted one foot to the edge, the waters below him roiled silently in the moonlight and a ghostly pale shape appeared just below the surface, almost brushing his keel. He let out his third breath and replaced his foot on the seat. He would call a bluff, but he could also recognise a lost hand and fold it to await the next deal.

"*Number Six,*" repeated the amplified voice, "*would you care to come aboard?"*

Number 2 stood up and waved at the launch which rose and fell gently beside them. "Yes, certainly," he called back. "We'll be right there. I think this is snug . . . er, belayed."

He squeezed between the side of the car and the hull towards where a short ladder came down from the bigger boat. "Aren't you going to 'give up the ship,' captain?" he asked Number 6. "Or do you prefer to ride back into port on the end of a towrope?" He waited a few seconds, then shrugged and turned to the launch. "Go ahead," he called up to the shadowed deck. "We'll follow you in."

The mutter of the twin diesels deepened its pulse and the launch moved slowly ahead of them, easing into the slack of the towrope as Number 2 flopped into the passenger seat again. "Really, Number Six, you can't expect to just keep sitting there. You have taken absolutely no part in your own rescue; you refuse the hospitality of your rescuers and obviously do not intend to thank them."

"I don't really feel they deserve my thanks. As for going aboard your yacht, I frankly feel safer in a boat I built myself."

"*Our* engines don't just die, Number Six. No, you hate to give up your role, even though your one-and-a-half ton twenty-footer isn't much of a prize at the moment. You are too sensitive to the trappings of power, I think – even when you have relinquished effective command you cling to your position as Captain of the Good Ship . . . What is her name, by the way? I don't recall the launching ceremonies too clearly."

"This thing? You accuse me of clinging to a title, but you seem to be more prone to labelling things. My boat, my cat – do you expect me to have pet names for my shirts as well?"

"It's considered a normal human trait to anthropomorphise certain types of things – perhaps I had forgotten you are less prone to 'normal human traits' than most of us. Labels may not be as necessary to you as to me; labels are tools for communication, and you seem reticent to the point of taciturnity, especially when you suspect me of something. You seem almost afraid to speak during times of emotional stress. You are a lonely man, Number Six. You hold yourself apart from everything. Why? Why, Number Six?"

The roar of engines eased ahead of them, and they slowed as the rope went slack. The launch began backing water, taking up the line. Moments later the amplified voice spoke again across the moonlit water. "*Number Two, stand by to come aboard.*"

Making a trumpet of his hands with one elbow braced over the top of the windscreen, Number 2 called, "Thank you, no – I'm quite comfortable here."

"*We are taking you aboard, Number Two. There is an important call for you.*"

"It can wait."

The stern of the launch drew alongside them, this time on the port side, a short rope ladder dangling beside Number 2.

"I think they want you to go aboard," said Number 6.

"Well – it *is* chilly out here.... Will you come if I do, Number Six? Please? Your boat will be in the safest of hands. I'll go first and you can pass the cat up to me."

"The cat? Where is the cat?"

"I thought you had him. Well, he couldn't have gone overboard. Perhaps he jumped to the launch while I was attaching the towrope. Now come along up like a good fellow. I'm sure you'll have that engine running like a watch in no time – and it'll stay that way as long as it doesn't come too near the water, I promise you."

Reluctantly, facing the inevitable with patience and fortitude, he stood and followed Number 2, spurning the extended hand and climbing the four wooden slats alone.

As the launch picked up speed slowly to tauten the tow with professional smoothness, a glowing television screen in the main cabin showed a face which one of the two castaways recognised.

"Number Four – thank you for getting this launch out to us so –"

"I am the new Number Two. You are, effective as of this moment of notification and pending full investigation, Number One-hundred."

Number 100's face went slack. "You – you cannot assume this authority without ... without confirmation! This is unprecedented!"

"Not at all. You assumed your recent post when our beloved Number Six defected, pending full investigation which later proved you justified. As for my designation, officially I am Two Prime. But my friends," he added meaningfully, "call me Number Two."

Number 100 seemed staggered. "But – but on what grounds can you possibly base this impossible action?"

"Their full extent has yet to come to light. But the most obvious include conspiracy, assorted charges of treason and attempting unauthorised departure by stealth."

"And piracy," Number 6 suggested.

"That is impossible! I was kidnapped! Number Six – you will admit you did not receive my aid in your suicidal scheme; I was trying to dissuade him from it when –"

"Save your defence for the hearing, Number One-hundred. If anything Number Six might say could be admitted as evidence, use will be made of him. You are remanded to the custody of the Rescue Unit – Number Seventy-seven, you will follow the usual procedure." And the screen went dark.

As it did there was some trouble in the stern, and the launch seemed to lose way. Another voice called, "Slow! She's sprung a leak!"

Number 6 hurried back to the rail in time to see his craft, his days and months of work and care, his hour of freedom, yawing fiercely at the end of a hawser, nosing down sluggishly in the swells and rolling with them.

"She's shipping water," said someone in a natty cap. "I don't know how long we can keep her afloat."

Number 100's voice was at his elbow, subdued, bitter. "So we have both lost that which we most prized, that which represented our greatest labours. You could have driven happily on your track. You didn't have to take your beautiful car out to sea in your perishing fibreglass sieve – and now you're going to lose it in fifty fathoms of salt water!"

"Seven fathoms, sir," said someone. "We're only a mile or so out now."

"We may have to cut it loose," said someone else. "It seems to be going all to pieces. Looks like the towing is too much strain on the hull."

The power launch lost way and the towrope dipped back into the water. "Can we keep it afloat?" asked one of the crew. "It'll hold us like a sea-anchor as fast as it goes under."

"Keep a steady thousand RPM," said Number 77. "We'll take it in as far as we can."

The rope lifted taut, and stretched to drag the nose of the wallowing derelict momentarily clear of the waves which threatened to swamp it. But the prow barely rose before lurching forward again, and they could feel the sudden drag on the launch.

"Stand by to release tow," said Number 77. "Sorry, Number Six, but we can't possibly make it in with the dragging. If we had floatation chambers we could buoy it up, but ..."

"Number Two, you could order a Guardian to come up under it."

"I am not Number Two, I am Number One-hundred; I cannot order myself a sandwich, let alone a Guardian; we are well inside the ring of submerged stations and the things aren't that manoeuvrable under water; and a ton or more would crush it directly back to the bottom, since they have only a few hundred pounds practical buoyancy. Other than these minor objections, your idea was a nice bit of creative thinking." Number 100's voice betrayed his bitterness.

The launch continued to slog towards shore, pausing and lunging against its load as the waves gripped and released the sinking hulk. Ahead, the lights of shore danced on the waters, and a white line of surf rose and fell in the moonlight against the dark deserted strand.

"It's going under," called someone from the flying bridge, and Number 77 said regretfully, "We'll have to cut it loose, Number Six. There's no way we could get it back to shore now."

"Could you float a marker over it?" asked Number 6.

"Certainly. Perhaps it could be salvaged."

His craft was now obviously beyond saving – it settled in the water even as he watched. The launch reversed as a crewman tied a yellow plastic can to a line, and they came alongside as wavelets began slopping over the thwarts. Cold, dark, corrosive seawater was lapping around the blind headlamps and almost to the tops of the doors. As a crewman leaned over to affix the marker buoy and sever the towrope Number 6 turned from the rail into the darkness of the deck.

Moments later the twin screws resumed their mutter and in the white noise of the wash astern he could not distinguish the slow, sucking gurgle of water surging over the sides of a sinking coracle. In his mind he concentrated on a single point – it had gone down dead level. He'd had it balanced precisely. Next time ...

Number 77 conducted him directly to his flat and saw him in. When he had gone, Number 6 tried the front door. It was immovable, as was the kitchen door. He picked up his telephone handset.

"Number Four," he said.

There was a pause. "That Number has been changed, sir. You are calling

Number Two Prime. I will connect you."

In a moment his television screen glowed to life. "I was expecting you to call directly, Number Six," he said. "First, I must apologise for the loss of your construction. We understand your emotional state of involvement with it, and are prepared to make it up to you. However, I am afraid you will not find me as approachable as my predecessor; your requests to me must pass through the proper channels. You will no longer be able to walk into my office at will."

"I shall miss those excellent tea-biscuits. The bakery doesn't stock them, you know."

"They may if properly approached. But you will be expected to behave yourself in the future, Number Six, or shortages may be expected to appear in various stocks."

"Behave myself? Number Two Prime, I intend to leave you undisturbed as soon as I have your permission to salvage my car. I shall need at least a set of diving apparatus, two floatation chambers and a boat of some kind. I can do the job myself, and you can watch me every minute to your heart's content. I shall shortly want a wagon, or truck, capable of carrying the salvage to my workshop."

Number 2 stared out of the screen at him.

"Let's not bump heads, Number Two Prime. I don't know what I could find to keep me occupied if I were to become overwrought with the loss of all those months of work. But I'm afraid my feelings toward the Village in general and yourself in particular are not especially *mutual* at the moment."

"Without your euphemisms, are you phrasing a threat?"

"Yes. I want my car back. I am willing to do all the work, but I can't do it barehanded and I will risk a great deal to get the tools for the job."

"You wouldn't dare cause too much trouble. You have already come closer than you know to neutralisation. With the slightest effort I could have you converted to Number Four-oh-six, with your entire personality reduced to so much suet. How would you feel about pushing a broom the rest of your life, Number Six? I can tell you now that you wouldn't mind it – you wouldn't mind much of anything after a few weeks of re-education so you could feed and dress yourself. Now have dinner and go to bed. Tomorrow buy yourself a needlework set and forget about your sunken treasure."

"Tomorrow evening I shall be comfortably in bed when your Green Dome catches fire and burns to the ground. Or I can start picking off your television cameras, one by one. Or I may even go out hunting Guardians with a sharp stick. Or distributing revolutionary pamphlets in the Village Square. Because I don't think you dare to damage me permanently. You are still only Two Prime, and I can tell you right now that I intend to call your bluff. I'll even wager that I could force you to destroy me against your will, and I really don't think you can afford to let that happen. All I want is an opportunity to salvage what I can, subject to the conditions already stated. Your investment and risk will be small."

Number 2 remained carefully expressionless. "We will have to take your proposal under advisement, Number Six. There is no precedent . . ."

"There are countless precedents for Villagers working on their own projects with Village help. As for thinking it over, every minute under the water means more damage to my engine. Tomorrow I must start devoting my full effort to one cause or the other – if I can't raise my car, then I will raise the very devil!"

"Don't push it, Number Six. There is no way you could start this . . . project tonight. With-hold your violent reprisals until tomorrow, at the least. It's late. Everyone is in bed."

"I will call for your final word at nine in the morning. Silence will be taken to mean refusal."

"Number Six, you don't seem to care for other people's problems. You are also dangerously peremptory for someone in your position."

"That may be – if you have any punishment you think will be effective under the circumstances, I invite you to try it. If I haven't heard from you by nine tomorrow morning, I'll call for your decision. Be seeing you." And so saying, he rang off.

Only then, as he walked out to the kitchen, did he realise his knees were shaking slightly. True visceral anger was a rare experience to him, and he found it less than pleasant. It was deeper and harder to direct than the cold intellectual anger which drove him night and day; it became dangerously elemental.

As he prescribed himself a stiff drink and dinner, he realised he had also come closer than he liked to admit to losing his temper. Even so, his decision stood logically. There would inevitably come a time, sooner or later, when he would have to force the Village to reveal itself or destroy him. Or free him. And now was as good a time as any.

A faint sound from the back door attracted his attention, and he put his ear to the panel. The cat seemed to be outside, meowing for admittance. He tried the latch, but it was still immovable. So he was locked in and the cat was locked out, at least until morning. Maybe they would keep him imprisoned here until they decided his violent period had passed.

He refilled his glass as he returned to the living-room. A cold draught made him turn to see the kitchen door closing silently as the black cat stepped unhurriedly over the threshold. When he tried the latch manually ten seconds later, it was again fixed.

One of the lessons the Village had taught him was patience in the face of helpless frustration – he did not even scowl as he refilled his glass and returned to the living room. The cat was standing in his chair, kneading the cushion with its forepaws. As he approached, it sprang lightly to the arm of the chair and balanced as he seated himself. It looked over its shoulder at him, then stepped carefully into his lap, one foot at a time. He rested his free hand on its head, and it butted up into his palm and began to purr. He was hardly aware of the distant sounds of London, muffled by the rain outside his windows, as he dozed in the armchair for half an hour before going to bed.

At precisely 9.00 by the tower bell, his front door chime sounded. Number 94 lounged against the doorpost, clipboard and ballpoint in hand; in the back of his electric truck were five bulky parcels.

"Number Two gave me to understand you would be ready at nine o'clock," he said. "I'm to run you and your gear down to the beach and stand by if you want any help."

"I'll appreciate the lift – you can probably bring me back here when I've looked over the job and found out what tools I'll need." He ran a mental checklist – lights, stove, windows – as he drew the door to and felt it latch.

He squatted in the back examining his loot during the cobblestoned ride down winding Village paths, while Number 94 tooted at passers-by. There were three military surplus self-inflation life-rafts, all still packaged; one had rowlocks and oars. All three opened automatically when water dissolved a protective seal. The fourth and fifth bundles were a complete wet-suit with accoutrements and two fully charged tanks of air. He leaned forward and addressed the driver. "Number Ninety-four –"

"Oh, he said the wagon would be ready when you are; I can bring it down to the beach for you."

"Thank you, but I'll only want you to run me back to my place and make a stop or two after I make a preliminary dive. I probably shan't want the wagon until past noon."

They parked two of the collapsed rubber rafts against the seawall, and Number 94 was set down to guard them. From the beach Number 6 could see the bright marker buoy, a yellow fleck against a grey–green sea. His first job would be to dive down to the wreck and study its position. If the bottom was firm and the wreck easily accessible from all sides as he hoped, he could have it afloat quickly and hope that the lubricants in the engine had afforded adequate protection during the immersion.

The bathing machines were vacant at this hour – he took the wet-suit into the nearest and emerged twelve minutes later wearing the dull black second skin. He hoisted the third raft with its oars under his arm and strolled boldly down the beach.

Knee-deep in the gentle waves, he shifted the oars to his left arm and tossed the rubber packet twenty feet out, beyond the edge of the surf. In seconds it grew, sections popping and puffing to full firmness as he splashed out to clamber into it.

Unshipping the oars, he rose to his knees on the rubber mid-seat and squinted across the water to sight the marker buoy nearly half a mile out from the shore in thirty feet of water. The sky was bright and the water clear – considering the depth, he could probably have done the job without the compressed air, but it would have taken longer. And time was his worst enemy now.

It took ten minutes to scull out to the marker; when he made the rubber raft fast to it he adjusted the belt of weights around his waist, took the mouthpiece between his teeth and drew a lungful of cool stale air before settling the mask down over his face and rolling backwards off the edge.

He sank slowly feet first. As the bubbles cleared around him he saw the line a few feet away extending down to a dark shape beneath him. He gripped the rope and accelerated his movement downward, swaying lightly to the faint regular surge of the water past the float above, feeling the soft fist of pressure squeezing his chest.

He swallowed hard to clear his ears and blew a little water out of the mouthpiece as he neared the bottom. There the derelict lay, still pointed towards shore, scarcely a drift of sand around the wheels of the drowned car which still stood squarely amid a bare wire-mesh framework.

He squinted through the dimness. Yes, the wires were bare. The painstakingly applied, supposedly impervious fibreglass they had sold him seemed to have dissolved in the seawater. It had been formed and solidified around that wire mesh, and soaked with "epoxy resin" – either it had totally dissolved or they had substituted an absolutely perfect replica of his frame, complete with a shimmering, quivering mass in the frame of the rear deck: fifty gallons of petrol still trapped in a tough plastic bag.

He studied the position of the car on the sea floor – and then noticed the floor itself, which not only bore no vegetation and concealed no visible marine life, but which, except for a slight wash of sand here and there, was nearly as smooth and clean as the floor of a swimming pool.

The bottom was hard, so his first plan still looked best. But his salvage scheme changed slightly; instead of taking everything with him this afternoon, he would leave the hull framework behind along with anything that would not be damaged by another day's immersion. He wanted an excuse to come back later and study this eerily empty world. A barrier somewhere must keep out the omnipresent life of the sea; even if this unnaturally bare floor gave no foothold for anchoring life-forms there should have been plankton and fish.

Now every minute his engine spent under water meant added hours of labour before he could drive it again. He had finished his evaluation; the last details of his plan came clear in his mind as he shot back up the long rope from where his car waited on the bottom.

Number 94 was lounging in the morning sunshine on top of the seawall with his straw hat over his eyes as Number 6 splashed ashore, dragging his raft up the sand above the line of the surf. He paused to shed his weights and tanks and replace his flippers with unstockinged sneakers, then trotted up to the electric cart. "Back to my place," he ordered. "I'll need a few things. And I want to stop by the Ironmonger's – I have a few quick purchases to make."

The cart hummed to a halt under the tree by the Village smithy, and Number 6 stepped out on to the bricks. Inside the shop Number 26 stood to greet him.

"I want about a hundred and fifty feet of quarter-inch cable and a dozen – no, two dozen thimbles."

"You're certainly the busy one," said the shopkeeper. "Always a project going." He found the heavy cable-cutters and crossed to the racked drums of ropes and cables. "That's a lot of cable – building a suspension bridge?" He chuckled at his own pleasantry.

"No," said his customer succinctly. "I'm floating a sunken ship."

"Do tell!" the other marvelled. "Well, I've got about a hundred and twenty or thirty feet left here on this one – would that do? I could cut into another roll for you if you want, but I'd sooner not."

"One hundred and twenty or thirty will be fine; I'd sooner have it spooled. You can put all this on my account, of course – and here is a sack for the thimbles." Number 26 counted out the small U-shaped bolts, threaded on both legs with a bar bolted between them. "Fine – be seeing you."

Back into the electric cart, lugging a massive spool of cable under one arm, Number 6 said, "Now go directly round to my workshop. I'll just need to pick up a couple of tools."

Still slightly clumsy in the wet-suit, he padded into his garage and spent most of a minute finding a ratchet socket wrench to fit the nuts on the thimble he held, and a bolt-cutter capable of shearing quarter-inch cable. He also cut two lengths of twine four feet long, and six inches of heavy insulating tape and took them all with him back to the cart.

"Now – back to the beach, and you can help me carry a few things."

As they drove, he busied himself fashioning the two lengths of twine into safety lines from both the socket wrench and the bolt-cutter to his belt. He was done and satisfied by the time they arrived at the foot of the cement ramp.

There were a few people on the beach by now, since it was past ten o'clock, but none of them paid much attention to the un-numbered man in the black wet-suit and his sportily dressed assistant carrying things down to the surf near the south end of the beach. They loaded the heavy spool of cable into the raft, which sagged alarmingly but held; added a heavy paper sack and two dull rubber bundles and a pair of large hand-tools on cords. Then with less help from Number 94, who didn't want to get his shoes wet, the raft was set afloat again.

Number 6 spent the next ten minutes rowing back out to the marker buoy and anchoring there again. For half an hour he worked with cable and cutters, thimbles and wrench.

Measuring the cable off the spool in double arm-spreads like a haberdasher, he formed a loop of twelve feet and clipped it with three thimbles. The U-shaped bolts fitted over the paired cables and had a crossbar tightened down over the open end by two nuts which could be snugged down in seconds with the socket wrench in his other hand. The closed ends of the thimbles passed around the short side of the loop; the long side ran out twelve feet more to its free end. He made four of these, then tossed them over the side.

Last, he carefully tore the insulating tape into four pieces and stuck two of them over the soluble seal on each of the uninflated rafts. Then he untied the cable-cutters from his belt and attached them to a loop on the raft, adjusted his mask and mouthpiece, and tightly rolled the paper bag which now contained a dozen thimbles, to squeeze excess air out. He gripped it around the wrench in his left hand, clamped his right over his mask to secure it, and rolled himself backwards over the side.

His four loops of cable lay half draped over the hulk of his car and its open-work hull. He started at once with the first loop, threading its free end around the nearest wheel, looping it snugly and clamping it with three more thimbles, his socket wrench tightening the nuts in quick, bright arcs. He moved to the next wheel, took the nearest free end of cable and did it all again. In ten minutes he had all four placed and connected, working with a fierce concentration in the dim light, soundless save for the drumming of his blood in his ears, the preternaturally sharp muffled clicks of his wrench and the alternate thunder and hiss of his slow, regular breathing.

Then back to the surface, pausing halfway up to swallow and yawn as well as possible through a demand valve. He stuck his head and an arm over the edge of the bobbing raft just long enough to grab the two rubber parcels, then doubled over and surface-dived, clutching them both in his arms. They fought the descent, but he kicked steadily downwards, breathing more rapidly until he reached the bottom again. There, gripping one package between his knees, he knotted the handrope of the other around the near front loop of cable. That temporarily secured, he let it bob up and took the other to the other side. There he drew both large loops of cable together around the raft and tied the handrope around both of them, arranging the raft so that when it opened, it would be upside down within the loops. Then, both hands freed, he went back and did the same with the first.

Now all was in place. He took off the handbrake, then bent to the nearer raft. He picked at the tape over the soluble seal with a fingernail until a corner came free, then pulled at it. In seconds the bundle began to unfold, slowly, because of the water pressure. As it did so, he swam around to the other and removed its seal as well. The irregular thuds of collapsed sections opening out beat against the eardrums as the compressed CO_2 fought the weight of the water to a compromise. They wouldn't be able to inflate fully under an atmosphere and a half, but they would buoy the weight enough so that he could lift it. Submerged, it couldn't have a dead weight of much over five hundred pounds, and if he could once get it moving upwards the rafts would begin to expand and increase their lift until he might be in danger of being sucked to the surface so quickly he could burst a lung.

When the second raft started to inflate, he swam back to the first. Bracing his feet against the sides of the car, he manhandled the flabby, struggling lump of rubber-trapped gas until it was roughly centred in its two loops of cable and hung half-folded, like a doughy puptent sagging upward as it continued to grow slowly.

Then back to the second raft. Already half-inflated, it had not fallen into the correct position. The aft cable was too close to the centre and slipping forward. More expanding gas swelled the larger end, threatening to pull free of its harness.

He kicked once and was above the wreck, already rocking with the lift of the under-inflated rafts. Taking the loop of cable in both hands, he drove his legs downward into the dense, springy mass of the float. Dragging the cable astern over the quivering evasive surface, he snagged it around a handhold two-thirds of the way back and got his fingers out of the way as he let it down gently and kicked free. It looked as if it should hold.

The wreck was almost ready to lift free off the seabed. It took many seconds to pick apart the water-swollen knot that held the marker buoy line to the bumper and refasten it to the hull frame. This done, he swam under one tentlike inverted raft and allowed a few cubic feet of his exhalation bubbles to collect in it, then swam around to the other and repeated the action.

It was stirring now – once it started up, it would accelerate as the water pressure decreased and the swelling rafts displaced more and more. He crouched cautiously by the front bumper, steadied himself, and lifted. It wasn't heavy, but it was massive. It gave perceptibly – it swayed and rose and he felt his legs straighten as the huge affair rocked and drew up, floating slowly at first, then falling away from him faster to soar gracefully into the light-hazed reaches of the upper depths above.

Suction pulled about him, but he clung to the framework until the dusty mirror of the surface far above shattered to greenish-white. Then he took a breath, opened his throat and kicked off for the top. Air surged from his lungs in an endless rush, expanding freely as he shot towards the daylight above. He was still ten feet below the dark cloud of his salvage structure when his lungs were empty, and he kicked twice more before his head broke the surface and he gulped cool fresh air along with a few droplets of spray.

He scrambled aboard his raft and shed the mask, weights, flippers and tank. There was half an hour's air left, and he had other uses for it. He sculled his raft around to shoreward of the car, which rode half-submerged between the bulky faded-orange waterwings that bracketed it, then pulled ten more feet of cable from the nearly empty spool. After anchoring the drum securely around a stern cleat in the raft, he made the free end fast to the bumper half a yard beneath the surface, leaning over the comfortably soft and sun-warmed rubber stern. Then he picked up the oars and began a slow steady stroke towards shore, just stirring the great mass that hung in the water behind him.

It was more than half an hour until, palms worn half raw and forearms throbbing, he felt the suck and slide of the surf behind him. He rested his oars and twisted on the seat, feeling his spine crack, to look over his shoulder.

It was nearly noon, and the tide was almost out. For a wonder, Number 94 had been paying attention. The promised wagon was waiting, with block and tackle and a small windlass, on the hardpacked sand at the edge of the surf.

He turned again to his oars with a different stroke. Now he pulled with the lift of each wave and fought its draw until he felt the scrape and drag of his burden brushing the sandy bottom. If the wheels still turned . . .

Another swell lifted it, and he pulled twice on the oars and gained five feet before his load grounded and bumped – and rolled. He shipped the oars and took the cable spool. Rising to his knees, he shook the last loops free and tossed it, unreeling, towards the shore from the peak of the next wave. Number 94 caught it and connected the bare end to the windlass.

In fifteen minutes the car was lashed to the low sturdy frame of the wagon behind the heaviest-duty electric cart available in the Village. The tower clock had not yet chimed the hour of 1.00 when it was let down again in front of Number 6's workshop. White crusts of salt rimed the drying body.

Without removing his wet-suit, Number 6 connected the garden hose to the houseside tap and turned it on his car. That salt had to be washed off as quickly as possible and fresh water was the best way, since its corrosive effect would be minuscule compared to that of the seawater. His KAR had been under water less than eighteen hours – if the lubricating oil hadn't dissolved, he could still save the engine, though he would have to disassemble it and clean it piece by piece. The engine should have had time to cool off before the sinking, so the block might still be sound. And still the challenge remained to determine what conditions were result and which cause of the unexplained failure of his engine. Only the symptoms he'd observed had given any clue. . . .

"Number Six – what about the rest of your junk? Your diving gear – and all those rafts you left lying on the beach?" Number 94 stood by the electric cart, watching him disinterestedly.

"They're well above the tide line. I shall want them tomorrow when I go down to bring up the hull frame. If you would be good enough to leave my things here – yes, right there will be fine – and call for me tomorrow morning at ten, I shall finish my salvage project and clear the area. Mind the hose!"

"Sorry. Good afternoon, Number Six – ten o'clock."

"Be seeing you."

He spent the next two hours working steadily. The KAR had to be put up on blocks so the wheels could be removed; the engine had to be laid open and stripped to its component elements. Bearings had to be extracted, washed, inspected minutely, carefully re-oiled and reassembled. Only the washing and drying must be done this afternoon – the rest of it could easily take him a few weeks. Possibly even many weeks. And what would happen then would depend on what happened before then.

The next morning he heard the 10.30 chime faintly across the water from the shore as he made his raft fast to the bobbing yellow marker buoy above the spot where he hoped the framework of his craft still lay, unless the aluminium bracing and steel screening had dissolved overnight as his "fibreglass" had.

He checked the tanks again – about half an hour's air. Skip-breathing could extend it to forty or forty-five minutes; there were no currents in this sterile sea and nowhere he could go too deep to return to the surface on his last lungful of air. He flushed his lungs with the last free oxygen he'd have until his bottled supply ran out or he found what he was looking for – and since he didn't know what he was looking for, the former seemed more likely. At any rate, he would have time to finish, dry and dress before lunch. Clamping a hand over his mask and gripping the mouthpiece between his teeth, he rolled backwards off the edge of the raft.

He came out of the roll head down and stroked for the bottom, drawing a long deep breath as he shot into the green immensities below and the light faded above him. There was the framework of his hull – the shore was *that* way – the first thing to do would be head straight out to seek the boundary that kept the infinitely viable life of the sea from this small bay.

Arms straight to his sides, legs straight and kicking smoothly, six feet above the bottom he bored through the unresisting water into featureless obscurities. Breathing in sips, holding each for ten seconds; *kick–kick–kick–kick–kick–kick–kick–kick (breathe) kick–kick–kick–kick–kick–kick–kick–kick (breathe)* . . . Wisps and curls of sand slid silently by beneath him, the only visible indication of his progress. Minutes passed. He must have been a mile from shore when something else appeared dimly ahead of him – a silent pale shape, large and indistinct.

As it approached, he forgot to release his last breath. Twenty feet away in the eerie green twilight he could make out the quivering, gelatinoid blob of a Guardian under pressure. It had compressed irregularly, like a half-empty balloon, in huge wrinkles which shifted and rippled like wind-driven grass as it fought through the water towards him, somehow maintaining a neutral buoyancy against all natural tendencies.

He couldn't distinguish its exact colour through the water – whether it was a killer or a herder. Since it was less likely to encounter Villagers down here than invading sea life, it was more likely to be a scavenger of anything organic that came beyond the beach and the proper swimming area. It wasn't a hunter; its movements were too slow, even as it seemed to sense him and start vaguely towards him. He twisted in the water and kicked away from it, leaving a cloud of exhaled bubbles fluttering upwards out of sight.

So the floor of this doubtful ocean was not left unwatched after all. Nor was it totally deserted, since the presence of the Guardian presupposed a need for it. But there was no evidence it had ever been called upon to function before – for that matter, he couldn't even be certain it had sensed him before he steered away from it.

He had taken off at roughly a right-angle to his left, which meant he should be paralleling the shore towards the headland to the south of the Village. It extended most of a hundred yards from the beach, so he should pass well seaward of it, but for the fact that it marked the southern boundary of the Village. Whatever defence preserved this shallow bay most likely came to land there. When he reached it, he could follow it in.

He swam swiftly, efficiently. *Kick–kick–kick–kick–kick–kick–kick–kick (breathe) kick–kick–kick–kick–kick–kick–kick–kick (breathe)* . . . His eyes scanned the visible area of the bottom for cracks, fissures, jetsam or any markings besides the endless calligraphy of lightly drifted sand constantly rewritten by gentle currents across the bottom. There was no evidence of any barrier at the surface – he must have been well beyond the Village boundary when they'd turned him back, and he had seen nothing. How far below the surface did it end? His boat had drawn three or four feet and hadn't touched anything. What could it be?

He broke himself away from the almost hypnotic fascination of the tangled non-pattern, the rhythmic beat of his legs and shallow breathing, for a glance at his wristwatch. He'd been swimming for seven minutes since he'd seen the Guardian – nearly half a mile. He should have come to the barrier by this time. Perhaps he had angled nearly parallel to it – without a compass, directions were uncertain. He had little more than half his air left; rather than waste it in a blind search, he kicked for the surface where he could re-orient himself.

When his head broke water, the glare of the midday sun blinded him briefly. When his eyes cleared, he could see nothing ahead of him but the foreshortened swells of the ocean. He seemed to be alone in the centre of an empty circle. With a kick and a twist, he swung about and saw his own yellow marker buoy some fifty feet away and the familiar beach and cottage-clustered hills beyond to the right. Instead of swimming parallel to the shore, he had somehow turned farther left than he intended and wound up nearly back at his starting point.

Still, fifteen minutes of air had not been totally wasted; even negative evidence could be useful data. Now what of his other fifteen minutes? Skip-breathing would stretch it to twenty or twenty-five; he could make it to South Point and back with a little margin. If he ran dry suddenly he could finish the return on the surface. It didn't especially matter if Number 2 saw him coming *back* from the border.

He took a careful sight on the tip of the promontory where it jutted out to rocks awash with waves. Then he dived like an otter to five feet below the surface, and swam with an eye on the dancing image of the sun to keep him headed roughly south. The bottom was likely to look the same as far as he went, and the shallow depth would deplete his air supply only half as rapidly.

After five minutes, he could hear waves shattering on the rocks and grinding pebbles to sand. The sound was peculiarly sharp and insistent, as all underwater sounds are; it guided him as it grew and the featureless plane beneath him rose and began to sprout natural-looking protuberances.

Now the waves were beginning to pull at him; he bore to the right away from them and noticed it was beginning to become slightly harder to breathe. Only about ten minutes of air left. If he used the last breath in the tanks on this quest, he would have to salvage his fifty gallons of petrol and the steel-and-aluminium framework which could still prove the key to his escape by free diving which did not particularly appeal to him. He could hold out here another five minutes and go back entirely on the surface, which meant much more work, and still have enough underwater time left to drop the ballasted keel which held the hulk to the bottom.

Where was he now? The endless applause of the rocks was behind him, the floor out of sight below. He angled downwards and away from the shore. And there was something on the bottom – dark, and round. . . . He stroked downward, feeling air force itself into his open lungs to balance the growing pressure on his ribs.

It wasn't something – it was a hole. A hole, six or more feet across – apparent sizes are deceptive underwater. He couldn't see its sides, or anything inside.

Then he heard another sound, building – a rush and burbling roar as of volumes of water rushing in and great bubbles surging upward towards the light. He beat his arms forward and swerved aside as something appeared below him.

Up from the opening came a glittering silvery mass, shaking with compressed energy, leaping past him, splitting into pair and multiple, trailing small eager miniatures of itself, accompanied by more leaping bubbles and finally in the midst of all, a pastel sphere which sprang for the surface.

Turbulence twisted him and flung him upwards in their wake. Air vomited from his lungs as pressures equalised, and he regained his equalibrium several feet below the bobbing, searching Guardian which he had apparently set off. It meant he would have to cover at least some of the distance back submerged – he rolled over and blew out through his nose to clear his mask of the water it had shipped during that brief violent rise, and then lifted the face plate just clear of the surface long enough to take a quick orientation from the promontory; then sank, turned and struck out for home. He sank to a cruising depth of five feet, laid his arms back, locked his feet together, kicking rapidly from the knees, rolling his hips and torso in the spine-aching spring of the dolphin kick. Skip-breathing lightly, he shot north with the sun's warmth faintly perceptible on his back.

He swam thus for two minutes, then surfaced and rolled over to look behind him for the Guardian. It was gone. He cut off his tank valve and spat out the mouthpiece. From here on it was straight Australian crawl for five minutes more.

He flopped into his raft and lay limply in the bottom for several minutes before he stirred. The pressure in the tank was dangerously low, but he had only a minute or two of work to do on the bottom and he might have as much as three minutes of air left. He lashed the wrench to his belt again, adjusted his mask, bit on the mouthpiece and rolled overboard for the last time.

It was becoming an effort to draw air into his lungs by the time he reached the bottom. He pulled himself down to the smooth stony floor of the lifeless sea and slid under the canted curve of the hull frame with his wrench extended to seek out the three bolts that held the ballast section in place. Since three hundred pounds of petrol and trapped air displaced some four hundred pounds of seawater, the resultant lift would carry his wire-mesh hull aloft nearly as rapidly as his expanding life-rafts.

His chest was beginning to ache with the strain of breathing from the depleted tank. He groped in the dimness for each nut and fumbled the wrench to grip them and turn. The first came out easily, as the frame was still held rigid. But the whole mass shifted microscopically as the second nut gave, and the bolt seemed suddenly fixed in place. He pushed at it with the handle of the wrench, then kicked at the handle to drive it through.

As it popped out, the whole hulk lurched and leaped against the weight of the ballast, which now hung from a single bolt. The nut eased, and the weight followed it down as he backed it off. Bracing his legs against the mass he drew the nut to the last thread, then gave a long sharp twist and pushed himself violently away as the keel dropped and he was sucked upward in a fierce, inverted maelstrom.

His vision blurred and his head was beginning to throb. He crouched and kicked for the surface, shooting upward through green infinities for an endless rush of time until light burst upon him and he gasped in fresh air around the exhausted rubber plug in his mouth before he fell back in the water and stroked feebly for the raft. There he secured a line from the bobbing stern of his hull to a side cleat and collapsed.

Ten minutes' rest restored him sufficiently to attach a tow line and begin paddling for shore. Number 94 was asleep on top of the seawall, knees up, straw hat over his eyes, and no amount of hailing would disturb his slumber. At length, as he neared the shore, Number 6 attracted the attention of an elderly gentleman who was persuaded to prod the napper awake with his cane.

The shell weighed only a fraction as much as the KAR, but it didn't have wheels. The windlass and electric truck were called into service again, and it was 3.30 before Number 6 was able to strip off his wet-suit, heat a can of soup, and flop into a warm tub.

No word from Number 2 came to disturb him – two days of backbreaking labour and two months of rebuilding might be expected to serve as his punishment for attempting to escape, but the SCUBA diving had been a thorough treat as well as most informative (in certain negative ways), and the opportunity to put his artificially maintained physical conditioning to use had been exhilarating. And he had come out of the entire exchange with nearly everything he had put into it – plus a number of new questions. If only he could be sure what had happened to his ignition system. . . .

SECTION IV: *Rondo Capriccioso*

He had to rearrange his afternoons to include three or four hours shopwork on the restoration of his derelict vehicle; it became his primary occupation. His mornings remained much the same, going about the Village in the streets, cadging pints of petrol from the Chemist's and solvent from the Artist's Shoppe.

Three days after his salvage job, he was sitting alone on the Terrace when a shadow fell across his table and he looked up. Number 18 was studying him uncertainly.

"Are you – uh – feeling sociable?" she asked tentatively.

He wondered what she would do if he stared blankly at her in total non-recognition, or grinned foolishly and began to babble inanities. But it would gain him nothing. So he said, "Certainly. Why shouldn't I be?" and pushed the other chair out from the table with his foot.

"Well, I'd heard – you'd built a boat, but it sank." She shifted her weight doubtfully, eyeing the proffered chair. "And I hadn't seen you here for lunch for a few days, and I wasn't sure how you were feeling. I mean, you might not want company."

"I appreciate your concern, but I'm feeling quite well. I've just ordered lunch – we can have the waitress back for you."

Relieved, she sat down and leaned forward over the table. "Did you really raise it after it sank? I'd heard you could be seen from the Lookout Tower with a pair of glasses, but I never got a chance to get up there during the day. You were only working in the mornings for a couple of days, weren't you?"

"Yes. I got it ashore all right, but it'll be some time before I can take you for a drive."

She pouted prettily. "Oh dear, and I've been so looking forward to seeing your car. Don't you ever allow visitors?"

"Some I can't keep out – Number Two used to walk right in whenever he felt like it, but that was his inalienable privilege. And speaking of Number Two, who is running things up there now?"

"Number Two, of course. Well, he's still technically Two Prime, pending the hearing."

"Hearing?"

"It's been postponed until Number One-hundred is out of the hospital. He's being treated for shock and exposure, and of course they can't hold a hearing until he's in condition to testify."

"What kind of hearing?"

"Into his desertion, of course. He was apparently running away with the help of one of the guests. Leaving the Village leaderless until Number Two Prime took responsibility."

"What about Number Three?"

"*What* about Number Three?"

"Number Two Prime was Number Four before; why didn't Number Three become Number Two Prime?"

"Why should she?"

"Because three follows two, as a general rule."

"Oh, silly! You don't *elect* your Members of Parliament in alphabetical order – you just seat them that way. I don't pretend to know what goes on up at the Green Dome, but I presume whatever happened there was some perfectly good reason for it. There's nothing I could do about it either way anyway, even if I cared."

"So regardless of reasons, Number Two Prime is effectively in charge of things for the time being."

"Well, yes! Somebody has to be."

"Why?"

"Well – because things don't just take care of themselves."

"Are you ready to order?" The waitress stood, pencil poised, to change the subject. When she had departed, Number 18 showed no interest in returning to local politics.

"I saw you out walking with your cat this morning – out of my window. That was why I came here to look for you."

"I'm flattered. I walk every morning – sometimes the cat follows me. Where's your window? I can wave to you."

The cat had taken to following him on his daily walking tours of the Village. One morning it was scampering ahead of him through one of the leafy lanes that surrounded the Village, and stopped suddenly by a low mint-like shrub. Number 6 stopped as well, some distance away, to observe the animal's uncharacteristic behaviour.

It sniffed at the dark green leaves, rubbed its nose up against them and bit a piece from one. It backed off, shook its head, and then nosed insistently at the plant again, nipping at the leaves.

Number 6 marked the spot in his mind, and shortly before midnight, on his evening round, he stopped there again for a closer look at the shrub. As a matter of policy, he kept his real interests as covert as possible in the Village. The leaves were small and pointed; he pulled one off, crushed it between his fingers to smell the oil. It was minty, but sweeter; correctly, he identified it as catnip. It might prove useful to have available; he loosened the earth around the root system with his fingers and lifted it, dirt and all, into a small paper bag.

He stood, unselfconsciously brushing his knees, slipped the closed sack inside his coat, and continued his evening constitutional. On his return, he came around the workshop at the rear of his cottage. There he knelt again to scrape a small hole in the soft earth of his own flowering border. Gently he slipped the rootlet-laced dirt lump with its leafy crown from the bag and into the hole. He tamped the earth lightly down all around and sprinkled it well with natural nitrates before he went inside.

He seldom thought much about his life outside while he was in the Village. The other world was a place to try and reach – a goal, rather than an urgent detailed reality. But he remembered, in an odd flash of memory, how a girl had offered him a kitten once, years ago when he had first moved to London. She had said he was too lonely for his human good, and needed something else alive around him. But his work had been irregular, even then – he could not afford to keep anything dependent upon his continued existence from one day to another.

The entire memory came back to him in one piece as the black cat stood up on the sofa and stretched, then ambled over to see if his arrival indicated food or attention. Number 6 bent to scratch him behind the ears, then hung his blazer over the back of a chair and sat down at the computer terminal console.

His evenings were now occupied with another design project – one of intricate and exquisite complexity, of the next order of difficulty beyond his late hull, and he had a large amount of study to put in on it. He had taken several books from the Village library on model airplane construction, and had pieced their contents together into complex formulae of lift and drag, centres of gravity, cambers, stresses and loads. Designing something that could maintain an even keel and support itself in midair was by no means as easy as balsa gliders might lead one to expect; he found a stimulating challenge in the problem he had posed himself.

The terminal he treated as a toy, and took a simple delight in its usefulness; not only could it accept his sketches, correct them and vary them as he directed, it could print out a reference copy on white paper in seconds on command. Its capabilities were not limited to engineering drawing: he produced a passable sketch of a sleeping cat in two evenings' work, ordered the machine to make three copies, serially numbered in the corner, and erase the picture. One he intended to give to Number 100, if he ever saw him again, and if it would have any reference to him by then – the other he considered for Number 40, Number 18, or Number 61, and decided to postpone a decision.

While he worked patiently at recovering lost ground and forging ahead theoretically, one week followed another. Four of them paced through the Village, carrying summer into autumn while Number 6 continued restoring his engine. It involved a complete disassembly of every moving part, its individual cleaning, drying, inspection and oiling before careful re-assembly. It was a gigantic three-dimensional jigsaw puzzle – a familiar puzzle, about as interesting as building a car from a kit.

He had discovered quite by accident one morning that the cat was likely to chase a ball of crumpled paper if it was thrown nearby him; it did this with every evidence of enjoyment, and he took to carrying an old tennis ball in the pocket of his blazer when he took his regular walks about the Village. From time to time he would throw it and the cat would leap after it as if it were a bird. When it landed and bounced and rolled, the animal would wander up to it, sometimes sniff at it, then lose interest. A harmless enough diversion, surely. The cat would never be trained to fetch like a dog, offering slavish devotion in return for attention

His days blended slowly into one another. Nothing ever changed in the Village but the slow clock of the seasons. Escape was still his goal, but he saw the path clearly ahead of him and was proceeding with all deliberate speed towards his goal. No more particular concentration was needed on the problem. His work progressed automatically from day to day as the KAR gradually grew back together, regenerated by his own two hands – and a wall full of tools.

The pieces were nearly together when Number 18 invited him over for dinner one evening and he accepted. Their luncheon conversation, somehow, had turned to fish and devolved to a debate between poached and broiled whitefish. This had led inevitably to her offer and his acceptance.

The butcher had a fresh catch on display, which had inspired the discussion, and his finest and firmest fillet went into her bag with a double handful of chipped ice.

"That's a fine piece of fish you've got there, Number Eighteen. Going to fry it?"

"Oh, no. It's quite fresh enough to poach."

"That's a delicate flavour for poaching."

"Poaching can be the gentlest way to cook something light – when it's properly done."

"I find it a little dry to be broiled," she added to Number 6 that evening as they resumed their discussion in her quiet cottage unit after dinner. He had to admit he had been well fed, and she had some valid views on the subject of food.

He smiled. "It takes a good deal of heat to broil properly. If the juices are sealed instead of being driven off as steam, it's quite juicy – and less oily than most fish. Why not be my guest tomorrow night? There should be a fresh catch in, and if not, broiling is more forgiving of an extra day in the ice chest."

"Honestly, I thought you'd never ask me. Have you got your car fixed yet? I'd love to come. I heard . . . Is your place really done up exactly like a city flat? With windows and all? How exciting!"

"Yes. It was done especially for me with no little trouble and expense, as Number Two would have been able to tell you at great length."

"Speaking of Number One-hundred, the hearing was announced this afternoon by the *Village Voice*. It's a month away. They probably want to be sure he's recovered completely."

"Oh. Is he out of the hospital?"

"I don't know. I don't know whether he's been mentioned recently at all, come to think of it. Would you care for a drink?"

"Gin."

"Anything with it?"

"Water."

The waning moon was high as Number 6 walked a leisurely, circuitous route homeward. The Village seemed to sleep, with only a few dim lights left on – though the silent traverse of a concealed camera studying an esoteric spectrum might go unobserved, and microphones might lie as silently as sprinkler heads in the grass. The Village was always awake somewhere, watching, listening. And a lone figure passed along the paths, with a faint regular crunch of rubber-soled shoes on gravel.

His steps became silent as he cut across the wide green lawns, past the empty flagpole; crunching twice, sharply, on lateral paths, then turning up a narrow lane between two comfortably nestled cottages. The sound of his soft, springshod feet padding on cobblestones diminished into the darkness.

The dim glow of a lawn-lamp showed him his own doorstep seventy yards away when suddenly the light was blocked by a figure which stepped out of the bushes ahead of him, and spoke urgently.

"Wait, Number Six! Please –"

The voice was less steady than the last time he had heard it, but there was no mistaking the metallic harshness of Number 100's voice. The raucous quality was still there, but an edge of tension and fear lent it a grotesque quality, like a puppet screaming.

"– I must talk with you!"

"By all means, Number One-hundred! Come inside and we'll talk over plans for our next escape attempt!"

"Number Six, you swine! I never did anything but what was best for you – now that I stand on the brink of extinction, when a word from you could save me, your first words are a shoe planted in the middle of my back! I must talk with you – we must talk alone. We are safe here only for a few minutes – not long enough to explain what's going on and answer half your questions. But I will answer your questions, I swear, if you'll leave me a chance to do anything."

"Where would we be safe for longer than a few minutes? You should know that better than anyone."

"Your workshop out at the track. If you'd been anywhere near going out there I'd never have dared come this close to your place."

"Why is *it* safe?"

"You are the Elephant's Child with your questions! I can't stay. Meet me there tomorrow afternoon. You could have any number of perfectly good reasons for going out there. Make it four o'clock. I shall arrange for tea to be prepared, come to think of it. Yes – make it four o'clock. Be seeing you." And he was gone.

Number 6 stared after him. After several seconds he shook his head doubtfully and started up the walk again. The Village more than once reminded him of Lewis Carroll's *Wonderland*, but he didn't think he had ever met the White Rabbit before.

At about a quarter to four the next afternoon he laid down his tools and wiped most of the grease from his hands. He pulled his second blazer on, saving his best to wear for dinner, and made a mental note to stop by the butcher's for the pick of the morning's catch on the way home.

The distant bells of the Village clock were chiming the hour when he arrived at his workshop, and there indeed was Number 100, uncommonly clad in grey overalls and a peaked cap. A metal tray with a grim tin military tea service stood in the corner.

"Ah, Number Six. Punctual to the moment. You must forgive my playing host this time, since I welcome you to your own shop, but do sit down and have a cuppa. The water's just on the boil."

Momentarily speechless, Number 6 sank to rest on one of the corners of the framework which lay about the shop awaiting some kind of re-assembly. A moment later he found a steaming cup balanced on his knee. He took the saucer gingerly and stood to help himself to the sugar as he spoke.

"You suppose I'm wondering why you called me here."

"I'm sorry the location isn't more palatial, but I am not exactly a free man at the moment."

"Ah, which of us is!"

" 'No man who lives can be said to be free', after all. But I must confess I did not intend this purely as a social occasion. I arranged this meeting (with no little difficulty) because I must have your help in setting things to rights. Since you are responsible for my being placed in this position, you owe me your assistance in getting out of it. Number Six, you know I've done everything I could to help you while you were here. You owe me at least a little consideration, on that basis alone."

"Very well – I'll consider you. What else do you want me to do?"

"Help me. My record is stained, my career wrecked because of you! You can help me by telling what happened that – that *awful* night – at the hearing. But if Number Four thinks he can –"

"You mean Number Two Prime."

"Number Two Prime is his own invention. He has taken this excuse to seize executive control of the Village, and is intent on destroying me to assure his position. But several people – some in high places – are aware of what he's trying, and with their help I hope to defeat him and regain the Chair."

"You talk as if you were autonomous. Doesn't Number One have anything to say about this? Go ahead – I believe you promised something about answering my questions. Do we have enough time to start now?"

"We have nearly an hour."

"Where am I?"

"In the Village."

"Thank you. Where is the Village?"

"On the western shore of one of the Balearic Islands. If you were to sail north three hundred miles, you'd hit Barcelona."

"Who is Number One?"

"There is no Number One. The founder and first administrator of the Village was Number One. When he – left us – his Number was retired. Chief administrators since have been Number Two, reminding us that ours is not the supremely dominant power, but the subservient."

"Then, in whose name do you administrate? The government – or whatever – behind all this?"

"In the name of Her Royal Majesty, Elizabeth Regina. This is an unofficially unrecognised cranny of the Civil Service. Surely you didn't think the Mongolians had built and peopled this place!"

"Who did people it?"

"Believe it or not, most of these people are here voluntarily. When the Other Side retires their code clerks, they run away to Canada. We offer ours a comfortable, secure resort."

"And if they're not ready to retire?"

"You are a special case, Number Six. Surely you were aware of that much! You are here for a reason, rather than an excuse. Attend: your precipitate resignation from your – ah – sensitive position came as less than a total surprise to your superiors: you were under scrutiny for some time before you took that step. There had been some evidence of your dissatisfaction with the job you had to do, and you had already been considered for review. Your resignation was regarded as a definite sign of emotional instability – naturally, you could never have been allowed in the field again under such circumstances.

"But you were still a brilliantly trained man – a valuable expert whose knowledge and talents were still needed by his country. And the Village had an important use for someone of your formidable abilities. Much of our automation is in the experimental stage; all our defences are still being tested. It was, of course, essential that you should remain unaware of the nature of the project in which you were participating so that you would put forth your most sincere efforts towards confounding our systems."

"I am the Fool you found to determine whether everything was Foolproof."

"I shouldn't have put it quite so bluntly, Number Six, but you do have a certain turn of phrase there."

"Let's get more specific. What were you in the hospital for, and why are you free of observation now?"

"Frankly, I was there for Corrective Therapy. But due to the ... *personal* nature of Number Four's usurpation – and partly out of friendship – a number of the technical staff have remained loyal to me and my cause. With their help I was diverted from most of the treatments Number Two Prime had me scheduled for. Also, I am able to evade his surveillance from time to time. This workshop is an example. The camera group that covers this area was installed while we were building it – since it was part of my own project, it was regularly monitored by staff who shared my interest in it. Now they remain loyal to me. Number Two Prime need never know anything that goes on here. We can arrange to signal you should he ever demand to see the coverage of the place and show him instead a videotape of the entire area deserted."

"And all I have to do for you is ... ?"

"Be my ally. I've spent my life behind a series of desks – you're accustomed to direct conflict and physical confrontation."

"I've retired."

"Yes, of course. *Too many people knew too much*, I believe. *Too many people were being killed.* But this is hardly a military operation, Number Six – murder is not an acceptable part of intra-departmental politics at this level. Only my career is at stake – and perhaps part of my mind."

"You seem very concerned for my testimony at the hearing."

"The hearing? That's a farce. Number Two Prime will have rigged it in his own favour; he wouldn't take so great a risk to seize power and then chance losing it on some slight whim of fact. We still have some time before this hearing – it may even be postponed. As long as it is still pending, I can remain in the Village; once I am taken away, I can never return to my old classification.

"Number Two Prime is only allowing you to continue working on your car because he cannot change my established policies until the hearing confirms him and dissolves the Prime. Because of this, you need make no attempt to disguise your covert activities as long as you do nothing obviously illegal and *demanding* action on his part. But if this hearing goes against me, he will immediately institute his own policies and you will be cut back to a Meccano set. Honestly – haven't I done more for you than Number Two Prime? Is he likely to continue your petrol supply? What would his reaction be to another attempted extension of your track? Do you really expect him to help you obtain replacement parts for those ruined by immersion?"

"Can you? Or is this job payment-on-completion?"

"I can't give you more track or guarantee petrol until I'm back in the Chair. But I can get you some things. I should be able to get whatever parts you may need through my remaining contacts; I've not lost all my influence along with my official position. So you see, we can help each other in many ways. If we succeed, I can promise you immunity for almost anything you do even nominally on my behalf – if we fail, I think you now understand enough about your position here to know that your punishment would perforce be perfunctory."

Number 6 studied him for several seconds. "Do you mean you want me to set up a palace revolution for you? A bloodless *coup?*"

"I fear it amounts to that. I have already hopelessly compromised your necessary ignorance of the true situation. The die is cast, the Rubicon crossed, the cat out of the bag and the fat in the fire. I am wholly at your mercy. You could march up the front door of the Green Dome tomorrow and destroy the entire experiment which is centred around you. Or you can ... well, continue as you are. Do your best against our defences. Plan ways of getting past them. Keep working on your machine. In short, act as if you knew nothing. It shouldn't be difficult."

"Thank you. But since I don't know the way things are put together behind the scenes, you will have to direct me. What specific combination of circumstances could replace you in the Chair?"

"Why ... I don't really know, exactly. We couldn't do it with him actually there. *He* had to wait until I was miles outside the Village before he dared."

"Did he? Or was it only that he needed a legal pretext? Couldn't he have accomplished the same thing if you were, say, out of the room? What if you were on the far side of the Village? What if you were out at the track for half an hour?"

"Why ... I think it took him nearly an hour to establish complete command. My friends were trying to find me, to contact me, to warn me to take action against him. As Number Two I could have stopped him with three words. But as Number One-hundred ..."

"Would it take you an hour to resume command?"

"I . . . I don't know. If he hasn't destroyed the voice-coded over-rides it shouldn't take that long. He was unfamiliar with much of my equipment, which must have delayed him as well. . . . Given advance warning for adequate preparation, I could sit in the Chair for ten minutes, free of interruption, and pick up all the threads to a point where he could no longer pose a threat."

"What is 'adequate preparation'?"

"My friends, my associates, would have to be alerted. There is bound to be disconcertion in the Village when the change in administration becomes known, and they can explain the situation directly to anyone who asks, thereby averting any loss of faith in the stability of the Village power structure."

"You want me to lure him out of the Round Room for ten or fifteen minutes, at some pre-arranged time. How far in advance will you have to know?"

"A day – eighteen hours at least."

"You know Number Two Prime far better than I; what do you think would bring him out of his shell?"

"It shouldn't take much at the moment. Remember, he thinks he has nothing to fear from us. Perhaps if you appeared to be planning some particularly outré device, he might be tempted to come out and take a look at it; what are you doing with your hands these days, by the way? Still digging seaweed out of your cylinders?"

"The engine's nearly reassembled. But your mentioning seaweed reminds me – your fee for my talents includes answers to direct questions, and I have several more."

"I don't know everything, Number Six. But you are welcome to the answers I have.'

"Why is there no seaweed or any other form of marine life in the Village Bay?"

"Isn't there? How odd!"

"That's why I asked."

"I'm afraid that's something I don't know anything at all about. I have read of areas of the sea where some freak of ocean current sweeps everything from the face of bedrock and allows nothing to grow. Or perhaps submarine oil seepage sterilised it. The Village was here before I was, Number Six, and I never doubted there were things about it I didn't know."

"What are the Guardians?"

"This I know, but it may be difficult to explain. Are you at all acquainted with Fluidics?"

"Only vaguely."

"Fluidics studies the flow of fluids the same way electronics studies the flow of electricity. Fluid flows can be modulated in much the same way as electric current: amplified, switched off and on with great speed and accuracy – and all, in a properly designed system, with no moving parts. The flow patterns of the fluid medium itself can be made to vary each other in stable, metastable or oscillating states – I don't fully understand it; as I may have mentioned, I'm not at all technically minded. It's analogous to but not at all identical with resistors, capacitors, valves and things in electronics, and there are many applications where fluidic controls are more efficient than electronic.

"Next, do you know what a Colloidal Mechanism is?"

"Is a Guardian a colloidal mechanism?"

"Not entirely. Please, Number Six, I don't mean to seem to evade your questions, but my position is awkward. Suppose a Hottentot attends a Peace Corps school and gets the equivalent of primary school physical science. When he goes home, he takes a transistor radio with him, and his whole tribe orders him to tell them how it works. You must have patience with me."

"Do I need to understand the theory behind them?"

"Do you want to? You'd probably best find someone else who could explain it. Or ask your terminal. Perhaps you could simplify your question."

"Are they alive?"

"Not as we understand life. No."

"Are they conscious?"

"They are aware, but they have no self-awareness. They are partly self-programming, an advantage fluidics has over electronics, requiring fewer and less delicate transducers to interpret its environment and learn from experience. That's something I know about. Events leave resonant waves in their control systems, and these waves predispose the thing to act in certain ways. When we first receive them, they are as small as soccer balls, and must be programmed to their basic moves in conditioning rooms.

They're rather cute when they're small."

"Then they grow."

"Oh yes. They are also self-repairing, unless severely damaged. Another advantage of Colloidal Mechanisms. Do you have the time?"

"Half-past four."

"I'd best be getting back. I'll have to take the tea service with me; I borrowed it from the hospital ward. You may finish the biscuits – they get stale quickly if left out."

"Where can I deposit a list of replacements parts I want?"

"Prepare three copies and I shall pick them up from you the next time your residence is safe for me."

"Triplicate?"

"There are three different places – departments – which might have anything you could want. I don't know who would have what. It will be easier if I can give them each a copy than if they have to pass one around. Faster, too, I shouldn't wonder."

"I must be off – they're expecting me for hydrotherapy at a quarter to. Be seeing you." Number 100 shouldered the spent tea-tray and departed.

Number 6 rose, picked up his straw hat and the rest of the biscuits and left as well, down a different path, towards the centre of the Village. He had a dinner engagement with a whitefish.

Dinner was successful on all counts. His original Hock sauce worked out perfectly, and Number 18 was properly impressed with the entire production. When it was over and the dishes were stacked, she picked up her light coat and said, "It's such a lovely evening – could you show me your workshop out at the track? I'd love to see it, and besides, I think a walk would do us both good after that marvellous dinner."

They chatted idly for the twenty-minute walk, but once inside the shed her manner changed from flirtatious to conspiratorial. "Number One-hundred was to see you today, wasn't he," she said. "I do hope you've agreed to help us."

"To overthrow constituted authority by force and violence?"

"Oh, certainly not! Besides, Number Two Prime isn't constituted, just *de facto*. And there isn't supposed to be any force or violence, either. If we can just get Number One-hundred back into his rightful position, there won't even have to *be* a hearing and the status can go back on being quo."

"Number One-hundred didn't go into detail about his supporters in the Village, though he gave me to understand they were numerous and ubiquitous. Still, I must admit I never thought of you as a political activist."

"It isn't a matter of politics, Number Six. I just feel that Number Two Prime is being unnecessarily high-handed about all this, and is really not justified in punishing Number One-hundred for what was, after all, mostly your fault."

"You seem to have learned a lot in the last month – did Number One-hundred tell you what happened?"

"Well . . . I think he exaggerated some of it. But you were with him all the time he was away from the Village, even when your boat sank, weren't you?"

"Yes."

"But you didn't really kidnap him on purpose, did you?"

"No."

"I couldn't see you going out of your way to take him along in a boat, no matter what he told me."

"Thank you. Did he mention anything about what happened to the boat's motor? Why it stopped?"

"Stopped? No – just that it had sunk while the Rescue Unit was towing you back to the Village."

"The engine died suddenly, and I believe some outer defence line was responsible. I'd like to know what it is."

She flushed. "Really, Number Six – I'm sorry I brought the matter up. This – this fixation of yours seems to become involved in everything you do. I hope you can suppress it if you intend to help Number One-hundred's cause."

"Pardon my honesty. I didn't mean to embarrass you."

"Now about the . . . What is this, exactly? It's not a revolution, or even an underground . . ."

"A counter-coup?" he suggested.

"Anyway, if you want to get in touch with Number One-hundred bring your message to me at lunch on a sheet of paper in an envelope. I take memos and things from my boss, Number Eleven, to the Central Kitchen every afternoon. I can meet one of the hospital therapists there and pass it to him, and he can see that Number One-hundred gets it by six o'clock. Number One-hundred can usually get out after dark; if he can't, I'll come, because I can get in to see him once a week."

"How many people are involved in this network? I begin to get the impression Number Two Prime stands nearly alone. Why don't you just pull his power points?"

"I guess there must be fifty or a hundred people, inside and outside, who are willing to support us to some extent."

"How far is that?"

"Well . . . that depends. Some would even be willing to sign a petition. But not enough, I guess. Most of them will help if it doesn't mean going much out of their way and if nobody's likely to find out they're helping. Like carrying notes, and skipping log checks, and passing falsified test reports – if they're well enough falsified. You know, that sort of thing."

"I know that sort of thing." He stood up. "I'll want to make out a list for you to deliver to Number One-hundred through your 'underground'. I can give it to you over lunch tomorrow."

"By the way," she asked, pointing, "are those big metal things all that's left of your boat?"

"That's all there was of the boat – except for the car."

"Oh. . . . Wasn't it kind of small?"

"It did well enough – as far as it went."

"As far as it . . . Number Six, I wish you would control your gift for innuendo – isn't any subject safe from you?"

"You asked about my boat – weren't you aware of its purpose?"

"Well . . . I just don't like to think about it. I admire it as a boat – I don't know anything about what else you may have done with it, and please don't tell me."

"You don't object to the boat – you only object to its being used as a boat."

"No – not exactly. I mean . . . a boat is a nice thing. It just shouldn't be used for . . . *anti-social* purposes."

"If you will pardon my crudity, why would my departure – *alone* – have been antisocial?"

"Well, because you are rejecting society! Anti-social means against society. And if you want to get away from us, reject us, that's against our society."

"But I'm not doing anything *to* your society."

"Yes, you are – you're rejecting us."

"It is my right to reject it."

"No, it isn't! You can't live outside society. Not and remain human."

"There is the kernel of our disagreement. I wish Number One-hundred were here to demonstrate his Famous Mathematical Proof that there is no such thing as an individual except as a reference unit in statistical aggregations."

"What? I don't really understand statistics."

"Never mind. He said the same thing you did with more numbers and less emotion, and took ten times as long to say it. As your host I apologise for this disagreement of opinion, but I beg the right to maintain my own."

"But it's *wrong!*"

"I also have the right to be wrong."

"But why do you want to be wrong?"

Number 6 sat down. He regretted the turn the conversation had taken, but refused to default. "I don't *intend* to be wrong," he said patiently. "But I want to be able to make my own mistakes and learn from them."

She stared at him. "And if somebody saw you were making a mistake, you wouldn't want them to stop you."

"Essentially."

She shook her head slowly, keeping her eyes fixed on his face, and chewed her lower lip in sincere confusion. "I'm afraid I don't understand you, Number Six."

"I'm afraid you do. Perhaps we'd better get back to the boat. Or perhaps, considering the hour, we'd best be getting back home."

"Well . . ."

"I'll take you for a drive when I have the KAR running again."

"Then you will help us."

Number 6 shrugged. "I'll co-operate in return for certain concessions," he said. "Such as replacement parts. I'll bring you an itemised list for lunch tomorrow."

"It sounds unappetising after your dinner tonight," she said with a tentative smile.

"Thank you," he said, rising to his feet and extending his hand. "Shall we toddle back to my place for dessert?"

"Just a bit – I have my work to do tomorrow."
"And mine."

The requisition he drew up for Number 100 to put into his channels was the subject of much thought and intensive calculation. Only certain items of the highest priority were called for. Most, but not all, of them would incidentally be essential for his most revised private plans, a fact which he chose not to bring to his benefactor's attention.

As it was, it ran six pages in three copies, with detailed specifications on several entries. Number 18 frowned when he passed the bundle to her under the table on the Terrace.

"I offered to smuggle him notes," she murmured. "Not the *Encyclopedia Britannica*. I hope this will fit in my folder."

"I should have written smaller. Could you supply me with a microfilm camera?"

"Shh. The waitress cannot be trusted."

"Sorry."

The following afternoon, when he unwrapped a beautiful butt of ham Number 61 had carved for him, he found a note stuck to the side of it. The paper was translucent with absorbed fat, and heavy pencilled block letters were almost legible through it. He peeled it off with a bemused smile and wiped the faint black smears of graphite from the tough, slick rind.

SAME PLACE. 9 P.M.

He wondered if he were expected to devour the note once he had memorised its contents. Number 100 must have some purpose behind this charade; perhaps he could be persuaded to offer an explanation this evening.

"Why this amateur underground of yours? You gave me the impression my testimony at the hearing would set things legally to rights."

"Frankly, Number Six, I hadn't told you this before because I wasn't entirely sure how far Number Four – Number Two Prime I should say – had got in his mad clutch at power. But it now seems extremely doubtful that your testimony would even be admissible at the hearing. You would be held in the position of co-defendant of the second order, whereby you would be presumed to be pleading your own case in such testimony. Number Fifteen explained it to me last week."

Number 100 was clad in the ice-cream uniform of the Village Neatness Committee; it was one size too large for him and lent the shards of his raucous arrogance a certain bedraggled dignity. He paced nervously back and forth across the closed end of the workshop.

"But even without your testimony, you are the only man who can help me regain my proper position. Let me explain to you what we have in mind. Somehow or other I must be got from the hospital up to the Round Room while you devise some way of distracting Number Two Prime from his position there."

"How long will it take you to cover the distance?"

"Why, I don't know. It depends on how, and when, and how soon."

"Fine. You know the Village backstage better than I; why don't *you* determine a time, based on when you'll be ready, and let me know. Since I'm working alone, I can prepare a sufficiently attractive distraction on relatively short notice."

"How much notice?"

"Eighteen hours – a day at most."

"That will do nicely. I really daren't stay much longer or they'll be looking for me. Some time in the next day or two we should be ready to move – I'll send you word."

"What if I don't happen to stop by the butcher's for two or three days?"

"Oh, something will turn up, Number Six. My people are everywhere."

"I don't doubt it."

"One other minor thing – that list of materials and parts you sent through yesterday seemed a good bit more extensive than your automotive repairs would warrant. You aren't planning to try to leave us again, are you?"

"Would you believe me if I denied it?"

Number 100 sighed and leaned against a rough bench. "Candidly, no. But if you would only agree to wait a few more days, I shall be back in the Chair. When matters are set right, you may find your status in the Village changed favourably."

"I'm quite satisfied with my present position."

"But you're wasting yourself. You are a rare and infinitely valuable man.

Most men have the souls of slaves – perhaps they could be said to have voluntarily surrendered their souls. They lack whatever elemental drive, or awareness, or other quality is supposed to make man more than a reasoning animal. It is best for most people that they be . . . taken care of. Tended. Guided. Told what to think and feel. Generally they seem to prefer it that way, you know. Certainly it's easier than having to make up your own mind and take all your own responsibilities. It's so much simpler and more practical to share out responsibilities and decisions.

"*Man* is a collective noun. His greatest strength is in union, in co-operation, in Society. Submerging his own will and his whole being in the greater whole."

"But *men* are singular. And some of them will take pains to remind you of that fact."

"Individuality is a valuable talent, Number Six. But so few people actually have it – and so many think they do. You have it, Number Six. You have defended your individuality with the greatest of brilliance and exquisite courage and faith in yourself. You have proven you have what the poet called 'that spark of fire divine'. Don't divert it to disorder, destruction, disorganisation and chaos. Man's purpose in the universe is to bring order out of chaos. Help us here in the infinitesimal portion of the great task we are attempting."

"Odd how we can never seem to agree, Number One-hundred. I had always felt the universe was already in pretty good order. It seems to tick along quite nicely without our attention. How do you suppose the Andromeda Galaxy has managed to hold together all these years?"

"'Lift not your hands to it for help, for it as impotently moves as you or I'," Number 100 quoted mournfully, if obscurely. "The universe I was referring to, on a practical level, is the universe that pipes in your water and keeps your lights burning, that delivers your milk and distills your precious petrol, that slaughters your meat and mixes medicines and paves the roads for you to drive on. The social universe, Number Six. You may be reluctant to admit it, but it supports you and makes your way of life possible."

"And denies me the right to enjoy it."

"It does not deny your right – only limits it for the common good. Order induces uniformity where it does not find it, but rejecting the order of society as you do involves your rejection of the foundations of human civilisation."

"I don't reject civilisation out of hand; it has a number of redeeming features. But I will not have it thrust upon me – nor will I thrust it forcibly upon others."

"And what if they come to you and beg you for it? Come, Number Six – your collapsible cast-iron kayak isn't remotely ready for another attempt. We shall have adequate time to debate Social Psychology next week, when all this nonsense has been settled.

"Heavens, it's late. I must be getting back. I shall do what I can towards your requests, of course – but what on earth did you want all that sealed nylon fabric for?"

"I wanted it to be a surprise."

"Oh, very well. Watch for word, and be ready. And in the meantime, do try to behave yourself. Be seeing you."

The Village bell sent a single gentle chime over the silent woods, and Number 100 was gone into the darkness.

SECTION V: *Scherzo*

Two days passed without word. On the third day, when Number 6 made his regular call on the Village Butcher Shop, a stranger wore the apron behind the counter.

"Good morning, Number Six. What would you like today?"

"That's a nice set of chops, there. Is Number Sixty-one on vacation?"

"Number Sixty-one was taken very ill last night. The doctors said he might not be back for some time. I've no idea what it was, but apparently it came on very suddenly. I didn't see him, of course. Well, I hope to serve you as well as he did. Here are your chops – will there be anything else?"

"I think not. Be seeing you."

"And you."

Ninety minutes later Number 18 joined him at their table on the Terrace, her face forcedly bright and cheerful. Under her breath she greeted him with, "Things are in a mess. Number Sixty-one was picked up last night. Apparently someone let too much slip."

"Have you any idea who?"

"Well, I have my suspicions. I don't think it was anybody you know. Number One-hundred called me at the office just half an hour ago and told me to tell you not to worry about this little setback, and that he would get in touch with you. And he also said to be sure to explain that this will be purely a disciplinary problem with which he could deal on the executive level, and he emphasised that you would 'not be called upon to rub anybody out'. Those were the words he used."

"I see."

"And he said your order would not be held up by this incident and you should start getting things tomorrow or the next day."

It took another month before everything had arrived. Items came in various guises from week to week, and the KAR grew back together a piece at a time. Something was different about the ignition system – something which could not be observed without much closer inspection than a single remote camera afforded: now every lead from the distributor to each spark plug was of heavier cable – shielded cable, grounded inconspicuously to the frame.

It was observed in certain private places that Number 6 had taken up another of his apparently endless hobbies – sewing. What he might be making from fifteen square yards of heavy sealed nylon fabric was a matter for some professional speculation, but whatever it might be it seemed to grow larger and more complex every day.

Analysis of his computer time-use suggested a crude biplane, and the possibility of a gas- or hot-air balloon was considered seriously, but the question of what would fill it remained unanswered.

Meanwhile, the subject of this scrutiny cobbled together a new sort of structure from the bare framework off the old – gone was any pretext at a racing silhouette; it began to resemble a free-form sculpture with smoothly polished curves, jagged edges and ends filed, sanded and dotted here and there with dabs of soft solder – narrow curved ribs, broad-bellied in the middle.

Number 100 was conspicuous by his intermittence. Conspiracies were murmured under awnings with a few merchants and Villagers, though nothing ever seemed to come of them. Number 6 wondered from time to time at Number 100's melodramatic inventiveness, but was offered nothing specific to divert him from his regular daily rounds of the Village and meetings with his acquaintances and band concerts and for luncheons on the Terrace as the days grew warmer and summer began to bloom.

Finally his work drew to its conclusion. And one afternoon when the engine ran smoothly and the wheels rolled, Number 18 came back with him from lunch. Number 213 met them at the workshop and led them out to the track, proudly waving his red flag. Unexpectedly, they were met by a five-man welcoming committee, led by Number 11, a blandly personable cipher in his mid-forties.

"I gave my office the afternoon off," he explained cheerfully. "Number Eighteen expected you would be ready today, and we thought a small celebration would be in order. Number One-hundred should be here any moment – he was especially anxious to see that your automobile was running properly again."

"Yes, indeed," said the familiar raucous voice outside the shed as Number 100 entered. "I saw it as I came up. It seemed to be running nicely."

He was dressed in an ecstatic purple blazer with gold piping, and Number 94 dismounted from the silent electric cart behind him with champagne and glasses. "I was hoping to have all this ready when you arrived, Number Six, but circumstances forbade. Still, better late than never."

Number 94 and Number 11 handed glasses around, splashing a moderate amount of champagne in each; when they had poured for themselves Number 100 raised his glass.

"The lost has been saved," he announced. "By strength of purpose and unstinting labour, with a good deal of spare time, Number Six has won back to the level at which he started. I must admit I never thought you'd do it," he added. "Though I myself don't know much about mechanical things, I'd always thought salt water was absolutely fatal to engines."

"It is. And I'm ahead of where I started – look at the screenwork I have."

"So I've heard; I'd like to see it. Have you thought of doing it up on a base for entry in the Village Summer Art Festival?"

"Never seriously. I tried that once – didn't especially like it."

"Oh, come, Number Six! Surely you should be gratified that others found your work enjoyable. Though as I recall you offered the award to another entrant − I forget her Number." He raised his glass again. "But let the dead past bury its dead ... figuratively speaking, of course. I propose a toast to Number Six's success."

"Past or future?" Number 6 asked as they drank.

"Present. The past is problematical, the future hypothetical. Nevertheless may I propose a second toast − somewhat presumptuously worded, but not, I think, unduly: *to our future success.*"

All eyes on him over a ring of rims, Number 6 joined them. As he held out his glass with the others, he asked, *sotto voce*, "Will I be expected to make a speech?"

Number 100 ignored him. "The day after tomorrow will bring at last the confluence of schedules which will make our operation practicable." He motioned the four strangers Number 6 had observed forward for introductions. "These men represent personnel interested in this operation − they're the only ones able to get away from their jobs at this time of day, and they will advise anyone else who needs to know of our plans.

"Unless you have thought of an excellent diversion to draw Number Two Prime from his perch, we have developed an alternative plan. Instead of trying to lure him away, we could achieve the same ends by driving him out. If something like a smoke bomb went off in the Round Room, and two Service Engineers ordered the Room evacuated, Number Two Prime would go wherever he was told. I could be waiting in the wings, as I believe you phrased it once, and simply step in and pick up the reins where I left them on that ill-considered journey to the seashore in concern for your welfare."

"It sounds like a reasonable plan," Number 6 said noncommittally.

"Ah. Praise from a professional. There is, however, a technical problem. What might be termed a 'hang-up'."

"There always is."

"I should suppose so − it's awfully difficult when you've never done this sort of thing before."

"The smoke bomb."

"Ah − yes."

"You want me to build you one."

"Oh, no. That is quite a commonplace item. The difficulty is in its delivery."

"And you are here to invite me to beard the lion and bell the cat."

"It should be in your province. The way can be cleared for you of human observers, but there are certain security devices which cannot be disarmed except from the Chair."

"I expect you have a diagram?"

"We have a map with notes. You will have to go in tomorrow night after midnight; it shouldn't take you more than fifteen minutes – it daren't take you more than thirty. I can tell you where to hide it and how to set the timing mechanism. The delay will be twelve hours; if you and Number Eighteen are on the Terrace as usual, you may observe some consternation up on the Hill at that time. I trust you will show the same amount of detached concern as those around you."

Number 18 was delighted. "Then we don't have to do anything when it actually happens?"

"You may applaud quietly. Number Six, I will call on you tomorrow afternoon to discuss your exact schedule of movements and bring you the infernal machine. Now I propose we return to the business at hand: Number Six, your car is ready to run, and we are here to share this triumphant achievement with you as you take your first drive around the track."

"I'm afraid I can't fit you all in."

"Vicariously, Number Six, vicariously. Though there *is* space for one passenger. . . ."

"Oh, Number Six, you promised me," said Number 18. "And I'd be very happy to share it with you."

They crowded out to the car, and willing hands helped Number 18 to the left-hand seat as Number 6 slid behind the controls. The engine caught at the first touch of the electric starter, and the others stepped briskly back to a respectful distance.

He slipped the transmission into gear, then depressed the foot throttle as he let the clutch in. KAR 1260 moved gracefully forward, accelerating around the corner of the building on to the track. Behind the muffled exhaust, Number 100's voice could be heard leading the others.

"Hip-hip-*hoorah*! Hip-hip-*hoorah*! Hip-hip-*hoorah*!"

The projected Secret Route of Entry was comparatively simple, involving no laundry chutes, air vents or fire escapes – one side door would be opened for him on the last stroke of midnight, and a certain sequence of corridors would be safe for certain periods of time. There were also, of course, a number of specially defined hazards in the form of detection devices.

Number 100 insisted on taking the plans back with him, and Number 6 was obliged to commit them to memory during the remainder of the afternoon. The smoke bomb was a cylinder about the size of an old fountain pen; it was armed and set by twisting the two halves clockwise to a stop. When it was operating, a blue band would show on its grey plastic surface. When it went off, clouds of black electrical-smelling smoke would billow forth in profusion accompanied by a 13-Hz infrasonic for five minutes. The firing mechanism, he was told, was accurate to within five seconds over a twelve-hour period.

It was nestled in the breast pocket of his black blazer as he strolled late that night near a small green door, half hidden by ivy, off an unfrequented path on the south, or downhill, side of the Green Dome. As the twelfth stroke of the tower clock dropped into the gloom, a blade of greenish-white fluorescent light stood and widened, and he hurried forward to enter the long empty hall opened to him, deserted but for himself and one of the four men who had attended Number 100's recent fete. This anomial worthy greeted him with a forefinger raised to his lips and a terse whisper.

"That door is now locked. You can open it from the inside when you're through. Give it a good push when you go out, to make sure it's closed. I think you know the way from here."

Number 6 nodded. Straight ahead to the fifth pair of double doors, rubber gloves for the handles. Through the doors to the first elevator bay. The bay monitor would be distracted from 12.02 to 12.04, and the monitor from 12.15 on was One Of Us.

He checked his wristwatch and wondered just how much of this charade was for real. If he walked into the lift bay thirty seconds early, would the bluff be called and Number 100's real control revealed? Probably not. There would be great opportunity for tocsins and alarms in the night and all sorts of running about and shouting, which would delight his theatrical heart; but this game board might be armed. The question was perversely tempting, but someone might get hurt in the confusion. Besides, the pressures lent a semblance of reality to his role.

Not for the first time he wondered if he would get enough out of this escapade to make up for the sleep it would cost him. A chance to get into the basement of the Green Dome was not that lightly passed by since the new administration had sealed things over – Number 6's innate curiosity had incited him to inspect the weak points with which he had been familiar and he had found them uniformly reinforced.

Even if Number 100 were being completely honest with him, pains would doubtless be taken to keep him shunted away from anything really interesting. He gave the bay monitor thirty seconds margin, then walked casually across the open space before the cold eye of the camera and stepped through an unlocked door into a vertical-access stairwell. It would remain unlocked until half past twelve

Up three flights to another door which should have been unlocked at 12.05; he laid his ear to the crack and listened for a full minute before easing it open. The curved hall was deserted. He let the door close silently behind him and lay down on his stomach.

Cautiously he crawled under the invisible beam which crossed the corridor thirty inches from the floor, then rose to his feet, dusted the front of his trousers and blazer, and continued around the curve. Fifty paces took him ninety degrees, and there another of Number 100's ubiquitous friends sat, his feet up on a small desk with a tiny TV screen, a double row of buttons and a side-hung handset. He looked up as Number 6 passed him and nodded recognition, gave him an amiable salute and returned to his magazine.

Twenty paces beyond him a door opening inward stood invitingly ajar as his instructions had promised. Through the gap he saw darkness intermittently lit from flickering display units; the spherical silhouette in the centre was the vacant Chair. With feline silence he moved along the curved wall. Diagonally from him, dimly spotlit like a deserted stage set, a ramp and double doors led out to the foyer. And beside him now, the Ordinary, its penny-farthing wheels and awnings an *outré* dissonance amid the glittering steel and shifting coloured patterns, like a balloon in a museum. Why was it the symbol of the Village? he wondered. Why did flags, buttons, stationery, mastheads show it? He must remember to ask Number 100 and see how believable his answer was.

The base of the stand that held the antique bicycle erect was high enough and deep enough to hold the grey cylinder; Number 6 took it from his pocket and consulted his wrist-chronometer. 12:14:25. He took just half a minute for a piercing look around the room, then watched the second-hand snip off the last five seconds. At precisely 12.15 he gave the cylinder a firm twist and felt something click into place; looking closely in the unsteady light he saw the blue band which meant it was armed. He set it gently in place and stepped back to study it critically.

As he did, the room brightened. He looked around quickly to see lights coming up on the main doors and the Chair. It no longer seemed like the time for an extended investigation – he withdrew as gracefully and silently as he had come.

Out in the hall the guard looked up inquiringly as he came past, and Number 6 held up his right hand, thumb and forefinger tip to tip, other fingers extended. The guard smiled, nodded, and returned to his magazine.

Number 6 squirmed gracelessly under the electric eye beam. As he did so, tensing for alarms but curious enough to take the risk, he carefully raised himself on his knees as he crawled through high enough to break the beam. It would look accidental and unconscious from any angle.

The silence remained unbroken. Without pausing, he gained the access stairs and looked up them. He could afford a moment to try. . . . Two at a time, he took the next flight up. The door was immovable. He had eight minutes until the door on the ground level would be locked – time enough to check every door from the top of the stairs at the end of the second flight up to the lowest level four flights down from his entrance. The bottom one was not locked.

Beyond the door lay darkness. Cool white light from the stairwell spilled across a cracked concrete floor, stained with seepage and cellar damp; a musty smell wafted out in exchange. On the edge of visibility two or three large dark shadows stood farther back in the unguessable extent of the room.

Number 6's hand felt lightly along the wall for an electric switch, and met nothing but a wisp of spider-web. He looked at his watch again – 12:26:40. Just over three minutes to climb fifty feet. He didn't especially look forward to meeting whoever would be coming to lock the stairwell again, and two minutes in total darkness would be worth little. He released the door and scaled the stairs.

He came out into the familiar elevator bay, tossed an ironic salute to the glassy eye of the camera, and passed through into the hall. He had not removed his rubber gloves since coming in; now he swiftly tried every other door in the long silent hallway. All resisted his touch but one – and that was the last he tried, for it was the door he had come in by and when he pushed it solidly closed behind him he was outside and there was nothing left to do but go home.

A small black shape extruded itself from the bushes as he came out and the cat wandered up to rub against his leg. He unpocketed the ratty tennis ball he'd carried for his evening walk and tossed it down the homeward path; the cat bounded after it, happy with the pretended quarry. Number 6 smiled wryly and followed the cat at a leisurely pace into the night.

He joined Number 18 on the Terrace shortly past noon and ordered a light lunch. When the waitress had gone, she leaned across the round white table and eagerly asked, "What time does the balloon go up?"

He looked at her with quizzically canted eyebrows. "Odd you should choose that expression," he said. "A quarter past, give or take five seconds."

"How long do we have?"

"Another four minutes."

"Did you have any trouble?"

"Not a bit."

There were all sorts of plausible reasons why there had been no response to his single unprogrammed departure from assigned precautions, but the most likely under the circumstances still seemed to be some degree of duplicity on the part of Number 100. Now as the time approached for his planted device to function, he sat facing the sea, one eye on his watch and one ear focused behind him.

"What will happen when it goes off? What'll we see?"

"It will make a lot of smoke and some noise, but not likely anything we can see from here. Presumably Number Two Prime will dash in a panic to safety, and the Village Fire Brigade will be summoned. That will probably be all we shall see – or hear."

"Now how soon?"

"About a minute."

Number 18 sat, staring fixedly over his shoulder at the Green Dome as he attacked his watercress sandwich, pausing between segments to call off for her benefit, "Five – four – three – two – one – pop! Now to see how efficient the Brigade is on a top-priority call."

He finished his sandwich and picked up his steaming cup of tea. Long moments passed as he stared mistily out to the distant uncertain line where sea and sky ran together, and heard the peaceful sounds of Village life continue undisturbed behind him. Number 18's whisper broke his unconsciously growing tension at last.

"How long has it been?"

He looked at his watch and was faintly startled. "Five and a half minutes."

"Nothing's happened. Could it have misfired?"

Number 6 shook his head. "I have no idea. Number One-hundred gave me to understand it was a simple foolproof mechanism, and checked me out on its simple foolproof operation. It's quite possible anything could have gone wrong with it – or it could have been found and removed or disarmed. It may show up in my bed tonight. I suggest you ask Number One-hundred. He'll have an answer – he always does."

He didn't. He had no idea what had happened – if anything had been suspected, it could have incited a complete search of the Round Room. And the device had not been indetectably concealed. A pity, but nothing could be done now. It would be best to wait a bit longer before trying anything else – if the bomb had been found, their entire group could be threatened.

For the next two weeks, the only communication between Number 6 and Number 100 was relayed messages carried by Number 18. His working hours centred more around the redesigned framework aluminum bracing and re-formed layers of wire mesh. Now in three sections, two light and one sturdy, it did resemble blunt wings and a platform as large as the car. Only the wings were covered with fine mesh; the open bracing of the small box would open out to a platform with crossbraces locked in place. Intricate and ambivalent as it was, it certainly didn't look as if it would fly.

His sewing project, the sealed nylon fabric, lay apparently forgotten in a heap in the corner of his shop. The cat often curled up there to doze away the warm afternoons of fading summer while its host tinkered and banged happily at whatever monkey-puzzle he was building.

Number 100 appeared around the corner of the shed one such afternoon with his customary unexpectedness, looked around disapprovingly and said, "Still bent on leaving us, I see."

'I'll thank you to watch your language in my shop, Number One-hundred. What's new with the Underground?"

"They've opened a Southern Extension with twenty trains an hour. Commuting from Bromley is much easier now. But that's not why I called, as you may have guessed – I thought you might like to know what happened to your infernal machine."

"The smoke bomb?"

"Apparently it was found by the cleaners and thrown out with the morning's trash. And that, of course, was incinerated at dawn. So there was never any suspicion. We could do it again, an hour later to miss the cleaners, and there's no reason why the entire operation couldn't succeed the second time through. Consider the other a dress rehearsal."

"When did you have in mind?"

"We'll have to resynchronise schedules with a Zero Time of one a.m. Certainly within a week – the next two or three days if we're lucky."

"And you want me to repeat my previous performance?"

"Precisely. It was *such* a fine job last time – pity the thing attracted the cleaners' attention. They must have come in just as you left. A good thing you didn't meet them! Well, I can't stay – I'll send you your bomb by Number Eighteen along with instructions on day and timing, since I likely can't get away to wish you luck. I must be going – I have an appointment with a remarkably lovely therapist." He smirked roguishly, and was gone.

Number 6 had carefully, in fact rather pointedly refrained from saying anything that could have been construed as acceptance of his visitor's proposal. In the privacy of his own mind he held deeper commitments to other schedules for the next few days.

He passed the next two sunsets studying wind currents over the cliffs north of the Village. A seagull would zoom in, wings rigid, folded yellow feet nearly brushing the waves, then bank suddenly into a tight spiral and climb the jutting seaward face. His observations did not pass unobserved, as he expected, and comments were made upon them in high places.

"He's out watching the birds again."

"You don't actually expect him to try to fly that thing!"

"I expect him to try. There'll be a Rescue Unit right under him with a net. And I don't believe he's seen the Flying Guardians – imagine his surprise when we send them up a mile inland."

"You've mastered their direction?"

"They're helpless against a ten-knot breeze, but Number Six will need fairly still air for his daring ascent, and once aloft he must fly before the wind."

"Suppose he needn't? If he can fill a gas bag he can power an airscrew."

"Reinforcement of one area does not weaken another. Number Six will not pass our outermost border."

"You're confident."

"This is the Village."

Three nights later, when the moon was at the quarter, he had not heard again from Number 100. Towards dusk he loaded his KAR 1260 for a drive down to the shore. The black cat, like a mascot, leaped into the passenger seat at his invitation and rode with him to the foot of the track.

The sun on the horizon was a football of gold which dazzled the eye. It squatted there at the end of a broad shimmering highway across the waves, and Number 6 permitted himself a smile at the thought of the open road that waited for him.

Quickly and efficiently, as though he had assembled it many times before, he went through the steps of surrounding the bracing with the shaped and watertight fabric like fitting a slipcover. As he did so, his alert senses caught the incoherent whuffling roar of a Guardian behind him. He turned to see it rolling down the beach towards him, accelerating into a wobbling charge.

Number 6's hand ducked into his pocket and produced the cat's old tennis ball. Clicking his tongue to attract the animal's attention, he let the cat sniff the ball for a moment, then tossed it in a long underhand to the landward side of the approaching Guardian. The cat sprang from the car and darted across the sands after its toy. As the furry shape shot past, the Guardian swerved and veered to follow it.

Immediate danger of interference diverted, Number 6 quickly bolted the open framework between two parallel pontoons and pushed the structure forwards into the surf.

His engine caught at the first touch of the starter. He let in the bottom gear and eased the KAR forward on to the structure. It settled lower, bobbing unsteadily until he reached the balance point. Then he shifted back into neutral, set the brake and hopped over the door. Balancing on the starboard pontoon, he bent to slip a rubber belt over the rear wheel. Then back into the car, and he erected the aluminum mast, braced between the seats. Shaking out the neatly rolled sail of nylon fabric, it was a matter of moments to snake a heavy cord through eyelets along one edge and line it up along the boom.

The ungainly catamaran rig was lifted now by the risen tide, and as he fed power to the rear wheels he felt the vibrations of the engine and the thrashing of the power screw push him away from the shore. Glancing over his shoulder, he saw the Guardian rolling about the beach in a widening search pattern as though it had lost him entirely.

Before him the last bright line of the sun was vanishing, and Mercury stood bright above it like a yellow beacon. His craft steadied as he drew past the gentle surf to deeper water, and he sped the screw until his engine was ticking at a comfortable three thousand rpm; then he set the rudder and clambered over the body of the KAR to run a quick inspection for stowaways. He was alone.

Already he was past the rocky point where Number 100 had shown himself – now he was approaching the area where his engine had died so mysteriously those many hard-won months ago.

His theories now would be vindicated or he would once again be returned to his Lifelike Habitat. It seemed whatever had affected his car had struck through the ignition, and he suspected the cause. Early in the Second World War there had been a device capable of stopping an internal combustion engine by radio-frequency induction – but the same shielding which prevented ignition systems from interfering with radio communications shielded them from induction as well and it was never used as a weapon. If the Village now were using a related method, his carefully shielded ignition should immunise him against it and at the very least give him a look at their next line of restriction.

The darkening coastline, rugged and sparsely wooded, drifted slowly past a mile away in unreal perspective for many minutes, and still the engine throbbed on. He estimated his speed at a comfortable ten knots – he held it while the sky darkened and the stars appeared. Mercury was gone below the horizon to port before the Great Bear became visible and directed his gaze to Polaris, halfway up the purpling infinite dome of the sky.

Now he steered away from land and raised his sail. As it filled with the seaward breeze he disengaged the engine and switched it off. He trimmed the sail manually until it was as taut as the following wind would make it, and secured its lines.

Again he set the rudder, and rode west with the breeze. The near-quarter moon shone high to his left, and ahead the fading glow of the sunset summoned him. In less than an hour he was out of sight of land.

The breeze held steady for another hour, until the last western glow was extinguished beneath the great dark sea, and a confusion of stars dusted the velvet blackness of the night. At length he brought his sail and rudder about in smooth coordination until he had the prow centred beneath the Northern Star. Then he fixed his sail again, lashed the rudder, and set about one last thorough checkout of everything.

Both pontoons now floated half-filled with petrol; beneath the seat and packed in the boot of his KAR were bottles of water and cans of food, fish-hooks, ropes and the usual gear for extended survival on the open ocean. He no more believed Number 100's statement that they were in the Balearic Islands than he believed his old superiors had been suspicious of his sanity before he'd resigned. He smiled. What a strange set of games Number 100 – if he had ever not been Number 2 – had chosen to play. And how fortunate for *him* that he had been willing to offer real stakes.

Watching the foam fleeing past him in the faintly moon-silvered darkness, he estimated that the continuing breeze now bore him north at a brisk twelve or fifteen knots. The hiss and slap of the bow waves was the only sound in the midst of a silence as vast as the night and the sea. All around him the infinite distant circle of horizon continued unbroken, and the constellations in their circling courses gave him his steadfast direction to the north.

The running swell of falling tide would carry him further seaward, but the wind should hold until morning. Then he would have to find what wind he could or make do with the engine. At least the skies were clear. Lulled at last by the silence, the release of months of accumulated tensions and a vast sense of accomplishment, he drifted thus in and out of a watchful sleep for some hours.

The first time he woke, the moon had set and Mars was low in the west. The sky seemed paler, somehow, though it was scarcely midnight – he looked up at the stars which no longer seemed to throng uncountably in the black of the sky and realised a thin curtain of mist had been drawn across them.

When he woke again an hour later it was gone, every star as crisp and sharp as pinholes in black paper. And eventually, Number 6 slept, half-stretched across the cushioned leather seat of his boat, uncomfortably wrapped under the steering wheel, a heavy beach blanket over him to ward off the damp chill of the night.

He didn't waken until the morning sun was bright through the clearing haze. Then he sat stiffly erect, rubbing his eyes.

Ahead of him a dark area on the horizon looked like land. Could it be the coast of Spain? Could Number 100 have been telling the truth? He squinted through the clearing mists of morning towards the dim uncertain shore.

The wind had failed sometime around dawn, and his sails hung limp in the faint movement of air that remained; now he struck the sail and started his engine again. As the machine warmed up he freed the rudder, let in the clutch and speeded the screw.

The distant blue haze resolved. He saw boats on the water, a town above the beach – small stone houses among trees, nestled between two rocky promontories. He couldn't see more, squinting into the newly risen sun.

As he drew nearer, the light dazzled him. But beneath it, on the rising ground above the small buildings like a watchful mother hen over her brood, stood a Green Dome. And the boats, he could now tell, were coming out to meet him.

He put about, knowing he couldn't hope to outdistance forty-knot power launches, and found a pair of twelve-foot spheres floating lightly on the water to seaward of him. His pointed ram was still ready – lifting it to position he gunned the engine towards the nearer Guardian, and without more than a moment of surprise felt the throbbing of the motor cease beneath him.

One sphere spoke with the raucous voice of Number 100, hugely amplified and resonant. "I'm afraid, Number Six, that you simply cannot be trusted with tools. And after all we've meant to each other. I found the sketch of the cat you made for me – I shall treasure it always. But you must come back – give us another chance."

"Another chance?"

"To make you feel at home here. We only want you to be happy, Number Six – and we want you to know that wherever you go, we will always be waiting to welcome you back. I do hope you have had a pleasant sail, though. Be seeing you."

And by then the boats were around him and hands were reaching down from them to help him aboard.

A Day in the Life

Music pounds out of the car's speaker with a steady insistent rhythm and the singer's voice sets up an eerie summons, high and compelling. It is a rock song, *White Rabbit*. Hard as daylight, the song wails on – the shadows of overhead trees dappling and swirling off the car as it roars down the highway and into the city.

The driver's face is grim and set. Eyes, chin, plane of the face, tightness of mouth, determined, stubborn and intractable. A dark blue scarf blows back from the throat of his jacket and his eyes stare intently ahead. The woman's image is conjured in the darkness of his mind, behind the brightness of London, its flat greens and sooty stone.

The car moves smoothly through the traffic, passing, turning and accelerating with a swift, sure expertise. The man's face is set unswervingly into the pounding uncertainty of the music. His eyes glitter and he smiles grimly, taking out a cigar and bringing it to his lips. Music and city blend into one kaleidoscopic rhythm: concrete and drums.

The music reaches an eerie, wailing climax, and the car drops down a ramp into an underground garage.

He gets out of the car and goes up to giant, double doors, throwing them open with a defiant downward jerk of his arms. He comes to a desk, glares at its occupant, whips an envelope from his pocket, slams it on the blotter, turns, exits.

A card goes up from a computer. Typewriter keys slam against it. The man's photograph is xxx'ed out.

The card passes down a conveyor, drops in a file. The file shuts. Its legend moves into the light: RESIGNED.

The man's car roars back through the traffic. His eyes gleam and there is a ruthless tilt to his jaw. A hearse is parked at the kerb before his house.

He gets out and goes in. Two men in black high silk hats, with black kerchiefs at the neck, look up after him.

He throws a group of travel folders in an already packed valise and begins to close it. A white fog swirls up about him. He turns and looks. A jet of gas comes in through the keyhole.

He straightens: the room spins.

The spire of St Paul's, seen through the window, spirals in against him. As he falls, his arm knocks the valise to the floor. Clothes and folders spill upon the carpet.

One of the folders falls flat beside his face. A name is printed beneath white gingerbread houses with grey-gabled roofs: PENRHYNDEUDRAETH: PORTMEIRION.

Section One

Some mornings it was:

"*Guten Morgen, Nummer Sechs.*" Number 105 straightened from her rose bushes and fluttered roughened, pudgy fingers at him.

"*Wie geht es Ihnen?*"

This interest seemed to please her, and she smiled, tucking a straying grey hair back beneath her scarf. "*Gut, danke, und Ihnen?*"

"*Gut, danke.*"

Beyond her yard, the street widened, winding down along the green, past the grocer's, to the sea.

Ting-a-ling-ling.

The bell above the door rang sharply in the dim, musky interior.

Number 87 looked up from the morning paper. "Ah, it's you, Number Six." His fat cheeks bowed in a smile. "I've been expecting you. That order of pickled herring just came in."

"I'd also like a half-dozen eggs, a five pound bag of flour, and some especially sharp cheddar."

"Cheddar?" Number 87 scratched dubiously behind his ear. "Oh, yes. Just the thing for you." He lifted the flap of the counter and came out around it, going to a group of wooden barrels in the shadow of one wall. He pushed back a cloth cover and produced a bit of rich golden cheese. "Try this."

"Satisfactory. Quite satisfactory."

"I thought you'd like it." Number 87 nodded and smiled. "How much?"

"A half-pound, I should think."

"Want to make it a whole pound, just to be sure?"

"No. Definitely a half."

"Right-o, Number Six." He busied himself weighing cheese, counting eggs, and getting the flour from its shelf. "Anything else for you today?" he said, doing the sum on a length of butcher's paper.

"Not today."

"That will be one point one five credit units."

"Charge it to my account."

"Good enough."

"And could you deliver this afternoon, about five?"

"Right-o." He rolled it all together in the paper and tied the bundle with a string. "I'll have Number Twenty-four bring it round. That is, if he ever gets here." Number 87 frowned, though his eyes remained merry and active. "Not dependable, you know. That's the way with youngsters these days. Not dependable." He shook his head in emphasis.

"Be seeing you."

Number 87 sketched a salute. "Be seeing you, Number Six."

Ting-a-ling-ling.

There was music playing on the speakers outside, and as the sun brightened, warming, people began to appear on the green and in the windy, gravelled lanes between the houses.

"Good day, Number Six." Number 237 appeared from a side street, sweeping off his battered fisher's hat and waving. Then he hurried and caught up. "Where are you off to today?"

"A chess game with the Admiral."

"Is that right? Never learned myself, you know." His scrubbed, honest face furrowed. "Not my sort of thing. More a hunting and fishing man, myself. Like to watch wrestling on TV. That sort of thing."

He was silent for a moment.

"You know something, Number Six?"

"What?"

"They're having a chess tournament in Village Hall next month, you really ought to enter."

"Why?"

"It'd be fun. I enter the fishing contest, myself. Won two years running. Not last year though. That was Number Eighty-seven. His first time, too. Going down to sign up now. Want to come with me and enter the chess tournament?"

"No thank you, Two Thirty-seven."

"Well, this is where I turn off. Some other time, maybe."

His hand swung in a hearty backslap, "Be seeing you," and he was off along the lane towards the Civic Centre.

Ting-a-ling-ling. The bell above the door rang. Inside it was cool, dark, sweet with the scent of tobacco.

"*Bonjour*, Number Six. How are you today?" The leathery old man continued rolling a cigar.

"Well enough, thank you, One Fifty-seven. And you?"

"Pretty well myself." He set the cigar aside to dry.

"You'll be wanting your specials, right?"

"Two dozen."

"Just a moment." He got up and went through a curtain to the back.

Ting-a-ling-ling.

"Number One Fifty-" The woman stopped. "Oh! Hello, Number Six." Her flowered dress swung against too full a figure. "I didn't see you here." She looked around. "Where's One Fifty-seven?"

"In the –"

"Here I am."

"There you are."

Number 157 placed a box on the counter. "Shall I wrap it?"

"No. I'll take it."

"There's the strangest thing going on outside."

"Here you are."

"Thank you."

"They're making some kind of film."

"I'll have to put in a new order soon."

"Please do –"

"Do you know anything about it, Number Six?"

"– and put this on my account. No, I don't, Number Thirty-two."

Her look was speculative and inviting.

"That's too bad, Number Six. How about you, One Fifty-seven?"

"What's this about a film?"

"There." She pointed through the window. Four young men stood around a camera, and a fifth stood behind it, eye to the lens, face hidden, looking through it towards the shop.

"*Qu'est–ce que c'est que ceci?* What are they doing to my store?"

Ting-a-ling-ling.

One of the youths came through the door, stuffing a handkerchief into the hip pocket of his denim slacks. "Hiya, pops. My mates and me" – he indicated the others around the camera – "are doing our term project in

Film-making. You remember, the course was announced last spring. And we were wondering if you wouldn't mind if we took some shots of you at work?"

"Me? Working? *Je ne compre* – I mean: Why?"

The youth shoved his hands into the pockets of his black leather jacket. "Well, it's a kind of documentary. There's so much to do and see here, so many interesting people and events, that we ... my mates and me ... we thought we'd try to show the old and the new. What it has been like and what it will be like."

"Oh. *Oui*. Whatever you like."

"And you, sir," the youth smiled: blond and engaging. "I didn't catch your number."

"Don't you know?" Number 32 said. "This is Number Six."

"Gosh, is that right, sir. I've heard a lot about you."

"Have you?"

"Oh, yes. A great deal. They think highly of you in this Village."

"Do they?"

"Yes. Me mother talks about you sometimes. And me mate, Number Twenty-four. He says you're a regular sort. Would you like to be in our film? I'm sure everyone would like to see you. You're not out much, I hear."

"No, thank you. I'm already late for an appointment."

"Say, that's too bad. Some other time?"

"Perhaps. Good day."

"Number Five Sixty-nine."

"And to you, too, Number Thirty-two."

"Where are you going?"

"To chess with the Admiral."

"The Admiral. Say, I'll bet he'd be a good subject for our film. He's been here longer than anybody."

"*A bientôt*, Number Six."

"Be seeing you, One Fifty-seven."

"Say, Miss –"

"Thirty-two. But it's Mrs really. My husband died."

"That's too bad."

"Oh, it was some time ago."

"Well, would you care to –"

Ting-a-ling-ling.

A sharp, cool breeze had sprung up from the sea, smelling of salt water in the sleepy afternoon sunshine. The group around the camera glanced up curiously, then turned back to their conversation.

Down the beach (past the deck chairs with their red and white striped umbrellas) the Village Restaurant was just opening. Number One Twenty-seven was busying herself about the patio tables, whisking off the night's residue of grit and moisture, and preparing for the day's clientele. She stopped for a moment and waved: the fragile face beneath her tarnished blonde hair showing no trace of the bitterness that had led her to attempt suicide in the water so near at hand.

"Ah, Number Six. Been wondering when you'd get here." The Admiral displayed the open board, figures ranked upon it.

"Good day, Admiral. Sorry to be late."

"Think nothing of it. Happened to be late myself. A touch of stiffness in my bones this morning."

"Nothing serious, I trust."

"Damme, lad, only an old man's aches and pains. Don't give it a second thought." His huge gentle fingers opened to reveal two pawns: one black, one white. He hid them behind his back, then held out both hands, palms closed. "Choose."

"That one."

The right contained: black.

They made the traditional opening: Queen's pawns to Queen's four.

The new girl came out, wearing a terrycloth robe over her swim suit, and moved one of the chairs into the sun, using a towel for a pillow. Sunlight gleamed off the silver lenses of her glasses.

"She's a looker, eh, lad? What do you think?"

"Haven't met her."

"Always a cautious one, you are." He brought his cane around and leaned his chin on the fertile. "Know her number?"

"No."

"Number Seven."

"Your move."

"Eh, lad. Oh, yes."

The Admiral's face composed itself line by fold by jowl into an exaggerated concentration, and he placed a finger beside his nose, peering blearily down at the board. Then he reached out, lifted an ivory figure, and set it down on a white square, vulnerable and tempting.

Reply:

Pawn took pawn.

The old man smiled, moved a Knight in reply.

"Knight to Queen's Bishop three. You prefer, then, Admiral, the Scotch opening?"

The play went swiftly.

"What? Castling so soon?"

Somewhere, out of sight, a brash young band swung into a Beatles tune, *Michelle*.

Four moustached young men in gaudy silk uniform led the band. Behind them a group of men marched in Salvation Army grey. Their leader had the hang dog look of the existentialist intellectual, steel-rimmed glasses, a French horn, and a chartreuse suit with red piping. He was followed by a shifty-eyed, big nosed trombone player in pink with blue braid; a sweet-faced choirboy fingering an oboe; and last: a stern-faced lad in a scarlet tri-corn.

Down the beach the girl in the bathing suit had turned in her chair and lifted her glasses for a look.

She was beautiful.

And some mornings it was:

"You there, Number Six, wake up."

The cool grey light of the television flickered against the living-room floor and its speaker rattled with sharp, insistent demands.

"Get up, Number Six. I want to talk to you."

The bathroom tile was cold, the tap water icy and fresh.

"You haven't been adjusting, co-operating. Why is that? Is there anything we can do to make your stay more comfortable? Is there something you lack?"

But the shower was hot. Steam rolling up the walls in a pebbly grey finish.

"We have tried to satisfy you, tried to help you fit in. Just what is your problem? We'll be glad to help, if only you'd ask. That's all we want, really, to make you happy here. What is it? What can we do? Answer me, Number Six Do you hear? Speak up."

A small sauce pan, a large pat of butter, a quarter cup of flour, some salt, a pinch of cayenne, and milk.

"Speak up. I will not tolerate this silence. It is your duty as a citizen to speak. I demand you answer me."

The yolks of four eggs beaten until thick (the shining metal blades cutting into the rich yellow vitelline).

"Answer me. Speak up. I'm warning you. I won't tolerate this kind of disobedience. You can't flout authority in this manner. You can be made to speak, you know. There are ways of dealing with you."

Then the whites, whipped to stiff peaks.

"Come in here where I can see you, this instant. I will brook no further delay. I want to see you and I want to see you now. I know you're in the kitchen. You're always in the kitchen. You'll make some woman a wonderful wife someday. Your culinary expertise is well known. Now get in here and listen."

Fresh, springy bits of cheddar dropped into the pan, and the flat plastic blade of the spatula stirring it in.

"There simply isn't room in this Village for someone who will not co-operate. We all have to work together to make it a fit place to live. And it will take all our efforts. The welfare of this Village must come before that of any one individual. Surely you see that?"

Then the yolk into the cheese batter and the mixture over the whites.

"We can only progress if we progress together. We must work in harmony and good fellowship. That's the only way we can build a community free from distrust, dissent, and unhappiness. One family, working together, playing together, living together. That's our ideal, a true mutuality of mankind. If you would seek to know what you could do for others, not what they might do for you, you would find rewards of which you have never dreamed."

The whole into souffle dish and into the oven.

"Our differences of opinion need only be set aside to achieve mankind's dream: Community. There need be nothing to mar our brotherhood. And in this golden isle, all will shine more brightly."

An hour of calisthenics and a fifteen-minute jog

Then breakfast.

"I want to see you here, in my office, at four o'clock. Do you understand? Number Six, answer me! Four o'clock. Not a minute later. I can have you brought, you know. I don't have to be polite. You've been allowed more than enough freedom in the past. It's a privilege you've abused. If you can't accept its responsibilities — Was that the door? Did you —"

The voice cut from speaker to speaker in the grey morning fog.

"I can see you, Number Six. I know what you're doing, where you're going. There are no secrets in this Village, no private existence. There is no need for privacy when all men are as one. Why not join us, give us a chance. We stand ready to help you. You have only to ask."

The tall, candy-striped poles with their square metal hoods and glittering camera eyes waited at each corner, speakers crackling with cool electric life.

"We are simply not going to accommodate ourselves to you. Get that thought out of your head. You're not that important. You have a certain value to us, yes. But nothing so great as you think. You are no more than a cog in our machine, and you must be made to work smoothly. You will be made to work smoothly. There is room only for harmony. And we will have harmony."

Number 105's house was shuttered and dark. The roses bright with dew.

"Think about that: harmony and beauty. A village living in peace and contentment,

a model for the world to follow. Oh, if you'd only let yourself go, you'd find us the best of fellows. There's so much to do, you could really be quite comfortable here. It's only your attitude that can't be tolerated. We love the real you."

Ting-a-ling-ling.

Chop. Number 87's cleaver cut through the beef. Chop. Chop. Chop. Steady, even slices, the silver wedge of the blade striking down against the wooden cutting board. Chop. Chop. Chop.

"Good morning, Number Eighty-seven."

A mean, resentful look from tiny eyes set deep over quivering, sullen jowls. "Number Six."

"And how are you this morning?"

"Well enough, thank you. Your order?" He produced pad and pen.

"Chopped liver."

"Off today."

"In that case . . . Kippers, definitely kippers."

"Off today."

"What would you recommend?"

"Couldn't say."

"One of those steaks . . . No. Not the fat one. That one there."

"Some people . . . know-it-alls . . ." he muttered. "Disparaging a man's. . ."

"What was that, Eighty-seven?"

His hands moved deftly, folding the meat tightly into paper. "Here. That'll be point eight five credit units."

"Charge –"

"All right." He frowned down at the register. "Getting quite a balance, you are."

"Bill me at the end of the month, as always, and have this deliver –"

"No deliveries today."

"No?"

"No. Number Twenty-four quit. Taken up a new career. Film-making it is. Just like these lads today: no sense of values. This profession was good enough for me father and it is good enough for me. Don't see why they have to go off and get themselves involved in that foolishness." He picked up the cleaver and made an abrupt downward motion. Chop.

"Be seeing you."

Chop. Chop. Chop.

Ting-a-ling-ling.

"– in the Cultural Centre at two o'clock . . . And the Women's League for Better Government will hold a benefit showing of Gone With the Wind in the Little Theatre this evening at half past seven. I repeat: There will be a display of the sculpture of our own Number Three Thirty–six this afternoon at two in the Cultural Centre. And this evening at half past seven the Women's League for Better Government will hold a benefit showing of Gone With the Wind. It's for a good cause; please come and help promote mutuality in our Village. It is forty–two degrees centigrade and the wind is two point three miles an hour from the north–northeast. This is your Hostess, Number Two Fifteen, turning you over to the music of Mantovani with his arrangement of Yesterday."

The day was grey, heavily overcast, the underbellies of the clouds moving in dark, ragged streamers. The wind chill, a faint foretaste of rain in the air. Gravel popped underfoot and the white gingerbread houses stood out sharp and vivid, grey-gabled roofs like battlements raised against the sky.

Ting-a-ling-ling.

The man sitting behind the counter, bent over a rolling machine, was large and beefy, a thin reddish beard covering his cheeks. The shop was pungent with the aroma of tobacco.

"Yes. May I help you?"

"Where is One Fifty-seven?"

"He is no longer here." The man did not look up from his work.

"What do you mean, 'no longer here'?"

"He left."

"For where?"

"I wasn't told."

"People do not just leave this Village."

"He did."

"Why?"

"He was no longer wanted. He was not mutual." The man lifted his massive head, eyes fierce and black. "Why? Was he a *particular* friend of yours?"

"No. I merely came to inquire about my order."

He pulled a ledger towards him. "And you are?"

"Number Six."

"Yes, of course," he nodded. "I might have known." He pushed the ledger away. "I'm afraid your order hasn't gone through yet."

"What do you mean, 'not gone through'?"

"All orders have to be initialled by Number Two, you know."

"And he hasn't initialled it?"

"He could be busy. You know how these things are. I'm sure he'll get to it soon."

"In the meanwhile, do you have any left?"

"A few."

"Might I have them."

"Yes. Of course."

He brought out a box. "There's one more. Do you want it now?"

"Will you hold it?"

"If you wish."

"Please."

"You're a polite one, you are."

"Be seeing you."

Ting-a-ling-ling.

On the opposite side of the green the young filmmakers were grouped around their camera, one of them panning it slowly across the Village. A woman stood next to the blond leader. She raised a hand in greeting. "Yoohoo, Number Six. Come here a moment, won't you?"

"Good day, Number Thirty-two. How are you this morning?"

She regarded him thoughtfully, brow dimpled faintly in a frown. "There's something I want you to hear, Number Six." She turned to her companion. "Tell him about it, Five Sixty-nine."

"Uh . . ." He scowled and fingered a calibrated lens hanging from his neck. "It's like this." He looked around warily. "My mates say you're O.K. Thirty-two, well, she says you're a regular bloke, too. So I guess I should tell you. I hear you're in trouble, in dutch with the authorities, see. They wanta get you, you know?"

"Get me? How?"

"Oh, well." He looked at the ground and then up towards the sky. "I don't exactly know. I just hear it, that's all."

"Where?"

"Oh, come on, man. Don't push me That's all I know. Period." He walked off towards the camera.

"Number Six?" Her eyes were troubled, worried.

"Yes?"

"Why do you persist? You can't defy them forever. My husband – poor Harry – he tried it, and look what it got him. Ah, don't you see," her voice fell to a whisper. "You could at least pretend to give in, like the rest of us."

"I'll keep it in mind."

"Hello, Number Six." A boy with a large nose greeted him.

"Hello, Number Twenty-four."

The boy looked worried; nervous.

The beach was cold, rank with a stench of ocean and seaweed.

"There will be a class in 'The Village – Its Charter and Government', seven p.m., Tuesday the nineteenth, in the Civic Centre Meeting Hall. You're all urged to attend. Citizenship is your right and privilege. Exercise it. Become more mutual today."

"Ah, lad," the Admiral waved from his umbrella, "a bit brisk today."

"If you'd rather –"

"No. No. That's all right. A drop of wine to take the chill off and I'll be fine."

A pawn was offered and rejected.

The new woman, Number Seven, came past them down the beach.

She was young, in her early twenties, with dark hair and a slender figure. She had a wistful expression, compounded of bitterness, disappointment and hope. And she looked at everything with a quick, uncertain glance, as if hoping in it she might find something of value, but knowing she would not.

Their eyes met for a moment, then she moved on, not quite smiling.

It was raining. He could hear the drumming of it against the roof. And, as simply as that, he was conscious.

He lay quietly for a while and listened to the rain. It was a good sound, clean and substantial: above suspicion. The weather was (save himself) the only thing he could trust.

He drew in a deep lungful of the sweet morning air and sat up, flesh contracting at the chill. He got out of bed, went into the grim, intestinal pink bathroom, rinsed his teeth and emptied his bladder. Then he stepped into the shower and turned the hot water handle all the way around.

The water smashed against him, icy cold, shrivelling his scrotum and sending a hot flush up spine and neck into his face. He picked up the soap and began to lather.

The shower turned warm, then searing.

"Good morning." The tinny shout of the television was louder even than the steaming crash of the water. "A cheery good morning. It's seven–thirty here in the Village. Time for us all to be out of bed and about our business. We've all got to do our bit, you know. A job for everyone and everyone at his job.

"Cloudy today, with a strong chance of showers, clearing late tonight or tomorrow. Be sure to wear your rubbers and carry your umbrellas. It will be wet."

He turned off the water and got out, towelling himself dry and combing his hair.

Two eggs on to poach, a muffin in the toaster, and ham set sizzling. He melted a little butter, beat in a tablespoon of flour, a pinch of salt, some nutmeg and a dash of pepper. Then he mixed it with a third cup of cream and stirred till it was thick. A capful of white wine and a palmful of Swiss cheese finished the sauce.

He buttered the muffins, set ham on each, an egg on the ham, poured the sauce over the egg, added green pepper and chives, and sat down to breakfast.

There was a blistered, discoloured spot on the moulding by his feet. Must be a leak somewhere. He glanced up – the enamel was unblemished. Either water was trickling in down a beam or there was faulty plumbing behind the wall. This wasn't a reasonable place for plumbing, though, and he'd gone over the rooftiles quite carefully this summer.

He dressed warmly in underwear, trousers, sweater and jacket, then laid his topcoat on the bed and turned to the mirror. He parted his hair high on the right side, sweeping it back straight at the temples.

His reflection stared back: brooding, enigmatic brow, straight nose, severe mouth, determined chin, fair Saxon complexion and wheat-straw hair looking stubborn and defiant.

Finished, he draped the overcoat across his arm and went into the living-room. He took the polished mahogany lid from his humidor and selected a handful of cigars, fitting them into a silver case and pocketing the case. There were less than a dozen left; he would have to see about his order. It might well have been filled by now. They had always gone out of their way to supply his individual brand before. Had, in fact, placed them here in anticipation of his arrival.

He had not (on that first day) been surprised to find them. Thoroughness (he had already surmised and was later to accept) was one of their characteristics and, however difficult the obtaining of these cigars must have been, they had not stinted, nor had he suspected any motive beyond thoroughness.

But now (replacing the lid) he wondered: Had so trivial an annoyance been prepared even then? Was everything, from the colour of the bathroom (so hideous he almost could not resist painting it) to the leak behind the wall (which he would, here at the beginning of winter with no chance of escape in sight, have to repair) a part of their plan? Did they hope, ultimately, to diminish him with minutiae, one grain at a time?

Quite deliberately he stilled his thoughts and gave himself up to the savouring of a cigar.

He opened the door and went out.

The rain had stopped and a cool golden light shone on the whitewashed buildings. Drops clung like crystal to tree limbs, sparkling in the sun. And in the fragile, translucent air even the distant, gabled skyline was clear and sharp.

Then a cloud rolled before the sun, plunging the Village into shadow.

Something scraped, struck metallically behind him. He turned. The long bony fingers of a branch stirred against his window. It would have to be pruned, of course, otherwise it might shatter the pane during a storm.

He moved down the moist, gravelled lane towards the green.

Number 105 was already out, stooping over the roses in a far corner of her lawn. A drab brown coat hung round her shoulders and flapped in the wind.

"*Guten Morgen,*" he said.

She did not turn or seem to hear.

The sea wind touched him, acrid and strong. He slipped his topcoat on and cinched it tightly, thrusting his hands in the pockets for warmth.

Number 237 emerged from a house, rod and reel in hand.

"Good morning, Number Two Thirty-seven."

The man looked up, a frown wrinkling his brow, sun striking flame from the fish hooks in his hat. "Oh, it's you, Number Six."

"Going fishing?"

He grimaced, speaking slowly, reluctantly. "Yes, with Number Eighty-seven. On the boats. Sort of a holiday. Been planning it a long time. Damn rain. Special permission from Number Two himself. Not going to let the weather stop us. Must run, you know." He set off down the road, not looking back.

Ting-a-ling-ling.

The new proprietor put down a pipe and stood up. "Yes? It's

Number ..."

"Six."

"Six. Yes, of course. Come about your order I imagine."

"Has it come?"

"Part of it. Humm. Yes, part of it."

"That's never happened before."

"No. I dare say it hasn't. Rather unusual I should think."

"How many have come in?"

"Six dozen. Six dozen all together."

"Have you reordered?"

"Yes; expect I'll hear something most any day now."

"Could you send a dozen round my way this afternoon?"

"Can't say, Number Six. Really can't say. My assistant's quit. Gone into film-making."

"Yours too?"

"Yes. I heard tell Number Eighty-seven's quit yesterday."

"Curious. I'll come back myself. About a quarter to five."

"Very good. Be seeing you."

"Be seeing you."

Ting-a-ling-ling.

It had grown darker, greyer outside, and a chill mist fell, descending on neck and brows. He turned up the collar of his coat and moved quickly across the green, soggy turf.

"Hey, lad, wait up."

He turned. The Admiral hurried towards him, brandishing his cane for emphasis.

"I had –"

"Expected to find me home, no doubt." The old man stopped and caught his breath. "Would have been too, but my charwoman didn't come. Had to go out myself. Weather like this is no good for a man my age. It's mortal cold, Number Six. And the cold hurts. My bones ache and I feel a touch of fever. Still up to a game of chess though. Nothing better. A warm fire, a drop of wine, and an afternoon with a pleasant companion. That's the ticket. Come on."

"My place or yours? Mine is closer."

"Mine. Mine, of course. Expecting a visitor."

"Who?"

They started across the green and the mist condensed, became rain.

"Eh, lad? What's the matter? You're looking thoughtful again. Dangerous sign. I've marked it before. Bound to get you into trouble."

His hand indicated the Village. "What more trouble could there be?"

"Don't say that lad." The Admiral shuddered. "Don't say it. You're bound to find out if you ask. I always have and I've never liked the answer."

They let themselves into a small, brick cottage set towards the southern edge of the Village. A great fire roared in the hearth and he was warm almost before they had entered. Papers, glasses and ashtrays were scattered around tables, desk and floor.

"Damn woman always comes Thursday. Why didn't she come today?"

"Didn't you call her?"

"No answer."

Then he remembered. "Isn't Number One Hundred five your charwoman?"

"Eh? Yes, yes she is. Why, lad? Have ye seen her?"

"This morning, pruning her roses. I called to her, but she didn't answer."

"Maybe she's heard."

"Heard what?"

The Admiral settled back and narrowed his eyes. "Don't tell me, you really don't know?"

"Know what?"

"You're *persona non grata* these days. There's a new Number Two and he's put it out that you are no longer to receive special treatment. I think he let it be known that he didn't consider you exactly kosher, not mutual, you know. That anyone seen with you might be suspect too."

"What about you?"

"Bosh. An old man like myself? No one pays any attention to me."

"Thank you, Admiral," he said.

"Ah ... here. Set up the board, while I find the wine."

They played for some half-hour in silence.

"You there, Number Six. We know you're there. We know everything about you." The television across the room had come on, and a man's face took form. Though the background (a wall-sized bookcase and lamp) were in normal colour, the face had a bluish, almost purple cast, lips dark as

dried blood. The man had close-cropped hair, a bullet shaped head, small feral features and a sharp smile.

"Not everything surely?"

"We've had enough of your boarding–school humour, too. Times have changed. We can no longer afford the freedom you enjoyed in the past. We've allowed you certain privileges before. That's over now. You've got to get in line like the rest of us. The age of the individual is past. This is the age of the common man. There was room for your kind once. No more. We must all march together, the same step, the same direction, the same goals. This is the road to progress."

"An excellent move, Admiral. I have rarely seen a rook used to such advantage."

"Nothing to it, lad. Just a sharp eye and an orderly mind."

"Number Six, answer me. This minute! I want to talk to you. In fact, I want to see you right now, in my office."

"Might I have another glass of wine?"

"Certainly, Number Six. Allow me."

"You too, Number Three Hundred seven. We've had our eye on you for quite some time. You had better mend your ways."

"Number Three Hundred seven. Is that your number? I didn't know that."

"Just call me 'Admiral'."

"Of course."

"The world has been tamed. There is no room left for rebels. We have a peaceful Village. Our citizens are content. I will not allow you to disrupt them. You're setting a bad example for our youth. They are becoming upset and uncertain. We cannot allow that. You must be stopped."

"Excuse me a moment, lad." The Admiral rose and went into the kitchen. He came out carrying a large pewter vase. He tilted the television set face down.

"What are you doing, Number Three Hundred seven? You can't shut me off –"

The Admiral poured the water from the vase into the back of the set. There was a sharp glare of electricity and the voice went dead.

"We can expect a repair crew momentarily."

"Right you are, lad. They won't leave you alone a minute in this damned place."

The doorbell rang.

"Good after –" She caught herself and stared up at him through the darkened lenses of her glasses.

"Number Six," the Admiral said, coming forward. "And this is Number Seven. She's a newcomer."

They made themselves comfortable.

"You surprise me, Admiral."

She lifted her sunglasses and looked at him thoughtfully. "The Admiral's been good to me. I ran into him my first day here. I was upset." She had fine, sharp features, clear youthful skin, and wistful, disappointed eyes.

"Eh? That's all right, lass. Think nothing of it. We were all put off a bit, our first day here."

"Your television ... have you dismantled it? I tried that with mine, but they came right away and repaired it. There's no way to shut it off."

"A little butter to make it run smooth."

"Yes." She gave him a final, wondering glance and then replaced her glasses. "It is rather Alice in Wonderlandish, Number Six."

"You're an American?"

"Yes."

"What's an –"

Outside they heard the high, piercing warble of a repair truck.

The door was flung open and four men came in: two of them wore blue uniforms and severe expressions; the other two wore rumpled green jumpsuits and carried rectangular metal repair kits.

"Number Six?" said one of the men in blue.

The repairmen went to work on the set.

"You, mate. I'm talking to you." He pointed a hairy finger.

"Yes."

"Come with us."

"All right." He turned to the girl. She tilted her head up to look at him. His reflection stared back from the lenses: a tall substantial looking man in a dark suit. "Number Seven."

"Number Six," she replied.

"Thank you, Admiral. I enjoyed the game."

"I'll see you later, lad." The old man's eyes were apprehensive.

"Be seeing you."

"Come on, mate."

Number 2 looked up, frowning. "Good afternoon, Number Six. I trust you were not inconvenienced."

"Not at all."

"Good. I'll take that as a sign of co-operation. I shall expect to see a great deal more of it from you, now that I am in office." His eyes narrowed. "You don't remember me, do you?"

Should he? or was this just one more slight-of-hand? Then, for a moment, he could almost (like a ghost image in the far recesses of his mind) remember this face, this voice, this precise tilt of head and gleam of demonic eye. Then, as he reached, it was gone, like mist, before daylight of reason.

"No."

"I was –"

"Number 4!"

"– Number Four then."

Yes. And for a moment the period stood out with utter clarity. There was a sense of water, the sea, a small boat, a quarter mile of dirt track, the use of his car ... Realities he could almost, but not quite make come clear, but which, if he could penetrate their centre, would be his. Then the vision was gone, only a dim impression remaining like a hauntingly familiar scent.

"You weren't so highly placed then."

"I am now. That is what concerns us. That and your intractable attitude. My predecessors have been too lenient with you. They sought to win your cooperation with kindness. I've had experience with your peculiar kind of mentality before. I know how to deal with it. You will co-operate or you will obey, but you will change. Have I made myself clear?"

"Quite."

"But" – his voice was built for harshness; it could not easily make the transition to conciliation – "things could be made easier for you. You could be set free. If only –"

"I'd tell you why I resigned?"

"I don't like that attitude of yours, Number Six. And I intend to do something about it." He looked back down at some papers. "Dismissed."

The rain fell heavier and heavier, whispering over the ground and drawing premature twilight across buildings and shrubs. Purple clouds boiled across the sky, running before the wind. Leaves whipped up about him and the rain stung his face.

He turned the collar of his coat up against his neck and went down the street to the tobacco shop. It was dark and shuttered, a CLOSED sign hanging in the window. He glanced at his watch: four thirty-five.

He walked down away from the shop and went home.

Number Seven was waiting on the steps.

"May I come in?"

"Yes, of course."

"I was curious. Exactly what do they *do* when they are displeased?"

"It depends." He took her coat and put it in the closet, switched on the stereo.

"On what?"

"I don't know."

"You don't seem to have come into any harm."

"Not this time."

They sat down.

"You have before?"

"On occasion."

"What was it like?"

"Would you care for tea, a drink?"

"Not now, thank you." She took off her glasses. "In a while."

"I started to ask you something earlier."

"Yes . . . Number Six is it? I'm not very good with numbers."

He smiled.

She laughed and crossed her legs. "Yes, it is rather absurd, isn't it. I wasn't very good with names either. Just faces."

"Number Six."

"Of course. I always remember them when I hear them and think myself a fool for forgetting."

"How –"

"How did I come here?" She raised her eyes and met his. "I was going to ask you the same thing. You see, I haven't learned much, really. Nobody here will talk, except the Admiral. I like him. He's the only person I've met here I feel I can trust."

"I feel very much the same."

"And I haven't been able to get in touch with the authorities – Number Two, I think he's called."

"Yes."

"And it's been rather hard, all in all. I tried to get out, of course, but that's almost impossible. There's no train or bus or car. And when you try to walk out, those . . . I don't know – they're like balloons, only I think they're alive – they stop you. And they're heavy."

"Guardians."

"Is that what they're called? How appropriate. Anyway, there doesn't seem to be any way out, not easily, and the natives won't tell me anything, and the Admiral's rather vague. I thought perhaps, well, you looked decisive. That's a rare quality anywhere. And I thought, Sandra, that's my real name, Sandra Champaign. Ridiculous isn't it? But it's the truth, I swear it. Sandra, I said to myself, maybe he doesn't know anything, and maybe he does, and maybe he's one of the ones responsible for your being here, and maybe he isn't, but you've got to talk to someone sometime and he looks worthwhile."

"I see."

"Who goes first? What's your name?"

"You might not believe it either. It's the British equivalent of John Smith."

"Then perhaps we had better stick to numbers."

"Perhaps we had, Number Seven."

"I'll go first, if you like, but I'd like that cup of tea, now."

"I don't talk like this all the time," she said when he'd brought in the service.

"Imagine you did."

"It's . . . I don't know, like giving up cigarettes. There's a tension, it crawls right up and gets inside you and fills you with a kind of evil energy. Do they have grass here, do you know?" She cocked her head and watched him with a half-amused curiosity.

"No I don't. How old are you?"

"Twenty-five." There was something appealing and pathetic in her eyes. "I saw some kids making a film around town. I imagine they'd know if anyone would."

"Your reason for being here?"

"I don't know" – she leaned her head to one side and looked at him again – "if there is a reason for my being here. But what happened was this: I was hitching by plane from Los Angeles to New York. Dylan is giving a free concert at Woodstock."

"Hitch-hiking by plane?"

"It's something I learned when I was married. My husband was a very successful insurance broker and so we were given a lot of credit cards. Anyway, one day he came home and said he couldn't stand it any more at the office, that the way we were living was sick and that we had to go out and find out more about life and ourselves. We used our cards and went around the country. We were with the Poor People's March in Washington when the troops came in and levelled their shacks. We used to sit outside in the evenings and look through the smog, rolling dope and talking. After a while, we split up. He just dropped out of sight, and since he wouldn't go back to work, there was no way they could collect their money. I was in Florida so I went to the airport and after a while this gay cat took me to his mansion in the Bahamas." She shivered. "I'm talking too much. I better drink some of this tea. Delicious. God, I'd like some grass. Got to come back down to reality. This place is too much."

"You were in Los Angeles –"

"Yeah, and this spade cat, he came up and said I looked like I was going to New York to see Dylan and he had a plane and he'd like some company to keep him awake. He was loaded – a TV star, I think – and he was going there to give acid away. Just for the vibes, you know?"

He stared back at her.

"So I got in his plane, and we went up, and I began to get sleepy, and he said, relax, go to sleep, he'd wake me up after a while. I did and I woke up here."

"Remarkable."

"You don't believe me?"

"It's no less likely than my story."

"Say." She looked around. "Your place is groovier than mine. I mean, I haven't got a stereo. And that's a good one." Her eyes narrowed. "Why is that?"

"I asked."

"And they gave it to you."

"Yes."

"Why?"

"I don't know."

"How did *you* get here, anyway?"

"I had a job, a job in . . . security."

"You were a spy?"

"Something like that."

She smiled wistfully. "I've known rock stars and dope dealers, but never a spy."

"I resigned."

"Why?"

"I'd rather not say."

"I can see that."

"It was my refusal that brought me here. It's a rather bizarre detention camp, as far as I can make out."

"A detention camp?"

"For a certain kind of person. Men and women for whom their government has the highest regard, but who possess information which is thought too delicate to risk in the world at large."

"But surely, not all of these people . . ."

"Not all of them. Some, as far as I have been able to determine, are what they seem."

"And of course some aren't either, but are the watchers."

"Apparently."

"Then what am I doing here?"

"Exactly what I was wondering."

"Do you come here often at this hour?"

"Yes. Quite often."

"It's beautiful, isn't it."

"Yes, very."

They stood, not quite touching, watching the steam rise from the ocean, a rose mist above bronze metallic waves. Dawn had turned the western sky ivory, and the morning breeze, chill and damp, blew up, tugging at their clothing. A few grey birds wheeled across the sky, levelled and shot past in a great beating of wings.

She turned to him. "People here don't trust each other very much."

He started to speak.

"Oh, I see the reasons. But . . . people can't live like that. It isn't good for them. They become hostile and remote, willing to do anything. Their lives and other people's lives become valueless and meaningless. I can see that it's even happening to you."

A bird cried.

"You don't like that, do you? But it's true. You're like a boxer out of training – I knew a boxer once, lived with him in New Orleans. You're not fit. You're restless and uneasy, out of your element. Do you really think you could have retired?"

"Yes."

"Some people *are* like that. They can relax as hard as they work. Not me, though. I wish I could."

He shoved his hands into his pockets and stared down at her.

"I've got to get out of here, you know." Her voice was sharper, desperate. "This place is no good for me. No good for anyone."

"What do you want?"

"Don't –"

"I'm sorry," he said. "I've heard all this many times before."

"And yet, you don't look like one of them. I can tell a lot from a man's face. And you don't look like one of the sheep, either. I don't understand you or the Admiral. I would have thought either one of you would have escaped by now."

"It's harder than it looks."

"Is it? I thought it might be. But you do want to escape, don't you?"

"I will escape."

"You sound so positive. When?"

"I don't know. When the right time comes."

"And when will that be?"

He shrugged again.

"Hey, there! Number Six."

They turned.

It was the blond, gangling Number Five Sixty-nine.

"Number Five Sixty-nine," he said, "Number Seven. Number Seven, Number Five Sixty-nine "

"Hello, Number Seven." He looked up. "Number Two's really out to get you."

"How flattering."

"No, mate, I'm serious. Me sister, Number Seventy-three, she's 'is secretary, and she's heard. He give orders you was to be picked up and brought to trial."

"On what charge?"

"Search me. But I do know this: Me and my mates, we been thinking. This being called Numbers, that's for the straights. Get me – the establishment. Names is where it's at. And we been watching you. You don't put up with much. You don't take no bull – pardon me, miss."

"You know where I can get some grass?" she said.

"Oh, wow, yeah, sure. See me later, we're growing some up just east of town." He pulled out a handkerchief and wiped his face. "Like I was saying, you don't put up with too much, and well . . . we dig that, get me? We think you're okay. If we can help you we will. But from now on, we're gonna be more like you. You know, independent."

"Far out." She smiled.

"Well . . . I gotta be on my way, Number Twenty-four wants to see me. In some kind of trouble, I think. A nice bloke, but careless. Good day." He went back up the slope and walked away.

"You seem to be quite popular."

"In demand, at any rate."

"What are you going to do?"

"Have breakfast. Care to join me?"

"Oh yes. This looks interesting. What will they do to you, do you think?"

"I don't."

They mounted the steps to the restaurant terrace and went in to the steamy warmth of the dining room. He drew out a chair.

The corners of her mouth quirked. "Are all British men so polite?"

"I don't know."

"You don't give a lot away, do you?"

Before he could answer, she was looking out the window.

Number One Twenty-seven appeared beside them, producing a pad from the pocket of her uniform and staring down at the table. Suddenly she turned and looked straight at him. "Oh, Number Six. It's all right. Really it's all right. I forgive you. I do. I understand now. Can't we just be friends and forget it?"

"Yes. Yes, of course we can." He smiled.

"Good." She seemed satisfied. "Now, your order?"

He lifted a brow. Number 7 bit her lip. "Coffee? You do have coffee, don't you?"

"Oh, yes, Miss. Though we don't get so much of a demand for it."

"Good. Coffee and a roll."

"What kind of roll?"

"Any kind. It doesn't matter. Choose one yourself."

"Anything else?"

"No."

"And you, Number Six."

"Steak and eggs."

"I didn't know Englishmen ate steak and eggs."

"I picked it up in America, Number Seven."

"Aught to drink?"

"Tea, please."

She went away.

"What was all that about?"

"One of the less creditable episodes of my life."

"You'd rather not talk about it?"

"No."

She turned and stared out a window. "Look." She pointed.

A group of women, mostly in their forties, were marching across the green, looking angry and carrying placards. At the distance it was impossible to read the legends.

Her eyes met his. "You know, I don't understand this place. Look over there."

A television camera stared at them from high on the far wall.

"They know where we are and what we are doing and what we are saying. Your place, my place, all the houses I've been in, and every street corner, all have cameras and speakers. And yet, they're looking for you, and they haven't come to get you. Why is that?"

Number 127 returned just then and they ate.

Afterwards they went up the street towards her house.

"It's incredible, really, to think that this place exists. In the outside world, you'd never imagine it, not in a million years. Oh, some crackpot type who really believes in a 'they' might. The kind who get their kicks seeing vast conspiracies behind every setback and pigmentation of skin. The kind of guy who watches *The Fugitive* and *The Invaders and The F.B.I.* But no one else would really take such a place seriously. And yet, being here, it all seems so inevitable. Insane, but inevitable."

"Yes, I had that impression myself."

"I mean, they never leave you alone and they never make sense, but they control you completely, and you never asked to be controlled or to be part of their system, but here you are, and there's no way to resist or to escape. The Establishment's Establishment, in a way. Disneyland with J. Edgar Hoover at the helm."

They rounded a corner and the mob of women was before them.

They stood gathered around the bookstore window in an angry snarl of conversation. One of the placards turned full on:

VILLAGERS FOR DECENT LITERATURE

BAN SMUT!!

PORTNOY'S COMPLAINT MUST GO!!

One of the women detached herself from the mass and came towards them.

It was Number 105, wearing her drab brown coat. Her face was pale and her eyes red-rimmed from crying.

"*Entschuldigen Sie, Nummer Sechs.* No —" she caught her breath. "I will the English speak. I must, Number Six. I must speak with you."

"I was just going," Number 7 said.

"Is. Please. Is not necessary." The old woman stopped and clasped her hands. "Not necessary."

"No, really." She put on her glasses.

"Be seeing you," he said.

"I hope so." She pushed through the women and went into the bookstore.

"Oh, Number Six, I've wanted to talk with you for long."

"I called out to you this morning."

"And I didn't hear! How stupid. I'm so upset. Please, you seem like a kind man, a . . . modern man. I don't like to ask —"

"That's all right. Let's go this way. It's quieter."

The sun came out from behind a cloud and suddenly the day was dazzling white.

"I don't know what to do, myself. I'm only a woman from the old country."

"What country?"

"And these times, they're different. Things are not what they were in my youth. They say it is progress and change. Maybe so, I don't know these things. But the way I was raised was good enough for my *mutter* and *grossmutter* and it has been good enough for me. It's these children I don't understand. Do you?"

"In what way?"

"It's my daughter, Number Six. My *liebling*. She's . . . she's gone off and . . . She's . . ." The old woman began to cry.

"In trouble?"

"*Ja.* Exactly so. She has gotten herself with child."

"She has?"

"Yes. It's that awful Number Twenty-four. I told her not to hang around with him. Trash, that's what he is. Him and that bunch he hangs around with. They don't work, they don't go to school, they just hang around and think up trouble. The devil makes work for idle hands. Many's the time I've told her that. There's the devil in that boy, I said. If only she'd listened."

They reached his walk.

"Won't you come in?"

"*Danke. Nein.* It wouldn't be right. But what am I going to do? You're a man of the world. You've seen much of life. Tell me. Am I wrong? Is this not so much of a sin anymore? What is happening?"

"Is he going to marry her?"

"Him? That good for nothing! Never. I'm sure of it. If he'd been any good, it would never have happened in the first place. Only, tell me, God, what am I going to do?"

"Have you consulted his parents?"

"No. Should I? Tell me what you think."

He looked into her worn, peasant face. "Number One Oh five, I think that's exactly what you should do."

"*Danke. Danke*, Number Six." She nodded to herself and went off down the lane.

He opened the door.

"Number Six?"

There were five of them standing just inside the door. They all wore uniforms. And they all carried guns.

"You are under arrest. Come with us."

Section Two

"On what charge?"

"A complaint has been brought against you."

"By whom?"

"By a party who considers himself aggrieved."

"In what way?"

"It is not my place to know."

"Whose place is it?"

"Those whose place it is to know such things."

"And when will I be advised of the nature of this charge?"

"At the proper time."

"And when will that be?"

"When it is deemed necessary."

"And who will decide it is necessary?"

"The proper authorities."

"Just who are these 'proper authorities'?"

"Those who have been duly constituted."

"And who constituted them?"

"The people."

"Which people?"

"The people of this Village. Now, you will come with me. There will be no further arguments."

They went out into the rain.

"Lack of mutuality . . . a capital offence . . . well, I mean . . . there's never been anything like it before."

"Number Two's orders."

"Well . . ." The desk sergeant scratched behind an ear. "In that eventuality . . . yes."

Their eyes met. The sergeant's lips were pursed in a faint, embarrassed smile. "I'm sorry, Number Six. Don't mean to hold you up. But this is not our usual job of work. Not at all . . . quite different, indeed. Not like that lot over there." He pointed across the room.

Number 24 sat on a bench next to a belligerent old gentleman. The old man had the clean, angry look of an IRA captain: bloodless lips, glittering eyes, taut skin. Number 24 had a large neb, wounded poet's eyes, an olive complexion, and an expression of bewildered suffering.

The old man caught the sergeant's gesture and glared, lip curling back in a sneer. "Fists like matured hams," he whispered, "for beating defenceless boys like you."

Number 24's eyes grew wide and fearful.

"Not like that lot at all," the sergeant repeated. "Just lurking about. More for their own good, really . . ." He brought his lips together and unbuttoned his jacket pocket, extracting a ball point pen. He lay the pen on the desk next to a ledger, opened the ledger to a half-filled page and began to write.

"Number . . . You are Number Six?"

"That is not my name."

"My dear sir" – the sergeant assumed an expression of almost bovine patience – "I am aware that your name is not 'Number Six'. That is your *official* designation – as I'm sure you know. The question is: Are you or are you not known as 'Number Six'?"

He lifted a brow at the sergeant. "The question is: What do *I* wish to be known as? My name is –"

"My good man!"

"And I am not your man."

"Number Six!"

"And I am not 'Number Six'."

"What would you have me call you?"

"By my name."

"But that would be impossible. You can see that, can't you? Surely a sensible man like yourself can see that. So many men have the same name, but there is only one Number Six."

"I've been told that before."

"Then, what would you have me call you?"

"What are men in my position usually called?"

"But" – the sergeant's eyebrows rose in astonishment – "that would be most unmutual."

"But truthful."

"The truth can only be an embarrassment."

"Not for me."

"You're only making it harder on yourself, Number Six. Now – Number: Six. Charge: To be specified –"

"When will it be specified?"

The sergeant gave a patient, forbearing sigh. "I am hardly the one to know."

"Who is?"

"Now look here! I have my job and doubtless you have yours. Mine is to process people as speedily as possible. Nothing more. Now, may I get on with my work?"

"As you like."

"Cell: Six." He turned to a constable: "Take the prisoner to cell six."

"No fingerprints?"

The sergeant produced a document. "See. Here: your photo."

"Photos can be changed."

"So can fingerprints."

"I should have known. But, tell me, how can you be certain of my identity?"

"They know everything. If they say you are 'Number Six', you are."

"And who are *they*?"

"The monitors."

"What monitors?"

"Number Six, I have no time for nonsense. Take him away."

"Be seeing you."

He was taken to a cell. The door opened, he was let in.

Across the room (mounted above the tiny, barred window) was a television camera. Below the camera sat Number One Fifty-seven, the old tobacconist.

He lifted his head, eyes dark and reddened. "*Bonjour*, Number Six," he said. "I'm sorry I've gotten you into this."

"And just what have you gotten me into?"

The rabbity little man looked down at his hands. "I've been selling the marijuana."

"Selling dope?"

"*Oui*. Just so. You understand?"

"No."

"I brought it with me from my home. My father had smoked it" – he gave a little smile – "and his father before him. All our family and our town."

"How did you come here?"

"On a boat." He made a ducking motion.

"What brought you here?"

"An advertisement."

"What kind of advertisement?"

"For a position." He seemed genuinely bewildered.

"Don't you find this village a bit peculiar?"

"*Je ne comprend*, Number Six. These things are not of importance. It is important only that I brought these seeds" – his palms opened as if the seeds themselves lay within – "and that I planted them and that it was wrong."

He sighed and his shoulders slumped. His hands came back to his sides. "I do not understand, but it is wrong. They tell me it is wrong. All my life I have done it. It brings a man relaxation and peace. It is one of the good things in life. Why do they always take away the good things? They take away alcohol. And women. They take away tobacco and money. They even take away God. Why they do this, I do not know." He looked up. "Do you understand, Number Six?"

"No."

"My father, my grandfather, even my priest. Could a thing be bad if a priest partook without harm? He was a very holy man – even the Bishop once spoke favourably of him. But they have arrested me for it. And here I am."

"And why –"

"And you are here because it is believed you were one of my associates."

"One of your associates?"

"So they think." Number 157 lowered his eyes.

"Why do they believe that?"

He made that peculiar ducking motion again and held out his hands. "It is my fault."

"*Your* fault?"

"Number Twenty-four's also. But really it is mine."

"What happened?"

"Long ago – before you came here – I lived in the house that is now yours. I built a compartment to hide it behind the shower." He sighed deeply. "I thought no one would look there. I made a mess. I am really not very good at these things. The room had to be repainted. I went to the hardware but the paint was so expensive. I have never been a rich man, you see." His spread fingers indicated poverty. "Not at all in the old country. And after we settled here, my wife became ill." He shrugged. "I bought some paint. It was the cheapest they had. A clearance, I think."

"*Rohz?*"

"*Oui, Rohz.* I painted it and then I had" – he spoke depreciatingly – "some trouble with my heart." His hand moved up towards his chest. "I was in the hospital, you see. While I was there, it was decided you should be given my cottage. I was to be moved to one larger."

There was a crack of thunder outside.

Number 157 started, and looked about anxiously. "I became agitated; I asked Number Twenty-four to move my crop for me. But he neglected it until you were here, and then it was too late. When they arrested me, they searched your house too, and it was there."

"*A very pretty story, Number One Fifty-seven –*"

They turned.

On the wall above the door was a television screen. Number 2 glared down at them from it. Light gleamed on his high, bald forehead.

"– but hardly one to charm the court. I think the two of you had better come up with a better defence than that or we shall very soon be forced to forgo the pleasure of your company."

"Forgo?"

"Don't be coy, Number Six. You understand me quite well. The penalty for frequenting a place where narcotics are kept is: Death."

"I am hardly surprised."

"I wonder if you'll be as smug when you face the firing squad?"

He smiled without emotion.

"But you'll be well treated until then. You're still a valuable commodity: no sense damaging the goods prematurely. And, since you're deprived of the pleasures of your own kitchen, let me offer you the hospitality of mine."

"Is that proper?"

"In this case."

"The menu?"

"Whatever you like."

"Thank you." He had, after all, been certain.

"You may order now."

"Shrimp cocktail, a green salad, welsh rarebit, red wine – not too sweet or dry – a sherbet for dessert."

"And you, Number One–Fifty–seven? What would you like?"

"For me?" He was astonished. "Nothing thank you. My stomach . . ." His hands spread. "I could not eat."

"Perhaps later? No? You're certain? Very well. Good afternoon, gentlemen." And Number 2's image faded from the screen.

There was the sound of rain and a cool wet breeze came through the window.

He turned around.

Number 157 had sat down on a cot. "Oh Number Six. They are going to shoot us." He shook his head in distress. "I just know they are going to shoot us."

"Do the defendants," the judge said, leaning back in his chair and folding his arms, a stern figure in periwig and robes, "wish to make any statement in their behalf?"

"*Excusez moi,* your honour." Number 157 made the small ducking motion of his head. "*Je ne comprend —*"

"Please use English in addressing this court."

"*Je regrette —*" He shook his head. "I'm sorry, your honour. I can speak English, yes. I am upset. I become confused . . ." He spread his hands in abjuration. "I speak in French."

"That's quite all right. Take your time. This court assures you a fair trial."

"Well your honour" – he looked timidly up at the judge – "I want to say: This man, Number Six" – he pointed – "is innocent. He knows nothing. It was accident these things were at his house."

"Excuse me."

The judge turned his head. "Yes, what is it, Number" – he hesitated – "Six?"

"Aren't these proceedings somewhat irregular?"

The judge assumed a kind of patriarchal indulgence. "Number Six, I've heard a number of things about you. I won't say I believe them; I won't say I don't. But I will say this: You wouldn't have to ask me that question and you wouldn't be here today to ask It, If you had been more mutual in the past. The manner in which we conduct these affairs here is clearly set out in a course on the charter and government of this Village which the public was offered an opportunity to take last month."

There had been such a course. He remembered the announcement distinctly.

"The procedure is quite simple," said the judge. He lifted two stacks of IBM cards. "These" – he hefted the one on the right – "contain all the information relevant to your case. These" – he indicated the second stack – "Number One Fifty-seven's. We will insert these, together with any facts you might care to present, into a computer. The computer will weigh the evidence and render an objective judgement."

"What kind of 'facts'?"

The judge smiled slightly. "Just that. The factual evidence: fingerprints, photographs, tape recordings, film, chemical composition, the like. No biased testimony. No prejudiced witnesses. Just the truth. And an honest objective evaluation based on the facts."

"But your honour," Number 157 spoke up again. "I tell you this man is innocent. He knows nothing."

"He is not charged with knowledge. He is charged with 'habituating a residence where narcotics are kept'."

"But your honour," 157 said, "this is not right. He knew nothing."

"This law was enacted to punish participants at a narcotics party who were present but did not possess narcotics when arrested. It appears you are telling the truth. Number Two has even made an appeal in your behalf."

"He has?"

"Yes, Number Six, he has. And very good of him too. But the law is specific, whatever its intentions: if marijuana was, indeed, stored in your home, however unwittingly, then you are guilty. If you are guilty, the penalty is death."

The spray whipped back icy and sharp against him and he looked out over the bow of the boat at the building before them.

It rose up dark and square into the night, waves beating the cliff at its base. A dim phosphorescence clung to the rock, wet and gleaming.

The boat, caught between wind and ocean, tossed violently about.

He kept a firm grip on a stanchion and reached out to steady Number 157.

The little man looked up uncertainly. "Where are they taking us, Number Six?"

There was nothing to say.

This building had certainly not been here a month ago, and yet he was sure that walls, floors, fixtures and cement, it would be authentic to the age of the smallest stone in the paving.

They were closer now, and heard clearly the crash of wave against rock. (Great foaming breakers smashed unyieldingly against the cliff.)

They slipped in along the base and entered a harbour. A guard stood on a dock and helped them make fast to the moorings.

Lightning flickered and there was the flat concussion of thunder. Rain poured down, blotting out sound and vision. A cold, miserable ache went along his back and a dull pressure started in his head. Suddenly the cold was piercing.

They were hustled off the boat and into a guard house. The room was hot and steamy, a dozen armed men swarming about. Number 157 turned to him. "What is this place? I've never seen it before."

"Neither have I."

The room opened on to a lift. They were herded in. It began to rise.

"There are prisoners here, aren't there?" he asked.

"Yes," one of the guards replied.

"Not by any chance an abbe?"

"No."

"I thought not."

The lift stopped and they went out on to a windswept courtyard and across to a door. There were steps in a chill corridor and they went down them carefully, one at a time.

The light seemed strange and his eyes ached.

They paused before a wooden door. Number 157 was thrown inward. The door closed, locked.

They went on. Another door opened. Hands closed on his arms. He was thrust inside.

He fell to his knees, in the deep pile of the carpet. A slender modern lamp lit the room. There was a red velvet divan at his elbow. He stood up dizzily and sneezed.

"Well, Number Six. It sounds as if you have a cold." Number 2 grinned from the television.

An hour later his temperature was over a hundred and two.

Some days it was:

"Good morning, Number Six. And how are we today?"

He looked up at the starched white length of the nurse. Her face was lean, unblemished and plain. A stiff white cap sat on her hair. Her eyes were intense, almost maniacally cheerful.

"Did we sleep well last night?" She thrust a thermometer in his mouth before any reply was possible.

"We're certainly sulky today. Why is that?" She took his pulse. "And our bowels – have we moved our bowels yet this morning?"

"Hello, mate." The man on the next bed waved a red, freckled arm. "What you here for? . . . Don't feel like talking, eh? I can understand that. Makes you miserable, don't it – the flu? I'm not really too sick, myself. But I figured, I got to do time, I might just as well do it as easy as I can. Of course, they aren't exactly stupid, get me. It ain't all that easy to put one over on them. But it can be done. I et soap myself. Made me sicker than a dog. I puked all over. Really something. Of course, I'm fine now, but they don't know that. Made 'em think I'm sicker than I was."

"Breakfast, sir."

Oatmeal, a poached egg, orange juice, two vitamin pills, one penicillin pill, one aspirin and two tablets he didn't recognise.

"Now me, I'm in for bombing a synagogue. Can you imagine that? For nothing more than trying to run those Jew bastards out of town. I say we don't need none of them in this Village. Hell, they use Christian babies in their services, don't they? Always lording it over everyone else, pretending to be so smart and so persecuted. I mean, they make their money off us, don't they? They exploit the working class, don't they? We gotta show 'em we're through with that, don't we?"

His lungs were dry and his lips were cracked with thirst. A fever burned behind his eyes and his face was hard as stone. There was no strength in his chest or arms; they seemed empty and bloodless.

"And how is the patient today?" The doctor took his pulse, glanced at a chart. "Yes, yes. Very good. A touch of the flu. Nothing serious. You'll be right as rain in a day or so." He looked at the chart again. "Well ... humm ... uhhuh." He left.

"Hello, Number Six."

"Number Seven!" He was astonished. "But –"

"How did I get here?" She grew thoughtful. "I don't know. I heard you'd been arrested, and I asked them if I could see you. I didn't know you were sick too."

"Yes."

"What –" She looked around the sunlit infirmary. "What are they going to do to you?"

"Kill me, they say."

"Kill you? Do they do that?"

"Sometimes."

"Do you –" She shook her head. "It's hard to know what to say. Do you think they will?"

He looked into her eyes. "I hope not."

She smiled. "I hope not either. But –" she shivered – "this place seems less and less real all the time. How do you stay sane?"

He was sorry the question was suspect. Suddenly he felt weak. "It isn't easy."

"I'm sorry. You look tired. I'd better go. Perhaps they'll let me come again." She looked around at the room. "Has this place always been here?"

"I don't think so."

"Amazing," she said, and left.

They brought him lunch.

"I tell you, mate, it was a hell of a night. Them Hebes come running and screaming out of the place. Some of them was on fire and the women was mad to find their babies. And them kids, them kids were the best of all. They were crying for parents and some of 'em were so terrified they ran right back into the fire. Man, it was something to see."

"A call for you, sir." An orderly stood by his side, a plug-in phone in one hand. He fitted the cord into a plug.

"Hello? Number Six?" The voice was cool, young, vaguely familiar. "It's

Number Five Sixty-nine; remember me?"

"Yes."

"I called your home and they transferred me here. Where exactly are you?"

"A prison of some sort. An island in the bay?"

"Yeah, I seen 'em putting it up. Funny, isn't it, them doing that? Well, we ain't gonna stand for it. We're all on your side."

"How kind."

"I mean, it's an unfair deal what you got, mate. You was innocent. Number Twenty-four told me all about it. This law's crazy, man. We tried to talk to someone. We tried to get through to Number Two. But nobody would give us the time. They said they was too busy. So we're gonna make your case known. We're gonna make people aware of this. If they won't listen to us when we ask polite, we'll force them to listen, get me?"

"I get you."

"Well, I just wanted you to know. It's funny, in a way – them letting me talk to you."

"I had that feeling myself."

"Okay then, 'bye."

"Goodbye."

The receiver clicked off.

And some days it was:

"And then mate, we took the little vixen, well . . . she didn't go back to her German momma exactly the way she came. I mean, hell, it wasn't nothing to what the Jerries did to some of them Polack women. Why one time . . ."

The smoke from the man's cigar cut his lungs with a sharp, stabbing pain. Ceiling and walls boiled with colour. There was a dull pressure in his eyes and his ears rang dully.

"You, Number Six. We've come for you." Two guards stood at the foot of the bed. "Come on, get up."

The words made a kind of dim, fevered sense. He could almost remember what they were. They had come to see him about something. Yes, they had definitely addressed him. He had heard them say, "Number Six". The words had roared distantly in his ears. "Number Six," they had said. "We have come for you." Now why had they done that? Thought moved reluctantly through his mind.

"The doctor says you're better today. We're moving you to a safe place."

Moving? Today? He could not make sense of the words. His head was a blazing, flaming agony and he was only dimly aware of his body.

"Don't give me that. I ain't falling for it. They've tried that one before."

The two men took him by the arms and lifted him from the bed to his feet.

"Come on. Get up. We ain't so dumb as you think."

They let go of him and he collapsed.

"Ah, come on. Get up." One of them kicked him in the side. He felt the blow dimly.

He was lifted again and carried out of the room. He never remembered anything more.

"*Good afternoon, Number Six.*" The television woke him and he came slowly to consciousness, eyes burning and dry, throat parched, lips cracked, tongue stale.

A group of men appeared on the screen. Soldiers in uniform, carrying rifles and surrounding:

Number 157, head down, stumbling forward, hands chained behind his back. A priest walked at his side, reading from a book.

The soldiers led him to a post, lashed him to it.

He was crying, face swollen with fear. He closed his eyes and bowed before the priest.

The priest touched a hand to his head, made the sign of the cross.

The soldiers put a blindfold over his eyes, stepped away.

The priest followed.

"*Ready!*" He heard the call faint but clear.

"*Aim!*"

There was a pause.

"*Fire!*"

The after silence was loud and sharp.

But today it was:

"*FREE HIM NOW! NOW! NOW! FREE HIM NOW –*" The cry was deep and loud and threatening. "*FREE HIM NOW! NOW! NOW –*" It had the rhythmic inevitability of a freight train roaring past in the night. "*NOW! NOW! NOW –*" The faces of the protesters (young, long-haired, lank and angry) smouldered with resentment. "*NOW NOW NOW –*"

"*Your advocates, Number Six.*"

"Your rebels, Number Two."

"*They are trying to save your life, after all.*"

"I'm flattered."

"*It won't do you any good, you know.*"

"I hadn't expected it to."

"*You're really a fortunate man you know. If you hadn't caught cold when you did, you'd be dead by now. This is probably the first time in your life you've ever been thankful for the flu.*"

"*NOW! NOW! NOW!*" They were on the steps of the Village Hall, fists raised to the blank grey windows. A line of guards stood before the doors, arms linked, faces bewildered and uncertain.

"*And why,*" an announcer's voice crackled from the speaker, "*are you doing this, Number Five Sixty–nine?*"

"*Cause it's unfair, man.*" His thick blond hair stirred in the wind. He looked strong and righteous. "*Number Six didn't do anything. He didn't know anything about that dope. The courts proved that. It was left there by the guy who lived in the house before. Number Six is innocent. He should go free.*"

"*I see.*" The newscaster was in his thirties and had close-cropped hair. "*Well, why are you marching on the Village Hall?*"

"*Because we've tried to talk to these people, with Number Two particularly. And they've refused to reconsider the case or even to speak to us.*"

"*And what do you plan to do if the police block the way?*"

"Then we'll break through."

"You're willing to use violence."

"If they won't listen to anything else."

"But isn't it true that Number Two himself made a personal plea for –" The sound cut off.

"An amusing situation, really. This young man thinks he can intimidate us."

"What will you do?"

"That's right. You won't be around to see it. Will you, Number Six? That's too bad. I'm afraid we haven't made a decision yet. But we will and it will be an effective one. We have our ways, as you know."

He said nothing.

"And yet, Number Six, you might still save yourself. You have only to cooperate and be set free."

"No."

"You're sure?"

"Quite sure."

"Don't be too hasty. Is this secret more valuable than your life?"

"Apparently."

"Then I wish you luck with it. Tomorrow is your execution."

It seemed likely, then, that whatever they were going to try, they would try tonight.

He was standing before the window, looking out at the phosphorescent surge of the waves.

"Number Six."

"Yes, Number Seven." He had almost been expecting her.

She hesitated in the doorway, silvered lenses catching the light. "You're not surprised?"

"To see you? No. You were too good to be true. Out of place, even here."

Her mouth moved in a smile. "Well, I'm close to true, you know."

"Everyone always is."

"The Colonel sent me."

"The Colonel?"

"Colonel Schjeldahl, your superior."

"My *former* superior."

"Whatever, Number Six. I'm here to help you."

"And how am I to take that?"

"Any way you want." She took off the glasses and put them in the pocket of her coat. "The Colonel wants you back. He has a project you may find tempting."

"Is that the price of freedom?"

"Would you pay it if it were?"

"No."

"He wants you to destroy the Village."

"He does? Why?"

"Let him tell you." She reached in her coat and produced a squat little gun. "Here, I had to break in. There's a helicopter waiting on the roof."

"From the Colonel?"

"Yes."

"What about radar?"

"It's been taken care of. Our men are on staff tonight."

"Our men?"

"Ask the Colonel, I haven't time to explain now."

"Why is everyone always in a hurry just as things become most interesting?"

"Isn't life always the most interesting when the most is happening?"

They went slowly round a corner. He held the gun in a hand. A guard sat by a door.

The man looked up, the meaty pockets of his eyes creasing with apprehension.

"Be seeing you." He squeezed the trigger. A jet of vapour hissed from the nozzle and shot up around the guard.

The man opened his mouth, straightened, and collapsed.

"It works."

"Didn't you think it would?"

"Should I?"

"Think whatever you like, Number Six."

He opened the door and they were out in the face of the wind.

The ocean was on one side, a stone wall on the other. Yellow light shone from windows above their heads and fell down against the flaggings. The night was black, and through it they saw the stationary lights of helicopter blades.

"*Your* men are on duty tonight?"

"It's a faction. Don't you understand, a faction. The Colonel's group is opposed to those who maintain this Village. They have tried to have it phased out for years. But the men in charge have a great deal of influence. No one knows why. Maybe they like power."

"What does he want me to do?"

"There are three directors. Collectively they are Number One. If they are removed the Village can be declassified and its prisoners released."

"Removed?"

"Killed."

"And where are we going?"

The cabin light came on and a man in a blue flight suit waved at them.

"To that unpronounceable place you chose to retire."

"It's easy to pronounce."

"Your car is at the hotel. We're to get in it and drive to London."

They were almost at the helicopter. The pilot had switched on the engine and the blades were beginning to rotate.

"We're on Aran Island, you're sure of that?"

"Positive."

"The north coast of Ireland?"

"Yes." She brought out some keys. He took them. "To your car."

"Be seeing you," he said, and shot her with the gas.

Section Three

He stood in the foggy Welsh morning and lifted his arm to look at his watch: the hands stood frozen at six.

The watch began to run.

The second hand swept forward and down. The works began to tick. He knew with a cold, sharp certainty that it actually was six: that their power extended even this far. He dropped the arm, lifted his shoulders to settle his jacket, and stepped forward on to the path.

Gravel crunched and popped underfoot as he went around the hotel to the drive.

He had glimpsed the emerald of his car from the air (moment's shock of recognition marring the landing as he brought the helicopter down, stirring up a fine wet lather from the golf course green). And now, as he moved through the misty, silent dawn its dew condensing on his face, he felt a terrible unease to know it stood there, defying logic in the chill reality of the day.

He turned the corner and saw it, shining and sharp, the long, clean lines of the *Flamberge* body, so much like the Rolls-Royce of MGs; the jaunty yellow hood, the green carriage, the polarised windscreen, the driver's door open and ready: engine running. He went round to the side and looked down at the interior. Yes, it was his, even to the scar of Janet's cigarette on the passenger seat, the tape in the player as he'd left it: *Surrealistic Pillow.*

The keys glittered, trembling with the low throb of the motor – gold chain hanging from them, his initials, J.D., on the fob. He reached in his trouser pocket: there was only the starched vacancy of the cloth at his fingertips. Yet those keys on that very chain had been there. He'd been given them as he climbed in. How, then, had they come here in the sun-filtered reality of the morning?

He looked across the sparkling lawn to the whitewashed façade of the hotel It was silent and empty; nothing stirred behind the dark, shadowed windows. Yet he knew that this was the most popular resort in the Kingdom. And even it (as real and incontrovertible as the familiar tooling of the car here at his side) held a faint suggestion of unreality, like a set not yet in use.

Building (sharp and solid in the pearly light), air, shrubbery, worn stone fences: these were of the world he knew. Surely there was nothing sinister or harmful in them.

He turned his head and looked right, down the road. It wound up away from the grey-gabled houses of the village beyond. This much was familiar. This was real. This was the home he had chosen for his retirement.

It's easy to pronounce, he'd told the girl. And it was. Portmeirion, on the Pembroke coast of Wales, second home of Coward, Shaw, and Russell. As real as it was easy to pronounce. And, weirdly, less real – for this was the world he'd left: the mad Disneyland of the village.

Somewhere, a cock crowed, and he stepped into the car, settling back against the seat, and swinging the door shut. He closed a hand on the gear stick, shoved in on the clutch, and let the engine rev. It gave a deep, full-throated roar, and he smiled, shifting into first and rolling forward over the drive and out on to the road.

The wind whipped in against him as he picked up speed, and he stared out through grey, polarised glass at green fields, hilly and rough.

The tarmac angled up, climbing the mountains, and he looked into the rear-view mirror, catching, for a moment, the reflection of the resort behind, its grey gabled spires the last visible reminder of the Village so far behind.

It dropped behind and was gone.

Then there was only the wind, the mist, and the roar of his exhausts in the primordial stillness of the dawn.

For, if he could not really trust this engine, at least he did not mistrust it. It felt right, as perfectly tuned as when he'd driven it last. This, then, was where he would let reality take hold: here, in this car, on this road, in this world he knew to be real.

Something in the harshness of the land, the strength of the rock, the preternatural silence of day, suggested a deeper, older, stronger reality than any they might alter or create. For the first time in two years, he let himself feel that there might be, outside himself, a place as secure and inviolate as that within.

The sun rose, a bloody disc behind the enshrouding fog, evaporating the dampness from his clothes, and the sleepy mutterings of birds, the bangings of sheep, the vague lowing of cattle woke to a clear, bright day.

He reached into a pocket and closed his fingers on a cigar, bringing it to his lips. He changed hands on the wheel, slid a hand into the other pocket and found the lighter.

The tart smoke filled his mouth. He let it out, changed hands again, propped his arm on the door, and relaxed.

There was much to decide, and his mind felt eager for it, ready and straining as if released from some ponderous weight. The question of reality (for all his determination) still plagued him, though he could no longer consider the green farmlands passing by a dream. The day (slender trees, blue sky, wind, car beneath him, the smooth grey surface of the paving) was too vivid, too real, too complete for illusion.

He rejected the possibility (not allowing himself to know that in illusion he might necessarily do the same).

He must, in any case, assume he saw a pattern behind their pattern, saw somewhere close to the truth. He had only one question: Where in reality would he find an answer to explain their madness? That he could predict them seemed a small enough victory if he could not understand them. He must see not only their design, but its source; otherwise he could at best counter them, never win.

He was, of course, even without that knowledge, still at an advantage. They could not control everything, he had to believe that. The reality of wind and storm, these (surely) could not be faked. They must count, ultimately, on his own self-betrayal: that he would become inundated by trivia and collapse from exhaustion.

Certain things were obvious. (A post stood at the corner of the road. Its faded iron sign read: SHREWSBURY, 38. He turned right with it and came down a levelling of the mountain into a valley.) The girl: she was fake, this much was easy to see. His escape was part of their plan. Only this present freedom was not faked: this was the real world, they could not be in control of it. He was free at last, and he must not miss his chance.

It was not so important that he remain free as that he reassure himself of the things freedom held. He must put his finger on the pulse of reality once and for all, that they might never shake him again.

He would have to see Janet, of course. She, at least, was the one thing on which he could depend. She and his mind. With so few weapons he would conquer.

He took a final puff of the cigar and flung it into the wind. The road dipped and the speed of the descent rushed through him, wind blowing back against his face, cooling the perspiration from his brow.

The miles swept by as the road rose and fell, curving past thatched-roofed houses, tall hedges and rocky fields, running south and east towards London.

He kept his foot on the accelerator until the last possible moment, then, just as he nosed down the ramp into the garage, he pressed in on the clutch, pulled back on the gear shift and then pressed forward: down-shifting. The engine roared sending high, whining echoes along the grey concrete walls and into the dimness below. Then the car levelled and he reduced speed, emerging on a vast level lot that shone harshly beneath a few fluorescent lights.

There were other cars around him, parked in neat, civil service rows, and he rolled forward, towards a gate. The gate guarded a steel-link cage. Before it, just to the side, and level with his right arm (as he pressed the clutch, the brake, and shifted into neutral, coming to a stop), was an orange box with a slot in front.

He took a hand from the wheel, bent towards the glove compartment and thumbed the latch. The card was there: on a pile of maps, exactly as he'd left it.

He picked up the card, leaned to the right and inserted it in the slot. As it went in, the interior lit and the box began to hum. When the card was fully inside it pressed back against his fingers and the light went out. The box clicked once and the gate began to rise.

He put the card back in the glove compartment, shut the panel, and settled back, shifting into first. The wheels bumped on to a steel platform caged on two sides with steel links: the front and rear were open. When he was just inside the gate dropped back, and as he braked to a stop, the lift rattled and sank with a hiss of compressed air.

He felt a tense anticipation of the coming meeting and sensed that one more erosion in him. He was being immersed in an illusion so great it seemed to be reality itself. That was the core of their game: to create the illusion of illusion where only reality existed, and the illusion of reality where only illusion existed. For on the day he should readily fail to distinguish the two, their game would be won.

(An empty lot opened at his feet, rose, passed.)

He could not believe they had not seen that flaw: he had only to wait. So complex an illusion could not be maintained without error. And the moment they slipped he would know where reality lay. Proof lay on every hand (like substance within illusion) as solid and real as the chimes of Big Ben.

It was as if, in their determination to undo him, they sought not to ensnare him, but to subvert him. How else was he to explain it? Surely they saw the truth as easily as he.

(Another level, its Euclidean geometry vacant and empty, gaped, and closed.)

If they knew him, why did they labour so long against him when he gave them not even the satisfaction of his anger? Why was he thought a fit subject for their purpose? Unless it was in his very intractability that their desires lay: an awful perversion of reality in which their actions had no motives, their madness no object destruction without reason.

He was finally (in the concrete reality of the lift, sinking below level after level of empty, shadowy lot) convinced he would defeat them.

The platform moved past the interface between floors and he saw the flat, stained surface of the bottom lot.

The lift came even with the floor and stopped. Compressed air sighed, became silent. The metal gate lifted.

Something seemed to tug at the muscles of his neck. He turned his head: there was a camera mounted in the rear corner of the cage.

He looked down at the dash, shifted into first, pressed in on the accelerator and shot down the aisle towards a set of double doors in the far wall. He braked and swung left, switching off the engine.

He dropped the keys into his pocket, swung open the door, put a foot to the floor and stepped out. He strode directly to the metal doors, twisted his wrists out, seized the two handles, flung them wide behind him as he went forward into the room.

There was a square desk set in the middle of the floor: an intercom on its surface. A thin clerk with dark hair and dark eyes sat behind the table. There were four doors in the wall behind him.

The young man looked up. His chapped lips parted:

"Zed M Seventy-three!" he said in astonishment.

"I wish to see the Colonel."

"Yes, Zed M Seventy-three. Right away."

The young man pressed a button and spoke: "Zed Em Seventy-three to see you, sir."

The reply was low, tinny and indistinguishable.

"Go right in, sir. It's through –"

"I know the way." He walked around the desk to the left hand door. It slid aside as he approached. He went down a panelled corridor and turned right. A plaque on the door read PRIVATE. He rapped perfunctorily and let himself in.

The Colonel (for just a moment he had a sensation of utter wrongness) stood at the other end of the room adjusting the curtains on a night-time view of Piccadilly Circus and the jungle at its feet. The Colonel turned (and the feeling vanished beneath his need to know: how much truth was to be found here?), bushy hair and cotton-fluff eyebrows luminous in the shadow. His skin was smooth tan, liver-spotted, his eyes old and tired.

"Zed Em Seventy-three." Eloquent brown eyes looked out from beneath tangled brows. "I am pleased to see you."

The old man limped up to him and stopped, gaze searching and intent. Then he sighed and turned his head, staring out at the metropolis below. "Zed Em Seventy-three," he said wearily, "you are suspicious. That place" – the words were bitter – "has had its effect, even upon you."

He followed the Colonel's gaze through the window to the smoky lights of the cars and the harsh neon of the marquees. And, with a numb start, like the beginning of fear, he remembered where he was, how far below ground. (The illusion had been so real he had not stopped to question, had had only that moment's unease for warning.)

The old man's head jerked around. He smiled. "How do you like my toy?" He was proud. "Never could abide these underground rooms. You remember? I asked to be moved upstairs from the beginning. But Housing refused, said they were hard put enough for space even with all these new excavations. So I demanded this." His hand indicated the false window and he grinned. "A television screen connected with a camera on the roof. It makes me feel less cooped up."

Images (had they seemed like buildings, cars, streets only the instant before?) moved across the pane/screen: flickers of light, suggestions of motion, darkness in irregular patterns. He seemed to be looking down the very centre of the maze to a place where, like an unanswered question, only blankness lay. Was this credible, or was it not? He could not escape the knowledge that, before the Village, he would not have paused to wonder.

"Interesting," he said.

The Colonel's eyes grew thoughtful, sad. "You've not come back as you went, that much is certain." He shook his head and made his way to the opposite side of his desk. He drew out a high backed leather chair and sank down. "Take a seat, Zed Em Seventy-three."

"Thank you, sir." He brought a plastic stool up to the desk.

The Colonel continued: "They've changed you. You're tense and run down. You're no longer a healthy, thinking animal. You're apprehensive, nervous, suspicious." The old man's eyes sought his and locked. "Do you think you're up to killing?"

The question was like a knife-blade of reality, cutting at once – as if (and perhaps it was) deliberately planned – to the heart of his uncertainty: Would the murders be real or not?

"I think I am ready to do the job." He was ultimately brought to so fine an equivocation as this.

"I'm glad to know that," the Colonel said.

"I have some questions," he said carefully. This was where he stepped fully into the unknown.

"I thought you might," the Colonel answered.

"You sent for me?"

"Yes."

"Then, it is a British installation?"

"The Village? Yes, it's ours, right enough."

"And I was taken there because I refused to give the reason for my resignation?"

The Colonel nodded, sighed. "Yes. You were so adamant that Sir Charles became suspicious." The name sent a jolt down his spine, and the old man looked at him pityingly. "Yes, Zed Em Seventy-three, your fiancee's father. He reasoned that if you were to defect, no matter what motive you might have, your veracity would prevent you from lying and that you'd refuse to answer altogether."

"Perceptive of him."

"Your loyalty was, after all, Sir Charles's responsibility."

"And" – this seemed the worst treason of all – "Taggert went along with it?"

The Colonel's eyes were bitter, frustrated. "He hardly had a choice."

(That was true enough. It had been, after all, one of the reasons for his resignation.)

"You cannot imagine," the Colonel said, and he felt a mortal dread, knowing what came next, "how much easier it would be for all of us if you would just" – the old man's voice hardened – "explain your . . . retirement."

"I think that best kept to myself," he said, and felt restless at the limitation.

"I understand. This is no more than I expected. You see why I want the place destroyed."

"Then," he said abruptly, "let's get on with it. Who are the men I'm to kill?"

He pulled in before the familiar red brick of his mews, shut off the engine, dropped the keys in his pocket, got out and went along the walk to the door.

(He tilted his head, staring through a chink between curtain and frame in the tall bay window: his front room was lit.)

The door closed and he went towards his apartment, body held tight in the expectancy of some further illusion.

The door swung open before him.

Beyond it the short, obsequious body of his butler stood framed in the light. The severe black of his suit curved round him like the carapace of a giant and sinister beetle. His face was swart, solemn, angelic (or stupid). There was something Montenegrin in the man's tiny smooth features, dark skin and bland expression.

He stalked into the room, wheeled (a warm 18th century landscape to his left, above the fireplace), staring down at the dwarf and frowning.

The little man stared back impassively, face a round rubbery mask, eyes flat and a little stupid.

"A Pernod, Sancho," he ordered. He had, after all, a great deal to do. Tiredness was a hard ache between his shoulders.

The dwarf bowed, closed the door, and went past the bay window to the kitchen.

He let his hands fall and turned about, going over to the shelving.

The pale grey screen on the television was unlit, dustless, the blue wood shelves enclosing it dustless. He grasped the edges of the screen and pulled out: the front section of the chassis rolled towards him, swung to the side, revealed a wall safe in the back of the cabinet.

He knelt, reached in and twisted the dial to 0, turning it slightly to both sides, clearing it. Then he rotated the dial right to 21, left to 33, and then back to 12. The tumblers clicked. He let go and seized the handle, pulled down, then back.

The door came open. There were three stacks of twenty pound notes (four hundred pounds each) on the top shelf. A wide, flat box took up the bottom. He took a stack of notes and placed it in his inside coat pocket. Then he closed the door, raised the handle and spun the dial, locking it.

The dwarf was behind him, Pernod on a silver tray. He took it and sipped. It was almost disgustingly sweet: but the aftertaste – He shuddered.

A soft, muted chime rang at the door.

He looked up and nodded. The dwarf went to the door and opened it. *Janet.*

She stood still, brown eyes staring, mouth (in the moment before surprise) precise, full, English. Her dark brown hair (cut tight around face and shoulders, as it had been when last he'd seen her) stirred him.

Then she was moving towards him and he took her in his arms.

"John," she said and pressed against him, too relieved even to kiss.

He held her tightly and, after a moment, said brutally: "I can't tell you anything."

She shivered and went tense.

"Isn't ... Can you at least ..." She hesitated, chose carefully. "Is it a mission for my father?"

"No," he said. "I certainly can't tell you that."

She straightened and pulled away, smoothing her dress. She looked up at him evenly, face strained and hurt in a way he had never seen before. "I can't take much more of this."

"Do you remember the message I sent you?" he said gently.

"John." Her eyelids trembled in bewilderment. She seemed reluctant to speak. "That was you, wasn't it? Tell me it was you."

"Yes," he said. "It was."

Her eyes, on his, were uncomprehending.

"There won't be much more," he said. "I promise you that."

Her eyes were wide, the deep, luminous brown of the iris hesitant but hopeful. "Is it over?" she asked.

"No," he said, "but it almost is."

He stepped away and raised two fingers to the dwarf. "Brandy."

The little man inclined his head and went off.

Janet's hand reached out, seeking his: her eyes denied it, fixed on the cold brick hollow of the fireplace. He closed his fingers around hers (cool and strong to the touch) and moved towards the antique leather divan opposite the logs. Her eyes came around, puzzled, then understanding.

She settled herself back against the corner, face pale above the stark black of her dress. Mouth and chin were strong, severe, unyielding. There was something sullen and defiant in her expression: an unnatural gauntness in the cheeks.

"All right, darling," she said. "But it's a little hard to believe in a man for two years without seeing him."

He went to the fireplace, knelt, and grasped the screen, shoving it aside so that he might reach the logs. He brought out his lighter, flipped back the top and snapped the wheel, watching the flame spring from the wick. He leaned forward and extended his arm until the lighter was under the shavings.

The flame licked out, singed the blond wood black, and a tiny nimbus of fire spilled up across the dry, splintered kindling. It blazed immediately, blue flame cooling upward to yellow. The fire seared the underbelly of the logs, popping and snapping.

"What's happening now," he said, "is so different from anything I have been through before that you cannot guess what it is like. Nor can I tell you. Yet it is, in its way, far more important than anything I have ever been involved in." He leaned forward and looked straight into her eyes, seeking, by as much as it lay within his power, to ensure her understanding: "But you must understand this: I will not allow it to come between us or to hurt us any more."

She looked at him for a moment, sighed and smiled with a deathly weariness. "Yes, John." She reached long, slender fingers to him.

He stepped forward and took them, the fine cool tension of her body (even if by so little) within his grasp. "To tell you more would be to endanger you. And I won't do that."

A tired, unhappy look came into her eyes. "You are over protective, darling. Not knowing hurts more than anything that might be done to me."

"Then I'm selfish," he said abruptly. "But I need your love too much to risk losing you."

There was a sound of plastic on metal and footsteps coming across the carpet. The dwarf rolled the teacart up to them and stopped, uncorking the brandy and pouring equal amounts into snifters. The liquid fell and splashed, sparkling darkly.

The little man recorked the bottle and bowed stiffly, then stood, waiting.

"Good night." He dismissed the butler and seated himself by Janet, watching the dwarf go back to his quarters at the rear.

He closed thumbs and forefingers on the stems of the snifters and handed one to Janet, offering the other in toast. She took hers and sat back, watching him over the rim. Her eyes had a cautious, nervous intensity.

"To us."

They drank the toast. Fire like velvet over his throat.

"How long will it be, this time?" Janet's face was tense, smooth, under control.

"How long . . ."

"Until you have to go back?"

He shook his head, "I'm not going back. But there are a few things yet to be cleared up."

"Are they –" She hesitated, visibly trying to come to grips with the question: eyes narrowing, mouth tightening. "– urgent?"

"Yes."

She sat the snifter down and brought her gaze to his, catching her lip between her teeth. "Then I must go. You see that: don't you?"

"Yes," he said reluctantly, "I see it."

"Listen to me, John. There are only a few times in our lives when we are given the chance to love greatly. That kind of love is like a work of art. It's as difficult and demanding a creation as a painting or a symphony. You know that and I know that. We both know how magnificent its rewards can be. Now understand me. We have a chance at that kind of love, and if you think I shall let it be destroyed, you are mistaken. And if it comes to a showdown between you and father – father be damned. I love you and I will have you."

He waited.

"There is much I have to ask you," she said. "But it can wait. Will have to, I suppose."

"Goodbye," he said, and she was in his arms, crushed to him as his lips met hers.

They broke apart.

She smiled, touched his cheek, and was gone.

He knocked at the door: a sharp penetrating rap and the sound echoing away into the house.

A sheep bawed in the field behind and he caught its reflection in the great picture window just to the right of the walk. Then he heard the resonant silence of the wind as it rushed swift and cool across the earth. Down the road, near Kingsdown, a horn blared. All else was serene.

Something moved in the house. There was the muffled sound of a door closing. Then footsteps came towards the front.

The knob shook, rasped as if the other end were being turned. The door moved inward, opened the length of a chain. A short, white-haired man in a blue denim smock peered up at him.

"Yes?" the man said. "What do you want?"

"Sir John Wilkinson, Bart?"

"Yes." The repetition was shorter, harsher: impatient: "What do you want?"

"I bear a message from Colonel Schjeldahl."

The eye visible through the doorway grew brighter. "Your identity badge?"

He slid a hand into the cool lining of his jacket pocket, fingers closing on the stiff plastic card, and brought it out, pushing it forward through the crack of the door.

Sir John took it (hands as smooth and pink as a child's) and lifted it to his face, peering at it carefully. Then he looked up, eyes bright and penetrating. He stepped back and closed the door, there was a scrape of metal on metal, and the door opened wide.

The hall was a sunny amber. An umbrella stand to one side of the door, a porcelain vase to the other. The pile of the carpet was thick and deep, yielding easily to the foot.

He went into the living room and turned to the baronet. Sir John offered him the card. He took it reading the familiar words as easily up-side down as right-side up: BY COMMISSION OF HER MAJESTY, THE QUEEN and pocketed it.

Sir John's face was kindly, softened by an amiable squint, flesh translucent and freckled. But there was something almost too companionable in its friendliness, as at the sharing of some off-colour Rotarian joke. Something too corrupt in his smile: the knowledge of some universal and unconfessed guilt.

There were gold leather divans along the wall facing the window, and antique writing tables at either end of the room. The whole had the faint decadence of eighteenth century Paris: gilt and lacquer.

Through the window he could see the damp countryside and the blue dome of sky. There was a rainbow over the road and the sun gleamed wetly in the grass.

Sir John gestured vaguely towards the divan. "Make yourself comfortable."

"I think we'd better have these shut," he said abruptly, walking over to the drapes, shoving them aside, and closing his hand on the cord. He drew it down and the fabric swung out along the track, shutting off the view.

The old man gave him a sly, delighted grin. "You know, I thought you were the one. I really thought I remembered your number." He seemed to pause and consider. "Yes, it was sent to me on a telegram. I've got it around here somewhere." His head moved in little jerks, like a bird's movement, more excited than nervous.

"So it's finally come, has it? You know, I've always thought it would." Sir John turned his head towards the divan. "Is it all right if I sit down? I mean: is there enough time?"

"Sit down."

"Good." Sir John went over and sat down. He looked up, face relaxed, boyish. "I've always speculated about what kind of person it would be. Just exactly what they'd be like. I wanted it to be someone, you know" – his eyes had a bright, far away look "someone sensitive, intelligent, charming. Not a mindless, guttural assassin. Perhaps that's only vanity. Maybe I just want to think I was deserving of the best." His eyes narrowed and he leaned back against the couch. "If it's not asking too much: for which agency am I being *hit*?" He seemed enormously pleased with the word.

"None."

"But surely I am to be killed? I would hate to think my gesture had gone for nothing."

"If I kill you," he answered, "it will be a personal matter between us."

Sir John looked at him slyly. "You know, that's very interesting. I had a conversation with Sir Charles Portland on that very subject." He cocked his head. "You do know Sir Charles, don't you?"

"Yes."

"Good. Then you'll know Sir Charles is a very determined man. Well, I said that no one killed for purely personal reasons any more. That it was old-fashioned. That most men suffer so overwhelmingly from corporate guilt that they rationalise their guilt away by placing its responsibility on some larger object. That then they can commit any crime, on any scale, and be free of its consequences. Thus they can start at some relatively minute level, such as cheating on income tax, by deciding the bloody government takes too big a bite of their wages, and hang their guilt on the impersonal workings of the government."

He paused and picked up a pair of wire framed glasses, settling them around ear and over his nose. "Sir Charles, on the other hand, said that he knew of at least one person who did not suffer from collective guilt and who claimed he killed only from his conscience. Now in light of that, I find your arrival almost too opportune. Don't you?"

"It seems improbable."

"But I had the distinct impression," Sir John said, squinting upward and removing his glasses, "that you wanted to question *me*. Is that right?"

"I have a few questions to ask."

"Is that right? Will you use torture if I refuse to answer?"

"I hadn't considered it, no."

"That's too bad. I've done a lot of thinking about pain and I've decided that, today, we are all too susceptible to pain. We are no longer conditioned to endure it. The surrender of our conscience has only been a symptom of an aversion to hardship. The public figures of our time condition us away from it. They endure nothing, are devoutly corrupt, and profit from their corruption. These are the people we seek to emulate – they fill the vacuum of our need for guidance." He brought out a handkerchief and began to polish the lenses.

"People simply refuse to acknowledge evil in themselves or in others. It's a kind of societal blackmail in which everyone agrees to everyone else's equality. We expect and give no better than the other man – and we expect and give nothing. We never strain against opposition and our muscles atrophy. Ever wonder why so many American spies sign confessions when they're caught?"

"What do you know of the Village?" He had some time (after all) to ask the question.

"Which village?" The old man peered distrustfully through the lenses. "The one just down the road? It's much like any other."

"It's a place where a certain kind of person is sent. Persons who have held positions of some delicacy. Persons who are possessed of secrets vital to their governments. Persons whose freedom might represent a vital threat to their nation's security."

"Do you by any chance mean a retirement village?"

"Persons who have been detained against their will."

Sir John tilted his head to one side and peered at him from a single, intent eye. "But surely, in these times, none of us are where we are entirely from choice. It seems clear to me that the forces of environment and heredity have channelled us down certain *inescapable* paths. What Negro in America is entirely free; what white in China is entirely safe? Aren't certain of your thoughts and attitudes a result of your upbringing? Too rigid and controlled a personality because of a strict father; a defiance and resentment of authority because of such fettering strictness."

"I was thinking rather of deliberate, severe and brutal manipulation."

"But are we not, in this world of ours, subjected to constant and inescapable manipulation? As subtle and persuasive as mother's instructions not to play with our penises, and advertisements that link smoking with sex appeal. As crude and overt as the public school's indoctrination of its pupils with Judeo-Christian morality, or the knowledge that if, alone, we indulge in certain pleasures, our entire society will punish us. And these pressures affect us in ways that are not entirely conscious; for the mind is not meant to be aware of its own defaults. Is not such manipulation, after all, common?" The old man gave a brief, questioning smile.

"How can you morally justify the existence of such a village?"

"One can't, of course. But morality has become old-fashioned and without it anything can be justified. You see, when men begin to justify their actions in terms of something besides morality" – he hooked the earpiece to one lens around his ear, and paused "their country, for instance, or their family, or their race, you can be pretty sure they've done something wicked. Since they are no longer acting morally, they do not wish to be reminded of morality, and if you talk of other things, they will not mention it."

"And how do you, personally, feel about this?"

"Personally?" The glasses went on. "We are no longer allowed personal scruples. If our government wages a dishonourable war, do we not have to serve? If our employers engage in shoddy practice, is it safe to protest? If our neighbours are offended, do they not threaten our lives? We are intimidated and circumscribed on all sides. We are forbidden personal feelings. There must be mass approval before we can act."

"And the people who are injured?"

"But isn't pain a universal of our lives? The pain of too loud a commercial, too long a queue, an unjust remark, a spiteful law, a loved one we cannot trust. Are these not the common experience of our age? And these people you speak of, who are they? Numbers, now, statistics, aggregates, masses, cogs in a system too vast to resist. How much do their individual lives differ – their problems, agonies, pressures and frustrations? Are they not the same in one village as another? Do men not carry their selves, their true problems, from one place to another as they move?"

"What about dignity?"

"Now? Dignity is dead. It went out with high button shoes and honest government. It was not compatible with computers and cost accounting. When a balanced book becomes more important than a human life, there is no room left for dignity."

"You feel no responsibility towards these people?"

"Responsibility? We have been denied that privilege for some time in the search for a grosser national product. We have forsaken responsibility with guilt, and placed them both on the shoulders of something more nebulous than ourselves, something less accessible to punishment."

"And" – he had to be absolutely sure – "you feel no responsibility for the lives you have ruined?"

The old man sighed and shook his head. "There are no lives anymore, only statistics. Any statistic can be sacrificed."

He reached into his coat pocket and closed his hand around the chill grip of the Colt. "Even your own?"

Sir John Wilkinson lifted his head and looked up out of tired, cynical eyes. "Even my own."

"What it means," the Field Marshal said, leaning forward on the frame and panting heavily, "is fitness. We have to keep fit."

His haunches lifted and his legs pumped furiously, as if this were indeed a bicycle and not a wheelless frame bolted to the floor. The steel bars on which he was mounted rattled with the pumping, and even the floor seemed to shake slightly.

"We have a duty, as a people and a nation, to keep fit. We cannot afford to be soft at a time when our enemies so completely surround us. It would be a flagrant invitation to conquest." He stopped, panting heavily, and looked up. "What newspaper did you say you were from?"

He got off the bicycle, took a few deep breaths, then lay down on the floor, pressing his hands flat by his chest and straightening his legs, rising on his toes. He began doing pushups, talking in measured breaths. "Our enemies are ready. They will attack at the first sign of weakness. We must offer them the only thing they will understand: a solid, determined front. We must be strong, alert or they will destroy us."

He stood and seized two handles set in the wall. There were weights connected to them. He shoved his right hand forward and a weight rose. "What some people fail to realise is that, while freedom's the ideal goal, you can't have freedom without discipline."

He let his right hand draw back to the wall and extended the left. "I'm all for freedom, of course, but it does have its limits. Take a soldier at war: if he's allowed the freedom to talk out of turn, he may give his unit away and they'll be killed. Bet you don't think he should have it." He let his left hand go back and began to raise the weights, one at a time: a hard, dynamic rhythm – arms extending, then returning. "And what about a clerk who knows a state secret – how much freedom should he have?"

He changed rhythm and shoved both handles forward simultaneously.

His face became red and sweaty. "It's the same with a civilian. Country's full of them. If they're soft, the country's soft. If it's soft the enemy will attack. A certain discipline must be maintained." He let go the weights. "What newspaper did you say you were from?"

He took a rope down from a peg. "Now I say: If the army can maintain discipline, the civilians can maintain discipline. After all, it's them we're fighting for." He began to skip with an easy, loping stride. "Now some people say the military's getting too big for its breeches. Well, that's a lot of loose talk. But a country is only as safe as it is strong. Any nation that thinks it can conquer it, will. Without strength, a country's lost."

He coiled the rope and hung it back on the wall. "In here." He led the way into a smaller, padded room. There was a trampoline in the centre. "You have to be able to defend yourself or they won't leave you alone." He climbed on to the trampoline and began to turn smooth, quick somersaults. "Of course the enemy wants to undermine you any way he can. He'll try to get you with chemicals. And with slogans. And with fear. He'll pollute your water and corrupt your youth. If he's not stopped, he'll subvert the whole population. And do you know how he'll do that?"

"No, I don't."

He got down off the trampoline and they went back in the gym. He worked his shoulders, flexing the heavy, slabbed muscles. "What they'll do: They'll get people to be soft in the name of humanity. They'll lead people to believe that mankind is more important than survival. But a country has to be realistic."

He scurried up the horizontal wooden slats lining walls and ceiling then grabbed hold of the overhead bars and crawled directly above.

"Sometimes, to save a country, a few of its citizens must be sacrificed. It would be foolish to risk national security because of one man."

The Field Marshal bent his head, looking downward. "Or don't you agree, Mr Drake?" then let go, falling, crashing down against him.

An elbow cracked his head and the room rang with darkness. He was slammed into the wall and air rushed from his lungs. Something sharp and wicked jammed into his back.

He was down on the ground with the other's body across his waist. The Field Marshal struck at his head. He dodged the fist and seized the arm, thrusting it sharply up behind the shoulder. There was concussion and he was asprawl the man's back, chin against spine, shoving up the hammerlock with all his strength

They were rolling across the floor. He could almost see the face above him: it was hot and contorted, flesh bulging, whites of the eyes glistening.

Then he was on top, fingers deep in the other's throat.

He lay on the floor and a fist smashed into his face, splitting lip and cheek. He reached up and toppled the Field Marshal sideways, slamming his knee into the other's groin.

They were up against the pulleys. He was being held firmly back against the wall (fist clenched in his collar) and something hammered his face.

"Thought I didn't know who you were, eh?" The fist struck him. "Thought you had me fooled, huh?" And again. "Knew who you were the minute I set eyes on you." His right eye was dark. "Heard about it the minute you escaped." His lip seemed raw and burning. "We all did. Even that old fool Wilkinson." Again and again. "It's not so easy as you thought, eh?" Again and again. The blows were powerful and stunning, almost painless, and in a moment he would be able to think.

"Been in condition every day of my life." Again. (It was only a blur of motion and a distant sense of concussion like the foundations of reality being struck.) Again. "Knew what you were out for. The girl talked." AAGGAAIINN!! "No need to call the guards. I'll take care of you myself." AGAIN! "Learn your lesson once and for all." There was a dim, shattering red like the pounding of some cosmic pulse and a terrifying force tore through him. "You're nothing special, after all."

The mute appendage of his fingers clenched on a surface round and cool. His hand jerked upward against weight and there was a crack like a rifle shot.

The Field Marshal's head went sideways in a gout of blood. The drops flew out, gelatinous and warm.

His hand fell against the wall and closed on a slat. His muscles clenched and the chest was dragged upward. He came to his feet with the weight of the room at his back, skull empty and sore.

The Field Marshal had been knocked across the room and had risen to his knees, knuckles braced against the floor. "Very clever. But hardly sufficient." Blood ran down his cheek and his right eye was a raw, oozing mess.

He shook his head and threw himself at his opponent. They jammed against the bicycle frame and rolled into the room. He kicked free and sat up, bringing his hands together and clenching them into a fist. He turned quickly and smashed the other man in the neck. The impact jarred up the bone of his wrists and came together in his chest..

The Field Marshal fell back and kicked under the ribs, the pain like an axe blow to his heart. His lungs caught and he felt death in his throat.

The Field Marshal crawled over and drove shoulder into breastbone. His bones seared and turned to chalk. His left arm was grasped, and driven between metal sprockets.

He saw the Field Marshal's hand close on a pedal and shove forward. The chain bit into his palm and clamped down, the sprockets crushing through his hand.

Agony arced down his nerves and he heaved up, a single convulsive movement that knocked the old man loose and tore flesh from hand. He threw himself forward and caught the loops of the jump rope, jerking it down and over the man's head. He braced feet against body and drew sideways on the ropes. They tightened and gripped.

"Good evening, Sir Charles."

"Good Lord, Zed M Seventy-three, your face!"

He took a seat opposite the desk, and settled back, gun aimed at the older man's breast.

Sir Charles looked surprised, even concerned. "What happened, man?"

"I had a fall."

"Can I do anything?"

"Answer some questions."

"I hope you realise the position you're in." Sir Charles paused, allowing silence to underscore the words. "There's no way in which you can escape. Security has been notified of your arrival and there are men outside every door. You were mad to come here."

"I think not."

"Surely" – Sir Charles's voice was incurious – "you don't think I'll let you kill me?"

"I'll kill you if I choose."

"Would you care," Sir Charles said, "to tell me why you resigned?"

"I'm sorry, Sir Charles," he answered. "That will not be possible."

"A pity. It's a decision you may someday come to regret."

"Sir Charles" – there was really no other way to begin – "why this charade?"

"Zed M Seventy-three, I wish I could tell you." Their eyes met, locked. "But I'm afraid that, as you are reluctant to confide in us, we are reluctant to confide in you."

"If you don't tell me, I'll kill you."

There was the sound of a door opening behind him and a rush of footsteps.

Sir Charles leaped to his feet, kicking his chair out of the way.

Men closed in and one of them grabbed for the gun. He twisted sideways and fired. The bullet shattered Sir Charles's head and blew the skull against the wall.

"Jesus Christ, the bastard's killed him," someone cried.

A fist slammed in against his already battered flesh, obliterating all consciousness. But as he was given up into darkness, he retained the memory of that shattered skull: the gleaming copper wires within the flesh.

Section Four

"Welcome back, Number Six."

He stepped out of the helicopter and brushed off his jacket. "Thank you, Number Five Sixty –" He noticed the badge. "Sorry, Number Two."

The youth grinned, half-pleasure, half-embarrassment, delight in his eyes. "How do you like the promotion?"

"I thought the black leather jacket looked better unadorned."

They went down the lane towards his house.

"You don't approve?"

"What difference does it make?"

"Well" – he scratched a leg – "I think a lot of you, of your opinion."

"I don't like it then."

"Why? I thought you'd be pleased."

"Pleased?"

"Sure; you know." He paused to wave at Number 87. The grocer waved back. "I can do a lot in this position. It was me helped you escape."

"Really?"

"Say, don't you believe me?"

"Aren't you telling the truth?"

"Yeah."

"Then I believe you."

"I just wouldn't want you to get me wrong, Number Six. I like you. You got class. They offered to make me Number Two if I'd call off the demonstration. There were no strings attached. I can run things pretty much as I like. Of course I gotta go slow with the changes, cause there are these three old men gotta approve them, but I'm in charge. I had the alarms switched off the night you escaped. That proves I'm boss, don't it?"

They came up to the house.

"I had 'em in a corner, sir. We outnumbered them."

"Well then, Number Two –" He turned at the door. "What do you plan to do with me?"

The youth's brows creased in puzzlement. "Do? I don't understand."

"What am I to do?"

"About what?"

"Do I have to make myself clearer? Why have I been brought back here? If you're in charge, am I free to go?"

"Free to go, sir? Of course you're free to go." The wave of his hand took in all the Village, suggested nothing more. "Anywhere you like."

"Outside the Village?"

"Why would you want to go there? Everything's all right here, now."

Sometimes it was:

Someone knocked at the door.

"Good afternoon, Admiral."

"Damme, lad, I'm glad you're back."

They shook hands.

"Well." He settled himself on the couch. "I didn't mean it that way. Only, I thought you might not be coming back at all." He shot a look. "You get me?"

"I've enjoyed our games."

"Eh?" He brightened. "So have I. So have I." The old man paused and searched in his coat pocket. "A mortal drop in honour of our friendship. What do you say?" He produced a slender greenish bottle.

"I'll find the glasses."

The doorbell rang.

"How convenient. Come in, Number Seven."

She leaned curiously forward and looked over his shoulder. "Oh, it's the Admiral. Hello, Admiral. I'm coming in."

He stepped inside and went in after her.

"Join us in a drop of wine, lass?"

"Thank you, Admiral."

He got down three glasses.

"To Number Six."

"To Number Seven," he returned. And then: "Your health, Admiral."

"You know Number Twenty-four got married?" she said when they had all been seated.

"No, I didn't."

"He got someone pregnant."

"Would you care for tea?"

"Yes, please."

"Admiral?"

"No thankee, lad. I'll have a bit more wine."

"Here, let me."

He went into the kitchen and drew water into a pot. Number 7 came in behind.

"Number Six?"

"Yes." He turned to face her.

"What happened?"

"In London?"

"Yes, of course."

"Not much."

"I'm not mad, you know. About being left behind. There was no real reason for you to trust me. I know what this place does." She watched him.

"Not much happened," he said.

"Did you kill those men?"

"Yes."

"Then why are you back here?"

"There could be two explanations." He put the leaves in the water.

"Which are?"

"One: Momentum. The order to return me was executed before they realised their leaders were dead. Two: It was a senseless attempt to confuse me."

"Is that all you have to say?"

He poured through a strainer. "What else is there?"

"There ought to be something more. You can't go out and do something like that and have it mean so little. What's the point, otherwise?"

"It did, though." He handed her a cup. "You'll have to accept that."

"But I don't understand." She followed him out.

"Neither do I."

"Eh? What's this? Secrets? Don't tell me. I don't want to know. There's too blessed many in this place now."

"Then we shan't bother you."

And they let it go at that.

And sometimes it was:

"Yes, sir. May I help you?" The clerk came around the counter.

"I'd like a pane of glass."

"What size?"

"Thirteen by ten."

"Just a moment." He went to a cupboard, returned.

"All out."

"When will you have more?"

"Any day now. A shipment's past due."

"Will you notify me when it comes?"

"Certainly."

Ting-a-ling-ling.

The day was clear, brisk.

"Number Six."

"Good afternoon, Number Two."

"Where you off to?"

"The tobacco shop."

He slung his jacket over one shoulder. "I'm going that way. Mind if I join you?"

"Not at all."

Their shoes crunched against the gravel.

"I thought you were going to do away with Numbers?"

"I proposed that, but there's been no answer. In fact, I haven't heard from Number One in several days."

"Really? Is that usual?"

"I don't know. I haven't been on the job long enough to tell."

"What do you propose?"

"To wait, I guess. I'm bound to be contacted soon."

"Wouldn't care to send me out to investigate?"

"I don't think I'd better. I mean, I've got a position to maintain. A lot of people depend on me. I wouldn't want to disappoint them."

"Well, I wish you luck."

"Thanks, Number Six."

Ting-a-ling-ling.

"Yes?" The bearded tobacconist stood in the shadows, face hard and resentful.

"I've an order in for some cigars. Number Six."

"Yes. I remember. Well, they haven't come in. And I don't know when they will."

"But Number Two okayed them?"

"Yes. But nothing's come of it. Nothing's come in days."

"Let me know if it does."
"Be seeing you."
"Be seeing you."
Ting-a-ling-ling.

The breeze was warm and salty.

"What's that you're reading, Number Seven?"

"*Portnoy's Complaint.*" She held it up.

"Why?"

"I don't like censors."

"Want lunch?"

"No." She made a face. "I've orders to avoid you as much as possible."

"Why?"

"I don't know. Only that I must be careful not to be seen with you." She tilted her head back and looked at him, then went off along the street.

But this time:

"Attention! Attention pleased This is an announcement of importance to everyone. Attention! Attention please! An important announcement:

"Citizens of the Village, this is Number Two. You are all to be set free. Those of you who wish to leave may do so. Liners will arrive next Wednesday to take you to Southampton. Passage to the destination of your choice will be provided there.

"Those who require a more extensive relocation may remain here until the details have been worked out.

"But you do not have to leave this Village. You may stay if you like. Repeat: You may stay if you like. We are not being closed down, merely opened."

It was good to be in London again.

He leaned back against the bus seat and looked down through the window at the street below. A newsboy stood in the grey twilight: a red and white sweatered figure against asphalt grey paving. The buildings were red, soot-blackened brick with dun, soot-blackened casements. There was debris – old newspaper, bits of cardboard, shattered plastic, a weatherstained playbill – blowing along the sidewalk and out into the street, where it was flattened beneath the wheels of passing cars.

MINISTRY SCANDAL – HIGH OFFICIALS SLAIN
ROVING YOUTHS BATTLE POLICE IN PICCADILLY
COMMUNIST PLOT CLAIMS M.P.

"So, you know, I says to her: If you don't get your arse into gear and go out and get yourself a job, I'm gonna kick your butt. And she says to me – get this: the girl's been laying around there ever since she got outta school, doing nothing but watching the telly and talking to boys on the phone – and where they get the time, I don't know – and I tell her to go out and get a job, and she looks up at me and smiles and says, 'I don't know if I should, ma, I think I'm pregnant.' And you wanta know something else: she says she don't know who the father is."

"Well, I never. That's almost as bad as –"

KNIFING ON OMNIBUS
KILLER OF FOUR CAPTURED THROUGH ACCIDENT

There was a high-pitched scream.

"Leave me alone."

A young man glared indignantly at his companion, and as the bus came to a stop, he slapped the offender, leaped to his feet and stormed down the stairs.

The stench of sweat, wine and urine was unbearable. In the pastoral reality of the Village he had forgotten air could be so foul. The indulgent softness of the voices was like the sound of grease sputtering or the wetness of poured garbage. Their faces were coarse, hardened, impoverished, smouldering with resentment. He got up, went to the back exit and down around it to the street. A newspaper stand displayed its headline: OXFORD RIOT – 65 ARRESTED.

A sign above the door read: FISH & CHIPS. He went in.

"What'll it be, love."

"Fish and chips."

"Aught to drink?"

"Ginger beer."

She slid open the door of the fryer, reached in with a scoop. Two fat golden fish came out. She lay them on a paper and brought out the chips. Then she I folded the paper into a neat parcel.

"Vinegar and salt?"

"Please."

She got a bottle from the cooler. "That'll be sixpence."

He paid it and turned around.

A camera was mounted over the door, swivelling slowly from right to left. TELE-GUARD SECURITY CAMERA, the identification plate said. *Monitored twenty-four hours a day!*

He stepped out on to the street.

All motion froze. Reality ground to a halt. Everything was still, even (he was certain) the motion of particle and electron.

Some terrible dislocation wrenched through marrow and bone.

Alone on the suddenly silent earth, he was as frozen as they.

This had been reality: deep in the fibre of his being, in the bedrock of his mind, he had believed this reality. Each blade of grass, each breath of air, each glimmer of light had seduced and compelled him. He had given himself up to the illusion.

And reality had broken.

Then, from far away, like the distant wail of the wind, a force blew up, stirring the dry grey dust of reality, and rising along his hackles in a frigid, blistering gale.

It lashed up about him and the fabric of reality quickened, grew thicker, took on life. The figures began to change. First their expressions (little flickerings of eye and mouth) and then their bodies (hair, complexion, length of limb, torso, stance and personality) began to change. They became farmers, businessmen, politicians, and peasants in a flickering blaze of change.

He saw every evocation of each visible personality throughout every incarnation down all history, all space, all time.

Light, sound, vibration, solidity and surface flared up in a great tumultuous cry. And the electric circuit of his nerves fused beneath too great an awareness as perception multiplied beyond limit and the universe closed in against him in a total, inchoate mingling of interior and exterior. All tissues, membranes, surfaces, interfaces and barriers vanished in a single gestalt instant. And transfixed by the experience of reality, he came finally to the centre of existence.

His mouth opened in a frozen, silent scream.

There was a moment which he became everything, and then – Godhood.

His consciousness fled from the moment unable to accept, trembled and withdrew. It blanked out pain, blanked out cause, blanked out event, withdrew cell by cell, nerve by nerve through his every day in the Village to the time before that, to the source of the pain.

He fell, unopposed, to the day it all began.

The music pounded out of the speaker and the singer's voice set up an eerie summons high and compelling. The shadows of overhead trees dappled and swirled off the car as it roared down the street and into the city rising before it.

His face was grim, set. Eyes, mouth, plane of the face, determined, stubborn and resolute. The singer's image was conjured in his mind, behind the brightness of the London afternoon.

The car rolled down a ramp into an underground garage.

He got out and went up to giant double doors, seized the handles and threw them open.

He threw the resignation on Sir Charles's desk.

Sir Charles looked up. His lips parted: The question was hung from the very depths of the universe itself:

WHY?

It smote his consciousness – all time, all structure, all reason ringing with the blow. Present and future mingled in his mind. Like the ghost of reality yet to be, he saw the Village more clearly than the face of the man before him.

And the memory of copper wire and jellied flesh was a shield within his hand.

"No!" he cried.

It was the ultimate affirmation.

The universe came to an end.

"*Veuillez*, Number Six, how did you resist?"

"Number Four was too co-operative, feeding me in prison. It was out of character. I ate and caught flu. Why? Obviously so I wouldn't be with you for the execution. Having found one illusion, I waited for the next. And after it, the next. There was never a time I believed completely in my environment."

"*Merci*. At least I know." He made a defenceless motion with his hands. "What will happen to me now; I cannot say."

"Perhaps you'll be given your old job back."

"Yes, I rather like blending tobacco."

"Well, if that's all –"

"Oh yes. You may go, Number Six."

"Be seeing you, Number Two."

He stepped out in the street and started home.

Number 237 was talking to a shopkeeper across the street. He turned and waved his hat. "Hello, Number Six."

"How was your fishing?"

"Good. Good. You must come to dinner and see."

"I will."

He went on across the green.

Number 32 came out of a store. Her skirt blew up about her legs.

Some days he would play chess with the Admiral.

And some days he would struggle merely to remain alive.

Today he had a window to repair.

And tomorrow . . . he would wait and see.

For he had defeated them, as he would always defeat them, learning more each time until he set himself free and left.

For one man alone, each victory against so great a machine must be sweet.

He lit a cigar and smiled.
Life was very good just then. Just then.

"It is not the works, but the *belief* which is here decisive and determines the order or rank – to employ once more an old religious formula with a new deeper meaning –, it is some fundamental certainty which a noble soul has about itself, something which is not to be sought, is not to be found, and perhaps, also, is not to be lost – *The noble soul has reverence for itself –.*'

Friedrich Nietzsche, *Beyond Good and Evil*